Love
has a
Name

A Novel

Happy Reading!

Christina Hill

Chitin Hill ♥

Cover Design: Christina Hill
Cover Photo: Brenda Villanueva

ISBN: 979-8-9857199-0-1

To all of the brave birth mothers who have made an excruciatingly difficult choice for the sake of your child. You are seen. You are loved. You are my hero.

PROLOGUE
Nice to Meet You

June 2011—Age 20

"Hi, I'm Anne. You are?"

I pause before answering, wondering which name I should provide. I have gained a few at this crux in my life, and it felt especially important to provide the right one.

"Andrea," I reply, flipping my long brown hair over my left shoulder.

"It's so nice to finally meet you, Andrea. Have you ever seen a therapist before?" Anne asks with a serious expression.

I want to laugh at her question, but find the restraint to hold back. A therapist? Counseling? Absolutely not.

"Um, no. Never," I respond instead.

"Wonderful, I am honored to be on this journey with you at this point in your life. Therapy is not for the faint of heart, but from what Janet tells me of how you got here, I would say you are one strong young woman."

Anne's words feel like both a warning and a compliment. I really don't know what to expect in therapy. Janet, the resident floor director of this facility, told me the purpose was to talk about my past, present, and future and to provide me with tools to cope with messy emotions.

She noted that all counseling services were a part of the program and every resident was expected to attend. It isn't exactly my description of a good time, but I'm learning to trust the process.

"I don't really know how strong I am. I came here for help, didn't I?" I ask with an edge to my voice. My hazel eyes are trained on Anne, testing her. The facility I am staying in is the epitome of *help*. That's all they do all day, every day: help people who are the most screwed up. I fit that description perfectly.

"I don't see it that way," Anne says, unfazed by my attitude. "Not at all, in fact, you are here because you're ready to face the hard stuff, and *that's* what takes strength."

"Well, we can call it strength or ignorance," I state while running my right hand up and down my left arm. The tracks running clear up and down it are raised with scabs just beginning to form. I close my eyes and swallow, my body still craving what it can't have.

Anne sits across from me with her black, cropped pixie cut, warm brown eyes, and an intense gaze that bores into my soul and makes me wonder if she knows everything about my life's story before I've told her anything.

"When we start on a new path, we are all a bit ignorant. We can't say for certain what the exact outcome will be, but we still move forward in hope."

That word feels like a curse to my ears. I don't want hope. It has left me disappointed and hung out to dry more times than I can count. I'm not ready to make peace with hope, but I realize I do need help, as painful as that is to finally admit.

"I don't want hope, I just want help," I say forcefully. I let out a sigh. I'm not making this easy on her, but my blind trust has gotten me into trouble before. I've got plenty of people to thank for that.

"You're in the right place, Andrea. I want to help you," Anne kindly adds, softening the edges of my prickly exterior. "It may feel impossible to have hope for what's ahead but I want to assure you that I am in this with you. You are not alone."

Alone. If I could choose one word to describe the events in my life it would be alone. I was loyal to a fault to every person who walked into my life, and all they gave me in return was loneliness. Why couldn't I have learned better?

As though she can understand my inner thoughts, Anne presses, "We can't expect to have life all worked out. Our mistakes teach us, and our stories remind us of the roads we have traveled. I want the times we meet to be a space for you to share the roads you've traveled, Andrea."

That's why I'm here, to talk about my past and share how I got here. I knew this. I was warned of this. Yet, it is all sounding impossible now that I'm here.

Where do I even begin?

"My story is pretty long…and sad," I tell Anne.

"We have time," Anne reiterates. Her movements are slow and measured. I haven't noticed any unnecessary pen tapping or foot bouncing indicating there is somewhere else she would rather be.

I take a controlled breath in, trying to calm my irregular heartbeat. I am nervous to open the vault of my past. I have kept everything locked away, believing that if I was just more loyal, more trusting, more *everything*, that it wouldn't haunt me. Instead, I only added to those horrible experiences. Stacking the memories one on top of the other until they all came crashing down, nearly crushing me.

I am still here, however; I am still alive.

I guess that counts for something.

"We will probably jump around from your early childhood to young adulthood each time we meet, but why don't you start with a story that was a significant moment for you," Anne says, directing my thoughts.

"What do you mean by *significant*? Like, good, bad… what?" I ask, needing more information so I can know which cards to lay out in front of her. Anne seems like the kind of woman who has gained plenty of strategies over the years to deal with women like me.

"You decide. We don't need to label the significance of being good or bad, just a moment that feels important or momentous for you," she explains.

As she speaks, a picture falls into my mind.

Small. Fragile. Dependent.

The memory of *her* makes my heart lurch and my stomach drops. I rub my sweaty palms together, wondering if I can share the story. Anne seems to think I am strong enough. Janet said I was ready. I've given up everything in my former life, haven't I? Maybe I can open up to her. Maybe sharing these memories would help, although I can't really see how. It won't change anything about what I've gone through.

My eyes roam around the room, trying to decide if I should share about *her*, the one that defined the word *significant*. She was tiny, but her hold on my heart was considerable. Life-changing, world-altering, stop-your-heart-while-you-think-of-her kind of hold.

Anne waits patiently, likely sensing my pause in sharing such intimate details of my life. I don't feel ready, but would I ever?

I take another deep breath; I can see the memory filling my mind and the words settling on my tongue.

You can do this, Andrea.

It's time to let it all out.

"Okay, I know where to begin."

Part One
The Journey

CHAPTER 1
Tomorrow Will Come
July 17, 2006—Age 15

The hospital room was eerily quiet. No garbage trucks rumbling down the road outside my window, car horns blaring, or muffled chatter from folks heading to their nine-to-five jobs in the city where they earned more in one hour than I had seen in a week. Other than the occasional squeaky footsteps passing by my door, the sound of silence was something I wasn't used to. My ears were ringing with a dull ache but my body was completely at peace, and I was experiencing some kind of unknown euphoria. My limbs felt overworked and sore but my mind and heart were weightless.

It's over. All of it.

I couldn't help but think back on the events of the day without the corner of my mouth turning up into a giddy smile. The first moments after my pain subsided, the soft cries ascended into full blown wailing screams, filling the room with the sound of life, and causing my jaw to relax with relief. The nurses took a noticeable exhale with the victory of birth, and I admired the tiniest face I had ever seen as her scrunched form hung suspended in the air. I could have sworn she looked straight at me when the too-young-to-know-what-he-was-doing doctor slowly lowered her to my chest. I debated whether I should touch her or not.

Should I?

Could I?

I want to.

Her tiny form begged for reassurance, so I let my fingers hesitantly graze the back of this petite, naked baby, her screams quieting the moment our skin touched. She was softer than I imagined she would be, and so warm; her head almost slid from my chest with the weight of it until a hand shot out to catch it.

"She's a beauty, alright," the plump nurse with a thick southern accent said as she repositioned the baby girl's head on my chest so it wouldn't fall again.

My voice came out in a whisper. "Yeah, she really is."

"You just finished the hardest part, sugar, but you do have to deliver the placenta, so why don't I hold that sweet little thing for you while you finish up?"

"If I have to," I replied, looking up to see the warm brown eyes of the woman extending her arms out in front of her. I awkwardly handed her this tiny piece of my heart that now lived outside of my body.

"You do, but don't worry, it won't be long before she's back in your arms again," she assured me. I watched the woman's head full of counterfeit blonde curls, twist and turn haphazardly as she spun on her heels and walked away from my bed. My arms felt empty already. I didn't expect to feel this way, but now I can't imagine having any other reaction.

Don't get attached. Don't get attached. Don't get attached.

The woman, who I nicknamed *Curls*, snuggled the baby girl between her bountiful breasts and carried her over to be weighed and measured. I didn't have time to take another full breath before my placenta was delivered, and the whole ordeal was over, or, as over as the immediate pain of pushing a small human from your body could be.

"Well, Andrea Strivers, you should be very proud of yourself," the too-young-to-know-what-he-was-doing doctor declared after washing every square inch of his arms. "Your baby girl is happy and healthy. Congratulations!"

I smiled back at him because I felt every piece of joy I saw reflected in his eyes.

Don't do that, Andrea! I scolded myself.

I shouldn't let myself feel these kinds of feelings, not when I knew how things would turn out. It would only hurt more. I caught a glimpse of arms and legs flailing out of the corner of my eye and tried to look behind the rounded backside of Curls. The high-pitched crying started again and my body lurched to try and help her before slumping backwards on the bed.

You can't be the one who comforts her and gives her away, Andrea.

I clamped my mouth shut so I wouldn't ask to hold her again even though I wanted to.

Hours later, after so much screaming—from the both of us—and the aching bits and bobs and last minute decisions, I was beyond exhausted. I was laying in my stiff hospital bed staring up at the ceiling, my once prominent smile faded as I remembered what the doctor had said. "*Your* baby girl." He must not have known my... situation.

I looked over at the rolling bassinet she was fast asleep in beside my bed. This little girl was perfect in every way. Her small, pursed lips that moved steadily up and down in her sleep and the soft peachy skin I only dared to skim a couple times, hesitant to allow our connection to grow. She couldn't be mine. Her forever family would be bringing her home with them tomorrow morning, and I would be going somewhere else, my exact location still to be determined.

My smile was thoroughly obliterated now, and in its place were tears trickling down my cheeks that my eyes had unconsciously summoned. When I held this baby for the first time, I felt peace surrounding my whole body. It was only the two of us protected from a world of impossibilities and no second chances. I didn't expect love to enter the picture, but it did, and now I needed to figure out how to turn it off.

The peace I'd felt has since abandoned me and was replaced by a visceral loss that caused my sobs to grow in size and number. I shifted to my side and grabbed my tormented stomach to hold my body back from retching onto the freshly cleaned hospital floors. I'm guessing this isn't how you should feel after having a baby, but I had no one in my life to tell me otherwise. The closest thing I had to a loving family member was the nurse I named Curls who helped me shower and change into another paper thin gown and an adult diaper earlier, promising me I looked like, "a million bucks, sweetie."

I didn't believe her, but she was all I had now.

At fifteen years old, I had lived a lifetime and was a closer friend to pain and suffering then I would guess most kids my age were. Sure, I had a family, but I wasn't worth their time or effort to love so I left at the ripe old age of fourteen and had been on my own ever since. None of my blood relatives knew I was lying in this hospital bed with my knees curled up almost touching my chin, tears streaming down my face. They wouldn't even know where to look for me, but they likely hadn't even tried.

Of course they haven't, Andrea, my thoughts confirmed.

The loss that had come over me like a sudden wave transformed into fresh hurt and anger, feelings I was most acquainted with these days, especially when I allowed myself to dredge up memories of my family. I was angry at my parents for abandoning me. I was furious with my Aunt Cindy for pushing me away. I still seethed when I thought about the scumbag who threw negligence to my consent and knocked me up, leaving me to fend for myself. I was irritated that some lady I had never met, who the hospital staff called Wendy Dobson, would be handing over the baby girl I just brought into this world to a new family. A suitable family. A family that I chose but also resented. Anger was the shield that protected me, helping me brave the battle ahead of saying goodbye.

I flipped onto my other side, away from the faint sleeping noises coming from the bassinet. My eyes locked on to the bright glowing light peeking through the bottom of the door that reminded me there was a whole crew of nurses and doctors working through the wee hours of the night, caring for patients and delivering babies. I crossed my arms in front of my chest, fully aware of the tender breasts just below it that were swollen and sore from the milk that had come in with a vengeance. It had nowhere to go. No mouth to feed and no body to nourish.

My honorary family member, Curls, helped me wrap my chest to avoid waking up to soaking wet sheets. "This is just about the fastest I have seen anyone's milk come in, sweetie. It's painful but you'll be rid of it in a few days."

I didn't reply. I could only look down and blink away the emotion welling up again. Her words should have been reassuring knowing I would be rid of the milk faster, but it only served as a glaring reminder that my body was missing something—*someone*. Like ripping a band aid off, I just needed to get through it. My physical body had undergone so many changes in the last nine months, most of it incredibly alien to me and downright freaky, and all of them pointing to a baby that wouldn't be mine to hold.

It's better this way.

You aren't good enough for her.

I couldn't take this gripping pain lying down any longer and sat up on the edge of the bed abruptly, swinging my bare legs to the side and hovering my feet above the white speckled linoleum floors. I could feel the cool temperature of the room run through my body as I planted my feet on the ground to stand. The goosebumps on my arms rose with awareness as I hobbled to the mirror situated above the sink, to the right of the door. The door where hours earlier nurses and doctors had been bustling in and out of to have me sign papers, answer questions, and fluff my frumpy bed pillows. It was a revolving door of activity and now it was shut, blocking off the shadowy darkness of my room from being overcome by the piercing lights of the world beyond.

It took energy that I did not have to get there. My body was sore in more places than I could count but luckily my legs remembered how to move, and I soon found myself face to face with the worn-looking girl in the mirror. I was turning sixteen in a couple of weeks. There was no celebration planned, no friends to wish me happy birthday, and no money in my pocket for gifts. I would likely be posted up on someone's couch, trading my granny panties for regular underwear again and trying not to relive this day: *her* birthday.

Leaning closer, I braced my hands on either side of the sink, adding more weight onto the rough palms of my un-manicured hands. I inspected the tired girl looking back at me. I might consider thanking my mother for my long, dark brown hair that hung well past the middle of my back if she were still alive. My hazel eyes looked almost black in the dark room, the circular rings of exhaustion hanging out beneath them weren't helping any. Sleep was nonexistent since I was too afraid that if I did, the tiny baby my heart wanted to love so badly would be gone when I woke up. I feared not getting to say goodbye while also not knowing how.

I continued to stare at myself, noticing my slender frame, no longer sporting a basketball sized belly, my shorter stature being the only indication I was fifteen since my continually expanding bust line and curved hips alluded to a woman twice my age. My swollen breasts pressed into the horrid hospital gown they gave me to wear, revealing more than it tried to hide with its unflattering shape and ugly pattern. It was a fate I shouldered long ago to have grown physically beyond my years. My body carried power that I never wanted to possess.

I had stared at this girl countless times before, but in this moment, she morphed into someone else entirely. Someone I didn't recognize and never wanted to be. My cheeks glistened with wetness as I looked on, wanting to look away but forcing myself not to.

I saw myself as *he* must have seen me. The man who stole from my body, and left me the mess to take care of. And it was a mess. I was hooked from our first meeting of eyes, but he had other plans that included my body while never considering me. It left me feeling frail and weak, like a small animal crushed in the talons of a fiercer predator. My soul was damned to death the moment I felt his hands on me.

A darkness hovered around my shoulders, slithering up my neck and teasing my senses with the memories I could never expel no matter how hard I tried.

You're used and damaged goods, Andrea. The familiar voice in my head reminded me.

The memories that *he* gave me were seared into my bodily fibers; I could not think of them without having some kind of physical reaction. This time, alone in a dark hospital room with all of its white walls, cold floors, and covered windows, my body reacted. I began to dry-heave, and though I had escaped the queasy feeling that arose earlier, there was no stopping it this time. I ran to the toilet just behind another door in the small, confined room and made contact with the porcelain bowl just in time. My heart was thundering inside my chest and my eyes squeezed shut while my breathing became labored. The memories were flashing through my mind at warp speed, painting a full-color picture I didn't want to see.

His lips traveling the length of my jaw as my hands became intertwined in his dark hair.

Steady hands as they held me up against the wall.

Ragged breaths filled with anticipation.

"Ahh!" I groaned, pressing my palms to my temples, trying to block everything out. "They're just memories! Keep it together."

You can't lose it right now, Andrea.

I heard a faint sound coming from her rolling bed so I quickly grabbed a paper towel to wipe off the evidence of turmoil from my mouth, stood on wobbly legs, and walked back out to the sink.

Keep it together. She needs you right now.

No other sounds filled our shared room so I splashed water on my face, hoping to startle me out of my past. My body was shaking thanks to my now unsteady legs and the all too familiar awareness *he* always left me with. Not here. Not on this day. I closed my eyes tightly once again, begging my mind to stop playing those painful flashbacks.

I heard another small squeak from the tightly bundled baby and my eyes flew open and my head turned towards her.

She can never know about him, her birth dad. I adamantly told myself.

When I found out I was pregnant with her, I swore to myself this baby would never know him. He was an unnamed, unmasked monster that I have tried over and over to forget, but never could. She didn't have to know about him; I could protect her from him by protecting her from me.

I clenched my fists and pushed them into my eye sockets, trying to force the dark memories into the compartment they belonged in at the back of my mind, while also wiping the evidence of his effect on me away. Any resemblance of a smile was long gone.

Keep it together, Andrea.

I needed to learn to live with these memories. They were mine now, just like all the other ones that haunted me. I dropped my hands from my swollen eyes and walked back to the firm hospital room bed, ready to resume my fetal position. I laid down facing the bassinet that held every part of me that was good in it.

She started to move again, her tiny legs lifting beneath the swaddle and a small cry escaping her mouth. I reached up and settled my hand on her chest, hearing her cries lessen with my touch at the same time the pending loss in my heart ached more.

The adoption woman, Wendy, that the hospital staff put me in touch with said this was an important piece of the process—a proper goodbye. She told me over the phone I could have all the time I needed and the new adoptive parents wouldn't hover around or rush in to swoop her out of my arms and out of my life. The gravity of this decision I had gone and made was starting to sink in. It felt like I was continually being punched in the stomach, and I wasn't sure I could face this kind of goodbye tomorrow morning.

My hand was still resting on the small form sleeping soundly next to me when my eyelids became heavy and I could feel the weight of sleep pulling me under. I couldn't let any more time pass though before I asked, begged, prayed for this little girl.

Please, God, or whoever else decides things, don't let her be messed up like me. Keep her safe and loved even though I can't.

With this final plea, my lids fell fully closed and my world became smaller and less complicated for those few hours of sleep.

Tomorrow will come, but not before tonight.

CHAPTER 2

Just Keep Swimming

July 18, 2006—Age 15

I woke up after a few hours of welcome sleep to a hungry, crying baby.

I was disoriented and unsure of what to do so I pressed the "help" button next to my bed and waited an unbearable few seconds before Curls walked in.

"Someone is hungry! Good morning, sunshine!" she declared in a chipper tone that made me roll my half open eyes. I gave her a grunt as my only answer.

"Not a morning person, eh? Well, don't you worry. I have just what this little lass is looking for." Curls pulled out a pre-made bottle from the mini fridge in our room and plunked down on the chair across from me.

Her head snapped up to look at me. "Oh. Did you want to feed her darlin'?" she asked, ready to hand the bottle to me.

Was I allowed to?

I wanted to, but it didn't sound like such a good idea.

I really wanted to though.

"No."

"Alright then. If you change your mind, just holler at me," she said with a wink.

I rolled back onto my side, pulling the covers up to my chin.

You're not her mother, Andrea.

I didn't want to be thinking about Michelle at a time like this, but I couldn't help recalling the woman who despised motherhood more than I thought I did. Ever since I could remember, my mother refused to answer to "mom," "mama," or "mother." She insisted I call her by her first name, Michelle.

Michelle used to explain, "I've always called my mother by her first name, Jane, as a sign of respect. That's why I taught you to do the same thing. None of that 'mama' shit, you hear me?"

"Yes, Michelle," I replied with a quiver to my chin as a small child. I knew full well how it would set her off if I called her by any other name.

Michelle took it upon herself to teach me plenty of life lessons in my adolescence, most of which left me baked in fear. Childbirth being one of them.

"Andrea, you don't want to know what it's like to push a bowling ball-sized baby out of your nether regions. I will tell you one thing though: you can't sneeze, jump, or run without peeing your pants afterwards. Some women even have to wear a diaper for the rest of their lives."

The horror on my face was evident as I clutched my face between my small hands.

Gross!

"The pain is so excruciating that you'll be screaming loud enough for the whole hospital to hear you and begging

20

for all the drugs they have to stop it," Michelle said plainly as she lit her cigarette and blew out the first ring of smoke near my face.

This really happened to people? I thought, my mouth hanging wide open, when I started coughing on the smoke ring encircling me.

"Yup. Dan wouldn't touch me for weeks afterwards because of all the blood that just kept coming," she explained, shaking her head with a disgusted look on her face.

Michelle had a way with words. Meaning, her *way* was to never hold anything back. I was eight years old and knew far more about the graphic details of all kinds of topics. This one in particular was enough to make me dread having a baby and I vowed to never, ever get pregnant. Ever. Maybe she told me so I would avoid sex like the plague or because she wanted me to bow at her feet and thank her for all that I put her through. Either way, it didn't work.

In middle school, my human development teacher made us watch a video on the topic of birth that was particularly scarring.

"Today, class, we will be learning about one of the most outstanding phenomena in human development: childbirth. Buckle up for an incredible documentary!" The words flitted out of my teacher's mouth, but not before the horror stricken concerns rang out around the class like fireworks being set off in the night sky.

"Ew. Can't we learn about something else?"

"Are we going to see anything? You know, like the birth part?

"Is this even allowed to be shown in school? It shouldn't be."

"I think I'm going to be sick."

It seemed I wasn't the only one with a preference not to learn more about this wonder that was childbirth. I didn't learn much from the video other than that my suspicions were correct: childbirth was every bit as horrible as Michelle described. There was no way this was happening to my body. Nope. Not going to happen.

My younger self thought that giving birth was going to be the hardest part, and I was tormented by these experiences for years. Why did women *want* to do this?

Saggy breasts? *Yes, please!*

Flappy stomachs? *Absolutely!*

Stretch marks running every which way making you look like a zebra? *Sign me up!*

As a naive teenage girl, these all sounded like a death sentence to my body. Yet, here I was, a fifteen-year-old mother who survived childbirth (minus the mother part).

I gripped the blanket tighter in my hand, trying to ignore the gentle words I heard Curls speaking to the baby in her arms.

Curls must be a mother, I thought to myself.

An actual mother who really loved kids. Not a woman who hated the reality of mothering more than she hated the title, like Michelle. I didn't want to be a mom and swore to myself it wouldn't happen to me. Life is funny like that, giving you the one thing you never wanted and taking all of the things you did.

My reality was fixed. This delicate girl would live, but she was going to be mothered by someone other than me. Our impending goodbye was hours away. It felt like my heart was being squeezed too tightly, restricting me from getting a full breath even for a second. The loss was constant and stifling. Birth seemed like the easy part now.

I would be discharged this afternoon to resume my life, which only a few short months ago was the only thing I could think about—the only thing I had hoped for. Since finding out I was pregnant, the big life-altering decisions just kept rolling in one after the other.

Do I keep this child?

How would I provide for her?

Should I have an abortion?

How do I even get an abortion?

I had known girls who had made the decision to abort an unwanted pregnancy. This would have been my choice too had I not gone and gotten an ultrasound to confirm what those lines on the dollar store pregnancy test had shown me and seen the little kiwi size baby floating around in there. I bawled like a newborn baby right there in the exam room as the nurse confirmed my pregnancy.

"Oh, honey, congratulations!" the ultrasound tech said, reading the whole moment wrong, but I couldn't correct her through my Earth-shifting tears. I was pregnant. There was for sure a baby in there. I knew once I saw her swimming without a care in the world that I couldn't just get rid of this baby. I had to figure out another plan. It took the remaining months of my pregnancy to completely avoid this decision that followed me like a dark rain cloud, promising nothing but a torrential downpour in its forecast.

I thought briefly about dragging my sorry-self back to my Aunt Cindy's house to beg her to help me, but my pride wouldn't allow it. We said our words, however nasty they were, and we made our decisions. I wouldn't go back to another home that didn't want me. I stayed in this constant spin cycle until my water broke suddenly and I was being transported to the hospital for delivery, ready or not.

"Help me! Please, someone help me!" I screamed, but I wasn't screaming for the kind of help that would take the pain away. I was screaming for help in figuring out what to do with this baby after she was born. Where was she going to live? Who was the family that would take care of her, kiss her goodnight, and I don't know… love her? I needed help because I was jumping into uncharted waters without a life jacket and no clue how to swim.

"I… I can't keep her. She needs a family. Damn, this hurts! Ahh!" I moaned with another birth pain.

The paramedics made note of my desire for this baby to be adopted while I screamed with every contraction and cursed at them with every missed stoplight. Their main goal was to get me out of their ambulance and into the capable hands of the waiting hospital staff as quickly as possible. Mine was to have a baby without getting attached.

The name Wendy Dobson was thrown around by a few of the nurses assigned to my care, and I had enough wits to gather that whoever she was, she was going to be the one to solve this problem that I had saved for the very last minute. I spoke with Wendy on the phone right after the delivery, landing me in those high waisted diapers that gave me nightmares since I was eight.

"I just want to make sure you are positive about your decision. This is a big choice to place a child up for adoption and if you have reservations at all, I want to know."

I did not choose to be raped. I never asked to be pregnant, and I certainly didn't expect to feel so much love or care or something for this baby girl I never wanted. All of the events leading to this moment were out of my hands. This was the only choice I could make, and I was done delaying and second-guessing myself. I was ready to feel normal again. I just wanted to be fifteen.

"Yes, I'm positive." For once, my voice didn't shake with indecision. It would be decided and done with, and I could finally move on.

"This is absolutely your choice—100%. Adoption isn't about giving up this child but choosing to place her in a family."

It all sounded so simple, the way Wendy explained it, but I wasn't in the frame of mind to feel at all empowered by her words.

"Then I choose adoption," I spat out, mocking her words with my own.

Wendy told me she had two adoptive families and gave me a short bio on each of them. I chose the young, married couple that lived near L.A. where I had been living. They had no other children and hoped to grow their family through adoption. The woman enjoyed baking, which reminded me of my Aunt Cindy, the aunt who had loved me longer than most, but had eventually cast me out of her home and her heart. The woman's husband enjoyed fishing, which is something Dan, my dad, liked to do on the weekends once-upon-a-time. It was the only thing he allowed me to join him in, and I soaked up the time spent in his presence, even if we never spoke. I took this all as a good sign that these people were going to be the new family, the *right* family, for this baby girl.

"I think they will be an excellent choice, Andrea. I will be there in the morning to speak with you in person and discuss the next steps in this process."

"Thank you, Wendy, for helping me out," I said, forcing the words out of my mouth before I could change my mind.

"Always." She cleared her throat and lowered her voice. I was not ready for the words she spoke next. "You know, Andrea, you are making a difficult but courageous choice to place this child with an adoptive family."

I swallowed the lump that had been creeping higher and higher in my throat as she talked and I listened. I was far from courageous. I was a coward.

Keep it together, Andrea!

When the call ended, I chided myself for the tears I had almost shed for the millionth time that day. I would be meeting Wendy in person soon, twenty-four hours since our phone conversation, and I wasn't ready. I'm not ready for any of it, the goodbye, the perfect family to take this baby, the tears that I would cry. I wish I could skip all of it.

I flung the covers off of me and sat upright in bed. "I'm going to shower."

"Okay, sweetie, do you need any help?"

I paused, hating how my heart leapt at Curls' kindness.

"I haven't forgotten how to shower," I retorted, reminding her and myself that I didn't need anyone else's help.

"No one said you did. I'm here if you need me though," she replied with an even softer tone that made me want to punch something.

I walked into the bathroom, slammed the door instead, and cranked the shower nozzle to hot, ready to feel the steamy water pelt my back. I was never clean enough, even though I tried. I had scrubbed my body raw for weeks after the unknown man had his way with me and the news of my pregnancy came; I don't know whose body I detested more: mine or his. It was a shell I lived in, but also despised. My stomach gurgled, and I felt I would be sick all over again, like I had been last night. The daytime was supposed to push away the dark thoughts that the night always made darker.

I stepped into the water stream that would likely leave burn marks on my olive skin, and I let my mind wander. It's not like the memories were ever far from my thoughts. I was reminded countless times in the past nine months of the douchebag that gave me a reason to call Wendy, to be locked up in this hospital room with stitches flanking my underside and my will to see tomorrow only a wisp.

I thought by giving birth to *his* child that it would naturally cause me to reject her. The opposite proved true, however, and whenever I snuck a glance at this perfect little human, innocently unaware of how she got here, I was filled with adoration for her. I couldn't help it.

You can't touch her anymore, Andrea.

Not her tiny toes, her delicate skin, or the short tendrils of dark hair on her head.

You will change your mind and we can't have that.

Keep it together.

His face flashed before my eyes as the water pelted my shoulders. I saw the smile that hid a monster and the invitation that ended in deception. His lingering minty scent filled my senses, tugging me under the heavy cloak of memory.

CHAPTER 3
Lights Out
October 2005—Age 15

"Sadie, come on, you're taking forever to impress some random guy who likely won't care about how much glitter you have on." I told her from my spot on the couch in the front room of her cousin's house.

"I'm coming, I'm coming. Geesh, Andy," Sadie said, walking into the living room looking like a whole new person from the one I had seen walk in after work.

Sadie was the first real friend I had met when I moved to L.A. I'm not sure how much of a friend she really was, but we balanced each other out. She had been bouncing from one boyfriend's house to the other and stayed with her cousin in between. I, on the other hand, was happy to find a place to sleep that was off the ground.

"Who's going to be there tonight that you're… dressed up for?" I asked, pointing up and down at Sadie's get-up tonight. She wore an extra short jean skirt with a tight fitting tank that revealed more than it hid.

"You know that guy that was at Billy's party last weekend?"

"The one who gave you the hickey?" I asked her. Trying to keep Sadie's love interests in order was like trying to count the stars in the sky.

"No, no, not him. I was kissing him before I met Jack."

Naturally, I thought to myself and dared not say out loud.

"Alright, so Jack is who you are meeting up with tonight?"

"One can hope," she said with a sultry grin.

I first met Sadie at a party, and we hit it off from the start. She was standing by a group of girls that I assumed were her people until she broke away and joined me near the couch I had been leaning on.

"Hey, I'm Sadie," she said in her simple greeting.

I was taken aback at first, wondering if she was actually speaking to me. I had come with another friend I had known casually, and he was making out somewhere with someone that wasn't me so I had been navigating this party solo.

"Oh, hey. I'm Andy," I said, giving her the name I was using to reinvent myself in this city.

"Did you come with anyone or are you here by yourself?" Sadie asked, genuinely curious.

I paused, considering how to answer her question. "I'm here on my own."

"He ditched you, huh? Don't worry, it's happened to me before too." Sadie said with a smile.

I wondered how she knew—was it written on my face or something?

"You just have that look, you know, the 'pissed that he left you to fend for yourself' kind of look."

I never opened my mouth to confirm or deny it. I just let the truth sit awkwardly between us. I was embarrassed and figured she could read this feeling just as easily as she guessed I had been ditched. She didn't say anything, instead, she invited me into her group of friends like I belonged there, and for a while, I did.

Despite the endless California sunshine, the fall air was beginning to change as we walked the few blocks from Sadie's cousin's place to the raging house party down the way. It was mid-October, but the cooler temperatures meant nothing to the state of California that never truly cooled down.

The party scene in L.A. was tantalizing and exotic compared to the calm, relaxed way of life that I knew having grown up on a cattle farm. The land surrounding our family home was filled with rolling grass hills and winding country roads leading to somewhere and nowhere all at the same time. The property my family owned was nestled a few miles from town and set back from the road with a gate keeping the cows from leaving and the strangers from entering. It was an impressive part of the world to grow up in but lonely when most of your friends were trees and uncommunicative cows.

L.A. was like a feast for my eyes. I looked at the vibrant city as though it would make good on all of the promises it made to me. The loneliness of my hometown was replaced by a city that never slept and more people than there were hairs on my head. I was never alone, and there was always a party, a sidekick, or body to keep me warm. Usually, it was all three. In a city full of people, I met *him*.

I was fifteen when I met him, and I was fifteen when I gave birth.

He was the tall, dark, and handsome type that stood brooding in a corner, drawing more attention by doing absolutely nothing than all of the obviously drunk party-goers stumbling about. He was confident—I could tell that much—with billows of smoke rising occasionally from between his lips, and a bored expression situated on his harsh, startling features. He appeared unamused by the circus of people swirling around him at this crowded house party.

My eyes immediately found him when Sadie and I walked in, half-buzzed already. I scanned his well-dressed form, starting at his haphazardly styled, dark brown hair down to his pristinely white laced sneakers. His posture may have indicated that he was unimpressed with the party but that didn't keep him from keenly observing the activity of people maneuvering around him. There were two other guys beside him, drinks in one hand and a lady in the other. I had never seen him in this circle of people before, which wasn't uncommon living in such a large city like L.A., but despite my inebriated state, he caught my attention. He knew this, too, since our eyes locked momentarily before he did a slow scan of the entire length of my body, sending a shiver up my spine and a rush of heat to my cheeks.

Alright, game on.

I had worn my favorite jeans that night. The ones that hugged the curves of my hips as they trailed down my legs and flared at the bottom. My short sleeved, white shirt hovered an inch above my waistline, showing a bit more than a sliver of skin. I often swept my hair up to keep it out of my face but tonight I let my dark tresses waterfall down the length of my back. I knew I had rattled him from his seemingly indifferent disposition because his eyes bounced over my body once more before he looked away. I thought I held the power, but I was wrong.

I quickly abandoned my noticeable considerations of him; I was never one to seek out a guy, which was the complete opposite of Sadie, who had already deserted her post at my side, likely to find Jack, Billy, or whoever else she would meet before she reached the kitchen. I moved to the dance floor, finding a partner quickly, willing the unknown guy to come and join me. Before the third song was over, I had consumed a few more drinks, brought to me by my other dance partners, and now found myself face to chin with the sulky man who had emerged from his corner.

"Are you finally ready to dance?" I said a little breathless, either due to the rousing song that I had just danced to or the fast pace my heart kept in his presence.

"Finally." A man of few words.

His hands firmly gripped the sides of my hips, never leaving, as we moved to the beat. He wasn't grabby like the other guys tended to be. This man was fluid with his movements and led us with an observable insistence. He tugged and pulled, taking charge like I wanted him to, and making my body become loose and flexible in his arms. I could feel the warmth of his breath on my cheek, in my ear, and on my neck as we danced through two more songs.

I was lost in the moment when he reluctantly led me to the kitchen to get a drink. He knew the effect he had on me, and I wasn't afraid to show him. I channeled my inner Sadie and confidently slithered my arm around his midsection, claiming a place there.

In the kitchen there were stacks of cups, bottles of assorted alcoholic drinks, and a plethora of weed and other mind inhibitors available for party guests—at a price, of course. I would have asked him what his name was. I wish I had at least known that. Yet, we were interrupted by an approaching commotion that stole my attention.

Sadie was half-tripping, half-stumbling towards us; her unstoppable progress now undeniable. She made contact with the side of the counter and fell down with a thud to her backside. Without looking at tall-dark-and-handsome, I pushed off of the kitchen counter and was clumsily trying to help Sadie stand to no avail. I deserted my efforts to get her on her feet and instead, shifted her back until she was leaning up against the kitchen wall.

The guy she had singled out—Jack, Jake, or Jim—wasn't far behind her.

"Oh, damn, Sadie. Are you okay?" His worried tone caught my ear.

"Yeah, yeah. I'll be fine. I don't know what happened," she said, rubbing her head.

"How much have you had to drink, exactly?" I asked, hoping this wouldn't cut our night out too short, not when I had finally met someone worth sticking around for.

"I don't really know."

"Here's some water; take a sip," I directed her, grabbing a water bottle from the cooler nearby.

Sadie rubbed her head with her fingers and I noticed a few beads of sweat on her brow.

"Do you want to leave?" I asked, hoping for a different answer than the one my conscience was giving me.

"Ah, don't leave now, you promised me another dance."

I ignored Sadie's new guy's petition and kept my hazy eyes locked on her.

"I'll be okay Andy, really. I just need a minute and then Jack will help me up, won't you?"

"Absolutely. I got you, girl," Jack said with a smug confidence.

With Jack's admonition and Sadie's playful grin, I determined all was well. My legs were wobbly as I stood back up, but I was able to make my way to where tall-dark-and-handsome stood waiting for me. He had a relaxed air about him and barely flinched seeing Sadie plummet to the ground the way she did.

It must have happened when I turned away to help Sadie. When I returned to the mysterious man I had ogled and danced with, I accepted the drink he offered me without question.

"Cheers," I said with a clink of our plastic cups.

He offered no reply other than a small grin behind the rim of his cup.

I tipped the contents of mine into my waiting mouth, and it burned the back of my throat as it slid down. The feeling wasn't immediate. I had enough time to set my cup down and follow tall-dark-and-handsome to a quieter part of the house, which didn't really exist. He positioned us in a corner and with my back pressed against the wall, his hands slid around my waist, enveloping my senses and causing butterflies to take flight in my stomach.

He left a trail of kisses along my jaw, and I wove my hands in his hair, gripping them even tighter as his hands explored the length of my body. When I looked in his dark brown eyes, I saw the intention of a kiss and I assumed my weak, tingling limbs were in response to this possibility. However, my legs felt too heavy, my mouth too dry and slack, and my head too dizzy. I tried to push the feelings away so I could be ready for the kiss but it was no use. Before I could utter a word, my entire world went black.

I would have been willing, but he just wanted the power.

I woke up in an unfamiliar room. It had no more than a single table lamp that sat on the floor, a light wood-colored dresser, and the bed that I was apparently laying on, fully exposed with zero blankets.

Where am I?

How did I get here?

I rubbed the tiredness from my eyes and propped myself up on wobbly arms. I had no recollection of being in this room. My head was throbbing. I wasn't *that* drunk.

Was I that drunk?

All of a sudden, awareness shot through me. There was no one else beside me and the blanket of silence that covered the room was tangible, which is more than I could say about the lack of covers on me. My head was pounding with every motion I made, and I noticed a discernible achiness in my body.

What happened last night?

I needed to know. I was almost desperate to figure it out.

My throat was tightening at the same time my breaths were demanding more of my effort. I sat straight up and frantically scrambled out of the bed in search of my clothes that I assured myself had to be there. I dry heaved once. Twice. Three times before I was forced to sit back on the edge of the hard bed. I spied my clothes scattered around the lamp on the floor and scooted over to pick them up, trying my best not to hurl. I shoved my legs into my jeans, disregarding the need to find my underwear, and hurriedly clasped my bra before I tugged my shirt over the drumming rhythm happening in my head.

This was all wrong.

Something happened.

What happened?

My vision blurred as I tried to focus on my surroundings. The room had dark, taupe walls with thin blue carpet that had stains in multiple places and only one window to let in what was likely the midday sunlight but was hidden by the shabby looking curtains.

One memory flooded my mind.

Tall-dark-and-handsome.

Another.

Sadie falling.

Then another.

Kissing… almost kissing… falling.

Wham!

The memories hit me like a cannon blast.

Interest. Desire. Confusion. Fear.

Fear chased the memories around my consciousness as my breathing picked up and the blood pumped quickly in my veins.

"No, no, no. Fuck, no!" I yelled to the quiet room.

Adrenaline finally propelled me forward, and I ran toward the closed doors, ignoring my need for a large cup of water, some food, or a bathroom. I was running, *fast*, as the long hallway became shorter with every step. My labored breaths echoed in my ears and my eyes were wide with fright and something else.

Oh. *Survival.*

A flight of stairs greeted me at the edge of the hallway, leading me closer to an exit that I so desperately sought. They eventually deposited me into a small entryway that held the beacon of light I was searching for—a door. I would take a door to anywhere else right now.

I didn't take any extra time to see if other life existed in the house before reaching for the knob to the red-painted door chipping in more than one place. When the light of day and a cool breeze hit my face, my eyes blinked rapidly to adjust, but I continued running as fast as my weary legs would carry me until I was in a small alleyway a few streets over. My ragged breaths, frightened and gasping were all I heard.

I looked around at my surroundings, blood pumping, adrenaline working overtime in my system, and realized my feet were bare. I had run on gravel, grass, and now asphalt, but my feet had not registered any pain. I was gasping for breath, having run to the boundaries of my lung capacity while trying to convince myself no one was after me, and I could slow down to steady my breathing.

My knees slowly gave way to the heaviness I felt in my body and my legs connected with the asphalt, no longer able to bear the weight of my reality.

He... I... we...

My eyes clenched tightly and I shook my head. I couldn't even allow myself to think what I believed happened last night. My hands shook uncontrollably as I tried to make sense of everything. I took inventory of the soreness that wrapped around my trembling form, stopping when I felt the sharp pain between my legs, the sensitive skin that would sprout bruises, and my trembling body, all confirming my suspicions. My breathing hadn't slowed much, and even though I knew I was alive because of the hectic pace my heartbeat kept, I had become powerless in mere seconds. I was a fool.

You willingly gave what he only wanted to steal.

How could you?

You are such a fool, Andrea.

I wanted nothing more than to sink further into the paved side street and disappear altogether. When sitting back on my knees was too much, I laid in the alley, curled tightly into the shape of a ball, protecting myself in a shield of fear and anger. The curiosity I had felt towards this mysterious man was replaced by *loathing*. The desire I had tasted when his mouth was on my neck now felt like burns covering my tender skin. I *hated* this man for what he had done to me.

I hated myself even more for letting it happen.

Shame kept me plastered to the pavement for an undetermined amount of time, and it shattered every last part of my confidence like an enraged lunatic wreaking havoc in a confined space. I was undone and exposed in the worst way.

When I got back to Sadie's cousin's house later that night with new bruises cluttering my body and soul, I made her swear to tell no one and to scope out every future party we went to.

"Of course, I will make sure he isn't there. I can't believe that dick would do that to you!" Sadie appeared outraged when I gave her the cliff-notes version of my experience.

"I can't face him again. It would kill me, or make me sick. Either way, I just can't see him again so if you ever want me to go out with you, you have to check and double check he isn't there."

She gladly agreed to do so, and whether it was due to the guilt of leaving me that night or because she wanted to be good friend, I couldn't tell.

"What happened to you that night?" A question that I wasn't sure I even wanted answered.

"Oh. Well, you remember Jack?"

"Barely. Is he the one who helped you up after your drunken fall?"

"Hey, it was more like a trip, really…" Sadie looked out the open window of the room we shared, a puff of marijuana leaving her mouth.

"I rewarded him for helping me that night," Sadie said with a casual shrug of her shoulders and a look of indifference. I wanted to know more of what happened between her and Jack in order to distract from what had happened to me, but I didn't want to hear more of why Sadie chose to leave me. I wasn't the best at knowing how friends should act, but it felt like some imaginary friendship line had been crossed.

Sadie came along when I needed her, but that night when I needed her the most, she was worthless. I could only blame her more when a few months later, I couldn't stop throwing up even though I was sober, I took a test and came to grips with the truth: I was pregnant.

I remembered how terrified I had felt waking up naked and unaware. That room, that *man*, tore me apart from the inside out. That fear never left me. It seeped into every pore of my body and made its home there.

• • •

July 18, 2006—Age 15

Curls traipsed into the room an hour after my curt remark about the shower, blissfully unaware of the barrage of terrible memories that tormented me. I was grateful, for once, that no one could read my thoughts; my stony disposition throwing them off the trail to the real brokenness that lived inside me.

"Hello again darlin'! It is a glorious day."

'Glorious' was the exact opposite of how I felt right now.

"Yup, sure is," I said through gritted teeth.

"Now, how is our sweet pea doing?"

"She's been asleep since you fed her and is doing fine. See," I replied to Curls while pointing at the sleeping baby.

"Oh, I know the baby is fine, but I was talking about you."

"I'm fine." Lies. Shorter answers, truth or not, meant less talking necessary.

"Good. Good…" Curls said, her voice trailing off. "Let me just check these monitors right here and I will be on my way."

Her curls were boisterous this morning, flamboyant even, as they clung to her head for dear life, bouncing to and fro every time she moved her head or did something simple, like breathe. I watched Curls perform her mundane tasks of checking monitors, blood pressure, pillows, blankets, temperatures, all the things, until she had nothing left that would keep her. Unfortunately, that didn't seem to stop her.

"You got something on your mind, dear?"

"Nope."

"You sure?"

"Yup," I lied again.

"You don't seem so sure." This woman wasn't going to stop. I needed to give her a bit more if I was going to be rid of this conversation.

"Just mentally preparing for the day ahead."

"Uh-huh. Say, did I already tell you that I was adopted?"

I stared at her with what could have only been a stunned deer in the headlights kind of look. She was offering me a piece of herself again, and while I felt bad about shutting down her kindness earlier, I still wasn't ready to accept it.

"You didn't. Sorry to hear that," I said roughly.

"Oh no, sweetie, I'm not sorry at all! It was the best thing that could have happened. Sure, it was hard growing up wondering about my birth mom since I didn't have contact with her, but I was loved beyond measure."

"Did you ever meet your birth mom?" I wondered, cursing myself for even entertaining this conversation.

"As a matter of fact, I did. Not until I was eighteen, but it was worth the wait. She was in a better place and so was I. We were both ready."

I was in too deep at this juncture. "Do you still talk to her?"

"Yes, I sure do. I love her and I know for certain now that she loves me. I doubted it for a while, but the older I get, the more confident I am that she made the best decision for me. Now I have two loving mothers, and they both mean the world to me."

My eyes shifted downward as I picked at a thread coming out of the blanket covering my bare legs. "I guess that's good to hear. I hope she doesn't grow up hating me," I said, pointing to the sleeping baby between Curls and I. We both stared at the sleeping baby, like she held more than just my mistake.

"You are giving her a beautiful gift, Andrea—to be loved twice as much."

I wished that I shared the same optimism that Curls had because all I could see was my long line of mistakes, and I desperately hoped they wouldn't follow this baby girl—*my* baby girl—as she navigated through life.

"I know it's probably impossible to recognize now, dearie, but you are making the hardest and most noble kind of decision."

"What do you mean?" I questioned.

"You are loving her the best way you can right now—by letting her go."

CHAPTER 4

Accidents Happen

1995—Age 5

There were very few things that I learned from Michelle, my mother, unless you consider swearing and gossiping as life skills. She didn't cook but was a regular customer at the local KFC where she purchased the family style special a few times each week. Michelle only cleaned when she was out of clean underwear, and even then she would rope me into doing the chores for her by the time I was five. I could barely reach the kitchen counters let alone figure out how to clean them.

Michelle wasn't like the other moms that kids my age had. In fact, I can't think of any other mom like her. She swore like a sailor, showed up an hour late to every appointment (if she showed up at all), and dressed like she was still in high school with short jean skirts, shirts that plunged too low and were cut too high, and her signature platform black flip flops. Her hair was a dark brown, like mine, but with bleach blonde highlights intermixed throughout that she did herself. She kept her long, wavy locks swooped up into a messy bun on top of her head that flounced around when she talked. I could understand why my father, Dan, fell in love with her in high school—not much had changed.

The other moms I had seen at school pick up and drop off wore t-shirts that covered their boobs and didn't cause you to question whether you were in the right place. They hugged their children and waved after them with tears in their eyes, not because they were sad they had a kid, but it seemed like maybe they would miss their child when they were off at school all day. As if children weren't all a nuisance.

Michelle was hardly the nurturing or empathetic type. Once while playing, I scraped my knee, tears welled in my eyes. "Ow! Michelle, my knee, I fell!" I approached her, scream-crying.

"It's just a scratch. You're fine. Go get a damn towel and don't you dare get any blood anywhere!" Michelle said, waving me off and quickly fleeing to another room.

My tears only multiplied as I watched her retreating form leave me to fend for myself. I seemed to be more of a burden to her than anything else. We both knew it.

She wasn't shy in sharing with me that my birth wasn't planned; I was an accident. An "oops" when the condom didn't work. I carried this with me like a brand seared into the flesh of cattle.

The name 'Andrea' that Michelle had chosen for me was another indication of my unanticipated arrival.

"We only had boy names picked out. Dan was sure you were going to be a boy. Holy shit, what a surprise! It didn't even cross my mind to have a girl's name picked out just in case. When we found out you were a girl, we couldn't think of a name and it wasn't until we got to the hospital and you were born, we had figured something out. 'Andrea' was the only name I knew of someone I didn't hate. So we agreed," Michelle explained as if it were the most natural explanation for my unwanted existence.

I knew there was a reason I hated my name.

She and my father were, however, madly in love, and this was one thing I was certain of. He looked at her with wide, puppy dog eyes like she was the most delicious treat. Michelle felt the same and took any chance she had to share their love story. I had heard it so many times, I practically had it memorized down to the way every cuss word drawled from her lips.

"Dan and I were going steady our senior year of high school and we couldn't get enough of each other. He would wait for me after every one of my classes and offered me the gum he knew I liked. That damn fool was lovesick, I'll tell you that," Michelle gushed, lighting another cigarette and taking her time to enjoy the first inhale.

"He never pushed or pressured me into anything like some of the other shithead jerks I dated. He was the silent, patient type, and I liked that. It was hard to know what he was thinking all the time but then he would *show* me how he felt and that was enough for me," Michelle said with a coarse laugh, coughing up smoke with it.

I stared at Michelle with rapt attention as I listened to her talk. This is often how it was between us, I stayed quiet while she talked. We both stayed in our lanes.

Michelle took a swig of her Diet Cola before continuing. "Dan would walk me home from school, lighting up a cigarette he had stolen from his dad's stash, and sometimes we would talk but most times we just walked, side-by-side with nothing but smoke clouds floating between us." Her lips tipped into a mischievous smile as she described the early years with Dan.

This was as good of a love story as I had ever heard, and I enjoyed it every time she told it. I begged her to tell me about their wedding day; it was pure magic to a young girl like me.

"I wore a slim, white silk, strappy dress that I found at Patty's Thrift Store and felt like I hit the jackpot: I looked damn good!" Michelle said, smashing her boobs together and hiking them up higher before trailing her hands down her body. "See, your Grandma Jane didn't have much money since your Grandpa Bill died, so a full blown wedding wasn't in the cards. We got hitched in her backyard with a few family and friends," Michelle recalled, as she smacked her gum and started painting her nails firecracker red.

I knew the topic of Michelle's parents was a sore subject for her and a complete mystery to me, so it had always left me itching with curiosity. When I saw the look that Michelle had in her eyes whenever she spoke of my Grandpa Bill, I left it alone, not wanting to incite unnecessary rage.

Michelle could be feisty and argumentative. I had witnessed it plenty of times when her anger let loose on either Dan or I, leaving both of us in a pile of confusion as to what we'd done.

Michelle picked up her story without batting a glued-on eyelash but not before I noticed the flicker of pain that quickly registered in her voice over her father's memory. "Dan wore his dad's blazer with tan khakis that he also picked up at the thrift store. He got my ring from his Nana who was already gone from this Earth, and even though it was just a simple gold band, I didn't mind. It was the best fucking day I had ever had." Michelle marveled as she recalled their wedding day.

"My best friend made our wedding cake... or I should say attempted! It turned out looking more like a drunk giraffe than a tall, elegant wedding cake. It tasted like heaven though. We did all the typical wedding things like throwing the garter and my bouquet, which was made up of some big-ass sunflowers that Jane had grown in her garden that spring. We danced until our feet ached something fierce and the sun had completely set. It was a day to remember, that's for sure."

At this point in the story, Michelle usually forgot that she was talking to her five-year-old daughter rather than a girlfriend that she was relaying all the juicy details to.

"Dan and I had sex together before, but there's something about a wedding night that made it all seem like magic. We kissed and touched and kissed some more until the early morning hours. We barely got any sleep! We were at it all night," she said laughing and almost dripping nail polish on the floor, "It wasn't until a few months later that I realized just what that passion had cost us." Michelle shook her head with the heaviest sign of regret.

I squirmed in my seat, not knowing how to react. It wasn't a secret that Michelle still held onto the regret towards her pregnancy—towards me.

She continued with her story, unfazed by my discomfort. "We didn't plan on having kids for another ten years at least… shit. We were only eighteen when I found out I was pregnant with you. That is just too damn young to have a baby. But there we were, newly married, just out of high school, and becoming parents. It was all just too much," Michelle said, staring off at something beyond my head before plucking the gum from her mouth and trading it for a cigarette, and holding it steady between her fingers. There was a hint of annoyance in her voice and a thick coating of bitterness.

"You were an accident alright, but Jane coached me through it and told me this was happening whether I damn well wanted it to or not. I was freaked out about having a kid. Losing my freedom and my body in one shebang! Stretch marks, saggy boobs... ugh, I was just a kid, but it was out of my hands and sitting pretty in my gut," she explained, lifting the cigarette to rest between her lips.

My father wasn't as particular about what I called him. "Pa," "Dad," "Father," or simply, "Dan," were all the same to him. I tried out a few over the years and eventually just stuck with "Dan." It felt more natural since I was calling Michelle by her first name. He was much taller than Michelle, lean but muscular, having helped his own parents work their cattle farm in the small town of Friant, CA, where I grew up.

Dan still helped out his parents, my other grandparents who I referred to as Nan and Pop, despite having little to no interaction with them. He took care of their land since our family lived in a two bedroom manufactured home right next door. Our 750 square foot house needed a good deal of work since the roof leaked in the kitchen right over the stove and the toilet in the one bathroom we all shared. It made for an interesting time cooking and peeing. The floors warped and peeled in different places, and the furniture was all thrifted and smelled of tobacco and old lady perfume. I did have my own room that boasted a twin mattress stacked on top of a ratty box spring, raising it from the ground slightly, but not much. There was a multi-colored dresser that smelled musty every time I opened a drawer, but it did the trick in housing my few second-hand clothes. It wasn't much, but to me, this was my whole world.

Dan also commuted a stone's throw away to Fresno to work at a hardware store in the area. I never knew exactly what he did there, just that he worked nights and slept half of the day. The other half of his waking hours he spent working on my grandparents' farm, going out with Michelle, or fishing on the San Joaquin River. He was quiet and reserved, which made it difficult for me to gauge whether I was a bother or cherished company. Dan did allow me to join him on a few of his fishing jaunts, but we never spoke. That was the rule.

"The fish won't bite if you're chattin' away like that," Dan explained to me.

I never wanted to disappoint him. "I'll keep my mouth shut then. Well, after I tell you I'll keep my mouth shut. Oops, sorry. Okay, I'm stoppin' now, promise." My mouth stayed shut but my mind stayed active thinking of all the things we could talk about.

Even though Dan didn't speak very much, there is one memory I have of him stringing more than a few words together at a time and shocking me in the process. It had been a particularly grueling day in my kindergarten class, when a girl who I thought was my best friend left me at recess to play with another girl, someone she had told me she didn't even like. I was confused, hurt, and felt the betrayal of a thousand knives in my small back.

I came home that day, stomping into the house after getting off the bus, throwing my unicorn backpack on the floor and racing to the confines of my room to let the tears loose I had been holding in all day. This was out of character for me since I usually took on the quiet demeanor that Dan had and that Michelle preferred.

Dan tapped on my door and entered after I aggressively bade him to come in. He sat uncomfortably at the foot of my bed while I sobbed, and he simply waited. He never acted like he was in a rush to get to the next project or activity, and this time was no different.

I never expected any words, knowing Dan, but he surprised me by speaking.

"Andrea, life won't always get you down. There are good parts, too, and we gotta have hope for those good parts." Dan said with as much gusto as someone who was half asleep and surviving on coffee could.

My sobs completely stopped after hearing the timbre of his voice speak the words that my heart longed to hear but didn't know it. This wasn't meant to be a lingering conversation where I shared the story and he provided the advice. In fact, he had no idea what happened that day; he never asked. It was simply an encouragement, meant to lift my spirits and remind me that I could keep going. I could survive hard things and make it to the other side.

And you know what? He was right.

With that, he put his hands on his knees and pushed up to standing without fanfare or drama, like Michelle would have done. He walked out of my room, pulling the door shut behind him until the soft click of the latch sounded and the door separated me once again from the rest of the big, mean world.

I thought about this instance with Dan often because it was one of the few times I felt heard or encouraged by anyone. Nan and Pop, though they lived right next door, were too old and crumbly to want a kid underfoot. Dan worked a lot and Michelle was too caught up in herself to notice me. I spent the majority of my days exploring the farm and playing with our cat, Tickle. This was a rare spark of connection that made me believe I was worth more than I felt. It was this memory that had me clinging onto hope, like I had a reason to.

That is, until one day years later, hope drove off of a winding road, rolled hundreds of feet, and was crushed with no sign of life left. That day, hope shattered into a thousand tiny pieces.

CHAPTER 5
Gone

July 2003—Age 13

Aunt Cindy shook me awake in the dead of night.

As I rubbed the sleep out of my eyes, I tried to register what was happening as I listened to her sniffling and nose blowing filling the silence of my bedroom.

"What? What's going on?" I asked groggily.

"Oh, honey. Something terrible has happened."

"What time is it?"

"It's 2 a.m. I wouldn't have woken you unless it was important," Aunt Cindy said through her tears. "I got a call from Sheriff Ted and got here as soon as I could."

I blinked rapidly, trying to focus on her face and shake off the lingering pull to turn over and fall back asleep. "Sheriff Ted? Why?" Everyone in town knew Sheriff Ted, even if we didn't want to, and he knew all of us.

The only sound I heard in my dark room was Aunt Cindy's muffled noises as her hands covered her mouth.

I pushed myself up to sit. "What happened, Aunt Cindy? Where's Dan and Michelle? Do they know you're here?" Her crying picked up again as I looked on with confusion and worry. At first, I thought she was actually Michelle since they looked so similar to one another, being sisters and all, but upon further inspection, it was indeed Aunt Cindy leaning over my bed in a near pitch black room.

She choked on her next words. "They're gone, Andrea. Dan and Michelle were in an accident earlier tonight when they were on their way home."

"Wait… what?" I said on an exhale that never seemed to put air back into my waiting lungs.

When the news finally sank into my waking consciousness, I was shocked and disturbed that this could actually happen. I never thought about my parents dying, even in spite of the difficulties we had. I just assumed they would live until they were old like my grandparents. They should have lived longer than my grandparents. That's how life was supposed to work.

Before I could think to cry or mourn their loss, I leapt out of bed and instantly started getting dressed, rushing around the room to find my discarded clothes from the day before or any other items that would be passable to wear in public. I was going to find them. I was going to help.

Aunt Cindy watched me frantically pace the room, each step making her cry harder.

"Honey, it's no use," she said, walking towards me as I was wrestling the sleeve of my sweatshirt over my head. When I realized my head wouldn't fit there, I began removing the sweatshirt with ferocious determination until it lay tangled up in a heap at my feet, I finally spoke.

"But...I need to go. I have to see them."

Aunt Cindy walked over to me and gently rubbed my back, "Nothing else can be done. They're gone." Dead before the first responders could make it and likely before the man who witnessed it could dial 911. Dead when Sheriff Ted called my aunt, and still dead as I slept, completely unaware.

All I had left was my aunt and a couple of grandparents that didn't like me. I was glad Aunt Cindy was the one with me. Where Michelle was blunt and moody, Aunt Cindy was soft and gentle. She was a saving grace at many forced family holidays and whenever she saw me, Aunt Cindy would come and sit by me and tell me funny jokes she read from her Far Side desk calendar. I only saw Aunt Cindy maybe once or twice a year but, to me, they were treasured times that I stored up like a squirrel gathering nuts for the winter. They were my nourishment during the hard times and I clung to them like I clung to her that night.

Michelle and Aunt Cindy had a strained relationship. It's not as if anything happened. You don't need a fight to create distance, two different personalities is all it takes.

I was glad Aunt Cindy was the one to tell me about my parents' accident because she proceeded to hold my thirteen-year-old self in her arms as tight as she could manage while I leaned into her chest and bawled my eyes out. The two of us stood in the middle of my bedroom, arms gripping and tears mingling until the burden of standing was too much and the grief brought us to a defeated seated position on the floor.

"W-Why did they die?" This question was less about seeking an answer than it was voicing the tragedy I had just learned of.

"I am so sorry, Andrea. No child should ever have to experience this." Aunt Cindy rocked me rhythmically while

I leaked tears on her shoulder. Losing two people at once was a cruel joke, chiefly if those two people were your parents. Our relationships weren't perfect, but they were all I had and all that I knew.

My heart was leveled by this news. I wanted to run and help and hide away all at the same time. I didn't know what to do.

"What do we do now? Should we go somewhere or call someone?" I asked in a rush.

"Sh-sh-shh. We don't do anything right now other than just absorb what's happened," Aunt Cindy said to me while smoothing a hand over my bed hair.

I wish I had something to do or someone to call. I needed something in my physical world to hold onto while my emotional one crashed down around me. It physically hurt to take a deep breath because on the other side of my parents' death was every one of my failures as a daughter. I was never enough. I couldn't make them happy and I couldn't save them.

At some point, I had fallen asleep but Aunt Cindy never left me. She laid on the floor beside the mattress I slept on and next to the clothes I had fought earlier that night. My heart needed her more than I needed air.

In the late morning, I awoke and the memories of what had transpired the night before flooded my mind and clenched my heart into a tight fist. I didn't cry, having shed more tears last night than I had in the last year. I felt beat up by the magnitude of such a loss and guilty wondering if I was grieving enough for the family that didn't want me.

Shouldn't I be crying right now?

Is this real life?

Did Dan and Michelle actually… die?

I had questions. I needed information. I wanted to know the details of what had taken place less than twenty-four hours prior. What I did know was that Dan and Michelle had gone to the movies in Fresno last night, and I had put myself to bed around 9 p.m., a regular occurrence. Everything that followed was still a terrible, heart-wrenching mystery to me.

Aunt Cindy, I thought when I saw her legs move.

I looked down at the form on the floor below me and saw Aunt Cindy was starting to wake so without missing a beat, my mouth started rattling off the questions that my mind thought up a mile a minute.

"Who found them?"

"Did they go to the hospital?"

"How did it happen?"

"Why are they gone?"

In her Aunt Cindy way, she sat up and placed her hand on my forearm that was resting on my crossed legs as I sat in bed, and with three soft pats, she proceeded to tell me all that she knew and had heard from the police.

"Dan was driving and Michelle was riding shotgun when Dan swerved sharply, likely to avoid a meandering animal, and he must have overcorrected. The momentum of the vehicle was too great and the back tires skid across the street before catapulting them over the edge of the road." She gave it to me straight without hiding the details that my mind craved. I had never seen a real-life car crash, but the scene that Aunt Cindy described played on repeat in my mind with every detail my imagination could conjure up. It was a horror scene.

"The man who lived just below that ridge saw the 1980 white Toyota Corolla flip multiple times as it descended down the hill, each time adding another crushing blow.

When the cops approached the vehicle at the bottom of the hill, they said both of them were gone. The vehicle totaled." The details were gruesome, and it made my stomach churn.

We moved about the house in a dazed stupor, unsure of what to do next. My Nan and Pop, Dan's parents and my grandparents, had talked to the policemen last night. They gave the officers the information they were after and the identity they suspected, according to my aunt.

Aunt Cindy combed through the kitchen cupboards and the refrigerator searching for food and something to do with her hands, I supposed. "Where is all of the food? How do you all survive off this crap?" she murmured, more to herself than to me.

I didn't answer. I was embarrassed, though I still can't explain how being embarrassed of my hunger as a teenage girl was possible.

Later that morning, after a barrage of questions, a half-eaten breakfast of rock solid toast, and a morning cup of coffee, my Aunt Cindy looked at me with a question behind her eyes.

She let out a long, slow breath. "So, Andrea, I know so much has happened. I can barely believe this is real, but there are some decisions we have to make."

In a flash of shock coursing through my body, I suddenly realized I had never asked one of the most important, pressing questions: *Where was I going to live now?* My mind flashed to the movie Annie I had seen once about a little orphan girl who eventually went to live with a family that would adopt her. It all ended well for Annie, but would it end the same way for me?

Aunt Cindy must have intuitively known the internal dialogue I was having because she looked at me with her red-rimmed, green eyes and said, "Andrea, your Uncle Roger and I want you to come live with us. You will have to change schools and you won't be living next to your grandparents anymore, but we think it's best for you to stay with us. With Nan and Pop getting older I just thi—"

"Yes." I didn't pause or take a breath before answering. There was no reason or explanation needed. I hadn't thought about having to be taken care of by my Nan and Pop but now that Aunt Cindy mentioned it, I was glad I had another option.

With that one word sealing my future and avoiding an orphanage, I packed my bags, grabbed a few family photos and memorabilia that I wanted and walked toward the front door with Aunt Cindy. She assured me that they would do a more thorough clean out of the house later on, but for now, everyone was focused on priority number one —properly burying Dan and Michelle and saying our final goodbyes.

I turned to face my aunt by the door. "There is one more thing I need to grab. I'll meet you in the car in a sec."

"Alright, take your time." Aunt Cindy's small smile gave me the reassurance to say goodbye to my childhood home. My heart was numb with all of the goodbyes.

I hurried past my bedroom door as I heard the front door click shut, snuck into Dan and Michelle's room and tiptoed towards the jewelry box. I paused, waiting for Michelle's voice to yell at me, but it didn't.

It couldn't because she was gone. Even if my brain knew this, my body didn't believe it. I stood there a heartbeat longer, waiting for tears to meet with this new reality I was living. They never came though I wished they would. I wanted them to punch some life and feeling back into the soreness living in my chest.

Her jewelry box sat on top of the dresser on the wall opposite the door. I lifted the top of the box and was welcomed by a familiar scent—Michelle's favorite perfume, Lucky, but the knockoff version from the 24-hour mart. My eyes finally started leaking but not because I was sad about losing her; there was a part of me that felt this, but I cried now because despite being her only daughter, she never truly loved me. That is what hurt the most. I was the mistake that she never had the opportunity to get to know.

She is probably glad to be dead and rid of me, I thought while wiping my eyes.

I poked around for a few seconds before my fingers landed on the item they had been searching for, a gold chain necklace with an emerald gem hanging delicately from it. The necklace had a gold metal band circling it like a continuous hug keeping it safe from falling and sparkled more than I had ever seen before.

Michelle prized this necklace most of all; she never let me touch it (like all of her jewelry), but she never wore it either. I had always wondered why she never wore this one, considering how much she loved wearing flashy, expensive looking things, and this was by far the most expensive piece she owned.

She would pull it out of the box and hold it up to the sunlight that streamed through the one window in their bedroom, twisting and turning it, clearly admiring its perfect cut and brilliant color, yet, she always placed it back in its place and chose another necklace to wear instead.

What was so special about this thing, Michelle? I asked in my mind, but wondered if her ghost could hear me.

I didn't have a magical pouch to put such a magical necklace in so the front left pocket of my jeans would have to work until I could find a spot for it at my new house, with my new family. Despite my world completely shifting on its axis in a little less than a day, I was relieved to be living with my Aunt Cindy and Uncle Roger. For once, something good seemed to be heading my way, and I wasn't about to mess it up. I didn't want to say or do anything that would disappoint them.

I shut Michelle's jewelry box with a trembling hand and walked out of their room, waiting for Michelle's crazed stomping and tousled hair to come screaming down the hallway for me to leave her room alone. She didn't, and that truth made me feel empty. Hollow. A truth I was forced to accept and live through.

They're really gone. Forever. As in, not coming back.

Sadness. Hurt. Regret. Relief.

The feeling of relief confused me the most. It was as if I realized this was my chance to escape. To start over. Become someone new, not the hungry girl with parents that didn't love her.

As I walked towards the front door and hesitated before opening it to exit this life and enter my next one, I looked around at the furnishings. I noticed the dilapidated walls that were begging for new paint, the discoloration on the ceiling from years of unattended leaks, and the familiar layout that I could navigate in my sleep. I wasn't coming back here, and for the first time since hearing the news of my parents' death, I admitted something to myself and the empty space around me.

"I don't ever want to come back to this place."

My admission was met with nothing but silence. Only a few tears slipped down my face at the finality of this moment. The door would close, literally, with me on the other side.

Relief.

I had a shot at a real family. I vowed to be a good kid and stay out of trouble. I would do my homework, say my prayers, eat whatever food they wanted to feed me, and I would never complain. I hoped to be good enough so I didn't end up like little orphan Annie.

I wiped my cheeks with the palm of my hand and gripped the door handle with fervor before stepping outside and closing it behind me as I walked steadfastly towards my future.

CHAPTER 6
Abandoned

August 1995—Age 5

"You'll learn letters and things at school," Michelle said as we ate dinner in the living room one night while watching TV. "We don't need to do that at home, that's why schools exist anyway."

I nodded my head, believing all the other kids going to kindergarten tomorrow wouldn't know the alphabet either. I had been so excited for weeks leading up to the first day of school and had bothered Michelle and Dan more than I knew I should have. I could hear the edge in Michelle's voice, but, then again, she was always annoyed.

"You have a book about letters, or something, right?"

"No." I replied, quickly noting the three books that I owned.

"It's fine. Just wait 'til school starts."

One of the books I had was about going to school, and I had flipped through it cover to cover multiple times a day, wearing down the pages in the process. It was the only guide I had.

"You scared about going?" Michelle asked, stabbing a piece of chicken with her fork.

"No… why?" I asked in disbelief, not knowing why anyone would be scared to go to kindergarten. I thought about all of the kids my age I would play with, having spent the majority of my life around adults and cows; I wasn't scared, I was raring to go.

She waved her hand with the fork in the air stabbing at nothing. "Like all the new shit you'll have to figure out: riding the bus, talking to a ton of new people… You know, those sorts of things."

I didn't know. I had never been and the book I had only showed happy kids, not scared ones. There had also been no talk about a bus until that very minute.

"I have to ride a bus?" My small eyes widened in fear. I wasn't scared; I was terrified.

"Yeah, duh. I won't be getting up that early and Dan will just be getting off of work so he needs to sleep."

My heart sank. I had never been on a bus before. "What if I miss the bus? Or don't make it to school? Where will I go to get on the bus?" I asked, my questions all crammed together in one long sentence.

"You'll be fine. It comes up the street a bit where the little shelter thing is. The bus driver will help you out or one of the other parents will," Michelle replied flippantly.

I pushed my crispy chicken and mashed potatoes around on my plate, making a new concoction that I knew I wouldn't eat. I wasn't hungry anymore anyway. There was no way I could ride that bus. I would get lost walking there, I just knew it. It's not like we lived in a small neighborhood; there were acres separating the houses from one another.

What if I got on the wrong bus that took me to a different school with mean kids and an angry teacher? Nope. I had to convince Michelle to take me.

"Michelle, please take me to school tomorrow! Please, I don't want to ride the bus. How will I get home? I-I'm scared," I pleaded my case with all of the fear that fueled me.

"Sh-sh-shh, quiet. This is the best part."

I turned my head to stare at the TV, watching half-dressed people run around in tight spandex suits on some beach in a dramatic way. I waited for what seemed like hours to a young kid. I thought about grabbing my book. Did I miss that part about a bus?

"I can't take you to school, you'll be fine," Michelle finally said, dropping her fork and wiping her hands on the paper napkin.

I wanted to cry, but I knew that would only make Michelle more irritated. Tears never worked with her. It's not like I had an angle, I just wanted to be taken care of.

Michelle must have seen the fright and changed her mind, or she just wanted to be rid of this conversation. "Fine. I'll pick you up, alright? But only tomorrow. I'm not doing it every day. You'll have to learn how to do these things on your own," Michelle said, pointing the straw of her paper cup in my direction.

"Okay, thanks, Michelle." I took the plea deal knowing it was the best I would get.

The next morning, I was up the moment I heard Dan get home, which must have been early because the sun was just barely peeking over the rolling hills in the distance. I had tossed and turned all night dreaming I would miss the bus and have to stay home all day. I didn't want that. I had been waiting for this day for too long.

I got out of bed to make some cereal; it was something I always did. Michelle bought dinner and said that was enough cooking for one day. Lunch was usually a cigarette and coffee for Michelle and whatever food I could find for me.

This morning, I pulled out a leftover KFC bag from the night before and began filling it with food that was both known and unknown. I had learned from my kindergarten book that there was lunch at schools but you had to pay for it. That wouldn't be happening, money didn't grow on trees, Michelle often reminded me. I packed leftover mashed potatoes, an apple that looked to be bruised in multiple places, two slices of white bread that I picked a couple of green spots off of, and a candy bar that I had been saving from my birthday.

I added a few more of the sugar coated, crispy cereal pieces to my bowl for added energy, got dressed in the outfit I laid out the night before, and brushed my teeth. All things I knew to do because of my book. I then walked to the bus stop using Michelle's directions.

"It's right around the corner. After Misty's property."

"Don't give me that look."

"I don't know why you're so scared to ride a bus."

"You'll be fine."

She dismissed my concerns with a wave of her hand and flip of her hair as she flopped onto the couch to watch another show and ignored my existence for the rest of the evening. I had already taken up too much of her time with my jabbering and knew how irritated she was.

This morning, I found the dilapidated shelter and sat there for a while, maybe hours, but I couldn't tell time either.

I started to think the bus had left without me, until a girl about my age came skipping down the street ahead of her mom. One kid after another started to arrive in cars after that. *Phew.* I hadn't missed it.

I boarded the bus carefully, doing my best to not miss a step and fall on my face. The girl who I had watched skip towards the bus stop earlier invited me to sit with her in the front row, reserved for kindergarteners only, so I did. My nerves relaxed with every mile we drove.

My first day was better than the pictures in my book made it seem. The kids were nice, my teacher was excited to be there, and learning letters wasn't as hard as I thought.

I was having the best day of my life.

Until I stood outside by the curb after school and realized she wasn't coming. I waited. And waited. And waited. There was no sign of Michelle or Dan or anyone that I knew, for that matter. The nice lady from the school office stayed out front with me for a while until she decided it was time to call home. The home phone she had on file continued ringing until it dropped her into our voicemail box at the end of every try. I could've told the office lady that Michelle never answers the phone, but I had hope that maybe today she would.

"Mrs. Strivers, we have your daughter here at the front office, and she said you were planning to pick her up. Please call us back so we can coordinate the pickup," the office lady said into the phone.

I could tell by the look on her face that she was worried. We were running out of options about what to do. I felt this weird shyness in front of the office lady, knowing she was doing all she could but it was no match for Michelle's heartlessness. I would have been better off riding the bus home. At least there were teachers here to help me get on the right one.

I stayed there for another hour, sitting in the hard plastic chair in the school office, without any whiff of Michelle. Eventually, the office lady huffed that she needed to get home and after exhausting the short but surprisingly existent emergency contact list in my file, she decided to take me home herself. Living in a small farming town had its benefits, one of them being that everyone knows where everyone else lives.

When I walked up the wooden add-on steps that Dan had built and pushed through the front door, seeing Michelle sitting at the table picking over the dinner she had likely just gone to pick up, my anger lit like a fuse.

"You didn't pick me up today!" I yelled after slamming the door and stomping into the house.

"Oh, shit," was Michelle's reply and her only words of apology.

The anger felt bigger than my small body and I thought I would explode.

"You better wipe that look off your face, Andrea, before I do it for you!" she sneered.

I stormed off to my room and stayed there for the rest of the night. I didn't want to see her and I knew she didn't want to see me. She wasn't sorry that she forgot about me. I was invisible to Michelle. A child she didn't want to think about or accept that she had responsibility for. I thought she would be there for me today; I trusted and believed I could rely on her, but it was only a glaring reminder that I wasn't important. I was forgotten. Left to fend for myself regardless of my age.

I was abandoned by my mother that day, but if I'm honest with myself, she abandoned me immediately upon realizing there *was* a me.

CHAPTER 7
Lost in Translation
July 18, 2006—Age 15

It was my first time meeting Wendy face-to-face; what a hell of a way to meet someone.

Wendy's short stature and narrow body made her appear like a wisp of a thing, but the grip she had on my shoulders was the only thing keeping me together. She dressed with the utmost care and attention. Her stylish, blonde bobbed hair curved close to her chin and mixed well with the gray that was highlighted throughout, a clear indication of her age and likely the stress of dealing with misfits like me.

I had handed Wendy the tiny, bundled baby girl to deliver to her new adoptive parents who were anxiously waiting in the next room. I had been a puddle in Wendy's arms ever since. I let myself fall apart, knowing when I walked out of those hospital doors, I needed to forget everything, even *her*.

"This is so hard Andrea, and that is okay. I've got you. You just let those tears fall."

I was speechless. I couldn't speak through the ache that sat in my chest and the lump that stayed trapped in my throat, threatening more tears if I opened my mouth to respond. It felt like I had a bullet lodged in my chest, but I imagine that would have hurt less than this feeling.

Now you can move on, Andrea, I thought, but didn't fully believe.

We stayed like that, Wendy sitting on the edge of my hospital bed and grasping my shoulders, inviting me to lean in and take refuge in her arms, until Wendy broke in with her delicate words of encouragement.

"We will get through this together, I promise you there is beauty even in the hard things."

My gasps and groans that I responded with sounded more like a frog trying to escape captivity in my throat than a teenage girl who just gave up her baby. I had drenched Wendy's navy blue blazer with the pink stitching that lined the sleeve cuffs and pockets with my tears.

She squeezed my shoulder and let out a soft sigh. "For tonight and tomorrow night I got you a hotel room down the street from here that you can relax in, sweetie. Maybe take a bath, watch some TV, and enjoy some take out. This time is for you to rest and recuperate. You have had an intense few months and could use a breather."

Wendy hadn't told me her plans to do this for me and I wondered if this was going to show up on a bill somewhere that I wasn't expecting, nor did I think to ask about, until that very moment.

"Will this be added to my bill?"

She studied me for no more than half a second before responding, "What bill?"

"You know, the bill you will probably try to stick me with when I leave here that shows all the line items of expenses you have spent. The bill that explains why you are doing all of this nice stuff for me."

Wendy burst into an unexpected laugh that made me confused. I just stared at her waiting for an explanation.

"Oh honey, there is no bill that you will get stuck with. These adoption costs are covered by the adoptive family and my agency. You don't have to worry about anything."

I must have been more tense than I thought because at her response, I visibly exhaled and sank deeper into the three hospital bed pillows I had stacked behind my back to prop myself up.

I don't know what made me trust Wendy. I don't trust many people, but there was something about her demeanor that said, *I got your back and I am not going to let you fall off the edge, even if you want to.* And boy did I want to. I was dizzy with so many competing emotions. I needed to smoke a joint and bring my nerves back down to Earth, or at least closer to it.

I did end up staying those two nights in the hotel she booked, and it wasn't a cheap motel where you wondered what would be hiding under the covers or lurking in the bathtub. Wendy rented me a room that she herself would likely have stayed in. I hated to admit this, but maybe Wendy wasn't after anything. Maybe she did just want to help me.

I took this gift as a kind send off from Wendy and the adoptive family, and, honestly, it was the nicest gift I had ever received. In that instant, I swore that I wouldn't be a bother to them. I wouldn't worm my way into their family and try to include myself where I wouldn't be wanted. I said my goodbyes to my daughter by birth alone, and that was just going to have to be good enough for everyone—including me. I couldn't even face the family that agreed to love her and hold her forever.

Before Wendy left me to dress and prepare to be discharged, she looked at me intently.

"Andrea, I know you said you didn't have anyone you could stay with after you left the hospital, but are there really no family members you can call? Maybe anyone that you can stay with after you check out of the hotel?"

My mind wanted to give a straight answer: I had no one. Yet, that wasn't exactly true, and something about Wendy just made me want to confide in her. Dammit. Why did she have to be so likable? I decided to come clean. It wasn't exactly a secret.

"I do, sort of. My Aunt Cindy, who I lived with for awhile after my parents died, lives close but she is so busy with work and life that it's just too hard for me to stay with her." I turned to look out the window, avoiding Wendy's gaze. This embellishment of the truth was probably the better angle to take here, not knowing how much Wendy would try to push back.

"I see. Well, I think if I were your Aunt Cindy, I would want to know that you just delivered a baby and chose to place the baby up for adoption," Wendy said, tilting her head to the side.

I couldn't argue with her. My Aunt Cindy would want to know this, but I couldn't burden her with my sad, depressing life when she had enough trauma of her own to deal with. She had endured many tragedies from her sister dying (and depositing me into her life), to losing her husband, my Uncle Roger, shortly after. It was best that I just kept to myself. Now I needed to convince Wendy of this.

"She probably would want to know, so I will make sure to tell her," I fibbed. Maybe I will send her a letter someday. That would be easier than calling her unannounced and dropping this kind of bombshell on her well-manicured life. I decided this little lie was warranted. I couldn't face my Aunt Cindy, especially right now when my sanity had been stretched like a rubber band pulled to its furthest boundaries. I was close to losing my shit, and I just needed to focus on getting out of this hospital. I could barely breathe here and needed to point this hot mess in a different direction.

"If you want me to make that visit to your aunt with you, I will absolutely do that, Andrea. Don't hesitate to call me, and don't hesitate to call her either."

In parting, Wendy handed me a card with her cell phone number on it and told me to call anytime, even in the middle of the night if necessary. I held onto the piece of paper, knowing I wouldn't call, but it felt comforting to know that I could. She had my number to update me periodically with photos of the baby, but I knew I wouldn't be looking at those either. Even a glance at that little girl, *my* little girl, would put me on an invisible hook that I wouldn't be able to release myself from easily. It was better just to cut the line altogether.

• • •

July 18, 2007—Age 16

I exhaled a moving cloud of smoke from my mouth, sagging further into the couch.

One year later, the wound of giving up my child for adoption was like a gaping hole in my heart, throbbing and pulsing when I pictured her tiny face in my mind's eye. You don't go through something like birth to up and forget all of the marks it leaves on you—body and soul.

My phone buzzed on the cushion beside me so I picked it up to see who it was, immediately feeling my stomach drop when I read her name on the screen.

Wendy: Thinking of you today. You are a strong girl, Andrea, and I am so glad to have met you one year ago today. Your birth daughter is thriving. Let's talk about getting together so you can meet her.

Wendy Dobson proved to be as faithful as ever and tried her best to stay in touch throughout the year despite me making it difficult on her. I could have thrown my phone in the ocean and moved to some remote farming village in the Italian hill country, and Wendy would have still found a way to reach me. It's not that I didn't want updates or pictures of how much this little baby had grown, but I couldn't face the shame I felt every single day for letting her go. It was best if she didn't know me and I wasn't in her life. At least that is what I kept telling myself, and I hoped that one day I would believe it.

It's better this way. Don't reply and open that door. Ignore Wendy, I thought, like it was an easy thing to do.

I needed to be at work in an hour and couldn't face it if I had these leech-like emotions hanging onto me. I had been bussing tables and washing dishes every night at one of the local diners, trying to earn enough money to pay for this couch I slept on, which came at a steep price. I had bounced around from one stranger's place to the next this past year but when I reconnected with Sadie at a party, she managed to convince her new boyfriend to let me stay with them. The entire apartment, including the couch, was shabby chic, emphasis on the shabby, minus the chic, but it was a roof over my head so I wasn't going to be picky. Her boyfriend, Todd, was adamant that I pay him almost half the rent even though I had to pick up my bedding every day off of the ripped up couch with a controversial history.

I turned my phone face down beside me, ignoring the twitch I felt in my fingers to send Wendy a quick reply. For all she knew, I was dead, or hurt, or both.

No one cares about you, Andrea. Wendy definitely doesn't.

I exhaled another puff from my joint. My due date, her first birthday, was today but I tried not to let it conjure up the mess of mangled emotions that had chewed up a part of my soul.

What would it be like to meet her now, as a one-year-old?

I quickly tamped out that thought, along with my joint.

Don't you dare interfere with her life. Remember why you gave her up—to get her away from you.

Reality was a bitch. I couldn't traipse into her life now, too much time had passed and I wasn't about to start expecting more from her new family simply because this little girl came from my body and shared my DNA. I was an almost seventeen-year-old who scraped by doing odd jobs like washing dishes in a kitchen or scrubbing toilets in public restrooms. I was someone who relied on other people to keep a roof over my head so I wouldn't find myself out on the streets with nothing but a cardboard sign to explain my woes and beg for help.

My phone vibrated again.

Wendy: It's never too late. Let me know where you are and I'll come bring you a meal. We can talk, or just share some food.

This was the way of Wendy I had come to know so well. She was persistent in finding a way into my life and in turn, a way into my heart. I couldn't allow this. I thought about chucking my phone against the wall. It would have made me feel better to shove Wendy further away from me, but I was finally able to purchase more minutes so I wasn't about to break it.

I set my phone down on the beat up coffee table and pushed off the couch to grab a glass of water to settle the sour pit in my stomach. I wasn't two steps into the kitchen with an empty glass suspended mid-air when Sadie and Todd pushed through the front door.

Breathlessly, Sadie started spitting words out. "Andy, we have to grab our things and get out of here. NOW. The apartment manager just called the cops and they're on their way. We have to go! *Hurry!*" Sadie said, with an emphasis on the *hurry.*

I set down my empty glass with an awkward thunk. "What do you mean the cops are coming? Why did the manager call them?" I asked, as I bolted to the small bag I had stored next to the couch with the few clothes and belongings I owned.

Todd rushed past us to the one bedroom room, completely ignoring my need to know more. Sadie turned, lowered her voice and told me. "The manager found out Todd was dealing behind the building and said he would call the cops if it happened again. Well, it happened again."

"Dealing? Todd?! Has he lost his damn mind?" I let out a groan of frustration and raced to slip on my sneakers, scanning the room for any items I may have missed. "What's he even selling?"

"Meth. And some pills. The usual," Sadie said in a more hushed tone than before, likely worried that her drug dealer boyfriend would get pissed about her confession and leave her to get caught by the cops that were on their way.

"Where are we going to go now?" I asked, worried as I slipped my hoodie on without zipping it since my hands were shaking so badly.

"I don't know but we need to split up. We are more likely to be caught if we're together," Sadie said, appearing more flustered than I had ever seen her.

With the few items they had, Sadie and Todd rushed towards the front door that they had entered just minutes before and raced down the steps to the back of the apartment building. I ran quickly, bending right to cross the street past the dive bar diner I was supposed to show up to work at soon. Apparently, I would need a new job and a new couch to sleep on. I couldn't show up there now, mere feet from where the apartment would be crawling with cops asking questions and trying to pin me to one of Todd's many deadly sins. I swore as my running turned into a fast paced walk and remembered I had no money. I had spent the rest on weed and rent money that I gave to Todd.

Damn you, Todd, I thought with every heavy footstep.

I recalled the conversation we had just two days ago when he pressured me to give him the money earlier than our agreed upon date.

"Andy, change of plans. I need the rent money by tonight."

"Tonight? What's the rush?"

"I won't be here for the next couple of days and need to turn it in before it's due on Friday." Todd said, eyes scanning everywhere other than my face.

I considered his serious but lame attempt at convincing me this was the truth.

"I can give you half now and maybe half tomorrow when I get my paycheck," I replied firmly.

He finally looked at me, bearing the full weight of his demand. "It's really gotta be tonight."

My eyes bounced to Sadie, who was lounging on the chair opposite me, painting her nails and pretending as if Todd's pushy demeanor was no big deal.

"I don't get paid until tomorrow morning when I show up for my shift. The best I can do is to come back here on my lunch break to give it to you." My teeth clenched together as I willed myself not to tell him off.

"Fine. Just don't be late or the rent will be." He picked up his sleek new phone and begged indifference while I sat irritated by our conversation. He held all the power and we both knew it.

The worst part was watching Sadie completely ignore these moments where Todd demanded control. She seemed content to allow his overreach on a few things and now it was coming back to bite all of us. Who knew if Todd had even paid rent this week or just used the money to funnel into his drug business?

This day was turning into a total nightmare. I stewed while stomping down the street, passing one business after another until I found a small neighborhood park that had a basketball court and a simple playground set. I set my bag down on the grass and plunked down beside it as though I had run a marathon. I hated running. I hated Todd for making me run. My shoulder ached from carrying my few items that bounced against my body awkwardly. I rubbed it with one hand while the other reached to pull my phone out of my jeans pocket.

Where's my phone?

I must have dropped it.

Or left it back at the apartment.

Shit.

I hadn't even had time to grab any of the food I had gotten from the food bank just the day before. I had nothing. No money, no food, no roof, no phone, no friends.

What the hell, Todd! I screamed internally.

"What the hell Todd!" I yelled out loud.

I knew something was off about that guy but Sadie was smitten, just like she had been about Daryn, Brandon, Bobby, and all the others. She really knew how to pick them, and I really knew how to pick my friends, apparently. Sadie always gave the impression of being an invested friend but all she really wanted was a wingman. I didn't mind it for a while but seeing that her boyfriend screwed things up, royally, I was fed up with her antics.

"Andy, there's a party this weekend in Hollywood. The guy used to be a former movie producer! Or, maybe it was a cameraman? Whatever. It should be a good time!"

"Andy, Byron said he would get us into the club he is bouncing at this weekend."

"Andy, there is a house party on the east side this week. You have to come with me!"

"Andy, why wouldn't you want to come? You're working? Just blow it off, come on!"

"Andy, how can you be tired? One more drink!"

This was Sadie. The life of the party, which is probably why so many guys were drawn to her in the first place. I had been too, but was becoming more exhausted by our friendship than I cared to admit. In this moment, when the possibility of not seeing her again for a good long while was more real, I let myself grumble about her.

I was still pissed about forgetting to grab so many things from the apartment when my eyes moved across the park and landed on a family playing with their small child at the playground. The lady, who I assumed was the mom, moved slowly towards the slide, pointing her digital camera towards the young girl who looked equal parts terrified and thrilled to be sitting at the top. Her dad was waiting at the bottom, eagerly clapping his hands in anticipation of catching the little girl after she bravely pushed off and descended down the slide. He swooped her up when she made contact with his arms, showering her with kisses all over her chubby cheeks. After filming this proud first, the mom came over and stood beside them, clapping her hands and rubbing her daughter's back in her own excitement over the brave feat.

Proud. Loving. Supportive.

My angry exterior started to melt as I watched this tender moment unfold, and I caught a small glimpse into the life of this family. I had never experienced a family bond like that up close and personal. Truth be told, I had never experienced it at a distance either. I wondered what it would have been like to have two doting parents cheer and clap over an accomplishment of mine. That was a life I had never known. The temperature of my anger began to rise again, and I remembered the feelings of abandonment when my parents up and died. In their life and in their death, one thing remained the same: I was on my own.

It was always just me. There was not an us, not a we, and never a family.

I hoped my little girl is experiencing more than I had with my family.

In my heart, I knew the adoptive parents were these kinds of people. Wendy told me that they would be. Still, the corners of my eyes filled with water that clouded my vision and caused me to rip my watchful gaze away from the loving family. I couldn't stand looking at them any longer, but it was already too late, the emotion found the corner of my heart I thought I had hidden well this time.

Screw it all.

My tears spilled over, and I let out a pained cry that I quickly covered with the back of my sleeved arm. I pulled my knees up to my chest and buried my face between them hoping to stifle the sobs that began shaking my body involuntarily.

Allison. This was the name I gave my little girl hours after birth; the girl who lived in my heart but no longer my body.

I remember Curls, the nurse, asking me if I was going to pick out a name for my daughter. "I don't see why it would hurt."

"But what if they don't want to name her that?"

"Then it will be written on her soul, and yours and you'll have a name just the two of you share. Either way, it doesn't hurt to ask them. Those adoptive parents seem like nice folk. Maybe they'll like the name Allison."

I nodded and looked away. It sounded like a bad idea to ask if the adoptive parents would accept the name I chose. I was hesitant to open my heart more than it had already been forced open. I didn't ask them because I couldn't face them. Curls told them though, and the parents up and named her *Allison.* I didn't think they would do it, but they did. It was only a sliver of what I could offer my daughter and yet, it felt like a piece of me I was giving to her forever.

I pressed my eyes further into my knees, trying to block the tears that wouldn't stop.

It's better this way. You aren't good enough for Allison.

I wrapped my arms around my legs even tighter, gritting my teeth and rocking myself forwards and back to keep from unraveling. Damn you, Todd, for ruining things! I no longer had my monotonous existence acting as the bandaid to shield me from Allison's effect on my sorry life. My heart was ripped open and exposed in a vulnerable way. I had been teetering on the brink of my emotions all day and Todd's idiocy shoved me over the edge. There's nowhere I could've hid that would have protected me from these feelings. They were always there, just a hair below the surface.

I stayed there in that position until I could only hope that the family had exhausted their play and returned home. I lifted my head, blinking against the dim light of the setting sun and scanning the playground for the family. To my relief, and despair, they were gone.

Of course they had a home. They were probably enjoying dinner together. Or reading books before bed.

It was my turn to leave even though I had nowhere to go.

CHAPTER 8
It's a New Day

August 2007—Age 17

I tried to keep my eyes closed despite the obnoxiously bright morning sun forcefully cutting through the dark shades of night. I didn't want to be reminded of where I was. I wanted to forget.

The city never slept and because of that, neither did I. I began to dread the night because of the constant activity of the shadows, stumbling by me in a dazed stupor thanks to alcohol and drugs. I had been startled awake many times by passing storytellers, begging for their crazed minds to be heard by anyone willing to listen.

My head rested on my arm as I laid on my left side, back facing the building's brick wall, ready to fend off any passersby if the need arose. I was piled on top of multiple cardboard boxes creating a barrier between me and the cold, hard cement, but the chill still found me. The speeding vehicles and screeching brakes woke me up so many times that I wondered if I had even slept. I had always loved the sounds of the city and once found comfort in its constant noise. Now those same sounds rung louder in my ears, and the once comforting white noise of city life was too close, too blatant.

It had been three weeks since I left Sadie and Todd's rundown apartment. I was now a seventeen-year-old girl with no money, no job, and no clue what to do. Things took a hard left turn, and now I spent my days holding my delicately worded sign: NEED FOOD SO HUNGRY! It didn't work. People were too busy these days, talking on their phones and walking quickly to wherever they needed to be. The gurgling sounds coming from my stomach came on a regular basis. It didn't matter that I filled it just days before. It was always greedy and asking for more.

As I lay there thinking about the gunshots I had heard in the distance last night, my attention piqued when I heard two faint female voices coming from a door that slammed shut further down the alleyway. They started walking across the street, heading in the direction of my makeshift cardboard bed, and I listened intently with my eyes still closed so I wouldn't give myself away that I was, in fact, eavesdropping.

"It is a great way to make a buck in the city. Thank you, Rachel, for putting in a good word for me. I can't believe I was on the streets like these bums just a couple of months ago."

This was city life, alright. There were more homeless people than there were sidewalks and once you got here, it was hard to leave. I strained to hear and willed my stomach to stop its noisy nonsense so I could make out what they were saying.

"Of course, Lin. Bernie always takes care of his girls. I couldn't imagine doing anything else now."

The two women passed me on the street, their voices becoming clearer but only momentarily until they started to merge onto the busy sidewalk that was already beginning to fill with passersby. My eyelids flew open and I peered in their direction. They had money, and likely enough to pay for food for a whole day and maybe even a little extra for weed or a pack of cigarettes. It was wishful thinking but it gave me the momentum I needed to peel myself off of my cardboard bed and follow them.

I hadn't eaten very much in the last two days so when I hurriedly stood, my head began to spin and I grabbed for the wall to steady myself before making off in the direction they were headed. How many times had I stood in some shelter's food line this week only to be turned away when they ran out of food? My odds were better using my sign and locating a busy street corner that wasn't already in use, which could also take a full day of searching.

"Wait!" I yelled out of desperation but the plea was stifled by my scraggly morning voice so I tried again after clearing my throat with a less threatening call. "Excuse me!"

Both of the women turned towards the sound of my misplaced manners, and I walked slowly towards them so they didn't think I was a lunatic trying to hurt them. I began speaking hurriedly, trying to spit the words out before they determined I wasn't worth their time or help, like many other people did when you were a beggar in a city full of beggars.

"I haven't eaten in days and I could really use a little bit of money to buy myself some food. Please. Even if it's just enough to buy a bag of chips, I'll take it. I am so hungry, I would probably just eat the bag along with the chips." I gave a small nervous laugh and realized how crazy I sounded.

Rachel or Lin, I wasn't sure who was who since my eyes had been closed when they were speaking, spoke up.

"How old are you, kid?" the tall, blonde woman with the full figure asked me.

"Old enough," I said, not wanting to break one of my street rules: don't share any personal information.

"You look young... don't you have any family that could help you out?"

I inwardly cringed, pretending that my age and family status didn't invoke a reaction I was ready to defend further. "No one that I would want to ask."

"Hm. Let me guess, you ran away from your family hoping things would be better and now you're here, begging for food and knowing things really aren't so great out on your own." The piercing gaze of those brown eyes stared straight into the raw areas of my heart. Was I that obvious? I needed to deflect, and quickly, before all hope of food was off the table.

"Something like that."

She let out a full sigh. "I know what it feels like to be desperate."

"Same. I was in your shoes not that long ago," said the girl with straight, jet black hair that had been quiet up until now.

I pretended not to bristle at the thought of running away from my family. It was a tender spot that wouldn't heal regardless of the time that passed. It did no good bringing it up, especially with these strangers.

"Why don't I get you something to eat and maybe help you find a better place to sleep. It isn't safe to be young and beautiful on these streets," the blonde suggested.

Food. Help. Beautiful. These words ran together until I realized they were meant for me. I was relieved that my quick decision-making landed me a meal for the day.

"Do you think Bernie could use any extra girls during the week, Rachel?" Lin asked, flipping her black hair over her shoulder.

"You know Bernie, he's always looking for new girls in his rotation," Rachel replied. "Looks like you have a decent body under all those layers, and your dark hair and eyes will draw some folks in, you know, the ones who have a thing for brunettes," Rachel said as her eyes trailed from my hair to my toes, inspecting my shabby outer appearance.

Did I even want to know what I looked like today? I glanced down at my baggy sweatshirt that I had picked out of a strange garbage bin almost two weeks ago to keep me warm at night; it probably hadn't been washed for months before retrieving it from the dumpster. It had that pungent, tattered vibe to it.

I stared with my mouth gaping open in complete shock. I stumbled over my words when I finally spoke. "Well, I... um... yes, I do have a body under these clothes. I can work hard and will do whatever I am asked."

"Good. Because those are the only kind of girls that Bernie likes working for him—hardworking and does what he asks without question." Lin nodded as she raised an eyebrow.

"Why don't you come to breakfast with us and we can talk over the particulars of the job. We were just about to hit up the bagel spot around the corner. We'll get you a shower and see if you'll be worth recommending to Bernie," Rachel said decisively.

I could not believe my turn of fate. I was not only going to eat breakfast for the first time in a long while but I also might have a job at the end of it all, pending their inspection. I didn't care what the job might be. I didn't even care who Bernie was. I was so damn hungry and too tired to care what the price of the meal might cost me.

Desperation set in, and my survival instincts took over. Not every question needed an answer because not every question had one.

CHAPTER 9

Strung Up

August 2007—Age 17

"How old are you?" Bernie asked.

I knew my age would be a deterrent. There was no way a seventeen-year-old should be working here, so I did what I needed to; I did what came naturally. I lied. "I'm eighteen."

"Alright, that'll work," Bernie huffed but didn't push any further. I counted myself lucky, for the time being. It turns out I was exactly what Bernie was looking for. I had enough youth in my features that would draw attention but enough curves to insinuate I was every bit a woman.

Bernie was heavy, bald, and wore fancy suits that made him appear bigger, scarier, and more boss-like. He gave me precisely fifteen minutes to interview for the open position but instead of sitting in an office facing one another with a large, oak desk in between us, he gave me a floor. A dance floor, that is, set atop a stage that was lined with a few poles reaching to the ceiling at varying distances, an audience of mostly rambunctious men, and a skimpy outfit that would eventually come off. I was more nervous than I had ever been in my life.

When was the last time I had shaved my legs?

What if I mess this up and everyone hates me?

I danced like my life depended on it, which at this point, it basically did. I envisioned another delicious, hot meal, and I kept this front and center in my mind as my arms and legs moved to a foreign rhythm. I had always loved dancing but dancing alone on a stage with ogling eyes, whistles, and catcalls from an audience, who were affectionately known as customers, was another deal entirely. I wanted to close my eyes but knew if I did, I would wind up wiping out, hard, on the slick stage in the seven-inch heels I wore for the "interview."

Have I ever worn heels this tall?

Have I ever worn heels?

"You got the job. I want to see you here for the next three nights at 9 p.m. sharp. You'll have time to get ready. Sally will teach you the routines, and if the customers like you, then you get more time on stage," Bernie said, pausing briefly. "Let's hope they like you."

"Thank you...um, sir." Or whatever they call a strip club owner. "I will work really hard to learn everything," I promised him, feeling entirely too dependent on the man in front of me. I hated feeling that way, but it was a necessary evil if I wanted to eat again.

He sized me up once more before nodding. Bernie started to walk away, his loafers making clicking sounds on the floor, before he turned to face me again. "I don't know where Rachel and Lin picked you up, and I don't give a damn, but don't make me regret not asking more questions," he said with an accusing finger pointed at me.

Don't mess this up, Andrea.

I moved into a dingy two bedroom apartment just down the road from my job at the *Wild Kitty* that Rachel, Lin, and another dancer, Sally, the one who would teach me the routines, already lived in. My roommates were sane and safe, something I couldn't always say about my former street mates.

Lin was the one who taught me everything about makeup, dressing my body, and working a room. "All of the power you'll ever need is right here," Lin indicated, pointing her finger up and down my body. "If you want to succeed out there then you need to unlock your sensuality here."

"Lin's right, the dancing part is easy, it's your confidence that will make them all fall to their knees, throwing hundred-dollar bills at your feet, and begging for more," Rachel said with a straight face.

The clothes and makeup helped some, but I still felt like a phony. I soon realized it was just a role, an act I needed to figure out how to play three nights a week, maybe more.

"Did you pick a stage name yet?" Sally asked me while lounging on one of the couches in our small dressing room. The space had a few vanity mirrors with chairs, a tiny bathroom in the corner, and a couple of couches we all used for our breaks.

"Uh, a stage name? Nobody told me I needed one of those," I confessed, inspecting the rack of outfits we could choose from and wondering where the rest of the fabric was.

"You can choose any name you want, but just know that when you walk in that door, that's the woman you become," Rachel said while pointing at the backdoor we all entered through.

"Does anyone ever really use that name?" I looked over my shoulder and asked.

Rachel flipped her blonde hair over her slim shoulders and her gaze bore into me. "If it were up to me, I would always use our stage names, even outside of work."

I met her gaze, feeling every bit as curious as I did exposed. "Why?"

Rachel exhaled and looked past me. "Eventually, we all become that woman on the stage and trying to pretend we are anyone else is a lost cause."

I focused my eyes back on the rack of clothes, swallowing the truth of Rachel's words. Well, *shit.* After years of despising the name given to me at birth, which seemed more like a formality to Michelle, the possibilities were endless. Who did I want to be?

"So what do you all go by on stage then?" I asked, finally choosing a slim pink number that looked somewhere between a bikini and dental floss.

"Sally chose Alana, I picked Lexie, and Rachel prefers Rita," Lin told me.

"When the sun goes down and the curtains go up, that's who we become," Sally added.

I slowly nodded, absorbing what they were saying but having no clue where to start in picking out a name I would likely come to hate, just like Andrea and just like Andy.

"You look like a Stella to me," Lin finally said with an assessing look.

"No way! Stella sounds too soft for Andy. Her features are dark and mysterious," Sally suggested, waggling her fingers like I was actually some mysterious person.

I felt awkward being the center of attention, but I was the new girl, so I supposed that's just how these things went.

"I got it," I heard Rachel pipe in. She leaned forward, resting her elbows on her knees and making me squirm a little under her scrutiny. "Alexandria," she finally said.

"Oooh, I like it! That's so exotic and... other-worldly," Sally said, clapping her hands in agreement with Rachel.

"I guess that works," I replied, having no better ideas and wanting to just be done with the conversation already. I didn't want to think about what Alexandria was about to do, I was too nervous.

"Remember, you're Alexandria now, more often than you'll be Andy. Got it?" Rachel asked, even though it was more command and less question.

"Got it."

Rachel gave me a small grin, the first one I had seen since we met. "Good, now go make those bastards drool."

• • •

January 2008—Age 17

Alexandria is looking tired and worn out tonight, I thought, looking at my reflection in the mirror in front of me. I had been working this gig for six months already, and dancing in heels at all hours of the night was taxing on my body. I often wondered how some of the older dancers made it through a night without aching muscles and blistered feet.

They make it look so easy.

As fresh meat, I wasn't always welcomed into the inner circle of dancers who had seen and done it all. If it weren't for my new roommates, I don't know that I would have survived the scathing looks and rude comments that came my way.

"Don't worry about it, Andy, just brush it off. They like to talk big but they don't really mean it," encouraged Sally, the one who always had something positive to say.

"Yeah, we have all had to go through the initial period of hatred before they started respecting us and calling us by name. Don't worry, they'll come around," Lin coached.

I tried to believe my roommates but I knew deep down that my downfall would be a cause for celebration for these veteran dancers. If I became a customer favorite, I was done for.

Well, it didn't take long before that happened, and my fate was sealed.

"They like you, Alexandria," Bernie told me after only a few weeks on the job.

"Oh," was all the enthusiasm I could conjure up, knowing exactly what this meant for any kind of peace in the workplace.

"I'm giving you an extra night on stage. Don't make me regret it." Bernie's famous last words, I had come to learn.

"Thanks, Bernie, I won't let you down," I said when I finally found my words.

"I know you won't," Bernie replied with a smirk before leaving the dressing room.

I knew the other dancers had overheard my conversation with Bernie; it's not like they could hear anything other than his loud, booming voice. My job may have become more secure but so did the resentment and hatred from all the other dancers. Even my roommates had an edge of envy when I earned that extra night of the week. There were rumors and talk that I had to be sleeping with Bernie in order to have earned so much favor from the big boss.

I wasn't... sleeping with Bernie, that is. Yet, I didn't deny it in case I needed to use it as leverage at some point. I soon realized I would be on my own if things went sideways, so being prepared was critical. You can't bring a knife to a gun fight or you'll be done for. A knife is no good when guns are involved. I had witnessed it plenty of times on the streets.

I was feeling extra tired tonight as I prepared to go on again and doubted it was because it was 1 a.m. My internal clock had adjusted to staying up all night and sleeping most of the day only to repeat it all over again the next night.

Dance. Sleep. Repeat.

I was tired of the grabbing hands that would, no doubt, test their luck. The lights that bore witness to every curve and dimple of my overworked body were extra bright tonight too. The work was more grueling than I thought it would be.

I looked at the mirror, pressing my lips together and moving them slowly side to side and back and forth to evenly spread out the red colored lipstick I chose. My eyes closed briefly as I took a deep breath. *In and out. Just get through it*, I told myself. When my heavily-lined eyes opened once again and stared at their hazel hue, I fluffed my dark curls and positioned the tiny outfit securely over my shoulders.

I was really lagging tonight, but the show had to go on. My one and only break already came and went earlier, and it was cut short after my first dance when the stage hand we called Big Joe told me to go back out for an encore.

"They want *you*, Alexandria," he told me with a crowd of cheers echoing behind me. "Get back out there and give them some more."

"Yeah? Well, I don't want them," I said, trying to walk past him, but he grabbed my arm, startling me with his rough grip.

"I said, get back out there." Big Joe was easily a foot taller than me, even when I wore my heels, and he didn't mind getting rough and nasty with us girls when Bernie wasn't there.

"What if I don't?" I challenged, puffing out my chest.

Big Joe looked at me with downcast brows and a harsh look. I wanted to break eye contact because I saw something in the intensity of his gaze that terrified me. I regretted my challenge, but it was already too late.

He tugged me closer, bending my arm at a funny angle. "I'm in charge tonight, missy, don't forget it," Big Joe said before spitting in my face. "Now get back out there before I give you a bruise you'll have to hide from Bernie."

I used the silk robe that was covering my naked body as a towel to wipe the spit from my face. I would have a bruise on my arm, that I was sure of. Big Joe was supposed to be there to protect us, I tried to remind myself while grabbing another outfit from the side of the stage to tear off once again. His threat had me trembling and was only made worse as I tried to dress with his eyes on me.

I don't know why I opened my mouth earlier. Now I was bruised, tired, and spooked by Big Joe. I decided to add an extra swoop of concealer under my eyes, hoping that would hide any circles that the lights wanted to make mention of. This was a good paying job. I couldn't risk losing it.

I set my makeup bag aside and stood to put the daggers of death on my feet, making my way to the side of the stage to clock in for work, and doing my best to ignore the sneer that Big Joe was giving me.

It will all be over in a few hours.

Keep it together, Alexandria.

We all have off nights, my new friends had assured me early on. Apparently tonight was mine. It happened in the last ten-minutes of my routine. I didn't notice until it was too late. I tripped on my discarded heel, my left ankle twisting as my body lurched forward and tumbled to the floor in the most unladylike fall.

Rachel was preparing to go on after me and called out to Sally for help. "Sally! Hurry, grab a robe and get over here. Alexandria just bit it on stage!"

Rachel strutted to the front, doing her best to distract our salivating fans so they wouldn't turn into disgruntled customers. I heard Big Joe yelling for Sally to hurry up before all of my attention moved back to my ankle.

"Ah, damn, this hurts!" I swore while getting up and doing my best to hobble back behind the protection of the curtain. "Thanks, Sally." I peered back over my shoulder to see Rachel playing her role to perfection and noticing not one eye wandering from the show.

Big Joe started laughing behind his closed lips.

"Ignore him. Here, put this on," Sally said, practically shoving me into the white silk robe she had waiting for me. Sally grabbed my waist as my right arm reached across her shoulders and we slowly shuffled back to the dressing room together.

I tried not to scream, cry, or grumble from the pain now shooting up my leg, but it was no use. "Ow, ugh, oh my gosh, I think I broke it. I must have broken it. Ow, ow ow!"

"What hurts, sweetie? Is it your knee? Leg?" Sally asked with a worried expression as she lowered me into the chair I had gotten ready in just one hour ago.

"It's my ankle," I spit out before mentally berating myself.

How could you be so dumb, Alexandria?
You've really screwed up this time.
Bernie is going to be so pissed at you.

The adrenaline and embarrassment pulsed through me quickly before both began to wear off, and the stabbing pain I noticed pinching my ankle jumped to the forefront of my mind.

"Damn, Andy, your ankle looks really swollen. I have a wrap I can put around it, but you may have to go to the doctor to get this looked at and make sure it isn't broken," Sally acknowledged, knowing full well the ramifications for my stupidity.

My breathing had settled, but my ankle still beat like a drum as she went to retrieve the bandage and started gently tightening it around my foot. I let my curses fill the dressing room that still held the competing scents of our perfumes when Sally returned and started folding the lengthy wrap around my swelling ankle.

"Alright, I will go now and get it checked out. I know I'm leaving early and Bernie is going to freak out; are you able to cover for me?" I looked at her with a pained but pleading expression.

"Of course, we'll cover for you tonight," Sally replied. "Don't worry about it."

"I can't believe this happened. I don't think I can dance for at least a couple of days so the swelling can go down," I finally said, admitting it out loud, and shaking my head in disappointment. I was so angry for letting myself get tired enough to make such an epic mistake that could cost me a few nights with no pay at best and a lost job at worst. Considering how many other dancers were hoping for my downfall, it had now been served to them on a silver platter.

Alexandria is ruined.

Sally finished her methodical work while I held back my screams.

"Here. I have a few Percocet left that really help me when my back starts acting up and it feels like I can't even stand, let alone dance. It will probably really help with the swelling and get you back out there sooner than you think," Sally stated, as she dropped two pills into my hand like they were nothing more than an over-the-counter pain reliever.

"Thanks. I will go get it checked out and see if anything is broken," I replied.

I wasn't naive. I knew what Percocet was and had seen enough buying, selling, and using on the streets to know how addiction stole someone's life. I thought back on one night in particular when a homeless man who occupied the same block as I did offered to give me a few of his opiates if I could show him a good time.

"Come on, princess, if you take these it will be an even *better* time," the man said with a growl and a look that made even my hair recoil in disgust.

"No, thanks." I quickly declined and found another block to sleep on that night, carrying my newly sharpened implement in case I was forced to use it. That is how it was on the streets. Buying, selling, or trading what you had for what you wanted. I had never taken any prescriptions or street drugs before other than marijuana. I slept in and around skid row, which meant I had to be alert and prepared for anything, so I never took any drugs that would inhibit my reflexes to survive. I heard the stories all the time about people being kidnapped, raped, drugged, or beat up —especially women—so I kept my mind sharp and my knife even sharper.

I dropped my gaze to my bandaged ankle as my mind pulled up a picture of the tiny, helpless baby girl. My body winced at the memory of the drugged rape that caused her conception. My throat tightened and my growing ankle was the least of my problems.

Keep it together, Alexandria.

I shook my head side to side not allowing my mind to go there. I had been in that position before, strung up and incoherent, and wasn't sure I could handle being in that place again. The only difference in this situation was... well, everything. I was choosing to take the meds and only enough to dull the pain so I could keep working. Sally was apparently using them, and she never seemed drugged out of her mind. I squeezed my eyes shut, letting the thoughts disappear just as quickly as they had come and dropped the pills into my purse. I would think about it.

Sally helped me slip my leggings over my wrapped ankle and I finished getting dressed so I could go catch the next bus to the hospital. "Bernie isn't here, thankfully, but if he comes in, I will do my best to curb his anger. Don't worry about it, Andy."

"What about Big Joe?" I asked Sally, trying not to sound as worried about him as I felt.

"Big Joe? I'll handle him," she said with a wink.

I looked at her with so much freaking gratitude. "Thanks, Sally." I knew exactly how Bernie got when this sort of thing happened, and I was afraid what that might mean for me when he found out about my incident tonight. I had seen him fire girls for less, but I tried to shrug it off. I had to. I needed to get this ankle checked out and get back to work.

CHAPTER 10
Desperate Times

January 2008—Age 17

The doctor held my x-rays up to the lighted board, somehow reading the black and white shades of my foot.

"You have a grade two sprain, so you will need to stay off of your ankle for at least a couple of weeks, alternating between icing, elevating, and wrapping your ankle throughout the day. It won't be fully recovered for another six to eight weeks."

Did he just say weeks? I thought, as my mouth hung open.

I tried not to sound too stunned, but that time frame wasn't going to work for me. "But I have to go to work. I won't be able to rest my ankle for that long. I can't afford to miss work. Two weeks is just too much time."

"I'm sorry, Ms. Strivers, but the only way to ensure your ankle heals is to keep weight off of it, which is why I am also going to place a prescription pickup for some crutches."

"Crutches?! So not only do I have to keep my foot wrapped but now I have to use crutches to get around? I won't be able to fucking do my job! Like, at all!" I had reached full blown panic mode at this point, and there was no hiding it.

The doctor stared at me, waiting for my melt down to settle before he spoke softly. "If you want your ankle to heal properly and not cause any further damage, you must stay off of it as much as possible. I would be happy to write a note that you can give to your boss confirming my diagnosis and treatment plan if that would help?"

"A note?" I asked, a breathy laugh escaping my open lips. I couldn't even consider how angry Bernie would be when he found out I would be out of commission for two weeks. I doubted a note written by this doctor or the president himself would help him understand.

"You can use the over the counter pain relievers every four to six hours to manage your pain, and I would encourage you to check in with your regular doctor in about two weeks to make sure your healing is on track. I will have the nurse come in with notes from our visit today." After dropping a sledge-hammer-like life change, the doctor stood and walked out the door, never looking back.

Just like that, my feeling of security had run its course. I had no backup plan in case of an injury like this one and certainly not enough money to live on while my ankle healed.

Could I keep my job?

Could I afford to stay in the apartment?

What about Bernie?

I feared the conversation with Bernie the most. Sitting on the exam table with my foot propped up and my head hung low, I imagined how this conversation might go.

"So I sprained my ankle in a tripping accident on stage and won't be able to dance for at least two weeks and possibly more."

"You did what, Alexandria?"

"I sprained my ankle," I would say stoically.

"You fool. I told you not to make me regret hiring you! Get the hell out of here and don't come back!"

I was done for.

Later that morning, as I laid in bed with Sally fast asleep in the bed next to me and the sun just starting to peek through the edges of our blackout shades, I thought about how desperate I was to keep this job. I hated feeling like this but, for some reason, my life just kept dropping me off at these dead-end places.

Rest was impossible when the pulsating around my ankle intensified and I could no longer ignore the pain. I never stopped by the pharmacy to grab the pain relievers or crutches; I was in denial that I needed them and too exhausted to care anyway.

I remembered the painkillers that Sally gave me.

I debated again whether I should take the Percocet but when my ankle screamed with pain and twinges shot up the rest of my leg at the slightest movement, I couldn't resist any longer. I pushed out of bed, hobbling towards the chair that sat beside the bedroom door in search of my discarded purse. When I found it and located the two small pills, I downed them with the lukewarm glass of water I had resting on my nightstand, not allowing myself to think any further on it. I felt them slide down my throat as I slid back into bed, hoping for deep sleep to overtake me, and it did.

I woke up seven hours later, feeling more refreshed than I believed possible. I swung my legs to the edge of the bed, stretching my arms above my head and relishing in the lightness I felt. I yawned and arched my back to get all of the kinks out before standing and walking to the bathroom. It wasn't until I was heading back to my bed that realization dawned on me. I looked down at my ankle, which was still wrapped but planted sturdily on the ground next to my right foot. It felt sore but, otherwise, completely usable.

"What the…" I uttered under my breath, as my unbelief morphed into hopeful relief.

Sally and Lin walked into the living room and plopped down on the couches.

"So, what's the news? Is it broken?" Sally asked.

I looked at her with a vacant expression plastered on my morning face. "It isn't broken, but he wanted me to stay off of it for at least two weeks," I began to explain. "When I got back, I took those painkillers that you gave me and they seem to be helping," I admitted, shock and awe still lingering in my voice. "I almost forgot about the sprain when I got up… Do you think I could get more of those for the next couple of weeks?"

Sally smiled. "I have a friend of a friend who has plenty more, and I am sure he would have some that you could buy too. The pills can get pricey but it's nothing compared to being out of work for so long."

"Thanks. I don't know how that doctor expects anyone to quit working for so long and deal with such horrible pain on top of it," I scoffed.

I just needed a few more pills to get me through these next two weeks and then I would stop taking them. I didn't have a lot of extra cash to spend, but I also didn't have any other options jumping up and down to get my attention. I needed to work so I could make money, pay my rent, buy food for myself, and maybe even purchase a new outfit. I couldn't risk losing this job because that meant I would be back to starving on the unforgiving streets.

When I walked into the dressing room, a tall, wide-set man, who had his back to me, filled the space and blocked my ability to enter the room further. He turned and looked down at me as I stared up at his shiny, bald head that I couldn't help but look directly at every time I saw him.

Bernie.

"Alexandria," Bernie said, turning around and crossing his arms over his chest. He knew my real name but refused to call me or anyone else by those names. To him, we transformed into our alias the moment we were hired, just like Rachel had said. "Just the girl I wanted to see."

Usually, his presence brought with it trepidation and worry but, tonight, I knew what was coming and I was prepared to deal with it. "Hi, Bernie," I started. "Yeah, so, about last night. I stupidly tripped, and Rachel and Sally helped cover for me while I got my ankle checked. Turns out, it isn't anything to worry about. I'm ready to go on in an hour." I met with Sally's friend of a friend earlier that day and bought more of the painkillers. They didn't come cheap, like she said, and the guy selling them gave me the creeps, but I was already amazed by how good my ankle felt tonight just walking to work. I could do this. I had to do this.

"Good. I would hate to lose someone with your talent over such a small thing as a broken ankle, but it's happened before. Finish getting ready. It's a packed house tonight," Bernie told me, slapping his palms together and sliding them back and forth against one another.

With that, I watched Bernie grab for the door handle and walk out in his tailored jacket and snakeskin loafers, leaving only the smell of overpowering cologne in his wake.

I exhaled a sigh of relief, walking towards my vanity mirror on shaky legs to put on my makeup and gather my wits. *A packed house.* It still made my stomach turn and my knees rattle thinking about the men that came to watch me dance and remove what little bit of clothing I wore out on that stage. Don't even get me started on the lap dances.

As I removed my ponytail and fluffed my hair, my mother's face came barreling into my mind. What would Michelle think of me now, knowing I was stripping to earn the money I used to feed and clothe myself? Would she be surprised or would she simply shrug and laugh it off as she waved me away. She would likely be jealous, knowing her. It was never a good look for her but the green, envious glow she walked around with became a permanent part of her skin tone.

My dark waves graced my lower back, and I ran my fingers through the loose, flowing tangles, taunting the memory of Michelle. *If she could only see me now.* I was more beautiful than her, undoubtedly. She would hate that, but I relished this fact.

Another face came to mind, but this time, I had to look down at my lap. Aunt Cindy had been in and out of my thoughts over the last couple of years, but I usually avoided her memory so that my heart wouldn't squeeze with regret. Tonight was no different. I didn't want to think about Aunt Cindy right now. I couldn't. I was about to go dance in front of a packed room of people that wanted me to be sensual and sultry, not depressed and moody. While Michelle and my Aunt Cindy shared similar features, they could not have been more different. We all had the same thick, dark hair but my Aunt Cindy never felt the need to push, pin, or plump up her appearance like Michelle always did. My aunt led the quiet, structured life that I craved as a child; Michelle only seemed to attract chaos in the form of personal drama. I, on the other hand, was somewhere in the murky middle of these sisters.

I hastily reached for my lipstick and started applying it, straightening my back in defiance towards the tender memories and climbing blush that made my cheeks look rosier than they already were. I had been through too much to feel embarrassed now. I found a way to put food in my belly and survive. I would wear whatever clothes (or lack thereof) that would let me keep this job and keep making this money. I wasn't going back; there wasn't anything left for me in the place I called home for a few short months. Aunt Cindy made it abundantly clear that my presence wasn't welcome in her home after we endured another loss, another death, but this time, it had been too much for both of us to navigate.

"Alexandria, you're up soon. Lin will meet you at the curtain to swap out," Rachel said interrupting my meandering thoughts.

"Great. On my way," I responded, with a quick nod. The pep talk happening in my head was over anyway, so I grabbed for my purse and found the bottle of Percocet. I popped the top off the bottle and shook two pills into my waiting hand, tossing them to the back of my throat and feeling their relaxing effect on my body before they even had time to absorb. I then tidied up my table space and slid my heels over my mildly swollen ankle, ready to take on whatever was waiting for me on the other side of that curtain. I just didn't expect him to be five-foot-nine with a rough looking exterior, a tender heart, and eyes for only me.

CHAPTER 11
Falling Hard
March 2005—Age 14

I had never been in love before. Sure, there were boys I liked. I remember one in particular, Spencer, who was, hands down, the best dressed ten-year-old in my fourth grade class. He had stunning blue eyes and blackish brown hair that made all the girls my age swoon. I fell hard for Spencer but realized my infatuation was just one out of roughly thirty other girls. My ten-year-old heart was broken into a thousand tiny pieces, and I was convinced I would never love again. However, after only a few short weeks, my heart made a full recovery.

By the age of fourteen, I had a few other unrequited loves and a handful of immature boys that I had dated, but there was one boy in particular who caught my attention. Brett was kind, cute, and athletic, a triple threat. He played basketball, baseball, and dabbled in soccer, although he could have fooled me the way he kicked a soccer ball around, making it seem like he was already in the minors— or whatever they call the semi-professional soccer team. I had never been into sports so I likely wasn't the best to evaluate such things. He called me every night to chat about our day, what homework we had due, which I faithfully ignored, and who his favorite sports teams were.

"I like the Dodgers but my dad is more of an Angels fan, what about you?" Brett asked.

"Oh, well, you know…" I paused, searching for an answer that would satisfy his question. "I like them both, but if I had to choose I would have to say the Dodgers." *Liar.* I knew nothing of baseball. The only thing I could assuredly say about the Dodgers is that they wore blue and white uniforms. My Uncle Roger had a felt flag hanging in his study that I noticed once or twice and was now coming in handy in a conversation I never thought I would be having.

"They have better players this year, and I really think they have a shot of getting to the World Series," Brett said on the other end of the phone line. I was sitting at the small bistro table in my aunt and uncle's kitchen, twirling the spiral phone cord around my finger and praying he didn't want to talk stats. If he did, it was all over for me.

What is so interesting about baseball anyway?

Brett was quickly becoming like water to my soul after going years without any. Sure, Aunt Cindy and Uncle Roger were doing their best to express their love, but my heart was longing for more; I felt like a cup that never stayed full for long, so I soaked up every last drop I could siphon. Turns out, Brett was just as thirsty.

I imagined his wide, sparkling smile with chocolate brown hair and hazel eyes, like mine, but more green. I fell hard for Brett, and my fourteen years of experience told me we were absolutely destined to be together for a lifetime. My heart had taken the plunge fully and completely, and I could have sworn he was right there with me. He would walk me to the bus after school where we stole kisses behind one of the brick columns near the gym. Brett was always kind and gentle but kissing him made my head swim and my stomach turn over, doing flips of delight and satisfaction. These were the moments of closeness I craved because I was the only one in the world that Brett saw. We were laser focused on each other and it felt good to be wanted.

"Andrea?"

"Oh, sorry, what did you say?" I asked, pulling my attention back. "I, uh, dropped the phone." I told him, not wanting to admit I had been thinking of our last kiss.

"Never mind. Hey, I was thinking maybe this weekend you could come over and hang out at my place. My parents will be home, but we can hang out in the basement. They never go down there. So... we could... be alone," Brett offered shyly.

Brett may have been my first boyfriend, but he wasn't exactly my first for other things. I had already stacked up quite a few experiences. I had never had sex before, so that would be a first, but my hands had roamed once or twice.

"I see, and what kind of activities did you have planned, exactly? Jenga? Maybe some Nintendo 64?" I teased. Both options would have been fine by me, but I knew these weren't the kind of games we would be playing, I just wanted to hear him say it.

"I was thinking more along the lines of... well, you know." Brett wasn't usually shy. In fact, he was the most cocky guy in school, and maybe the most cocky guy ever. I was enjoying listening to him flounder to find the right words even though I knew this wasn't his first rodeo either.

We continued talking for another hour, at least, and came back around to our weekend plans more than once, anticipation lining every said and unsaid word. Little did I know those plans would never come to fruition. Not because we weren't willing and eager to see them through. Life just has a way about making other plans. Plans I didn't see coming and never wanted to.

I had been living with my Aunt Cindy and Uncle Roger for almost eight months and was halfway through my eighth grade year before my world tipped upside down, again. A few days after that call with Brett, I was summoned to the principal's office. It was just before lunch and I worried my whole walk there that maybe Brett and I were discovered making out in the stairway between classes. We had been caught before and earned a talking to and were promised detention if it happened again. I didn't want my aunt and uncle to be upset with me, so I made sure Brett and I were extra vigilant during our top secret make out sessions. I was on edge, walking soberly towards the school office, assuming we hadn't been as covert as I thought. I started biting my nails and thinking about how I could pass off the kissing as just hugging and realized I was totally screwed.

"Come on in, Andrea. Take a seat, I want to talk to you," Principal Beth directed while wearing a distraught expression. As directed, I sat in one of the two upholstered chairs that were positioned across from her mahogany desk but, unlike other visits, she sat in the second chair right next to mine. I wanted to jump in and set the record straight before she could get the upper hand and shake my resolve by throwing off the assigned "principal" and "student" seats. No way was I going to let her catch me off guard.

"Principal Beth, about today. It really wasn't what it—"

She held up her hand to stop me from continuing. "Andrea, I want you to know that I got a call from your Aunt Cindy."

My body went still. "Wh-What did she say?" Deep breath. Don't let her rattle you.

Principal Beth reached out her creamy, ebony-toned hand and laid it on my pale arm that was becoming lighter by the minute with all this worry.

"She is at the hospital right now with your Uncle Roger. He suffered a heart attack earlier this morning. Your aunt wanted me to relay to you that she is at the hospital with him now and will call you after school when you get home to provide an update," she explained, but I stopped listening when I heard the word *hospital*.

My mind was clouded in confusion and I tried to switch the gears from kissing Brett to my uncle being seriously ill. The shift was awkward and clunky but when I finally got the gear to stick, the alarm in my voice ricocheted off of the small office walls. "Why didn't my aunt contact me earlier? Is my uncle okay? Is he awake and talking? When can I go and see him?" My mind raced with all of the worst case scenarios, and I was helpless to stop it.

My body took me back to the moment sitting on my bedroom floor, arms wrapped tightly around me while contemplating the news that my aunt had shared that left me parentless. I had been here before, and I could not stop my consciousness from believing the worst.

"I know you must be so worried about your uncle, Andrea. This is really hard news to hear. I want to help answer your questions and to pass on what your aunt has instructed."

My mind was spinning but I needed these answers. "What is the plan then? What do I need to do?" My palms lay open on the top of my thighs, helpless and pleading for some kind of actionable response from her. *Give me something,* I thought.

"Well, your Aunt Cindy wanted you to finish out the school day and then catch the bus home. This is a lot to take in so if you wanted to set up some time with our school counselor to talk, I am sure she can make time for you today."

I couldn't believe what I was hearing. Stay at school? How could my aunt expect me to do such a thing when my uncle was in the damn hospital?

I never saw Michelle and Dan again after they left on their date that night, and I had always wondered *what if* I could go back and say goodbye? There was no way I was dragging my feet through the rest of this tedious school day. There also wasn't a chance I was talking to the counselor. I had some cash in my locker that was supposed to be for lunch, but I decided I needed to catch a bus to the hospital as soon as possible. Now that Principal Beth had orders from my aunt to keep me here, I would have to sneak out undetected, which I wasn't a complete stranger to, but my aunt never knew about it and, this time, she would. I would have to break some rules that she would know about. I hated that.

I tied off my conversation with Principal Beth, assuring her that I would like to schedule some time with the counselor after lunch to distract from what I was about to do. I tried to end our conversation without being obvious of the plans forming in my head and walked cautiously away from her office, half-believing she would read my mind and thwart my plans like she had done so many times before. I made a left down the hallway and a beeline for my locker in order to grab the cash and leave out the back doors while lunch was finishing up. My feet moved faster than my legs, causing the rubber soles of my shoes to squeak on the floor in protest.

I knew the city bus system well since I didn't drive yet and my Aunt Cindy didn't like to drive in the dark, so I used it often to visit friends or hang out at the mall on weekends or after school. It stopped around the corner from the school and I quickly jumped on, paid my fare, and tried to act naturally in light of my panic that Principal Beth would wave the bus down and drag me back to school. She didn't, and I managed to escape without any trouble, but that didn't stop me from looking back out the window more often than not.

No more than ten minutes later, the bus approached the hospital. I had no idea what floor my uncle was on and hospitals always seem to have the most complicated floor plans, so after pulling the wire to alert the driver I was ready to get off, I made my way inside to find somebody to help me. After getting a few complex instructions, I nodded and began clumsily trying to navigate the many hallways that all seemed to lead somewhere and nowhere.

With every step, my panic grew more tangible. I worried about my Uncle Roger, but I was also worried about what my Aunt Cindy might say when she saw me. The train had left the station, so to speak, and whatever response I got from her I would just have to deal with. I hated disappointing my aunt and uncle, and I had always made a point to have the appearance of the perfect teenager so they wouldn't regret taking me in after my parents met their fate.

I finally found the right hallway on the right floor after getting repeat directions and I hurried towards the nurses' station to figure out which door my aunt and uncle were behind.

"I need to find my Uncle Roger and Aunt Cindy. Last name is Bolivar. They came in early this morning because my uncle had a heart attack. What room are they in?"

The nurse looked at me like I was a particular brand of crazy but softened when she noticed my age—young and frantic.

"I can't provide that information to you without some form of identification. Do you have anything that shows you are family?"

Shoot. I didn't expect to need identification and the closest thing I had was my student ID card sitting in my locker at school. There was also another problem—I didn't share their last name.

"I don't have my ID on me. But I really need to see my aunt and uncle. I need to make sure my uncle is okay," I said with a panic-stricken voice on the verge of tears.

The nurse briefly debated her next move and after considering me and confirming I wasn't a bandit, she tilted her head towards the door in the far right corner. "Room 367, just past the bathroom."

"Thank you!" I said with an audible relief as I sprinted down the hallway in the direction she indicated.

I swung around the door frame of the room, ready to help and be there for my aunt and uncle, but I wasn't prepared for what I saw. Directly in my line of sight was my Uncle Roger, lying completely still in the bed. I suppose I expected to hear the sound of beeping machines or the muted conversation between my aunt and uncle, but there was no life in those machines just like there looked to be no life left in my uncle. His skin had taken on a pale gray tone and his lips were a faint hue of purple.

"No," I said quietly, cupping my palm over my gaping mouth all while staring at the dead body that, beyond all reason, belonged to my uncle.

"He's gone." I heard the soft, defeated voice of my Aunt Cindy say from her chair in the corner nearest the window that was casting light into the room with more brightness than it had any business doing.

No...no, no, no. This isn't happening!

My eyes found my Aunt Cindy who was no longer the positive, self-assured woman I was used to. She was now visibly clothed in grief. Her cheeks bore red splotches and shone with wetness from the many tears she must have shed. She was wearing the same outfit I had seen her in that morning, an overly cheerful yellow short-sleeved shirt, which now seemed in total contrast to her inner and outer turmoil. She paired this shirt with blue denim capri pants and black crisscross strap sandals, inviting the first signs of spring that began to show outside but were severely lacking in this sterile hospital room. It only reminded me of how cruel this life could be. It took the people you loved away without warning and yet, life never stopped moving like it seemed to for me. The flowers would still bloom, the sun would still shine, but right here in this room, everything stood still.

He can't be dead. No, he has to be sleeping.

I was so surprised to see my Uncle Roger lying on the bed, eyes closed and pale, my feet felt like they had heavy weights strapped to them, and it made it difficult to move closer to my aunt, but I knew I needed to try. I treaded sluggishly in her direction, noticing that she wasn't angry by my presence or surprised that I had gotten to the hospital. Instead she was overrun by her loss and carried a physical burden of grief that caused her countenance to droop. She clutched her purse in her lap with both hands while one hand escaped periodically to wipe away the falling tears with the tissue she gripped like it was her lifeline.

Loss. Sadness. Goodbye.

He's really gone. He's not just sleeping.

I tentatively reached for her hand while I slunk down to my knees beside her. Upon touching, the grief she had so visibly carried now traveled up my arm and straight to my soul exploding at the center of my core. The pain sat heavy in my chest too, but I was still able to draw a breath, though I felt guilty doing so with my uncle lying mere feet away from us now lacking the ability to do so.

He's gone. Forever.

We sat like this for a while, crying and sniffling, neither of us speaking but both of us knowing there weren't any words that could change things. The room grew darker, and my body grew heavier as I sank back and leaned against the wall. We both knew in our hearts that when we left this room without my uncle, it would be over, like a more distinct finality would hit and we were both avoiding this. So I reached up and slid my hand into my aunt's, and we sat for a little longer.

The nurse who told me what room to find them in, bypassing the need for my ID, popped her head in periodically to see if we were still there. When she found us, still weeping softly and grappling with the impact of our shared loss, she exited the room to continue on her rounds, never rushing us. We eventually did leave that hospital room, more due to exhaustion from crying all the tears and feeling all the feels that we could both collectively handle for one night. Aunt Cindy drove us home and we collapsed in our own beds without any calls to other unknowing family members or understanding of what would come next. Tonight was all we knew.

In the morning, I listened to the few voicemails that Brett had left, clearly worried when I had abruptly left school without telling him or any other friends where I was going. I called him back despite the early hour and let him know that my Uncle Roger had died and I wouldn't be coming back to school that week.

"Oh. Wow. Sorry, Andrea. That really sucks." I can't say I expected the world from a middle school boy but I was left wanting after our short phone call. We hung up with a feeble, "I love you," and that was that. Not enough, but still something.

The next few days were filled with decisions that needed to be made, people that needed to be notified, and plans that needed to be solidified in order to host a memorial service for my uncle. Gone were those quiet moments in that hospital room with only Aunt Cindy and I, silently weeping and holding onto one another so that we wouldn't float away with our grief. I had been hearing less and less from Brett over the last few days, only texting back and forth to keep up appearances that we were still together despite the vast chasm that now lay between us.

My grief had become a burden that Brett couldn't shoulder.

"You know, everything with your uncle dying and me with baseball tryouts to focus on, we each just have a lot happening right now that is pulling us apart," he tried to explain over the phone one night.

"Right. No, yeah, that makes sense. I get it." I was crushed, to put it mildly. My heart was processing such intense levels of grief that trying to peel back the layers felt impossible so I let him go without a word. I was too tender, and too emotionally drained to wade into the ocean and try to keep my head above water with only the help of a pool noodle.

The funeral came and went, and my return to school was an awkward dance that nobody knew the steps to. My friends were unsure how to talk to me, my teachers were overly sympathetic, and both seemed to treat me like I was made of fragile glass and ready to shatter at the simplest touch. I hated being the kid with problems. I put on a brave face to try and steer clear of the forced empathy but also because my aunt needed me, and she wasn't going to be able to get through this unless I became the rock she could lean on that wouldn't budge. She had done this for me when my parents died so now I would be there for her.

I would be strong enough for the both of us.

. . .

January 2008—Age 17

It was no surprise that I had issues.

Every significant person in my life had left me either by death or by choice. The only place I had security was my work. I danced in order to protect myself, and it had worked... so far. I often met plenty of men who wanted to make me their girl whether for a night or a few nights, at most. Dancing on a stage for the enjoyment and pleasure of many eyes didn't exactly make it the easiest place to find a boyfriend, which is why I didn't expect to meet Mike or that he would stick around for long.

He was taller than I was, unless I wore my heels, and he had a completely shaved head accentuating his narrow profile. Like his bald head, Mike had a clean shaven face without any hint of stubble, and it had me wondering if he had to shave multiple times a day just to keep it so smooth. He had arms bulging with muscles and chiseled to perfection and I was not shy in admiring. It was camouflaged by tattoos with only a few areas that were vacant of ink, one of which was his clean shaven head.

We shared a drink after I got off work one night and from there, we were inseparable.

"You are so damn beautiful, Alexandria," Mike had said, pouring out compliments like water from a pitcher. "You're sexy on that stage too. I've never seen a routine like that one." He bought me a couple drinks that I never took my eyes off of, and we proceeded to talk until the late morning hours.

"If you're finished with your drink, maybe we could go to my car and uh… smoke a joint together?" he offered with a twinkle in his eye and I knew smoking a joint was only one of many activities we would be doing.

"Yeah, sure," I agreed, knowing the joint, and the sex, would help me sleep better that day and prepare me for another shift later that night. We smoked and laughed and continued talking until we weren't talking anymore. He was hurried and rough as he kissed me, but I matched his intensity with an increased fervor, playing the role he wanted me to, just like I did on stage. When we finally pulled apart, satisfied and breathless from the exercise, I wasn't expecting him to cry but he did just that. His forehead rested on top of my shoulder as I sat on his lap facing him, stunned and motionless while the sobs shook his body and drew on my sympathy.

"Alexandria," he whispered into my hair.

His tears reminded me of my own. They were brimming with anguish and marked by a painful story. I had cried those tears after Michelle and Dan died, and again when my Uncle Roger slipped away before I could say goodbye. Those tears showed up when I found out I was pregnant, and again when I said goodbye to that baby girl. These kinds of tears were more than sadness; they were misery bottled up with nowhere to go and no one to hold them. When they were finally released, the feelings came out sideways.

"My name is Andy," I said in a feeble voice, giving him a piece of me, or maybe just to prove to myself that this girl was still inside of me somewhere.

The tears I kept hidden from the world were now trailing down my cheeks in a continuous streak and, as I sat on Mike's lap in the front seat of his dark blue pickup truck, I realized that our bruised and battered hearts had found solace in one another. It wasn't love, I know that now, but it was comfort, and that seemed good enough for both of us.

CHAPTER 12
Love is Pain
February 2008—Age 17

"Price went up," he said with little care.

"What? Like how much?" I spat back.

"Double."

"Are you fucking kidding me? I can't pay double!" I could feel my anger rising as it crept up and settled on my face, burning it crimson red. I had been purchasing Percocet from that guy that Sally referred me to for the last couple of months, and he was as steady as ever in getting me my pills. Until now.

"I told you last time it was goin' up."

"I didn't think you were actually serious. Who can even afford that?" I scoffed.

Our regular meeting spot was near the train tracks that pierced their way through the south end of L.A. The metro dropped me off a few short blocks down the street and I strolled to where I met the unnamed man who often sat in the driver's seat and passed me the goods through the slim opening of his window.

"If you can't pay it then go find another dealer, but just know they likely laced it with something else. These are the only clean painkillers I know of in this city."

I swallowed my pride and begged for a discount but he wouldn't relent. I couldn't pay what he wanted, which meant I had to find another option.

"What am I supposed to do now?" I asked, my palm settling on my forehead.

"If you're so damn desperate, just go get the knock-off version, you know, the cheaper shit—heroin," the dealer suggested, sounding more pissed with every minute I kept him idled there.

I nodded my head and slowly backed away from his vehicle, running both of my hands through my hair from scalp to ends. My ankle no longer needed to be wrapped or iced, and I was making it through my shifts without so much as a twinge, but the pills gave me the relaxed energy I needed to get through the night. I enjoyed the euphoric simplicity. My ankle may not need the painkillers anymore, but try telling that to the rest of my body. If I tried to stop now, withdrawal symptoms would hit, and I would be flat on my back with cold sweats, shakes, and covered in vomit. I know because I've tried to stop.

I hopped back on a bus heading towards a place I knew would have what I now sought. Even though I never used heroin, I had lived long enough on the streets to know where to buy it. Heroin was easily accessible, everyone seemed to be selling it, and the dealer was right, it was a hell of a lot cheaper, I knew that much. It required a few more tools and pokes, but I would have to overlook some of these things to avoid the disaster waiting for me on the other side of withdrawals.

I got off the metro at the edge of the Arts District and Skid Row, walking up and down the streets and peering over my shoulder every few steps.

I shouldn't be here, I thought, but kept going.

I started asking around and it wasn't long before I found what I needed and caught another bus back home to meet up with Mike. He knew I had been taking painkillers because of my bum ankle and was cool with it. He probably wouldn't care about heroin either. The only thing that seemed to ruffle Mike was when I talked to other people. We had been dating for two months, and Mike had proved to be a steady, if not an annoyingly consistent, presence in my life. He insisted on driving me to and from work every day, and he also had a regular table to the back right of the stage that he occupied for the hours I worked.

I danced and stripped all night but that didn't seem to bother him. It excited him. Mike did contract work, whatever that meant, and he didn't have a consistent schedule, so this allowed him to be with me more and more. Bernie didn't care as long as Mike kept his distance, and he didn't imply he was my boyfriend while I worked. Bernie said it would be bad for business.

Mike didn't mind as long as he had a good view of the stage. He said he wanted the best angle to watch and admire me.

"You wore a new top tonight. It makes your tits look perfect!" He would tell me after my shift, his exuberance off the charts, and while I was the focal point of said exuberance, I handled it as well as catching a slippery fish with my bare hands. When I danced on stage half-nude, it didn't feel nearly as exposing as Mike's attention.

He noticed everything about me and for someone who wasn't used to being noticed, I was both unsure of how to respond and fully enchanted by his affections. Mike said he loved me, and I was naive enough to believe him. Hell, I was naive enough to love him back. He got my name tattooed on the remaining real estate left on his bicep after only a week of dating.

Alexandria, it read.

"This is how I express myself, babe. I put what's in my heart on my sleeve," he explained, flexing his muscles in the mirror while I watched that name dance too.

I stood beside him staring up at the fresh, black ink and wondered if this was what love was supposed to be. Is this what it felt like? *It had to be*, I convinced myself.

Mike was equal parts hard and soft, and this drew me in closer, believing his kindness smoothed out his jagged edges. There were parts of Mike's personality that made me question his intentions. He could be overly jealous, at times, of both men and women, both of whom I interacted with a lot in my line of work. I still lived with Lin, Rachel, and Sally, but I rarely saw them.

Before I met Mike, we talked about touchy customers, and gave each other pointers on new moves to add to our routines. We shared so much of our lives on and off the stage that Mike decided early on that he wasn't a fan of all of the time I spent with them.

"I don't get why you even want to hang around them. What do they have that I don't?"

"Well, for starters, Mike, ovaries, gossip, and advice on men," I said plainly.

Mike always seemed to bring the sass out of me. His jealousy played the strings of my defensiveness so well. Maybe too well.

"Eh. You don't need any of those things, Alexandria. You see them at work, isn't that enough?"

He was right. I did spend a lot of time with the girls at work already, but our time off the stage was different. I tried explaining this to Mike. I wanted him to understand.

"Yeah, but they're my friends. Don't you like to hang out with your friends?" I threw this question out there already knowing the answer. Mike didn't have friends. He only had me.

He didn't bother answering my question, but my saucy mouth made Mike visibly annoyed. "I just want to spend time with you, babe. Why is that such a crime?"

"It isn't. You're right. I'm just tired right now. I want to spend time with you, too," I said while trying to avoid any heated confrontation. He pulled me into a tight embrace, one that indicated ownership, and I let him. His hands possessively gripped my waist and he left a trail of firm kisses down my neck, leaving me breathless and confused in one stiff cocktail of emotion.

Mike's jealousy also found me when I was at work. I told myself that he liked to watch me dance and that's why he stayed, which was true, but there was one time in particular that made me realize that wasn't the only reason. I had just finished working the floor, providing a lap dance here and there before returning to the stage, when an arm reached out and grabbed my wrist.

"Sir, you have to let go," I said in a stern but noticeably shaky voice. Bernie had a no-touch rule but that didn't stop the customers from pushing the boundaries. That's why he hired Big Joe, but when it came to me, Big Joe kept his distance, even at times I actually needed his help.

"And why is that, sweetie? Isn't this what you're wanting anyway—a real man to take hold of you?" he protested, his voice getting louder and drawing more attention to us.

I had my fair share of grabby customers, but this guy oozed dangerous arrogance. His eyes told me as much. Before I had a chance to respond to this creep, Mike bolted towards the man, grabbing his shoulders, and swinging him around to plant a powerhouse punch to his right cheek. It was dark in the crowded room with only the hazy colored lights on the stage to guide the way. Mike fled shortly after connecting his tightly closed fist into the drunken man's jaw, but I saw what happened as clear as the morning light. The man stumbled backwards and tripped on a chair that left him laying on the dirty floor. I was stunned; unsure what to do with a hurt customer and a pissed off boyfriend. Big Joe finally showed up to lead the man out, casting shade my way with a glare that could kill. Bernie never found out, to Mike's benefit and my own, but I knew it would only be a matter of time before something else like that happened.

I told Mike later that morning after my shift and back in my tiny apartment that he couldn't do that again. "You could have gotten me fired. You can't do that shit, okay?"

"I love you baby, but that guy would have groped you more if I hadn't stepped in. You wouldn't want that to happen, right?"

Liar, I thought. He did it because he was jealous. It's not like this was the first time he threatened a customer, but it was the first time he used his fist to make the point.

"I knew he was fucking looking at you all night," Mike said, more to himself than to me while shaking his head in frustration.

I let the air escape my mouth in a huff. "I get that, but Bernie just won't want to deal with the unhappy customers and I could lose this job if he finds out my boyfriend is throwing punches at anyone who barely touches me," I told him, mustering all of the composure I could fathom in that moment.

Don't freak out, Andy. It will only make things worse, I told myself.

"Why are you pissed at me? That pig almost dragged you out of there! You think he had good intentions? He would have used you! I am the one trying to help you. Why can't you understand that I am just doing this for you!" Mike said as his voice crested a higher octave.

Mike had a temper. I knew this, but I didn't know how to deal with it. He didn't either.

Mike stomped out of the shared living space and paced around the kitchen, his anger visibly apparent in the now reddish hue climbing his neck and face. "You'd probably be dead in some backstreet alley if it weren't for me! You think that dick wouldn't have pushed his luck? You're so fucking dumb sometimes!"

He grabbed one of the half-empty beer bottles that had been sitting on the counter, throwing it against the wall, and shattering it completely in a shower of glass and the last dregs of amber colored liquid. "You ungrateful bitch! You can't even see when I'm trying to help you!" The word "help" rolled off of his tongue like a stronger curse word than the name he just called me.

My defenses were up, and I lobbed another grenade in his direction. "You didn't have to punch the guy! You could have just told him to back off instead of clocking him, but you always take things to the extreme."

That did it.

Mike charged towards the dining room wall, opposite the kitchen, and punched his fist through the drywall like it was nothing more than a paper bag. I watched in stunned realization. Mike's anger could easily turn on me.

Don't react, Andy. Keep calm and he will, too.

Tell him you're sorry. Apologize and he'll relax.

He hasn't hit you before, but it doesn't mean he won't.

My defenses had morphed into fear as my mind screamed for me to stop fighting and do whatever I needed to in order to protect myself. My chest rose and fell with every labored breath I took. I had to remind my trembling hands and quivering chin, which wanted to flee more than anything, that Mike stepped in for me. This was more than I could say for what Bernie would have done if he had seen it happen. Bernie usually pinned those situations on the dancers first, customers second, and rarely saw the need to throw anyone out over a little grab. I was still surprised Big Joe even did anything. Mike may have overreacted, but he did stick up for me.

Mike's fast breaths in and out of his nose were the only thing I heard as I tamped down the rest of my trepidations and plunged forward to save myself from further danger. "I'm so sorry, Mike. You were only trying to protect me and I freaked out. I'm sorry, I was wrong."

Don't make things worse with Mike.

Keep it together, Andy.

I had seen Mike's outbursts often enough to know how they started and ended. I saw his shoulders relax and his fists unclench and though he didn't say a word, I stood and walked slowly towards him until I faced his back, wondering what man I would encounter next. Would I become more acquainted with his wrath or would my courage tamp out the fire that I had started? I didn't give myself time to think before I started massaging his shoulders and kissing his neck. Mike softened like melted butter after I worked out the tension between us. My touch caused a current of desire for him and a jolt of panic from me. Mike's anger burned red hot, but my instinct to survive was stronger. He didn't know the survivor hiding inside of me. The one who had lived on those backstreet alleys, only ever doing what she needed to do to stay alive.

Just give him what he wants, Andy.

I swallowed my pride, my defensiveness, my hatred. I gave him what he wanted to smooth out the fighting words we had just volleyed back and forth.

Every thought and every word he spoke indicated he was unsure of my affections towards him, and trying to convince Mike of my commitment to him was like trying to fill a kitchen colander. There was nothing I could do to persuade him. Nothing.

But I gave him what I have. I gave him the best of Alexandria, but she wasn't who I needed.

· · ·

March 2008—Age 17

A few weeks after our fight, I had woken up after a long night of work, Mike lying beside me with his arm slung around my middle, when I jumped up and raced to the bathroom so I wouldn't discard the contents of my stomach onto the floor. I had been feeling extra tired lately since I had been working more nights during the week, and I was still trying to figure out a good heroin dosage.

The rest of the house was quiet, but as I trudged back to my bed, my feet laden with bricks instead of socks, I saw Rachel sitting on the couch drinking a cup of coffee.

"You feeling alright?" she asked behind the rim of her mug.

"Yeah, it's just been a long week of work. I am feeling a little extra tired. A few more hours of sleep should help."

"Hmm. You've been working a lot lately. It looks like you have been gaining more weight around your belly too and maybe even some on your hips…" Rachel could be brutally honest at times. She reminded me of Michelle—calling attention to the imperfections of my body or personality regardless of my feelings. I had thicker skin after being raised with this kind of "honesty," so I was pretty good at brushing it off.

Don't let her see you flinch, Andy, I coached myself.

"I guess I am a little heavier than usual. My clothes still fit just fine and the men like my curves anyway." I turned to leave and walked back towards my room, hoping my embarrassment wasn't obvious.

"You were pregnant before, right? I'm surprised you didn't recognize the signs this time around. Better take a test just to be sure," Rachel said casually from behind me.

My feet were planted into the ugly brown carpet that was old enough to have heard many secrets over the years, and now it knew mine. I thought back on the last few weeks scouring the calendar in my brain to try and remember the last time I had my period. Six weeks ago.

Shit.

I scanned through the symptoms I had experienced the first time trying to deny the obvious signs that my brain could not un-know after Rachel's admission. Tired? Check. Tender breasts? Check. Unexplained sickness? Check.

With my feet still anchored to the floor, my legs felt like jelly beneath me, but instead of sinking lower, I made haste back to the bathroom to relieve the growing worry that rose with the bile.

Two lines would flip my world upside down once again and one line would keep my life the same. Unchanging. Uncomplicated.

Once I found balance and my stomach stopped its convulsing, I grabbed my purse from the room while Mike still slept and made my way to the drug store down the street. I had done this before; I went through this same panicked sequence of purchasing a test, peeing on the stick, and waiting the required time to find out how radically my life would change. While many things were the same, there were also some new feelings that I hadn't expected.

Unlike my last pregnancy, I knew who the father was. He wasn't a mysterious, nameless man or a one night stand that I would never see again. I was in a committed relationship this time around, and something about that caused flutters of hope to rise up in me. I wasn't sure how Mike would take the news if I told him he was going to be a father, but I knew he loved me.

Love would be enough, right?

I couldn't sit on the edge of the tub any longer. I stood abruptly, which made my stomach revolt and my legs threaten to disown me, and walked hesitantly towards the test sitting on the edge of the counter. Before looking down at it, I took a deep breath trying to calm my jittery nerves and quench the ache that slammed doubts in my face. It had been only eighteen months since I had given birth to that perfect little girl. Only eight months since I had gotten a steady job and food to eat on a regular basis, and only three months since I had started dating Mike. My life had taken a mean turn when I found out I was pregnant the first time, and its cruelty persisted with the adoption of that first child. Could I do this again? Would I adopt another child to someone else to hold forever?

The questions darted around my head for some time before I closed my eyes tightly and I assured myself of the possibility of things being different this time around. I may not have to put this child up for adoption. I would have Mike's help this time. He would be happy about our love child, right? There was that hope again, knocking on my heart's door, reminding me that my story wasn't over yet.

I opened my eyes and blinked a few times to fan out my fake eyelashes that clung together with the support of day-old mascara. With another breath in and out, I looked down to read the information that I already knew.

Two lines. Positive. I was pregnant. Again.

I bought two tests in case the first was faulty. I peed on the second stick, waiting the few minutes it took for the colored line to strengthen. I didn't need to wait long; both lines started to show and darken into a deep pink hue that confirmed the results.

My hand found the swell of my abdomen and my other hand met it to encircle the life that my body was intent on growing. I pushed aside the worries that crept into my thoughts like a thief in the night and let myself camp on the idea of what it would be like to keep this child. Would I have another little girl this time? If it was a little boy, would Mike want to name him after himself or maybe another family member? I secretly loved the idea of having a family, a true family that loved one another and expressed this often. It was the opposite of what I experienced growing up, and maybe that is why I held this dream in my heart, never spoken, never shared.

I didn't know much about Mike's family; he kept that information to himself, and I didn't press him since it seemed like a sore subject, but he loved me, so why wouldn't he want this same kind of family with me? My dreams hinged on Mike, and I knew I had to tell him. In fact, I was excited to tell him. I wanted to see the surprised expression on his face when I told him he was going to be a father and watch as it changed into adoration for me, Andy. Not just Alexandria, but me.

I breathed deeply, feeling the warmth underneath my hands and the hope that caused me to float out of the bathroom to wake Mike and tell him what I thought would be amazing news.

CHAPTER 13
Goodbye to Love
May 2008—Age 17

It had been two months with no word from Mike. The conversation didn't exactly go as I had seen it in my head. I could still see the look on his face: his eyes grew wide and his jaw clamped tight while I watched his teeth grind together behind his smooth cheek.

"How could you have been so fucking stupid? We used protection!" He yelled out a curse before he shot such horrific bullet-shaped words of blame straight at the one carrying his child. "Is this some scheme to get me under your control? You think that's going to work on me?"

I had been so excited to tell him about the baby but with every word, every blow to my fictional future, my heart was crushed. "No, no, Mike, I swear to you! I didn't do this on purpose, it just... happened!"

"Wait." The word fell out of his mouth at the same time I saw his mind working out an alternative story. "Is this even my child? Did you really go and fuck someone else and then try to pass it off as mine?"

I could see in his eyes that these questions were rhetorical. As soon as he thought up the fictional tale, he was firmly convinced, but I tried anyway.

"Mike, no! I'm with you! I haven't slept with anyone else and I would never try to get pregnant! You think this is easy on me? I'm the one whose life is going to completely change here!" It was all hitting me. I would lose everything... again. Did I want that?

"You're disgusting. I can't even look at you knowing that *thing* is in your stomach."

My mouth hung open, unsure how to handle Mike's wicked anger. I didn't think sex would work this time, or I would have tried it. Instead, I made promises I wasn't sure I could keep.

"I'll get an abortion. That's it, we'll just go to the clinic and be done with all of this. I don't want to lose you, Mike! I can't." I knew I was begging, but I couldn't help myself once I got started. I could feel him slipping further and further away from me.

"It's no use. You're already ruined! I can't touch a whore like you again, Alexandria!" With that final blast, Mike fled from my apartment, leaving me to pick up all of the pieces of my heart that had just shattered.

"It's Andy," I said to the closed door. "My name is Andy."

I thought I would have an abortion, even though Mike wasn't in the picture to try and please anymore, but I was too depressed to think beyond the basics: work, sleep, eat, survive. The cloud of shame hovered above me, and I wasn't able to shake it. I hadn't gone to the doctor to confirm my pregnancy this time either. I took my bloated waistline and swollen ankles as evidence enough. I couldn't imagine looking at the monitor or hearing this baby's heartbeat knowing Mike wouldn't be there to share it with me.

By the time I was ready to start dealing with things again, it was too late to visit the clinic. After a few quick calculations from the first birth calculator I found online using Sally's phone, it told me that I was almost four months pregnant and due sometime in the middle of October.

The aches and changes in my body were expected this time around and didn't seem as foreign. However, stripping while pregnant wasn't an option according to Bernie. When I started to show, he finally had to address it.

"Nobody is going to want to see a mom-to-be stripping, Alexandria. You got one more shift and then I will have to fill your spot with someone else," Bernie said, looking at me with disgust and disappointment. "You should have dealt with *it* when you had the chance."

"You're right, I should have," I admitted, because if the depression hadn't wiped me out, I would have dealt with it.

For the time being, I still shared the apartment with Rachel, Lin, and Sally but with Sally moving out soon to live with her boyfriend, the rent would go up until someone else occupied her old bed. The girls let me stay even though I couldn't afford to pay rent, but I knew their kindness would run out eventually.

Pregnancy was like a freight train that didn't stop for anyone or anything, and the timing of my circumstances were pretty crappy. The train just kept on rolling regardless of how I was coping. I barely had enough money to keep buying heroin, and I wasn't sure how much longer I would be able to take it. Was it having an effect on the baby? I thought about what was happening to the infant inside my body while I pierced my waiting veins, but my despair over losing Mike and all that I was losing because of him weighed on me.

All I had left was my needle.

I decided to reach out to Wendy while I still had access to a phone, even though Sally was getting bothered by my constant pestering to borrow hers.

Me: Hi, Wendy. It's me, Andrea…

It didn't take long for her to respond.

Wendy: Andrea! I am so glad you reached out. How are you? Where are you?
Me: I'm fine. It looks like I may need your help, again, with another… pregnancy.
Wendy: I am so happy you reached out to me! Of course, I am here for you! Tell me where I can find you and I'll be there.

Wendy was undoubtedly overjoyed by my text. I could feel it in every exclamation mark. We hadn't spoken in a couple of years, and I am sure she was just relieved I wasn't dead. I sent her the address to the *Wild Kitty*, where I would be working my last shift, and instructed her to meet me in the parking lot around 10 p.m. when I took my break.

Wendy: Thank you, Andrea. And, one more thing…

I stared at the screen, waiting for her next message to pop up but also dreading what it would reveal.

Wendy: I love you and I am here for you whenever you need.

Love? What the hell was that?

Even as the questions crossed my mind, my eyes glossed over because I wanted them to be true. I didn't need her love, and I didn't know how to want it either. I couldn't get out of my fucked up situation alone though. I would need her help. It was probably a simple admonition on Wendy's part, a throw-away comment that was intended to comfort me, but I knew the emptiness of words all too well. I wouldn't be fooled by another *I love you.*

When I met her that night, I wasn't expecting to be greeted with a bright and cheery hello and a hot meal paired with a large cup of steaming coffee when I sat in the front seat of her car. My eyes pricked with tears, but I took a slow, measured sip of coffee to swallow the lump in my throat before it could expose me. Wendy was delighted to see me, but I wasn't sure why. This wasn't exactly the greatest of circumstances that we were meeting under but her response towards me never seemed to falter.

"Andrea, how are you doing? I am so glad that you texted me," Wendy said with a smile that I wanted to believe was fake, but I saw no trace of such a thing.

"Good. Tired, but good. This baby is taking up all of my extra energy." Even if I didn't have any extra energy to begin with. I felt a twinge of regret that I was sitting here with Wendy, ready to talk about adoption for this baby, too. I had hoped things would be different, but they never were.

We continued talking around the topic at hand but my engagement with small talk was finding its end when I abruptly changed the subject. "So, I would like to see if the other adoptive family would like this baby too. I don't know whether it's a boy or girl yet, but hopefully that won't matter to them. I just want this baby to be with family—with their sister," I explained, my voice falling to a whisper at the mention of there being a sister.

Wendy looked at me with intent focus, communicating her devotion to me and this baby, despite our mess. I had to look away as she started to speak, hoping there wouldn't be kind words at the end of her short silence because I knew that would likely be my undoing.

"I was hoping for the same outcome, but Allison's family is not in a position to adopt this infant. I brought a few profile books that you can look through and hopefully find another forever family for this child. For now, I do want to ask you a few questions about the birth dad and get more details on you and baby."

I tried not to clutch the steaming cup of coffee tighter or reveal the twenty flips my stomach just did at even the hint of discussing Mike. I wasn't ready for the emotion that would follow when I thought about him and his abrupt departure from my life. I still cringe when I hear his words replay in my mind the last time I saw him.

I needed to figure out how to get through this without showing emotion.

Just stick to the facts and basic information, I coached myself.

"I was seeing the baby's dad for a couple months before I found out I was pregnant," I said and my words sounded rushed and desperate, like I'm trying to convince her I'm not a slut. "I thought he might be on board with being a dad, but he wasn't and left as soon as he could. I haven't heard from him since."

Facts. I let out a sharp breath, concluding all I have left to say about him.

I braced myself for the look of sorrow that I expected to see from Wendy's freshly painted face despite the late hour we were meeting. Wendy was as thoughtful with her words as she was attentive to her bobbed blonde haircut and black pantsuit. I couldn't deny the peace I felt in her presence, but I couldn't risk letting my guard down and being slammed with all the humiliation of my predicament. I needed to be a rock: cold, hard, and factual.

Instead of disgust, Wendy looked pained as she reached across to the passenger seat that I occupied and gathered my cold, trembling hand in hers. She didn't immediately follow with any words, but I think she intuitively knew that more words would not make the truth easier to bear. I looked down at our clasped hands and it was this simple touch that allowed the dam to break and my tears to flow while sitting in the passenger seat of Wendy's car, right outside the strip joint that I wouldn't be employed at for much longer. The same job that got me off the streets, put food in my mouth, and a roof over my head. Soon I would lose it all... including my second child.

My tears were spilling faster now and a slow, rolling groan built in my chest and escaped from my mouth. So much for being a rock. Instead, I was putty. I tried to hate every tear, every sob that escaped from my quivering lips, and I tried to especially hate the soft hand that had escaped mine to rhythmically run up and down my hunched back.

My whole life I wanted to be loved. I wanted the feeling of being the center of someone's world, a prized and precious gem. It wasn't until I sat here with Wendy, one hand clinging to mine while her other caressed my back like the wounded child I was, that I released the pent up emotion in my caged heart. I had been touched plenty but being *seen* was a new sensation for me. I didn't want this baby to experience anything less than this feeling right here: complete acceptance. I knew I was broken beyond repair but this baby didn't have to be. They were being offered a better life, full of love, devotion, and mounds of affection. This child would be fiercely loved by their adoptive parents, their big sister, and somewhere in there, me too. However feeble my own experience with love might be, I would love this child. The anguish that squeezed my soul would be the reminder of the pain it takes to love someone.

CHAPTER 14
Second Chances
May 2008—Age 17

My feet ached, my head throbbed, and my body screamed to lay down. I just finished my last shift at work, hoping the amount listed on my paycheck would get me by for the next month. After that, I would need a new plan.

Kicking off my black flats, I rubbed the bottom of each foot until they believed I was done dancing. I couldn't stop thinking about my conversation with Wendy last night. Before she let go of me, she started to speak. Not to me, but to God. Every hair on my body stood to attention.

"God, you are here with us right now. We ask that you would be a comfort to Andrea in the midst of this hard season. You are faithful to meet us where we're at, Lord. Meet us here."

No one had ever prayed like that with me or around me. I pulled back when she finished, like her hand was too gentle for the war going on inside of me, and drank a few gulps of the now-lukewarm coffee.

That was weird, I thought, taking note of the new sensations rolling around my body.

Even now, as I rested my head on my cool pillow, releasing an audible sigh, I could feel the peace that coated every word Wendy prayed that night. I wasn't sure what to say afterwards, so I offered up a basic, "Thank you," while taking a bite of the dinner she had brought me, hoping it would mask any of the embarrassment I felt. I hated breaking down like that, and I sure hated that I had so many damn reasons to.

No one else in the apartment was awake, and I was glad for the quiet, but I couldn't sleep. I instinctively placed a hand over my small, rounded belly to reassure this little one. Of what, I don't know, but it seemed as natural a movement as breathing. Deciding how thirsty I was, I carefully rose from my bed, stretching out my left side and then my right, scanning the bedside table for any liquid. I found the cup I had earlier and drank deeply for several seconds.

It was moments like these when my body was still and the space around me was muted that I thought about my aunt. I didn't like to make a habit of it since the memories were uncomfortable. They sat funny in my gut. What Wendy did for me last night reminded me of something my aunt would have done.

Aunt Cindy had been as close to a real mother as I ever had. She made nourishing meals, used encouraging words, and really looked at me, not just past me. She and my Uncle Roger never had any kids of their own, but they were better parents than the ones I grew up with.

After returning the cup to the side table, I sat on the side of my bed, playing with the ends of my hair, lost in thought, and I remembered our fight; the one that catapulted me to a new city and separated us for good. On top of losing her husband suddenly and being consumed by grief, my aunt had to become the sole financial provider overnight. Some days she was in bed all day, and other days she was knocking on the door of every business around trying to find a job. I lost myself somewhere in trying to fill the gaps that needed patching, and it still wasn't enough. I wasn't enough.

My aunt and I drifted in our own worlds for weeks until our grief took a turn and shifted into anger that had nowhere else to go but towards each other. We fought, yelled, and made hurtful accusations that left open wounds, unable to heal. We tried to deal with the overwhelming sadness that begged to be released, but it wasn't working.

"You don't know what it's like to lose a husband!" Aunt Cindy screamed after I simply asked if she was getting out of bed.

I was shocked by her reaction, having never been yelled at by her. "You're right, I don't know what it's like to lose a husband, my only experience is in losing *both* of my parents at the same time. Sorry I can't sympathize with you!" I slammed her door and stomped down the hallway to my room.

She got up, flung the door open, and plodded after me. "Are you high? Drunk? Don't think I haven't noticed!"

I whipped around, ready to defend myself. "No, I'm not, but I'm surprised you've noticed anything other than your own freaking problems!"

"My problems? I lost my husband. My only problem is you!"

My next words left my brain faster than I could think of them. I had no response. I only had another stab of abandonment in my back.

Our anger kept us functioning, and we raged to keep from crumbling. I feared we'd never resume stable emotions again. I was used to having unstable adults in my life, but not Aunt Cindy. She was supposed to be safe, able to keep everything together.

I lost my words and my ability to move. I stood in the frame of my door and watched as the metaphorical earthquake destroyed everything else around me.

"You shouldn't have been at the hospital that day, Andrea. He wouldn't have wanted you to see him like that," my aunt threw back at me, her eyes wild with feeling, hands clenched into fists at her sides.

The ground was still shaking, just like the next words that came out of my mouth. "W-What are you even talking about, Aunt Cindy? How could I have stayed away? *You* were the one that didn't care to invite me to the hospital to say goodbye to my uncle." I took one step back, trying to distance myself from her words. "You got to say goodbye to his living body while I had to whisper to his dead one," I spit back at her with all of the venom I had stored in my soul, and there was plenty of it. It was as if the emotions I forgot to feel over my own parent's deaths were haunting me in the wake of Uncle Roger's.

The fight had drained out of her, whether due to her grief or me pulling it out of her with every vicious comment I could find. I stood in my room just beyond the doorway, studying the look on my aunt's face that said things wouldn't get better. She couldn't see beyond her grief, and I couldn't stand outside my anger. It eventually became a fatal combination.

I slammed my bedroom door in her face, blocking her out and protecting myself in the process.

A flutter within my stomach startled me out of the memories.

Was that… the baby moving?

I closed my eyes, remembering the distinct feeling from when I was pregnant with Allison. I held perfectly still, trying to feel it again, but I couldn't. I guess it was just the memories of Aunt Cindy churning in my gut. They were never easy to recall and left a sour taste behind.

It tore up my heart like paper being fed through a shredder knowing how much of a burden Aunt Cindy thought I was, so I left. When Aunt Cindy fell asleep the night after our final fight, I packed a bag and hitched a few rides to L.A. I put her and every other part of my old life behind me.

I leaned forward, resting my elbows on my knees and squeezed my hands tightly together. I physically remembered how angry I felt at Aunt Cindy, and how defeated her expression was before I slammed that door. Did she miss me? I hadn't seen or spoken to my aunt for four years; that might as well have been a lifetime. The time and distance was too great and far too wide.

When I left her house and her life, I traded my cell phone for weed and food. I didn't contact any of my old middle school friends after leaving, and I wiped my hands clean of the life I had under my aunt and uncle's roof. I wanted to start fresh, which meant I couldn't go back. I thought space and time would heal things, but time makes some wounds grow bigger.

I stood on tired legs and moved closer to the window, the warmth of the sun drenching me in its comforting embrace from head to toe. The California sun rose high in the sky every single day with its powerful rays. Even when the clouds tried to conceal its light, the day always came and the darkness always left. Isn't love kind of like the rising sun? It's always there, despite not feeling its warmth or seeing its brilliant light. It rises and sets like clockwork, but it is always there, a constant. I wasn't an expert on love; in fact, I barely knew how to recognize the real thing, but I figured it would be like this. It should be.

I breathed in the hope of the sun's beams and reminded myself that Aunt Cindy had loved me once. Maybe her love was like the sun—always there but hidden by the clouds of time and distance. I could only wish that her love could withstand the wake of disaster that seemed to follow me because, right now, I really needed her. I needed her reassurance that I wasn't beyond help. I was scared to face birth alone again.

I needed to call her even if just to apologize for messing up her life. I had to call her. I turned away from the window with sure steps, grabbing my purse, and slipping my black flats on. I wouldn't be able to rest until I talked to her.

Before I reached the door to my room, I felt the fluttery feeling in my stomach again. This time I knew it was the baby, and the movement was all the encouragement I needed to keep walking out my front door to make the call to my aunt.

Shame can't win every time.

CHAPTER 15

We All Need Somebody

May 2008—Age 17

"Andrea?" Aunt Cindy whispered tenderly.

"It's me," I said, barely able to get a word out of my mouth through the tears that flowed freely down my face. I found a few spare coins in the bottom of my purse and went to the pay phone near the drugstore down the street, knowing if I waited any longer, I would lose my courage.

"Andrea, oh my gosh, a-are you okay? I-I'm so relieved that you called! Oh, I am so glad you are alright!" Her words of concern washed over me.

I wiped the tears from my cheeks with my sweater sleeve. "Yes, I'm good. Really," I exhaled, trying to convince her even when I wasn't convinced myself. "I didn't expect so long to go by but I just, well, I guess things just ended so badly." I hated calling attention to the memory but couldn't tiptoe around the issue for long. It was the chasm that separated us for four long years.

"Where are you, sweetheart? Can we get together?"

"I'm safe. I live in the city right now," *but not for much longer*, I thought to myself. "Are you still in Anaheim?"

"Yes, yes, same house. Why don't I come to your place?"

"No!" It wasn't a good idea to bring my aunt into a house full of strippers, but I couldn't very well tell her this. "I mean... why don't we meet at a restaurant or something?"

"Sure, that works. Is this the phone number I can reach you at?"

Here we go, one small confession at a time that would point to the jumbled life I was living. "Um, no, this isn't my phone. I'm borrowing it." By borrowing, I meant paying to use it, but I wasn't ready to tell every one of my secrets.

We made plans to meet at a restaurant halfway between our homes, and just before we hung up, Aunt Cindy cleared her throat and said, "Andrea, I know we'll talk more when we meet, but I can't let another second go by without telling you how much I love you. I am so glad you are safe."

"I—" My voice caught and I couldn't finish my sentence. I wanted to tell her I loved her too, but I wasn't sure I was actually capable of love anymore. The tears were spilling out of the corners of my eyes again, reminding me that I felt something. I wanted her love, even if I didn't deserve it.

She doesn't know how much you've ruined things, Alexandria.

It's true, she didn't know everything I had done, but that just meant that the love she was offering me now was pure. It wasn't tainted by all of my mistakes.

"I love you too, Aunt Cindy." When the words came out of my mouth, I believed them. I just hoped she wouldn't regret her confession when she laid eyes on my growing belly.

Aunt Cindy looked so similar to the picture in my head. Her hair was still dark like mine, but I noticed more gray hairs on her head that lined her face. The parallel lines now permanently etched into her face increased in number as well but her wisteria-scented perfume and the brilliant smile that shone all the way to her sparkling, tear-filled green eyes were exactly as I remembered. We held one another for an extra length of time before sitting to enjoy a hot meal.

I couldn't avoid it for long. My stomach was protruding enough from my midsection to hint at new life beneath it. It was too obvious to ignore. My leg bounced under the table, and my hands were rubbing together from nerves and because it had been a while since I had a hit. I hope it only read as nerves.

"Sweetheart, you look so beautiful. Your hair is longer since the last time I saw you and your facial features make you look like a young woman now," Aunt Cindy said.

"Thanks. A few things have changed," I responded, looking down at my bulging belly, my hands instinctively tracing its roundness.

Aunt Cindy looked down where my eyes had fallen. "I couldn't help noticing. Are you ready to talk about it?"

I heard the care dripping from her words, but I only felt the blood pumping in my ears.

Go ahead, tell her how you messed up.

I took a deep breath and let it out slowly, buying time, and calming my fidgeting. "The baby is good. I mean, we haven't been to the doctor yet, but I am sure everything is fine in there." It wasn't the time to divulge that I had done this before. I had been in this exact position with an expanding stomach and an increasing number of problems. She didn't know about Allison and I wasn't ready to tell her. Not yet.

"Is the baby's father... involved?" she asked softly so only I could hear her.

"No." I said with empty emotion.

"Oh. Are you okay with that?"

"I don't have a choice. He, uh... he left when he found out I was pregnant," I said while forcing myself to observe Aunt Cindy's reaction. The look on her face looked akin to what mine probably mirrored when Mike dumped me. Stunned. Shocked. Confused. Like a punch to the gut that left my eyes wide and my mouth wider.

"Andrea, I'm so sorry," she said, pausing to gather her next promises. "You don't have to do this alone, you know. I'm here now, and I hope you'll let me stay," she said in a hushed voice so the other customers wouldn't hear.

I didn't want to need someone so badly, but that's how I felt with my Aunt Cindy. I may have needed her more at this moment than I needed food or water to survive. "Okay," I agreed, nodding my head. "I'm sure the baby is happy to hitch a ride on its way to breathing oxygen, but I won't be able to keep him... or her."

"Oh. So what is your plan?" Aunt Cindy asked me.

"Adoption. I've heard of someone who helps with that, so she is helping line up a family for this baby once it's born," I replied.

The look on my aunt's face went from concern to remorse in a flash. Her eyes filled as she admitted what troubled her. "I tried so hard to find you, Andrea. I-I just can't help but think that if I tried harder maybe I could have found you, and then maybe you wouldn't be going through all of this."

I heard her regret and absorbed the feelings as if they were my own. In some ways, they were. How many times had I wished the same thing? I blamed Aunt Cindy for not coming after me. I didn't leave a trail when I left, but did she even try to look for me?

"I don't know, maybe not. Maybe this was always going to happen."

"I felt horrible after some of the things I had said to you. I should have never told you about the burden it felt like to provide for you. For *us*. I was tired and overwhelmed by everything. I said so many horrible things about you not understanding death, when you lived through the grief of your parents," she told me.

I saw the sorrow covering every line and every movement that stole across her face as she apologized to me.

"I contacted the local police department in Anaheim every single week for the first few months trying to get an update on the missing person's report that I had filed with them. I also reached out to every family member I knew and thought you may have gone to stay with," Aunt Cindy said with a baffled look that I wore on my face as well.

She had tried to find me. I made it impossible, but she tried. I looked at her with more gratitude this time. "I thought about contacting you so many times but I just couldn't. I hurt you, and that's what kept me away. I knew I had become a burden, which is something I promised myself I... I..." My voice hitched as I tried to put words to the angst gripping my heart. "I promised myself I wouldn't be a burden again."

I didn't have much experience having conversations like this that involved apologies and forgiveness. I had never seen it done before and hoped my aunt could understand how I felt. "I'm just… so sorry, Aunt Cindy." I let the tears share my heartache.

"Honey, I forgive you, a thousand times over, I forgive you," her breath caught before she added, "I love you."

There it was again. My whole world was shaken by that one simple testament: I love you. My ears longed to hear it, my heart wanted to know it, but my mind still rallied against it, believing it had to be false. Somewhere along the way, I picked up the burden of regret, and I realize now that there isn't a heavier load to carry.

We continued talking in the same corner booth for hours until our waitress started wiping down the table in a not-so-subtle attempt at finally kicking us out in order to serve the next hungry customer.

"I know we are just now reconnecting, but I would really love for you to come back and stay with me again, Andrea, if you want to," Aunt Cindy stated with a questioning gaze and hopeful tone.

Could I try this again? Would it be different this time? I hesitated before responding but the fact that my current living situation was about to expire left me with only one option.

"Yes, I would really like that, but only if you're sure…" I responded.

"Absolutely," she assured me, with tears filling her eyes at her accepted offer.

We made plans to retrieve my belongings on another day before driving back to her cozy abode situated in the heart of Anaheim, CA. Every street sign and house color soaked me in a shower of remembrance. I sank into the soft mattress later that night, layering myself between the cool sheets after a hot shower, and relished the feel of being in this bedroom again. My bedroom that had once been my sanctuary. For the first time in a while, I was looking forward to what awaited me tomorrow.

* * *

Two Weeks Later—June 2008

I was curled up on my left side, sick to my stomach and shaking uncontrollably while staring at the closed hospital door. *Déjà vu.* I had lived this moment before; I laid there wondering if the night would consume me or if the daytime would highlight the loss, sending me deeper into a pit of agony.

When you lose a child to adoption, you mourn all of the moments you don't get to witness daily; their life moves on without you in it. When you lose a child to death, you mourn the moments you never got to have. I was now the bearer of both kinds of loss.

When I felt the cramps and saw the blood right after waking, it didn't register what was happening to me. I walked out of the simple bathroom that sat nestled between my room and my aunt's in the narrow hallway, holding my abdomen with one hand and the doorframe with the other.

"Aunt Cindy? Something is wrong," I said, barely above a whisper, my shock unable to get more words out.

"Andrea, what's going on? You look so pale…" These were the last words I remember hearing until I woke up some hours later in a hospital bed. I was briefed on what had happened when I awoke.

"Ms. Strivers, it appears you have miscarried. I would estimate you were eighteen weeks along. Were you aware you were pregnant?" the doctor asked hesitantly.

"Yes." My vocal cords still lacked the adequate strength to speak, and I cleared my throat, hoping it would clear my thoughts as well. My hands felt jittery, and I could feel the beads of sweat starting to form on my brow. How many hours had it been since I had pushed the heroin through the tip of a needle into my waiting body? Too long.

The doctor cleared his throat, "I see. Well, we got your labs back and noticed there were high levels of drugs in your system." He paused for my reaction, but all I could do was continue staring out the window, wondering how I would get out of here.

Keep it together, Andrea.

"I believe this may have caused fetal distress and triggered the miscarriage," the doctor said in a softer tone.

His words spoke the truth I didn't want to hear. Not yet, anyway, and especially not with my aunt sitting in the chair at the foot of the bed. I couldn't look at her, afraid to make eye contact with the woman who had welcomed me into her home. Me, the drug addict. Me, the troubled-girl. Me, the mother by womb-only.

"Andrea, is this true? Have you been taking drugs?" Aunt Cindy's voice came out shaky and confused.

I swallowed the extra saliva in my mouth, "Yes." I didn't try my hand at empty apologies or ineffective groveling. I had lost too much to care.

"How…I-I didn't…" Aunt Cindy's words faltered after my frank admission, but instead of finishing her thought, she left the room claiming she needed to take a walk and get some air. I couldn't blame her. The room felt stifling.

"Your nurse will be in shortly," the doctor stated at the conclusion of his assessment. He had said other words too before my aunt stepped out, but I don't know what they were. I tuned him out.

I was trying to rest like my body longed to do, but I also felt like I had run for miles. I was sweating but couldn't stay warm while my aunt was wandering the halls absorbing the information I couldn't save her from, and I wondered if she would return. The truth was finally out there, and it was as hard as I thought it would be.

I needed to find the right moment and then I would leave, this time, for my sake.

CHAPTER 16
Dead Weight
June 2008—Age 17

"Here, kid, take this," the stranger said, thrusting a cup of coffee in my face. I took the cup but when I looked inside, it was already half empty.

"Thanks a bunch," I said sarcastically to the man who was already walking away from me. It was the first hot drink I had in weeks, so instead of drinking it right away, I let the steam warm the underside of my chin.

It was June, and even though the temperature never dropped too far, the chill of the night still lingered in the morning. It had been one month since I delivered the severely premature baby that called my body home for four short months. It had been hard to come to terms with being pregnant, having Mike's child, and then just as quickly having it all disappear.

Poof. Gone.

I tipped the cup to my mouth slowly, taking a sip of the dark-roasted beverage and finding the bitterness tasted exactly how I felt. I still remember every achingly clear detail of the minutes spent in that hospital turned prison.

My aunt finally returned to my hospital room an hour after finding out I was on drugs and that's what killed my baby. She was back to her caring self, and it made me angry. I wanted her to be upset with me, to give me the reaction I deserved, but she didn't.

"Andrea, are you sure you're doing okay?"

"You are looking so tired right now, why don't you go lay down?"

"Are you feeling sick? Do you want a bucket just in case?"

"NO!" I screamed at her, letting out the pent up rage I wanted her to have. I had never gone through withdrawals that severely, even during times of having little to no money to pay for heroin. My body was expelling a child and drugs all at the same time and I wasn't sure how long I could hang on. I needed to escape.

Later that night, when my aunt thought I was sleeping, I heard her talking to someone on her cell phone in the bathroom. Her voice was hushed and I knew she was trying to be quiet, but I heard everything.

"She just seems so depressed. I am not sure what to do. Her body is really fighting," my aunt said. I can still hear the despair in her voice.

"You're right. She just needs time. I just wish there was something I could do for her. She seems to shove it all inside," Aunt Cindy replied, pausing to listen to the whispers coming through the speaker that was likely pressed close to her ear.

"She hasn't wanted to talk about the baby... I've tried... yeah, okay, I will just keep reminding her I'm here to support her," Aunt Cindy said with a sigh.

If my emotions were working, I would have cried hearing how worried she sounded all because of me, but they weren't. Her words hit my stone cold heart and fell to the ground.

"Thanks, Wendy, I've never done this before. I really appreciate your support right now. Everything is just so fragile." My aunt's voice caught on the last word.

Wendy.

The woman didn't know how to leave things alone. When she showed up to the hospital earlier, I refused to see her. I told her to get the fuck out or I'd leave. The nurses knew I was a flight risk, so they ushered Wendy to the waiting room to see if I would change my mind. I didn't. I had no child to give her, so there was no reason to talk to her. I was just as pissed at her as I was at my aunt. Why wasn't anyone angry at me? Why are they being so nice when they should be telling me how badly I fucked up for killing this baby?

I gave the memories another shove, reminding them who was the boss around here, and took a sip of my donated coffee, this time scorching my tongue and causing me to spit it out on the sidewalk in front of me.

I threw the cup of backwash coffee across the sidewalk I sat on. "Ugh, it tasted like dirt anyway," I muttered.

I watched the sun peak over the horizon. Another day to survive. There were countless homeless people lining every street, alley, storefront, and sidewalk in L.A. Most people were desensitized to seeing all of us out here with our own individual stories of suffering. They often looked at us like plants lining the streets rather than human beings.

This is what you deserve.

This is how Aunt Cindy and Wendy should have treated you.

My Aunt Cindy didn't know where I was. I barely lasted twenty-four hours in that hospital, trying my damndest to wean my body off of the heroin it craved more than oxygen and failing.

"I have to go, I have to leave. Get me out of here. I can't do this!" I repeated like a song on a CD skipping. My aunt did her best to calm me, but it only added more gasoline to the fire burning inside of me.

I grabbed at my still cramping abdomen that was as empty as a tomb, delirious with wanting it all to stop hurting so much. My body wouldn't quit shaking and convulsing, and I knew I needed to do something; I wasn't this strong. I had to leave. I craved escape.

When my aunt went to the cafeteria and the charge nurse came to babysit me, I sat up in bed, ripped off all of the monitors, IVs, and tape lining my arms, getting rid of the chains that held me in that bed.

"Andrea, stop, please, let me help you!" the nurse begged, but I ignored her. "Stop! Wait, you can't just leave!"

"You can't keep me here! I'm leaving! Get away from me!" I found my clothes and shoes sitting on the chair on the other side of the room, and I burst out of the door, the nurse's voice still ringing out somewhere behind me, but I had tuned her out. My head was throbbing, and I ignored that too.

It will all be better soon. Run!

My feet picked up the pace even though I was sluggish and wanted to be sick.

Keep it together, Andrea!

I pushed forward, through one door and out the next. I wasn't staying here for one more second. I was killing my aunt with every groan I made and the pressure to pull through felt overbearing and impossible. I could barely breathe.

Don't stop now!

You'll get relief soon.

I hitched a few rides up to the city before finding a dingy pawn shop. I had no money and nothing but the clothes on my back to barter with but I had something else.

I hurriedly reached into my left shoe. "Where is it!" I yelled at the shoe, transforming into the lunatic I felt like. I tossed it aside before digging my hand into the right one.

Bingo! Here it is.

I'm not sure how I managed to keep it this long. Whether it was the value of the necklace or the only memories I had left of my childhood, I couldn't say. I kept it with me at all times but never sold it and never wore it, just like Michelle. After hightailing it out of the hospital and a few hours of withdrawal symptoms later, I was willing to do just about anything to get out of this bodily prison.

I walked into the pawn shop, looking down at the emerald gem that hung like a brilliant star on a gold chain, and I clutched it tightly in my hand. I didn't know where it came from, but in an instant, I felt so jealous of this gem. It was precious and beautiful without even trying. I would never amount to this. I carried it around this long thinking it was special and maybe it would make me feel that way too. Maybe it would make me feel something for the mother that hated me. It didn't. Instead it just reminded me I would never be special. I was too impossible to love.

It's dead weight.

I thrust the necklace onto the counter and the shop owner gingerly picked it up. I was moving around the pawn shop in a mess of shakes and dry heaving, waiting for his appraisal and hoping it would come soon.

He cleared his throat and I flung my head in his direction. "Are you sure you want to sell a necklace of this value? You might want to take it to a jeweler to see if you can get more for it," the shopkeeper said.

"It's fine. Yes, take it. What can you give me?"

"The best I can do is $100.

"That's it?" My surprise was discernible even amidst my anxious movements.

"It is way under value for what this is probably worth, but I can't swing much more than that," he told me honestly.

"Whatever. I'll take cash," I huffed. The money was more valuable to me anyway. I could get some food and heroin and then figure out my next steps.

I stared down at the spilled coffee that created a wet spot on the pavement. I didn't want to be reminded of the decisions I made or didn't make. What I knew was that the $100 I made on Michelle's prized necklace was long gone, and I relied on strangers giving me cups of coffee or a spare granola bar.

I stood up from the step I had been perched on, tucking my hair behind my ears and smoothing out my clothes. I had a large, bald man that wore loafers to talk to about a job.

The *Wild Kitty* was boarded up.

Spray paint from city taggers cluttered the few windows that had boards over them, trash and debris lay all around the building and the sidewalk. My hope of a job was now shattered like the attic window above the front doors, which was the only one that hadn't been covered. I had my small duffle bag, my needle and spoon, and the last hot meal I could afford swirling around in my stomach as I contemplated my next move.

"What am I supposed to do now?" I said out loud, shrugging my shoulders. I didn't know any of the other strip joints in the city, and I was back to square zero.

I kicked at an empty water bottle that blew across the sidewalk in front of my feet, wondering how it came to be here in front of this deserted building. I felt a lot like that vacant bottle. The contents had been enjoyed by someone and then tossed out a window or dropped on the street without a second thought, just like me. Cast aside and forgotten. This bottle served no other purpose now; it was trash, and I couldn't help seeing myself this way too.

I walked a few steps to where I had kicked the bottle and bent down to grasp it in my palm, giving it a closer inspection. It was missing a cap and the label was faded and tattered, but the bottle still held its original shape, clinging to its last bit of pride. I knew a thing or two about pride; it's the fuel that has kept me going all these years. Pride stopped me from reaching out to Aunt Cindy for so long, and it would keep me from doing it again.

I stared at the bottle for longer than was socially acceptable and decided that I would keep it. I couldn't part with it just yet. Call it a strong sense of meaning or call it heroin, but I was taking that bottle.

I propped it upright in the side pocket of my small duffel bag containing the few items I owned and continued walking before turning down a side street a few blocks away to try and find a place to sleep for the night. More trash, used strollers, and tarps lined the short alley, but I knew what this spot meant for people—it was their safe haven. It was ugly to look at and most people hated seeing city streets crawling with crazies and filled with what appeared to be trash, but what most people don't know is what keeps people here.

Most of us who are homeless have families we could go back to but we choose this life because our problems are accepted. Being accepted as an addict by fellow addicts is better than facing your loved ones as a person with a shameful addiction; an addiction that needs to be fixed, changed, or gotten rid of. Other people outside of the lifestyle just didn't get it. On the streets, you aren't judged or berated to get clean. You are simply accepted as you are —baggage and all.

When I finally found the side of a building that looked habitable, I stepped past extended feet and smelly humans, turning my back to the wall and sliding down it until my butt met the rough concrete. The man sleeping next to me was shaking wildly and a shiver coursed through me, recognizing the bodily discomfort of withdrawals. I turned my head away from the inconsolable man and tried not to think of how I would be that person soon if I couldn't figure out a solution to my money problems.

I could really use a cigarette right now, I thought, while sitting on this cold ground watching the world move slowly in hazy existence around me. My mind chose that moment to replay a memory of Michelle standing on the front porch, leaning against the railing of the add-on porch smoking her cigarette. As a kid, I looked at her longingly, wanting to one day look just like her. The puffs of smoke escaped her pink lips and traveled in front of her face before they continued their journey upwards and, eventually, disappeared completely.

I was curious what the smoke tasted like and why it was something Michelle did multiple times a day. "Could I try?" I asked once when I was ten years old.

Michelle studied me briefly and then nodded, extending her cigarette for me to grab. I placed the lit cigarette between my lips as I had seen her do so many times before and took an inhale, making sure the sides of my cheeks had small cavities in them just like Michelle's did. It looked like she was sucking in air through pursed lips and so I mimicked it.

Immediately, a coughing fit grabbed hold of me, and I expelled the smoke from my mouth in fits. The smoke had tried to choke me. I felt like I couldn't get another full breath when I heard the laughter coming from Michelle growing louder and louder. When I looked up at her, she was bent over, unable to contain herself.

"Oh, that was… hilarious! You can't inhale *that* much," Michelle said between mocking laughs that made her grip her knee for support in keeping upright.

I tossed the cigarette on the ground and stormed inside, hoping Michelle didn't notice the embarrassment written plainly on my face.

"Hey! That cigarette was still good!" she yelled after me, all signs of amusement gone from her voice. I didn't care though, I just needed to hide.

I had plenty of opportunities to practice smoking in my teen years, proving to myself and Michelle that I could do it. I may not have shared a cigarette with Michelle again but every time I lit up and successfully exhaled the smoke like I had seen her do thousands of times, I thought about that time on the porch. I hated her for making me feel so dumb. Karma really was a bitch.

I felt like I was the one laughing now, because even though things were rough, I still had something she didn't: life.

CHAPTER 17

Manuel

August 2008—Age 18

Time flies when you're high and untethered.

My eighteenth birthday came and went without a second glance as birthdays typically did for me. I moved through the days in persisting existence without much to anchor me. My daily meal at the soup kitchen was both a physical necessity and a social outlet. I met a woman named Chloe who was years older than I was and had been on heroin most of her life. We often stood in line together for our one hot meal, passing the time by swapping stories and gossip on the streets.

"I just don't get how you got out here. I mean, you're young, you should find something better to do with your life than hang out with fools like us." She nodded towards the rest of the room as we straddled the cafeteria bench seats to finally eat after such a long wait.

"Young doesn't mean shit in this world, Chloe, and you know it," I said frankly.

Chloe looked down at her bowl of soup. "Eh, I just wish it did sometimes."

I had learned long ago that it was worth it to find allies on the street, and Chloe was mine. There were enough gang members and shady folks out there that I needed someone on my side. I did my best to steer clear of all that, hiding my head beneath my sweatshirt and acting crazy when I had to.

It was Chloe who finally convinced me to meet Manuel. "Andy, I know what you're thinking but just give him a shot. I swear he isn't like the other creeps and he takes care of his girls," she said, doing her best to sell me on this popular business venture for most young women in my position.

"Chloe, I told you I used to strip, not sleep around."

"This would be good money, though! You could actually live somewhere else other than our small little tent posted up at different spots around this godforsaken city," Chloe said before taking a bite of her chicken soup.

I could see the persistence in Chloe's eyes. I could also see they were bloodshot and glazed over.

"Money would be nice. I hate having to beg. People don't give a damn about helping and when they do, it's always so little," I complained.

"You have a shot at something better here. You'd be crazy not to take it."

"Why don't you take the gig then, Chloe, if it's such a great opportunity?" I looked up from my food, doing most of the questioning with my eyes.

"Because my tits are sagging and yours ain't! Simple as that. I'm too old, girl. You still have your whole life to make some money and get off these streets," Chloe stated.

She had a point. I could take the gig, make enough money, and then move wherever I wanted to. Maybe find a job or my own place to stay after I pocketed enough to live off of for a while. I could afford heroin *and* food and wouldn't have to choose.

"Fine. I'll meet him," I conceded.

I didn't know what to expect when I finally did meet Manuel. I had ditched my baggy sweatshirt, and rinsed my hair and face in one of the public restrooms to make sure I was more presentable. I convinced myself that this job was important. I didn't want to ruin it by looking like a frightened, drug-addicted homeless girl, even though that's exactly what I was under all of the pretense. I needed to shake off my helpless demeanor and put on the confidence of a woman who would provide for herself.

The man Chloe called Manuel couldn't have been older than mid-twenties. He was standing confidently before me and was a different play on the dark and handsome features I had once been drawn to. His caramel colored skin, buzzed, jet black hair, and deep brown eyes made up the *dark* part of his looks, but the *handsome* piece came more from the way he dressed and carried himself. His clothing was pristine, not a ruffle, crinkle or smudge to be found. Unlike my attire, where I had to turn my shirt inside out to hide the fact that it was constantly worn. He was my height so when he extended his hand in greeting, we looked at each other squarely in the eyes.

"Alexandria?"

"Yeah, that's me," I said, answering to my street name that I told Chloe to pass along.

When our hands touched, my stomach dropped. I wasn't sure if this was from fear or attraction, but I pushed both out of my thoughts just as quickly as they had entered.

"I hear you were a dancer once."

"Yeah, I stripped for a while."

"Did you have another name? Maybe I knew you."

"Same name. Alexandria," I offered, hoping he wouldn't press me for further details on my name. My heartbeat began to race at the thought of his possible recognition.

Did he know me?

Did I know him?

"No, I don't know that name but I like it," he confirmed. "You're eighteen, right?"

I nodded a few times before dropping my gaze to the ground. Unlike when I worked for Bernie, I was actually legal this time, even though that meant nothing in the line of work I would be getting into with Manuel.

His perusal was driving into me, scanning every part of my body, leaving a chill in its wake, and fear as its companion. "I think you'll be a good addition," he finally concluded and with this one statement, I was owned. I answered to a higher power now, and his name was Manuel.

The streets were filled with people who had stories; they had reasons for being here. Some got out, and others, like me, just moved up the chain a bit. That night, I got a job. One that afforded me to keep buying heroin safely, which meant no used needles. I had a boss, coworkers, and regular customers. I worked all hours of the night and slept a few hours during the day in between getting high in the small apartment Manuel had set up for me. I was no longer a homeless eighteen-year-old but an eighteen-year-old prostitute with a pimp. Manuel kept me for himself for a while, and I started to believe he would never add me to the rest of the lineup I knew he organized. I didn't mind. One man was enough to deal with and Manuel appreciated the favors.

"You're perfect," he whispered into my hair one night, nuzzling my ear in the process and sending my heart to galloping.

I gave a small laugh. "You must say that to all of the girls," I replied, hoping to get him to admit that there were others he was sleeping with too. Manuel didn't admit to anything he didn't want to. He was like a vault that no one knew the combination to, and I would venture to guess that not even Manuel knew the code.

He only smiled before crushing his lips into mine once more, tasting my question and sensing my longing for him. Only him. I responded in earnest, showing my appreciation rather than telling him. I told myself I was protected. I might have even been adored, but not loved. My heart was lost somewhere in the wild movements of his hands; the consistent attention that had me dreaming. My adoration for Manuel echoed off of his walls and returned void. Empty. Unavailable.

Mike's jealousy had been our downfall, but when I looked at him, I knew there was love in his eyes, or something like it. When I looked at Manuel, he looked hungry. I was terrified by what I saw because I knew that one day, it would overtake me and I'd be left with nothing.

• • •
July 2010—Age 19

"Stop!" I screamed. "You can't do this!" I yelled with all the lung power I had left but to no avail. The air was warm inside the bag as I begged for every breath and worried at every one I couldn't get. I didn't see him when I climbed into the SUV that pulled up to the curb next to me. The strength of the man holding me was unrelenting. My body was slow to react. My heroin addiction usually numbed the grueling experiences to make them bearable enough to repeat each night, but not tonight. It only dulled my response time. I still felt every rough movement, every push and pull of the unwanted touch.

I mostly worked on Figueroa Street where the 110 and the 10 freeways meet in downtown L.A. Where the cars lined up like they were going through a drive thru, assessing their options and ordering what they wanted. Tonight, I had gone rogue. I wanted to know what it would be like to hold all of the money in my hands, rather than the scant amount Manuel gave me. He was taking a greater cut of the profits now, and that pissed me off. I had worked for him for almost two years and I barely made more than when I started.

I couldn't see the man's face with the bag over my head when he dragged me into the trunk. *No!* I kicked my legs and felt like I was thrashing around but my body was exhausted and even weaker under the control of this burley man that held my life in his hands. Literally, since his large hand pinned my neck to the ground. My fingernails raked down his arms hoping to inflict even just a little bit of the pain he was dishing out to me.

This is the end.

Don't fight it, Andrea. It was bound to happen.

All of the battle drained out of me and onto the floor of that vehicle. I was raped that night, but before I lost more, which was shaping up to be the plan, my pimp, Manuel, stepped in with guns blazing.

Not every working woman has a pimp, and those women have to be cutthroat and ready for the inevitable violence that rears its head. I wasn't that kind of woman. I had an addiction that paralyzed my thinking at times, and without protection, I would have had to be more clear headed. I needed to be ready for the guns pointed in my face, the attempted kidnappings, and the bloody battles. I thought I could handle it. I was wrong. Manuel was who kept me alive out here. He kept the creepers away and the gang bangers out of sight.

Gunshots rang out as they pelted the back of the vehicle, windows, and tires. The sound of metal crunching under the impact was how I felt in the arms of my kidnapper. I tore the bag from my head when the large man that had painfully taken advantage of me minutes before lay screaming on the floor next to me, clutching his arm as it spilled the deep red of blood. I watched in horror as it pooled on the floor and colored my own arm in its unforgiving shade. I owed Manuel my life while he took those men to within an inch of theirs.

I started coughing and clutched my throat so the bile wouldn't escape. I was only now able to breathe again; the oxygen tasted like relief.

Keep it together, Andrea!

There was screaming, groaning, fast breathing, swearing, and the sound of knuckles connecting to flesh and bone. Manuel flung open the trunk, pulled me out of my crumpled position, and took me to his waiting car, which was still running. I wore less most nights than the outfits I had worn at the *Wild Kitty,* if that were even possible. I was missing some of my clothes now, but I couldn't care less. The distinct metallic taste of blood on my tongue warned me of an injury I didn't remember getting and the tenderness on my cheek and neck spoke of the bruises I would have.

Manuel swung me around, before I was lowered into the backseat, and pinned my back to the side of his car. My body was aching, but the look in his eyes made me forget every sharp pain. It was the look of a man ready to kill. Manuel gripped the underside of my chin with his palm, clenching so tightly, I let out a whimper of pain. All I could hear was his fast breathing through a clenched jaw and flared nostrils. When he released my chin, my hand went to soothe the ache he left me with only to feel the slap of his hand across my face.

"Don't you ever fucking do that again!" he screamed, so close to me that his spit flew in my face while his finger pointed at my bare chest.

I thought he was going to kill me; he *should* have killed me; I wanted him to because I deserved it.

I was shoved into the backseat of his car with little effort from him and a whole lot of cringe worthy pain for me. The door slammed and my hand went to trace the handprint he left on my sensitive cheek before we peeled away from the scene. This was the feeling of my unrequited love in all of its glory. My heart still longed to be close to Manuel as his hands were violating every piece of me.

I don't know if the driver of the other SUV made it out alive. What I did know was how livid Manuel was about the whole ordeal. His anger filled the small car, and it was choking me like smoke filling a room and stealing all of the oxygen I had just gotten back.

I got an earful from him in both English and Spanish

"You whore! How could you be so stupid!"

"*¿Estás demente?*" Are you crazy? he yelled, pointing towards his head.

"Don't you know I always have eyes on you? There isn't a finger you lift without me knowing about it!"

I had to look down, to the side, anywhere other than the condemnation being aimed at me through the rearview mirror.

"If you ever try to go behind my back again…" he trailed off after this veiled threat, leaving me to wonder and imagine what he would do if I ever did this again.

Would he kill me? The thought came but I couldn't find it in me to be afraid. *Kill me. I don't care.*

I had never heard of him killing anyone before, but Manuel had people who did all sorts of things. It wouldn't surprise me. Not much did these days. I was still alive and mostly unharmed, which is more than I could say for my two kidnappers that we left behind. I realized that night that I wasn't as afraid to die as I thought I would be. Death seemed to be an option I hadn't considered before but after the events of tonight, maybe I should. I wish this wasn't the first time a man tried to take advantage by forcing himself on me or stealing back the money he agreed to pay. Manuel was always there to deal with the fall out and, for that, I should be thankful. He saved my life regardless of how little I cared about it.

I wanted to die but I wanted Manuel's love more. "I'm so sorry, Manuel. It was a mistake. I will never do that again, I swear to you."

When we pulled up to the curb outside of my apartment, I stumbled out of the car, throwing my tremor-filled body at his feet using my words. With my body. Everything I had. This went on for weeks afterwards, begging for his forgiveness until words weren't enough and I needed something more. I needed the power of my body to smooth away the rough edges of his unforgiving gaze. I needed Alexandria to fix things.

Power. Survival. Loathing.

"I don't want your fucking apology," Manuel would spit back harshly.

He kept me close after my "stunt," as he called it. "I'm the one who keeps you safe out there; remember that when you think about running off. I won't be saving you next time." His words cut deeper than a newly sharpened knife.

"You want your drugs to keep coming? To sleep in a bed and not a cardboard box? Then do your *job*," he told me.

I knew I had broken his trust, and the worst part was knowing that Manuel wasn't the kind of man to ever give second chances.

Whenever I doubted Manuel again, I thought about my near death experience and how close I had been to death that night. I felt it in the grip of the faceless man and the lack of air suffocating me.

Yet, here I was. Alive. For what reason, I didn't know, but I thanked Manuel in the only ways I knew how. I did whatever he asked and pleased him in whatever ways I could so my alliance with him was secure even when trust was nonexistent.

Nine months later, I was paying for all of it. Again.

CHAPTER 18
Loss Like This
November 2010—Age 20

"Wendy. It's me, Andrea." I called her from the cell phone that Manuel had bought for me when I started working for him. He wanted to get a hold of his girls at all times. I wasn't sure how much longer the phone would be active, considering I wasn't one of the girls anymore, so I had to call Wendy while I had the chance.

"Andrea. H-How are you?" she replied in shock.

I knew I was catching her off guard with my call. Our last meeting hadn't exactly gone over too well. I cursed my body for its lack of novelty and wondered how it was possible to be pregnant *again*. It was against me and determined to carry children that I would never parent, leaving me in a puddle of heartache and a pile of un-dealt with issues. It was a sick cycle that I could not escape from.

"I've been better. Listen, I need to enlist your..." I searched my brain for the right word "... services again," I told her. Was there a more delicate way to say this?

Probably, but I couldn't think clearly enough and went with the first explanation that came to mind.

"Are you saying you're pregnant, Andrea?" Wendy asked.

"Yes."

"How far along?" Wendy gently prodded, seeking the information I wasn't readily offering.

"I don't know, but probably about four months or so." *Like the last time I called you,* I wanted to say, but didn't. I was far enough along for Manuel to notice. He immediately pulled me from his rotation and told me to deal with it, so I was dealing with it the only way I knew how.

"Are you telling me you haven't been to a doctor yet?"

"That's exactly what I'm telling you." I couldn't help my snarky comment from flying through my lips. I almost regretted it.

"We'll figure this out, Andrea. I am in this with you," Wendy replied, diffusing the tension I had created. "Can you tell me who the father is?"

I refused to tell Manuel it was his child. I didn't want to be attached to him like this. I didn't want another reason to be under his thumb, and bearing his child would secure this fate.

"No," was all I could say. My mouth couldn't form the syllables of his name without cringing in fear.

Wendy sighed into the phone, "Okay, alright... we'll figure this out together."

The admission slipped out before I could catch it. "I wish I didn't feel so alone," I replied, the sound coming out muffled through the gaps between my fingers as my hand covered my mouth. Before Wendy could reply, I dropped my hand and blurted out my next question. "Can you help me find a family for this baby or not?"

"Of course," she responded without any hesitation. "Can you tell me where you're living right now? Are you safe?"

I let out an annoyed sigh. "Yes, I'm fine," I said, even though I wasn't. I had locked myself in the apartment Manuel paid for, surviving off food scraps and heroin until I could come to grips with what was growing in my body.

"Have you called your aunt?"

"No, please don't tell her," I begged. "We haven't spoken since the last… incident. I don't want to worry her over this too."

"Andrea, we have to tell her. You can call her or I will."

Dammit. This wasn't going how I planned, but then again, I didn't really know what that plan was. "Fine. You call her," I huffed. The last thing I wanted was my aunt knowing I had another heroin baby to deliver.

Wendy gathered a few more details before promising to call me back soon. It was only a day later that she tried calling, but I didn't answer. I was too afraid to hear what she had to say, good or bad news. When I finally answered one of her many calls she told me about a few families she had lined up for me to review their profiles, but I could tell she had another idea.

"I had a thought after we spoke…" Wendy started. "What do you think about asking the family that you were planning to adopt to before?"

Oh, the family that never got a baby because it died?

I couldn't help the obvious guilt I still felt over my miscarriage a couple of years ago. I felt weakened by my dependence and causing the death of that baby. I would be lying to myself if I thought guilt was what I dealt with. No, guilt was child's play. Shame is the monster I carried now.

"I know it's been two years, but they are still waiting on a baby to join their family and since you chose them last time, I thought maybe you would consider them again?" Wendy was treading carefully in this conversation. Likely, since she had a front row seat to what shame made me do.

"I don't know…" I replied. That family knew I left the hospital with afterburners on and no concern outside of appeasing my cravings. Did I want to bring them back into my spin cycle again? What happens if this baby dies too?

"Think about it. You don't have to decide right now. You take some time to consider everything, this is a huge decision after all," Wendy affirmed.

I heard the confidence in her voice that a decision would eventually be made and we would start this dance all over again. Wendy would have to have enough confidence for the both of us. I had to keep reminding myself that I had no attachment to this child, and no matter what family he or she ended up in was fine by me. They were all deceitful promises, but they kept the peace in my head most days.

Wendy took me to the doctor's office a couple weeks later where they informed me I was, indeed, four months pregnant. They did an ultrasound, and I stared at the black and white movement on the screen with tears blurring my eyes.

"He's perfect," I whispered. A boy.

I felt a warmth encircle my hand. When I peered down, Wendy's hand gripped mine with a fierce protectiveness. I was barely keeping it together, and she must have known this because she became the sure footing that I needed. I told Wendy my decision when the ultrasound tech left and before the doctor came in.

"I want them to have the baby," I said before I could change my mind for the umpteenth time.

She gave my hand a few pats and then a squeeze, indicating her agreement before adding, "It's your choice. I will call them and let them know later today."

The doctor gave me a list of Methadone clinics that I should visit during this pregnancy. I had learned my lesson from the last one that I couldn't wean my body from the drugs, and Methadone provided a safer option for me and the baby. Next, I got the lecture that included how much I should eat and drink and when my next appointment would be scheduled. I was through living with so many restrictions and dreamed about a day I wouldn't be controlled by a pimp, a heroin needle, or my past. I had been told what to do by everyone other than myself.

• • •

April 6, 2011—Age 20

When I arrived at the hospital to give birth, Wendy met me soon after and stuck by my side the entire time. I begged for relief and cried out in pain while Wendy rubbed my shoulder. Aunt Cindy walked in the room no more than an hour later, and I sighed in relief at her physical presence in the room. Her green eyes held a sincerity beyond my understanding.

Wendy had called my aunt as she told me she would. Aunt Cindy was ready to see me long before I was ready to see her. Shame does that to a person. It wasn't until my legs were draped over the contraption the nurse called stirrups, and crying out in pain that I felt ready to face Aunt Cindy.

A guttural noise left my overworked and sweaty body when I felt the last contraction squeeze my lower abdomen in a vice-like grip that wouldn't let go.

"His head and one shoulder are out," the doctor cried from between my legs, only the top of her head visible from my vantage point. "One more push and then he's out. Come on, Andrea, you got this."

My head was dizzy with exhaustion and I felt I was going to throw up, but the grip on my stomach was tightening again; there was no time for being sick.

"Hold my hand, sweetie," Aunt Cindy encouraged from beside me.

"He's almost here!" Wendy said through her joy standing on the other side gripping my hand tighter than I held hers.

I threw my head back against the raised hospital bed and arched my back as much as I could, harnessing the pain swirling around my body to the one place it mattered. "Ahhhh!" I screamed until every twinge, every stab, every pinch was over.

My body slumped down in relief. Heavy breaths came in rapid succession as I loosely held Wendy and Aunt Cindy's hands in my own.

I waited. Listening. Watching. I could only see the soft caramel skin tone being held in the hands of the doctor, then I heard his faint cry... until I didn't. The nurses rushed about in a chaotic foot pattern, grabbing tools, asking for supplies, and speaking codes I didn't understand between one another. Something was off, and I was too out of it to gather what it was. I could only assume his fight through addiction was beginning when I wanted mine to end.

"Where am I?" I asked in a groggy voice.

"You are back in the recovery room, Andrea," my aunt's voice replied, rising above the intermittent beeping from the monitors around me.

I groaned, "Wh-where's the baby?"

"He is recovering, sweetie. They took him to the NICU right after birth. When you are feeling better, I can take you to see him," said an all too familiar voice that didn't belong to my aunt.

Curls. The nurse who had been there during my first pregnancy was here?

"No." I shook my head vehemently. "I can't see him. It's just too much," I said on the verge of an emotional breakdown. "I won't!" I screamed louder until I felt like someone could hear me. My body shook uncontrollably, and the blood that ran through my veins was like ice, chilling my skin as the adrenaline seeped out of me.

"Sh-sh-shh, it's alright, Andrea," my aunt consoled.

"That's right. We don't have to make any decisions right now, darlin', just rest as best you can, you hear?" Curls said, her words slightly above comforting as I tried to regain my senses.

I can't believe she is here.

Witnessing another birth.

Another mistake.

"I know this is hard for you, but you have to know that the story doesn't end here. There are bigger things at work here. Just hang on to that," Curls said softly over the hum of machines.

Hard being a complete understatement.

Asphalt is hard.

Decisions are hard.

Addiction is hard.

This was *agony*. Losing another child, being reminded of the first I gave up, and the second I killed. I was about to lose it. I needed air.

I left the hospital hours after birth; they all tried to convince me to stay but my body required medicine that wasn't at the hospital. It begged me to leave and, eventually, I surrendered to its demands. I wanted to close my eyes and forget everything. The nightmare would lessen for him, but it was just the beginning for me.

Wendy: Andrea, where did you go?
Wendy: Please don't do anything rash.
Wendy: I love you, Andrea.

The texts came through, continuously reminding me of the child I left behind; the story I didn't fit in. I guess I hoped the memory of his brown, limp frame as they lifted him up would fade, but that's not how brains work. They remember it all in painfully accurate detail. My body ached with the reminder of birth, and its dependence thrummed through my collapsed veins. I needed to find relief in the only way I knew how.

. . .

June 16, 2011—Age 20

Cindy: Andrea, are you okay? Please, text me back so I know you're alright. Please.
Cindy: If you need a place to stay, you can come live with me again, Andrea. I can help you. We will get through this together.
Cindy: I love you.

Those were the last texts I saw pop up on my phone before I set it facedown on the floor beside me. Manuel never did turn off my phone like I thought he would when I found out I was pregnant. Instead, he just assumed I would be back when it was all over.

He was right.

Manuel resumed his faithful position as overseer on my behalf but no longer did I have my studio apartment; the locks had been changed and I wasn't allowed such luxuries anymore. My cut had been decreased to pay for the time off I had taken, and every action that Manuel took spoke of my demotion.

"You'll get a more permanent place when you prove yourself," Manuel said after I returned, groveling for his management and love once more. "For now, try to stay out of any more trouble."

"I will do anything," I said, throwing every ounce of self-respect I had before him.

"Good, that's exactly the kind of perspective you'll need if you want to make it out here. You really screwed up with your recent incident," Manuel stated. He was colder than I remembered. Uninterested and bored with me. I noticed the other women he was with and hated them as much as I hated myself.

After I left the hospital in a rush two months ago, I met another prostitute who let me share her car, which was a marked improvement from a piece of cardboard on the ground of some random alleyway. I worked different blades in downtown L.A. now; wherever Manuel had me was where I went. No questions asked. I no longer had private clientele or friends of Manuel that I served, but rather any old or young male that happened upon me that evening was who I shared a bed, car, street, or room with.

There are plenty of prostitutes in L.A., but business was still consistent, and I was seeing four to eight men on any given day. Some days were slow, others were busy, and the rest were forgettable. I made some good money, averaging $80 per customer, but most of it went to Manuel, for retribution, heroin, and food. I carried a few belongings with me but always made sure I had my silver spoon for liquifying my heroin, a tube of gloss, and a knife. Heroin was my lifeblood and my addiction could be broken down very simply: make money, buy heroin.

The areas I worked were unpredictable, and I learned this the hard way. Every night seemed to bring with it new drama. It was standard behavior for a drugged out city, and I knew I had to be prepared. Even if my mind was a little altered, I didn't want anyone thinking they could take advantage. If my threats didn't scare them off then Manuel's gun would.

While most nights ran together, there was one encounter that was seared into my memory despite the cloud of forgetfulness I lived in. I gathered my purse that held all of my essentials and exited the car I had entered no more than twenty minutes beforehand. The man behind the wheel was at least thirty-five years older than I was, but I preferred the older men—less issues and little drama. I caught a glimpse of Manuel as he passed by in his black SUV, clearly checking out business and making sure everyone was playing nicely in the sandbox together. I slowly moved towards the wall where a couple of other gals were, and I lit up a cigarette while waiting for my next call.

There was nothing notably different about this night. The air still held a hint of garbage mixed with smog as I watched the sun dip below the cityscape. The cars still perused Figueroa Street at a snail's pace in order to sample the ladies on the menu. Pimps rolled up and down the block, keeping their eyes open, pocketbooks full, and guns loaded. All was in proper order for a night on the blade and while everything seemed the same, it all changed in an instant.

My life would never be the same.

CHAPTER 19
Hope Finds a Way

June 16, 2011—Age 20

Really, again? What is she doing here?

Janet was back. She had been coming here pretty regularly, talking to the girls and making friends. Rumor had it that she had been a street worker once upon a time; I had only talked to her once, but from looking at her, I would have never guessed. She usually didn't come alone, but brought another woman or two, you know, safety in numbers and all that. I'm not sure why a former prostitute would do something so foolish as returning to streets crawling with pimps, but that's exactly what Janet did.

Tonight, she had two men with her that I named *Blondie* and *Midnight*. The first man had short cropped, black hair and an even darker skin tone, hence the nickname, *Midnight*. The second guy, Blondie, had short, dirty blond hair that was shaggy on top and edged shorter on the sides with a dark beard that hugged his face. Both men looked young based on how they dressed—slim, dark jeans, hoodies, and sneakers, but none of it screamed "money," "thug," or "drug dealer" when I looked them up and down. I was used to sizing up potential clients, and these guys didn't look like the usual type that sought company for a night but I wasn't one to judge. Everyone looked for comfort in a prostitute eventually.

Blondie, Midnight, and Janet approached Mona first, which gave me a good angle to study them further. What was Janet thinking, bringing two handsome fellas out here? They were about to get a show whether they asked for one or not.

I looked on as Mona flaunted herself in front of the two men with a few well-timed giggles and smiles for good measure. It was all for show since Mona and the rest of the girls out here just wanted to get paid, caring little about who put the money in their pockets—or bra. The guys didn't seem to react. Instead, Blondie produced a red rose from the inside of his zippered jacket and handed it to Mona. Her face dropped as she stared intently at the rose, breaking contact only to carefully wipe the corners of her eyes so she wouldn't smear her eyeliner.

What are they saying to her?

What are they doing out here?

With a few final words that I could not hear from my position down the block, the three of them moved on, slowly, and with caution. They peered around as if to gauge how many pimps had eyes on them. As long as they didn't linger, their presence wasn't a hindrance to our work. These three didn't fit here, that much was obvious, but it wouldn't stop the girls from trying to persuade Blondie and Midnight to purchase their services. My eyeballs weren't broken; they were cute, but I was wary enough to keep my distance.

It only took one pimp to get spooked for the whole operation to crumble into foul words, serious threats, or a full blown fight. Sometimes, it was all three. These guys didn't look like they wanted to pick a fight, and Janet was smaller than me, posing zero threat.

They have to know what kind of street they're on.

I tamped out my cigarette and watched as they spoke to another woman, handing her a red rose, and a few words before moving on. Only one of the girls disposed of her rose after the three of them walked away, while the other girls seemed to clutch them tighter. I had done my best to avoid the trio by moving further and further down the street, side-stepping other street workers and evading their presence just a little longer in order to observe their tactics. I couldn't figure them out, and even though this made me even more watchful, my curiosity won out. I stopped moving further away and waited for them to approach me.

"What'll it be tonight, gentlemen? Are you all looking for a good time? If so, you'll each have to pay," I stated in my most confident, rehearsed *Alexandria* voice, despite feeling just a touch rattled and a bit confused by their unusual behavior.

"We aren't looking for that kind of good time, miss. We just want a chance to change your mind," Blondie spoke, kindness coating every word and an urgency in his tone. He had a strong stature and youthful features, but the depth in his eyes told a story I wasn't sure I wanted to hear.

"Why are you out here, then, if not to have a little fun? Maybe I should be the one to change your mind," I said, my words dripping with suggestiveness as I focused on the men and ignored Janet.

"You've lived a rough life, but you can choose a different path now. A path that doesn't leave you chained to a pimp or shackled by your disease. You can experience freedom. True freedom from addiction, your pimp, and this life." Blondie reached into his jacket and pulled out a red rose, extending it towards me like a beacon of hope.

I stumbled back a few steps and reached for the brick wall behind me, needing something to steady me. What are they thinking saying something like that to someone like me?

"You are worthy, cherished, and far more precious than this rose. If you want out of this life and you're ready to know what this kind of freedom feels like, meet us at Pam's Diner down the street. You know, the one that has the bright pink neon sign? We'll be in a blue van in the parking lot for the next hour and we'll make sure you get off the streets—alive."

Blondie waited for me to grab the rose, which I hesitantly did as I waited for my mind to produce a question, any question before they moved on. Nothing came, though. My mind was like a crumpled sheet of blank paper. I took hold of the rose and felt the weight of their promise sink in.

Freedom, I thought as I watched the corners of Blondie's mouth lift into a full smile as I stood glued to the spot that had become my identity. My mouth might have dropped open at some point while my composure continued to crash down around me.

They started to walk away, but I wasn't finished. "Wait!" I yelled, before they could get any further. They each turned around to face my perplexed expression as I crossed my arms over my chest, needing the protection. "Why me?"

It was Janet who answered my disjointed question, though I still took little comfort from it. "Everyone deserves a choice."

I stood, stunned by what she said and how it made my body feel. A rush of warmth coated me from my head to my toes, and the coolness of the brick wall touching my back was no match for it. "What the hell do you mean?" I said through my shock.

Janet smiled and tilted her head towards the rose I held in my hand before turning to walk away.

It was all I could do to not slump down on the sidewalk. It's not what she said that made me feel undone, it's how it made me feel. Those people saw straight through me, but instead of feeling powerless from their words, I felt the opposite. I was handed some power—some freedom. If I still had a lit cigarette, I'd think about touching it to the sensitive skin near my wrist just to assure myself my heart was still beating, and I was still here, like I did sometimes.

The three moved methodically down the block and out of sight before anyone had a chance to tell them to leave. The conversation was over before it had ever really gotten started but the shockwaves continued long after they left.

Could I be anyone other than *her*? Out here, I was Alexandria and only Alexandria. My real name was the last bit of control I had in my life. My customers took whatever I gave them, and it was never the real me. It was never Andrea.

Alexandria was the girl who slept with men her grandfather's age. She was the one who worked the stage and took off her clothes to appease the drooling dogs. Alexandria worked the street in nothing but her bra and underwear, despite her low self-esteem. She waved, flirted, and made faces toward anyone who slowed down and inquired of her services. Alexandria did all of this and more—for a price of course. Andrea wasn't this girl. I had no clue who Andrea was anymore. I lived and breathed Alexandria, but I fell asleep each night broken and lonely as Andrea.

I rubbed my chilled arms, trying to ignite some heat back into my body.

They used the word freedom like it was a choice, but what those three didn't know was that I sold my freedom a long time ago. We are all slaves to something. At some point, I became a captive but I didn't fight it; I *became* it. Freedom sounded great as an ideal but Blondie seemed to believe it was a reality for someone like me. They didn't know my whole story, though. They didn't know where I had come from or the regrets I lived with every day, or the depth that my addiction had plunged to, and how I sought to appease it with every moment of my existence.

There was so much hope infused in his offer. More hope than I had seen in quite some time and, yet, I wrestled with what to do with it all. I wanted to know more but if I had learned anything in my life, it was that hope liked to hold hands with risk, and risk I could not do. Risk required change, and whenever I pursued change, it leveled me. It brought me to my knees and forced me to beg for mercy.

However, hope doesn't go down easily. It holds just enough space to believe the impossible even if I would rather not believe anything at all.

I tried to push the thoughts away and bury the questions like they didn't matter; like what they said didn't change anything. But that wasn't true. There is something about hope that kept me coming back. Like the good addict I was, I knew a thing or two about returning when I should just walk away. I couldn't stop thinking about it. I looked down at the simple, red rose that held my opportunity. A chance to see if the other side even existed.

My mind was roaring STOP but my body was already walking. I was halfway down the next street when I contemplated the risk—Manuel would find me; he owned me, after all. I thought about the change; I would likely not be able to take heroin with me wherever this freedom would be. Could I survive that? I had more questions and enough reasons to keep my life the way it was. I considered the hope, that beyond all reason, always finds a way. Risk and change always seem possible in the light that hope casts, even in the darkest alleys. That night, freedom somehow felt attainable, help within reach, and the chance at knowing what worthiness felt like was drawing me in.

It would be a gamble, but I didn't have anything left to lose.

Love has a Name | Christina Hill

Part Two
The Rebuild

Love has a Name | Christina Hill

CHAPTER 20
Breakthrough

Six-months-later
December 2011—Age 21

"Andrea…? Andrea? Are you doing okay?"

I quickly shake my head and look up at Anne's pleading eyes.

"What did you say?"

"I just asked if you are doing okay. You got quiet and trailed off in the middle of your story," Anne, my therapist, says, her warm brown eyes studying me with concern.

I must have spaced out. My hands grope for something solid to grab hold of and confirm I'm here, in her office, in this chair, and not back on the streets where my memories had transported me to. It feels like my body is in another lifetime and, truthfully, it is. It had taken months to tell Anne about my history and to finally make it to the moment that changed everything.

"Yeah, yeah, I'm good. I just remember how it felt to make that decision to find Janet, Beau, and Jordan at the restaurant. I must have gotten caught up in the story. Sorry," I say sheepishly while bracing myself on the arms of the chair.

"That isn't unusual. Our bodies always remember our stories," Anne says in her measured tone of voice that calms my anxious thoughts. "You have made so much progress over the last six months here, Andrea. I'm proud of you."

I nod my head slowly, thinking back on our first encounter. I had no idea what I was getting into by seeing Anne regularly and spewing every feeling in my heart. It's refreshing getting everything out there. The memories try to pull me under as I speak them, and sometimes, like today, they do.

I rub my hand along the faded tracks on my arm. Those wounds have all healed, but they are still visible and are my own scars of remembrance from the hell my body has walked through.

Anne broke into my thoughts. "Since you are feeling a little disoriented, why don't you picture your safe place to help ground you in the present."

I close my eyes without instruction and recall the picture I can see so clearly in my mind's eye. It is the bay window in my Aunt Cindy's living room just behind the couch. The afternoon sun would burst through the curved window and warm the cushions and pillows that my aunt used to decorate the space. The warming scent of cinnamon filled the air around me either from my aunt's baking, or the fall themed candle she would light regardless of the season.

Vanilla. Cinnamon. Orange. Comfort.

When I first went to live with her and my uncle, I loved this spot and would often sink into the cushions and allow the warmth of the sunshine to coat my skin. I had fallen asleep there multiple times by accident or by choice, and it became a sanctuary to me.

Aunt Cindy. Her memory still pains me to talk about. I can see her clearly throughout my history as a steady constant, as well as the countless times I pushed her away. I remember those times the most. I know our time for healing will come, but the space in between now and then looks gray. Not now, not yet.

I open my eyes and reach for the glass of water sitting on the table between Anne and I. Anne has been meeting with me once a week (sometimes twice) since I moved into the Journey Center. My body has been detoxing from heroin… and fear.

"How long does recovery take?" I asked Anne during one of our first few sessions.

She angled her head to look at me. Her black, pixie style haircut hid no secrets and contained just enough edginess to trust her. "As long as it takes. Physical and emotional healing takes time," Anne said. "Addiction will always be a battle you will fight, but now you will have the tools to face it."

I still don't understand when things will get easier, but I'm here. Taking a long drink from my glass, I can feel the momentum of my heart rate settling back to somewhere in the normal range. It's people like Anne and Janet that remind me in times like this that my past is just that—the past.

Janet is now my floor supervisor and she is organized, scheduled, and straightforward with her charges. She makes sure all of our beds are made, chores done, and obligations met. Janet is shorter than I am with crystal blue eyes and honey blonde hair that she keeps in a tidy braid running down her back. Janet isn't much older than some of us and a lot younger than others, but her strong voice always takes command of the room.

It was Janet who held me during the many bouts of trembling, shaking, and cold sweats I had while I detoxed. I quit, cold turkey, in order to stay. It was a torturous five days and then some as the substance my body relied heavily on ran its course in my weak body. I wanted to give up and go back to the streets so many times, even though I knew what would be waiting for me: Manuel and death.

Janet would just rub my back and dab at the abundance of sweat hanging out on my brow with a cool washcloth.

"I can't do this anymore, Janet. I'm not strong enough. I don't want to do this. My body hates me. I fucking hate me. I just… CAN'T!" I screamed with every curse word I knew, trying to convince her of my need, but she held me closer, not allowing the waves to pull me under.

"This is hard, Andrea, but look—you're doing it!" she encouraged me while I wondered if her kindness had an expiration date.

Janet lives at a different location on campus but is on our floor so often, I wonder if she ever sleeps in her own bed. She has other volunteers that I see regularly, but none more consistent than her. She helped me fill out the application for the recovery program I've been in for four months now.

As I set the glass back on the small table in front of me, I look down at my arms again. My emotions are sensitive like the wounds traveling up and down my olive skin. My addiction reminds me hourly that I am missing what I need to feel whole again, but I don't feel completely numb anymore, and that should count for something. My eyes absorb the warmth from the comforting colors that fill the small space in Anne's office.

I know there is more to the story—my story—but I hesitate to continue, knowing the intensity just around the next bend. I clear my throat and briefly look over at Anne before lowering my eyes to my lap, "There's more."

"Whenever you're ready," comes Anne's soothing voice. I never sense judgment from her, only acceptance, and so much patience. I can do this.

I slowly release a breath that indicates the *more* that is still to come. I launch into the story, sparing no details of what I lived through, what I could never forget. "It wasn't that easy to just up and leave. I had a job and a boss to think of. I had an extra hit of heroin in my purse screaming at me like a needy child. My whole life revolved around those streets. I knew walking away meant I could die, but the pull to meet up with them was stronger so I went anyway."

It's easier to look down at the red and cream rug beneath my feet and the circular table that sits between Anne and I, then it is to look into her eyes. She's accepted me so far, but maybe that would change. Maybe I'm not strong enough to share.

She considers my hesitation. "You can do this, Andrea."

"You're right. It's just harder than I thought it was going to be to share everything." I let out a shaky exhale.

"It certainly can be difficult. Take your time," she says with a smile covering each word.

I let out my breath and continue. "I kept walking the few blocks to the restaurant they had told me about." I can still see the bright pink neon sign when I close my eyes, shining like a lantern in the dead of night, calling out to me with every flicker. "I stopped mid-step so many times and stomped back towards Figueroa, only to change my mind again and retrace my steps to the restaurant."

"Was there something that caused you to finally decide on going to the restaurant and not turn around to leave?" Anne pries further with a gentle question.

I couldn't decide what I wanted more—an unknown future or the miserable, yet, familiar present. Eventually, I balled my fists, gritted my teeth, and allowed the firm set of my jaw to point the way towards whatever awaited me in that parking lot.

"I was curious. A woman and two guys who show up on a block full of prostitutes and are not looking for sex? Doesn't happen. Ever. When they spoke to me, it felt like they had known me for a long time." They had spoken to the young child who lost her barely-caring parents, the teenage girl who was alone, and they spoke to Alexandria, the actress who only wanted to get through the next day.

"I couldn't understand how they figured I would be able to up and leave that life behind without getting killed. I guess I was done caring and figured I could die from heroin and Manuel, or I could die trying to escape them." I swallow, trying to coat the raw scrape of the vulnerable confessions coming out of my throat.

My body might still be sitting in the chair of Anne's office, but my mind has taken me back in time.

When I met them at the restaurant, they welcomed me, introducing themselves and ushering me into the van right away. Blondie was Jordan, Midnight was Beau, and Janet offered me her name, though I had heard it plenty through the gossip mill on my blade. Before I sat down, I looked into the back seat to check for any masked villains. Habit. Janet was the only person back there and she looked anything but a potential threat. She smiled at me and I felt a wave of panic grip me in that moment, remembering the last time I had left Manuel's covering. I sat down and Jordan handed me a blanket and water bottle. I was shaking but hadn't even noticed. I was too concerned by Manuel's anger taunting my thoughts.

Should I go? Manuel is going to be so mad when he finds out I left. Livid. No, bloodthirsty, *I worried.*

There was one other girl who sat behind the driver's seat that I recognized from the same street I had just fled, but I didn't know her. That was normal when you worked a street as busy as Figueroa with new women showing up nightly. The market was flooded but the demand was high.

I remember the two of us looking at one another briefly but the full weight of understanding passed between us in that one look. One nod of our heads. If anything suspicious went down, we had each other's backs.

"I'm…" I paused, wondering who I wanted to be. "Andrea," I offered weakly, the name still sounding like another language leaving my tongue.

"Mercedes… actually, no, it's Kit," she replied.

I nodded my head and looked away, not fully understanding the separation that was taking place between Andrea and Alexandria.

Kit wasn't on any drugs from what I could tell, and appeared mostly normal apart from her skimpy outfit and hooker vibes. She had long, dark, straight hair that hid the enormous gold hooped earrings dangling from her ears. Her eyes were dark and made darker by the smokey eye makeup that covered them; it seemed at odds with the bright pink lipstick she wore on her full lips. She was in a short, black mini skirt, and a jean jacket that did little to cover her bikini laden top. Kit's tanned skin made her appear mysterious and sultry—exactly the kind of qualities that were desired in our line of work.

Why was she leaving the streets?

Did she want this freedom, too?

The way they ushered us into the van definitely seemed like a shady encounter, but I didn't care. I wanted freedom now that I knew it existed. I had no reason for trusting them, but something in me told me I could.

We began merging into the light traffic that dotted the streets at almost 1 a.m. and had been driving for no more than five minutes when two black SUVs started tailing our van, and Jordan's steady voice assured us of our next move.

"Andrea, Kit—get down on the floor and don't sit up or look out the window, we're being tailed and I don't want anyone seeing you two," Jordan calmly encouraged. "Janet, you too."

The moment called for quick action. Alexandria and Mercedes knew they would die because they knew who was tailing them. Andrea and Kit, however, clung to hope for the chance at a life that remained.

"Oh shit! I knew I shouldn't have come! They always find you. No matter what, they track you down," said a very frantic Kit, who fell to the floor fast and was now simultaneously reciting prayers and swearing.

I followed suit and curled into a small ball behind the passenger seat, closing my eyes tighter with every mile we drove. I was frozen in fright and only breathing because of the adrenaline coursing through me.

"We won't let them get you, Kit. Your pimp and his men will realize this soon enough," Janet said with innocent encouragement.

My heart rate sped up, telling me fear was at work in my body, but I was so still. Unmoving. It wouldn't be long. This would all be over soon.

A confident Jordan picked up his cell phone and started calling someone while directing a focused Beau to turn left at the next street. "Hey. It's Jordan. We have two girls with us and we're being tailed… Yes, just like last time… Thanks. We'll be there in four minutes. Can you open the gate and have the guys out front?" There was a short pause while Jordan waited for confirmation from the person on the *other end of his call. "Great. See you soon," Jordan said, ending the call and pivoting in the passenger seat to peer out the back window. "We've got two guys in the vehicle directly behind us but I didn't see how many were in the other vehicle. Girls, keep low to the floor and when I tell you to get out—"*

Jordan was abruptly cut off when the sound of bullets making contact with metal deafened any ability to hear or speak. Kit had stopped reciting her prayers and, instead, started hysterically shrieking while covering her head. She was reacting enough for the both of us since I had lost my voice at some point. Fear had two, strong hands on my throat.

We aren't making it out of this, *I thought to myself. The bullets were flying and someone was going to die. I was going to die.*

"Stay down! Don't get off the floor!" Beau yelled from the front seat, hitting the gas harder than he already was. He had to have run multiple red lights at this point, knowing how the streets of L.A. were cluttered with them.

"They're still there!" Beau yelled out of pure adrenaline.

"Here comes the other car! It's getting closer to our side," Jordan spoke with an urgent tone, but maintained an irregular calm.

I heard a few other words being thrown around in the front seats but most of it was drowned out by Kit's sobs and pleas for her not to die. My forehead was pressed against the carpeted floor of the van, palms wrapped around the crown of my head while my knees were tucked beneath me. I prayed for invisibility, but expected to be blindsided by a bullet instead. The small hairs on the nape of my neck stood on end as I sent up a weak prayer to whoever was listening.

Please. We need a miracle. Please help us stay alive. I don't want to die.

I didn't expect to hear anyone's voice calling from on high or for the sky to split and a miracle to come down like rain. Praying, pleading, and asking were the only things I could do, so I did them.

Beau was still driving recklessly through the streets, keeping our minivan ahead in the race against the evil that tailed us. He swerved down a side street fast enough that I imagined there would be skid marks on that neighborhood road. He gunned it, topping out at the max speed that the car was capable of hitting. Kit grabbed my hand and squeezed; her tears were leaving makeup tracks down her cheeks when I turned my head to look at her. Void of emotion, I closed my eyes tightly wishing this race would end and to take my life swiftly without any pain.

"We're here. Hang on!" Beau shouted.

"Look, Beau! They're all here. I sure hope this works again," Jordan yelled above the screech of brakes as we made another turn.

The van bounced wildly as we jumped a curb and slowed to a stop. I couldn't imagine where we could go in the city that Manuel wouldn't have the advantage. He had eyes everywhere, as he often liked to remind me. I waited for a shower of bullets to descend on our getaway vehicle, ensuring we were truly dead and gone.

One frantic breath.

Two.

Three.

Four.

They didn't come. Beau and Jordan exhaled heavily from the front seat without any words between them. Kit was chanting unintelligible words as her body—hunched in the fetal position—was rocking back and forth. Janet searched for our crumpled bodies, rubbing our shoulders to assure us we were still alive.

"We did it. They're gone. They left! We made it back safe!" Beau heaved a sigh of relief intermixed with a nervous laugh as he slapped Jordan's shoulder.

"Andrea and Kit! You're safe! Let me help you out," Jordan said, emerging from our makeshift military vehicle. He slid the door open and gently peeled a haggard looking Kit off of me, righting my body until my feet connected with the pavement. I hesitated opening my eyes,

*believing there was no way I would exit this vehicle alive, and so I
waited for the firing squad.*

Nothing.

*My breathing was shaky, my body trembling. This was always
supposed to happen. Death was my only out, my only freedom.*

*"They're not here Andrea; you're safe now and they won't be able
to get you, I promise." Jordan's hands braced either side of my arms
with my back pressed up against his chest in case my body chose to fall
unannounced. His soothing words encouraged my eyelids to peel apart
and stare at the ground beneath me. My gaze slowly moved upwards
until I saw before me what looked to be a crowd of people creating a
barrier between our getaway car and the street beyond. I was puzzled
why Manuel and his gang left without a fight. In fact, I wasn't ready
to believe it.*

Did I miss the shots being fired?

Was anyone bleeding?

Who had died?

*My eyes roamed the bodies before me. They weren't holding guns,
knives, or other objects of destruction but most of those gathered were
men—big men. I tracked the length of the group and noticed some with
tattoos that lined their muscular arms and traveled up to shaved heads
filled with piercings; different shades of men that had likely known the
inner workings of gang life intimately.*

I left one prison to end up in a different one, *I thought.*

*They didn't rush me and no one was yelling. I wasn't sure if I
should run far away or fall to my knees thanking them for saving us,
but the consoling words that Jordan spoke told me what I needed to
know. "These guys have all lived that life. Some have recovered from
drug addictions, others have come out of gangs, and some have been
released from prison. They know the world you came from and now
you are safe from it, too."*

*I had no words to form a response. My right hand trembled as I
raised it to cover the sobs escaping in quick succession from my gaping*

mouth. The tears flowed as my emotions finally caught up to the developments that unfolded during the last hour. I couldn't believe we survived. Gravity won out as my shaking legs could no longer keep me upright. My body folded into a pile at Jordan's feet as the emotion rose up from the recesses of my body to greet me as if for the first time. I've never been so afraid and relieved. The pavement was drenched with my tears and the still night filled with my groans of relief.

It was over. I was safe. Kit was safe. Nobody died.

Alexandria and Mercedes were left somewhere on the floor of that van.

But Andrea and Kit had been saved.

I grip my hands together again, reminding my body and mind that I am here in the present as I describe to Anne how these strangers willingly faced my oppressors knowing we could all die. For those men to have lived the lives that they did before coming to the Journey Center, the place I now call home, meant that they knew those situations often left a bullet lodged in someone's body, and you just hoped it wasn't going to be yours. The tears involuntarily rise again. I have become better acquainted with them showing up like this.

My life changed forever in the span of minutes. I got the miracle I prayed for while curled up on the floor of our getaway van, but now, I think it was already on the way before I even opened my mouth to ask for it.

CHAPTER 21
Abuelita

July 2011—Age 20

"*¡Hola! ¿Cómo estás, Mija?*"

"Um. Come again?" I reply, a little dumbfounded. I haven't heard any Spanish since... since Manuel. It sounds familiar, but I don't want it to.

She smiles wide. "I said, hello and how are you?"

"I'm good. So, yeah, I'm Andrea, and I guess I'll be working here?" I am assigned to kitchen duty for the first year of the program, and I'm still scratching my head as to why Janet put me here. To be fair, I let Janet know repeatedly that I can't cook... at all.

This older *Latina* woman with dark eyes that shine brighter than the light bouncing off of the stainless countertops just stares and smiles. I shift my weight to the other foot, waiting for her to say something else, preferably in English. My nerves are already on edge.

"I'm Gloria Ramirez, but call me *Abuelita*."

"Alright. What does *Abuelita* mean?" I knew some Spanish but not enough, apparently.

"*Abuela* means *grandmother*, but *Abuelita* is a more familiar term. You can call me *Abuelita*," she says, again, with no room for argument.

"I can do that, I guess. You're a grandma then?"

"Of course, that is who I am, *Mija*, and I do it well," she proclaims. "I have many children and many grandchildren. I am a blessed woman."

I soon find out that *Abuelita* makes the best food I have ever tasted, so I will call her whatever she wants. I can tell just by the care she takes in preparing and serving the food each day how much she loves the work she does. *Abuelita* has vivid, sunny rays bouncing off of her at all times, and it doesn't take long for me to be completely drawn in by her infectious personality.

"*¡Ven aquí*, Andrea! Come here and dance!" she encourages me often. I listen because when it comes to *Abuelita*, I am helpless. Her joy is contagious, and when she cranks the stereo while we clean up the mess each evening, my hips start to sway.

"Okay, but just this once, got it?" I point at her as she grabs my hands and swings me around until I forget my empty retort. We shimmy around the tables as we spray, wipe, and sweep up the remnants of a meal that had been thoroughly enjoyed. Not everyone who helps in the kitchen is as keen on dancing while cleaning, but *Abuelita* will do her best to rope them in anyway. Watching her hip bump Anthony, the six-foot-five-inch beast of a man, makes me laugh, especially when I see the embarrassment creeping up Anthony's neck.

Abuelita hums while she cuts veggies, dances while she washes dishes, and flashes a brilliant smile and bubbling laughter as she serves each resident. Everything she makes is from scratch, and she takes great care in the food that comes out of this kitchen—her kitchen. I can tell how much she loves what she does, and *Abuelita* never seems to tire of the monotonous rhythms of it all, and because of her, neither do I.

One evening, as I sulk into the kitchen to don my apron and hairnet and ready the meal for the impending dinner rush, I try to hide the tangled mess of emotions sitting in my gut, but *Abuelita* is too observant. She pulls me aside while the others on the kitchen crew get to work.

"*Mija*, you are upset. Tell me—what is troubling you tonight?" Her brows scrunch together in concern, and I don't know how I'm going to get out of this. I'm trapped in the intensity of her care.

I look at her, fighting the voice in my head that says she doesn't care. "*Abuelita*, I had a really rough morning, and I don't want to talk about it right now. Can we just start prepping dinner, please?" I try to keep my emotions in check as I offer this feeble explanation but the insistent look she has on her face and her determined stance tells me it isn't enough. She sees the hidden corners of my soul even when I can't.

"You are hurting, *Mija*. I see the struggle on your face and in the slouch of your shoulders. Tell me this burden that you carry," *Abuelita* presses. I watch her cup my elbow. "Come, let your burdens out."

Her hands move from my elbow to an outward extension in front of her rounded body and towards me, welcoming the burden she insists I let her share. I only stare at her hands as my composure slips along with the tears that well up and distort my vision. I don't expect her arms to wrap around me, but hugging is a natural extension of who she is. My body feels so rigid and awkward in her arms but *Abuelita* simply strokes, rubs, and pats my back while squeezing me just a little bit closer each time. I let my tears fall, one after the other, having little control over them anyway. We stand for what feels like an eternity to a girl who has rarely ever been hugged in a soothing or gentle way.

When I pull back and look at the woman who I have become so fond of, I decide to risk it and share what I have been crying on *Abuelita's* shoulder about.

"I-It was a memory, a nightmare, actually," I start to say. "I mean, it wasn't a real nightmare, but it felt like one after sharing it with Anne," I say, attempting to wipe my tears away. "I told her about my pimp, Manuel. It brought up a lot of painful memories, and, well, it made me panic that maybe I'm not as safe as I thought I was. He is so demanding, and it terrifies me that he won't stop until he gets what he wants. What if he comes back and tries to break me out of here? He knows where I am. He chased me here." My panic is now on full display as I try to explain my troublesome situation to *Abuelita*. To convince her that everything could fall apart.

She looks at me with a creased brow and evident concern, but when her expression softens and she rubs both of my arms vigorously, I can translate her comforting touch.

"Manuel knows where you are, but he hasn't come. You cannot live your life looking back over your shoulder, *Mija*. Soon, you have to start looking forward," *Abuelita* says with a nod of her head and another embrace. "Don't forget to look forward."

She is right. I spent so much time living in my past, and at the Journey Center, I spent my time *talking* about my past. It's helpful, and the projects Anne has me doing to process through some of these things are interesting, but *Abuelita* is right. I need to start looking forward.

A few days after becoming a blubbering mess in *Abuelita's* sturdy arms, I ask Janet about her, no longer able to pretend *Abuelita's* story isn't calling out to me. Janet knows everyone who works at the Journey Center; she's been here long enough.

"*Abuelita* Gloria is one of the most genuine people I have ever met, truly. Plus, she has a way with food that goes straight to my heart," Janet explains, as we sit at the lunch table enjoying the food I had just helped make.

"While most of us have hardened our hearts because of the hardships we have faced, *Abuelita* has only become softer and more loving. She has had plenty of struggles but she is as steady and unmoving as a boulder," Janet says with a knowing laugh before her expression turns serious. "She has lost both of her children. Her first child died as a newborn only mere months after he was born due to heart complications. Her second child, a daughter, left this world after a serious drug overdose. *Abuelita* came to work here after her daughter passed away twenty years ago, committing her time and energy to care for those who were coming out of an addictive lifestyle."

I stare at the plate in front of me while Janet, sensing I am processing this information, continues after another bite of *Abuelita's* famous tamales. How can someone, a mother, watch her child overdose and then commit her life to working with people just like her? Like me.

"So… *Abuelita* doesn't have any children?"

"She has lots of children and grandchildren. They just aren't biological. I guess you could say she's adopted them,"

Janet says between bites. "*Abuelita* has been a constant source of encouragement for people who live here and seek treatment. She feeds them with food, but she also feeds their souls."

I take a bite of my own tamale, washing it down with water as I try to make sense of *Abuelita's* story. Over the many hours we worked together, she had become closer to me than most of the strangers I share DNA with. She is kind, thoughtful, determined, and pure delight all wrapped into a small, but mighty package. Most of all, *Abuelita* notices me. She looks at me with a fierce devotion even though it's no secret why I'm here. I'm an addict. Just like her daughter and just like most everyone else who walks through these doors. It is as if she looks at me and sees the version of me who is free of labels, free of addiction, free of my past. She sees the woman I desperately want to become.

CHAPTER 22

Everyone has a Story

April 2012—Age 21

Kit and I are sandwiched side-by-side on my slim bottom bunk, leaning against the headboard and whispering back and forth.

Our bodies connect at the shoulder, leaning in and on one another literally and figuratively. I've never had a friend like this, but I can't imagine it can get any better. I woke up in the middle of the night last night, sweat pouring down my forehead and adrenaline coursing through my veins and Kit was right there, dabbing my face with a cool towel. She doesn't complain or ignore me, instead, she only moves closer.

We often sit on my bunk or Kit's, just like this, swapping battle stories, funny tidbits from our earlier days, and who the cute guys are on campus. Tonight, Kit's telling me about her family. The one I've always known she had, but never really heard about. She's kept them close to her chest and as she explains, I understand why.

Kit pulls her long hair over her shoulder and starts to braid it. Her mouth falls open, and I can see the struggle she's up against in her mind, but I leave the space open, knowing it takes time to brush off the rusty words.

"My mother drank herself to death when I was thirteen," she begins to say and I stay quiet. "She was Catholic, you know, and always told me she'd be in a better place if she died. I hate that she gave herself the excuse to leave, that my brother and I were worth leaving," she confesses while moving her head back and forth in disbelief. "My papa was a Spanish-speaking Mexican who worked all of the time, so when my mom died, my brother and I went into foster care."

"Oh, Kit. That's… heavy," I say, consoling her as best as I can. In many ways, I'm looking at my own wounds in the reflection of hers.

Dominique, another roommate of ours, leans over the edge of her top bunk above Kit's bed. "You were in the system too, Kit?"

Kit cranes her neck to look up at Dominique. "Yeah, I was. I've been out for almost three years though. Were you a foster kid?"

"I was but I ran for my life when I had the chance," Dominique says, shaking her head to the point I thought she would be dizzy.

I lean forward and sit up straighter to see Dominique's expression sober. Her hands start fidgeting with the white sheet, revealing her anxious thoughts as plain as day.

"There isn't anything easy about abuse. It steals from you and tells you that you aren't good enough. You aren't worth lovin' and you sure as hell aren't worth likin' either."

My cheek might as well have started pulsing at the memory of Manuel's hand slapping me. The night he saved me from the kidnappers wasn't the first or last time he hit me, I just got better at shoving it aside like it didn't matter. Like I couldn't see or feel the bruises on my skin.

I study Dominique, really looking at this woman who is at least twenty years older than I am. In street years, add another ten years for the ones that were stolen. The additional wrinkles, missing teeth, and her slim figure indicate as much.

The women who come to the Journey Center enter through the emergency shelter, like Kit, Dominique and I had done, and some will start the program. Others will accept the help from the emergency shelter and be on their way the next day or transfer to another facility, sometimes in a different state, almost like a witness protection program situation.

"You know, I'm not sorry about my life. I spent a long time being angry and bitter. No more," Dominique says, shaking her head again in her very aggressive way. "It's hard to forget but I'm not going to forget about my future too."

I have been gathering up these stories like a knick-knack collection I never wanted, but my ears can't un-hear the struggles and they can't ignore the hope.

A soft knock sounds on the door. "I thought I heard voices. What are you ladies still doing awake?" Amanda, a graduate of the program and our floor mentor asks as she walks into our room.

"Hey, Manda. We were just talking," Dominique offers.

"We weren't going to stay up much later, promise," Kit adds.

"Like I believe that!" Amanda says with a laugh.

"Manda, have you told Kit and Andrea about your story?" Dominique says, sitting up further in her bed.

There it is again, the stories just keep coming. My collection is growing by another one tonight.

"I shared a bit with you ladies, right?" Amanda asks, walking further into our shared room and leaning against the dresser near the foot of our bed.

Kit and I shake our heads. "So what happened?" I ask, no longer able to hold my tongue.

"I was forty-six when I could no longer hold a steady job and pay my rent. Drugs took over my life until there was nothing left. At the time, I didn't think much of it, just that I had more time to get high. I lost everything, including my husband and kids. They stood by me as long as they could but, eventually, my addiction pushed them away too." Amanda tells us.

"Shit. Drugs really mess people up," I say, still carrying the burden of my own addiction.

"You're telling me. Drugs took away fifteen years of my life."

I am almost a year sober, and every day still reads like a bloody war novel. Back and forth, back and forth. I feel like it will never end sometimes.

"I started talking to my kids again sometime after graduating from the program. It took a long while before they were ready, but I just kept waiting and letting them know I was still sober and I still loved them. My therapist helped me learn that they would need to walk through their own forgiveness and it could take some time. It did, but they also saw what forgiveness had done in my life."

I think about Aunt Cindy and the chaos I had brought to her life when I stepped into her home and long afterwards. I don't know if she can forgive me. I've asked her too many times.

I may never be able to show my face to her again, I consider.

Kit and I are staying on for another year of the program in order to stay sober and make some extra money. I'm not sure yet if purpose is in my future, but hearing what is possible keeps hope lingering on the sidelines of my journey, waiting for a chance to jump in and play.

. . .

The next morning, I'm dragging. After Amanda left, Kit, Dominique, and I stayed up way too late talking, and the smell of the coffee waiting for me in the cafeteria is calling my name. Scratch that, *screaming* my name.

I see Beau, Jordan, and Kit at one of the corner tables and go to sit with them after grabbing a tray of scrambled eggs, sausage, hash browns, and one large cup of drip coffee, which I hate, but also need.

"What's up? What are we talking about?" I ask as I sit down next to Jordan with Beau and Kit sitting casually across from us.

"The guys were just reminding me it's been almost a year since the rescue," Kit replies.

"Oh yeah, another two months, and that marks our one-year-off-the-streets anniversary," I say jokingly, poking fun at the not so distant past. "How does someone celebrate a milestone like that?"

I had shared many meals like this one with the guys, each time not sure what to make of their kindness just shy of a year ago. Beau had outrun two cars, five pimps, and certain death, but why? What was in it for them? In my estimation, *absolutely nothing.*

Before anyone could answer, I asked a different question that I wanted the answer to. "So, why do it? Why come out to the streets in the dead of night to help prostitutes who are likely not going to follow you? You guys could have died that night right along with us." I say, nudging Jordan's side with my elbow, and still trying to understand after all this time, but failing to.

"You two chose to come," Jordan says, before taking another bite of his eggs and turning his head to the side to study me intently. Too intently.

I look away, unable to hold his gaze. It does things to me that I'm not ready to admit to.

"Yeah, but we were the crazy ones. It doesn't usually turn out this way if I had to guess." I know the kind of women that live on the street. There is power and money in our line of work if you play your cards right.

"If it weren't for Janet, the Journey Center wouldn't even have a rose ministry. She left prostitution after meeting a stranger one day, a stranger who turned out to be an employee at the Journey Center," Jordan adds, his fork diving into the pile of eggs on his plate.

"You're right, it usually doesn't work out that way for most women, but even if only one of you came that night, it would have been worth it because that's one less life being abused out there," Beau piped up on the verge of a passionate rant. "The rose ministry is hard, savage even, but when it clicks and two people are now in radically different circumstances because of it, the risk is nothing."

I try to swallow but something prohibits me. Blasted emotion.

"I saw my purpose laid out plain as day when I first got here to help serve right out of high school," Beau explains. "I didn't know what I was getting into, but I was naive enough to try, and I'm glad I did. You need to be a bit crazy to believe the impossible."

I look between Beau and Jordan. They hold zero regrets for putting their lives at risk, and I know I can't convince them otherwise. In fact, they have gone back to Figueroa with Janet a few times since. Don't get me wrong, I'm thankful beyond belief, and as I look at Kit, I know she is too. Maybe I'll understand one day… maybe not, but for now, I'll just have to stake a claim in their confidence.

"If Beau wasn't twisted enough to believe it was worth it, I wouldn't be here either. I was wasting away in my jail cell and would have spent the rest of my life hating myself if he hadn't shown up," Jordan says with emotion thick in his throat. I notice his eyes are filling with tears, and I suddenly don't know what to do. My breakfast is gone, my coffee too, and my hands have nothing left to occupy them. I'm not used to seeing emotion in men unless it was rage or passion.

I knew that Jordan had been through the program at the Journey Center, graduating two years before I got here, however, I didn't know it was because of Beau.

"How did Beau find you?" Kit asks, breaking the silence at our table.

"He walked into the jail and asked the warden who was the most messed up kid in the joint," Jordan laughs and we all join in. It comforts me to see him laugh.

"Yeah, and the warden didn't hesitate," Beau includes. "I knew when I saw the look on your face that I was in the right place; I was exactly where I needed to be."

It is clear to see the connection that Jordan and Beau have built over time. There is something about seeing someone at their worst and sticking around that binds souls together, and it's easy to see that with these two.

"I was pretty broken up, wasn't I? Still tweaking out from my alcohol addiction and withdrawal, and not coping well. You saw something when you came that day and even though I cursed you up and down, you still came back," Jordan says, tipping his chin in Beau's direction along with his words.

I was having a hard time looking away from Jordan as he shared. His square jaw would clench tightly when his emotion got the better of him, and his eyes would scrunch up when he laughed. I was mesmerized by the strength I saw in him. I want some of it.

Beau pipes up, "You were a hot mess, but, if *He* can leave the ninety-nine sheep for the one, then so can I, or at least I can try."

I don't know what Beau is talking about, another story, I'm guessing. Before I can ask, Kit speaks up. "What do you mean? How did we start talking about sheep?"

Beau looks at Kit with amusement sparkling in his bright brown eyes. "It's a story in the Bible. Jesus tells about a shepherd who didn't think twice about leaving his herd of ninety-nine sheep to find the one that ran off and got lost."

"And when he finds that one sheep, it's worthy of a celebration," Jordan adds. "Kind of like celebrating two ladies who left the streets." His eyes hold an obvious twinkle in them.

I look at Kit, another one of our knowing stares passing between us. There's something about the story that Beau explained that's hitting me square between the eyes. My mouth runs dry, and I start to see a glimpse of why Beau and Jordan rescued us that night almost a year ago. It's so small, but it's there.

They were looking for the one but found two instead.

CHAPTER 23

Ready to Jump

April 2012—Age 21

I don't think anyone saw me leave.

I walk a few blocks down the road to the bus stop, knowing the number I would need to catch to take me further into the city. It's almost 2 a.m., but when I couldn't get back to sleep, my mind started to race and I had an idea, an idea that I couldn't shake. My head is throbbing in pain and my veins are pulsing with need. I'm sitting on a bus in my sweatpants and the sweatshirt I remembered to grab with a few coins jingling in my pocket.

I wish this damn bus would move faster. My palms are sweaty and the nerves in my stomach are making me second guess everything. It's been ten months without heroin. They told me it would get easier, but it hasn't. Sure, some days are better than others. This isn't one of those days. I told myself before slipping out of my room, pushing through the entrance doors that morphed into my exit, and getting on this bus, that I would only hold it. I wouldn't use the heroin. I'm still telling myself this, but every mile this bus travels, my resolve starts to slip.

The scene outside of the bus window is familiar and I pull the lever to alert the driver I need to get off. When the night air hits my face, it's almost enough to startle me out of continuing this dead end journey, but I'm convinced it's too late now. I'm here. I'm walking.

I see the tents lining the sidewalks along skid row and walk towards them, knowing my little idea is being sold just inside one of them. I've got some cash too, along with my coins, and I'm just hoping it'll be enough. I still need to travel back to the Journey Center after this.

My feet stop moving when the risk of my actions start to catch up with me.

What the fuck are you doing, Andrea?

"What am I doing?" I say out loud to myself and the brick building next to me. I rest my hand on the cold, jagged exterior wall. It's the only thing holding me upright while my head swims and my eyes spin.

Anne told me once that our bodies always remember our stories. I consider that in this very moment, and I get it. My body remembers this place. The smell of urine and weed mixed with desperation; the sounds of a city not ready for bedtime; the touch of a stranger you already hate; the sight of encampments stacked on top of each other; the taste of heroin in my bloodstream. My body remembers all of it. I thought I would be stronger than this. I expected as much, but now I know I'm not. I'm not strong enough to leave here without it.

"Whatchu want, honey?"

I whip around with my fists raised ready to inflict damage. I forgot my knife, but I'll fight if I have to.

"Woah. No need to get feisty. You lost or something, sweetheart?" the woman with crazed eyes asks me. She doesn't look like a threat, but she doesn't look like a friend either.

"No. I'm not lost," I say to both of us.

"You know where ya are... right?"

"Yes," I reply, knowing where I am, but still trying to figure out the *why*.

The woman nods, her short black hair, that's standing on end, moves in sync with her head. "You here to see someone?"

My voice catches in my throat so I abandon my mouth and simply nod my head.

The woman is dressed in a few shabby layers that have likely not been washed in months, or years, and the only smell stronger than her body odor is the weed she's smoking.

"Whatchu want then?" she asks, jutting her chin towards me.

"I– I'm looking to buy," I try to explain.

"A-huh. What are you after?"

I clear my throat and try to use my voice this time. "H- Heroin."

The woman looks me up and down, assessing whether I'm worth the trouble or the risk. I don't look like a ritzy Bel-Air housewife needing a hit, but I don't look like a street dweller anymore either. I don't really recognize who I am at this moment, all I know is that I'm willing to be whoever this lady wants me to be in order for her to introduce me to her dealer.

"Follow me."

I trail behind the woman who stands between me and the small, glass vial I'm expecting to see again real soon. We

walk past tents, through an alleyway, and down another
street before we make it to the side of another building. I
try to keep my mind turned off the entire time because I
know what I'm doing, and I'm a fool.

The man who I expect is her dealer is smoking
something out of a pipe when we come up on them, but he
continues to inhale like we aren't even there. When he does
look up at me, I can see the glassy coating in his eyes; a
relaxed look on his face telling me he is high. I gulp down
the memory of feeling just like him. The weightlessness, the
ease; it's all on the other side of that hit. It's like a tease to
my senses, and I can't look away. Instead, I pay him what
he asks and put the vial and the tools to use it in my
sweatshirt pocket while I trudge back to the bus stop.

I pace back and forth while I wait the few minutes that
feel like hours before the bus arrives. All of the supplies I
need are tucked away and out of sight, but they feel like a
neon sign advertising their presence in my pocket. Like the
neon sign I met Beau and Jordan under when I left these
god-awful streets.

Don't think about them now.

They aren't here. They aren't in your body. They don't know.

I squeeze my eyes shut, trying not to think past the next
few minutes. I'm conscious and aware, but I don't want to
be. I don't want to remember the program, the friends,
Anne, anyone. I want that feeling of being high again, not
because I want to forget my past this time, but because I
want to remember the feel of it.

I step off the bus and retrace my steps into the Journey
Center, but I don't go back to my room. I've planned
everything out in my head during my ride back so I
continue down the hallway, past my dorm room, and into
the shared bathroom. I'll use just this once, get it out of my

system, or in it, and then keep things under the radar. I can't leave this place and end up on the streets again. I won't. The lights are off and the smell of cleaning products linger in the air. The memories try to remind me of how far I've come, but I'm tuning them out. I push them away just as quickly as they try to hit me.

I walk into the handicap stall, shutting the door but forgetting to lock it behind me in my haste, and I slide down the wall to the ground. Reaching into my pocket, I fumble for my recent purchase. It sits in my hand like a weight, pulling me down and ready to take me under. I can't believe I'm holding this, but then again, I can. Wasn't it all going to end here? Raising the glass bottle in front of my face, I twist it between my thumb and pointer finger, shaking it back and forth and watching the contents dance before my eyes.

It's too late to turn back. I'm staring at the only thing my body craves, but my eyes are blurry. I can barely see past the tears welling up, and I'm not ready when I feel the warmth of them slide down my chilled face.

I try to ignore the meaning of my tears by tipping the jar upside down and shoving the needle into the vial to fill it. I feel the regret like an old friend. The failure, the disappointment, the shame are all filled within the needle. My hands are shaking and I almost drop the glass bottle on the cold, tile floors of this empty bathroom, but manage to set it down unharmed, which is more than I can say about me. My shoulders are rolling forward and I'm hunched over my legs, knees to my chest as I hold the needle and cry. I hike the sweatshirt further up my arm seeing invisible tracks that will soon become visible again. The tears are blurring my vision and keeping me from shoving the needle into my anxious and waiting veins. They are no longer collapsing under their traumatic history and are easily visible, ready, expectant.

"What am I doing? What am I doing? What am I doing?" I repeat over and over as my words echo off of the bathroom stall, but my body is acting ahead of my brain. I tune everything out, including my own sobs that are now ripping through the quiet space. I can't hear my own pleas to stop, pause, wait, consider, and I don't hear the sound of another voice begging me to do the same.

I'm still gripping the needle, but I feel a hand encircle my own. It isn't trying to wrestle the needle from my hand, but it isn't letting me use it either.

"Sh-sh-shh. Andrea? It's Janet. I'm right here with you," the voice says.

My eyes are still blurry with tears but when I hear her name, I release the needle. I don't hear it drop to the floor, but I'm not looking. I can only see the familiar face that is now only inches from mine.

"I–I... don't..."

Her hand is rubbing my arm in a soothing rhythm. "It's okay. I'm here now," Janet replies.

My hands shake even more when the flood of remembrance fills my senses. It felt like a dream. All of it. Walking to and from the bus, being on skid row again, holding heroin in my hands and being seconds away from using it. I'm no longer able to ignore what's going on; I'm too conscious for that. Awareness hits like a lightning strike, and I realize what I've done.

"Oh no, no, no. What did I do? What have I done?" I scream, rocking back and forth.

"I've got you, Andrea. I'm not leaving you," Janet assures me.

I drop my head in shame. "O-Okay. Don't leave me...
Please," my heart implores.

"I won't. We're going to get through this," Janet
soothes, sitting next to me and wrapping her arm around
my shoulders, huddled up on the floor of this bathroom
stall.

I didn't use the heroin like I had planned to, but my toes
were hanging off of the edge of the cliff and I had been
ready to jump.

I would have done it, too, if it weren't for Janet.

. . .

"I failed," I finally say out loud, the words tasting acidic
in my mouth as I speak them.

It's been mere days since the bathroom episode. I'm
tired of replaying it, but here I am, across from Anne and
talking about it again.

"Why do you think you failed?" Anne asks, crossing her
legs and leaning her forearms on them.

My hand runs through my long, unwashed, and tangled
hair. "I was about to use. You all should be kicking me out
not... helping me," I say, shaking my hands in the air for
emphasis. As much as I want to stay, it doesn't mean I
should. I wanted to keep it all under wraps, but I was
caught. Laid bare in my breakdown.

"You never did use that night though... why?" Anne
asks me with a curious tone of voice.

I look out the small window to my left watching the
light stream in and coat the room in warmth. If it weren't
for the brightness of the sun, I'd forget it's daytime. My
whole world feels dark.

"I don't know," I exhale. "When Janet showed up, and I saw the look on her face…" my voice trails off as I imagine the concerned look in her eyes. "I realized what I was doing."

I can feel Anne study me while I study the sunbeam casting tiny rainbows on the wall behind her. I'm still wondering how it all happened. If I'm being honest, it freaked me out that I got all the way to skid row and back with a bottle of heroin. I was present for the whole thing, but I wasn't aware of what I was really doing. My body was acting while my mind was watching. They became separate.

"Do you think God believes you failed?"

I finally look over at Anne, wondering if my body and mind are back in sync again. "Hell if I know," I mumble.

"The Bible is filled with stories of troubled people," Anne says.

I look away again, trying to find the tiny rainbows I found earlier. I've heard some of this before. The Journey Center is a faith-based organization and lives and breathes all of this God stuff Anne is talking about. I have a regular morning devotional time and a weekly Bible study too. I have participated in all of it while caring about none of it.

"King David had a woman's husband killed because he got her pregnant and didn't want him finding out. Moses killed an Egyptian and then ran away to hide for forty years. Don't even get me started on how many times God's people, the Israelites, failed. Andrea, failure is part of being human. We can't escape it, but we can always repair. This is why God is so big on forgiveness." Anne leans back in her seat at the same moment I move to the edge of mine.

I keep my head turned away from her. I'm not ready to talk about forgiveness—I don't deserve it. I have too many questions bouncing around in my head.

My curiosity can't seem to stay quiet and soon my questions are given full reign.

"Why doesn't He step in and help? If He is so powerful, why didn't God stop me from buying heroin? Isn't that what a *helper* or *friend* should do?" I ask, letting the questions slither off of my tongue and using the names Anne has referenced when talking about God.

"Absolutely. A friend also sits with us in our failures, in our suffering," Anne responds calmly.

I think about her words while fiddling with my fingers in my lap. I wish there was a door to slam or a window to break, but instead, I grab the tension ball that sits in the middle of the coffee table like a centerpiece. My hands grip, squeeze, and twist, giving my frustrations a place to go. I don't speak because I don't trust my words.

"Suffering is inevitable but God is right there with us when we go through it. It seems to me that Janet was there when she needed to be."

I look up at Anne's expression and see the sincerity written there. I can't deny the obvious. Janet came in the nick of time and stayed with me for the rest of the night because I couldn't stop crying. She held me together, but it's not like that took away my pain. It didn't take away my mistake. I felt sick to my stomach waking up the next day and remembering all of it, every painful fucking detail of my failure.

"I will explain it this way," Anne says, shifting in her chair and clearing her throat. "Two things are true here. The first is that God is always with us. The second is that we will experience suffering. He doesn't always rescue us from the hardships of life, but He is always with us when we face them."

I'm absorbing this information and trying to decide how I feel about it. It sits like a wad of tension in my stomach. The reality of my suffering hits me, and I snap like a rubber band being stretched and released. "Oh yeah? Where was God when I was living on the streets and had to dig through trash cans for scraps of food and clothing to stay warm? When I was trying to earn enough money to fucking survive? What about when I was high out of my mind or sitting in the hospital after saying goodbye to my babies? Huh? What about when I thought I was better but still bought heroin like nothing had changed?"

There they are, the tears. The angry tears. Flooding my eyes until they are so clouded that I can barely make out Anne's patient form sitting across from me. She is so calm; I want to throw something and jolt her from her composure. All I have is my tension ball so I throw it on the floor, but it doesn't bounce, and that only irritates me more. Hot, angry tears slide down my cheeks when I see Anne get out of her chair and sit beside me with a tissue extended and a soothing voice in my ear.

My arms are slack in my lap, and my back is hunched over. I feel defeated by myself, by God, by my past.

"He was right there in your darkest moments, Andrea, and God is here with you now."

"What if I don't want Him to be?" I petition weakly, tired by my own questions.

"When you're ready, He will be too."

CHAPTER 24
Love Can Do That
April 2012—Age 21

"*Abuelita*? Are you here?" My voice echoes, reverberating off of the stainless steel countertops. No pots and pans banging. No laughter or Spanish singing bursting through the sound system. *It's too quiet for Abuelita to be here*, I consider.

I peer up at the kitchen clock indicating the early hour. I assumed she would be here because it seems *Abuelita* is always here. I push through the revolving door exiting the hushed kitchen and enter the quiet dining hall. My eyes immediately focus on the only other body in the room who is sitting at one of the long cafeteria tables—Jordan.

I don't know why my heart leaps when I see him. I'm guessing it's because he's become such a good friend, but it's also easier to lie to myself that I don't feel more. That I don't see more.

He looks up and pulls his earphones out. "Hey, Andrea. Are you working tonight?"

"No, I have tonight off," I say. "I was just hoping *Abuelita* was here so I could talk to her. Looks like it's still too early. I'll just talk to her tomorrow." I rub my right arm, wondering if Jordan can sense my anxiety. I took a week off from working in the kitchen after my almost-relapse, or whatever we're calling it, and I miss *Abuelita*. I want to talk to her after everything that's happened.

"You know, I'm a pretty good listener if you want to sit and talk?" He leans forward, resting his elbows on the table, intent on talking and making me feel... something.

"It's okay. You look pretty busy typing away on your laptop."

The idea of talking to Jordan about my relapse makes me nervous, but I guess I could talk around it. He has always proven to be a good listener.

"It can wait. Here, sit down." Jordan stands and begins pulling the chair out directly across from his seat, and I fear making him feel bad if I deny his gesture now.

"Alright, thanks," I say quietly while taking the offered seat.

"So how have things been going?" Jordan starts.

Well, let's see. I left the center, I bought heroin, and I almost used it last week, and now I'm questioning everything in my life. That's pretty much how it's going.

"Things are going good." I dare not open up too much. I was told everything I shared or experienced was confidential unless I decided to open up about it. I have that choice and I'm not letting it go.

"You said you were wanting to chat with *Abuelita*. Is there anything you could share with me?" Jordan asks cautiously.

I exhale slowly and gaze down at my fidgeting hands beneath the table, trying not to let on that I'm dealing with more than I am. My mouth opens and then closes again.

Why does this have to be so hard?

In the span of a few heartbeats, Jordan speaks up again and fills the void between us. "I know talking to *Abuelita* is probably a lot more intriguing than me, but if you want to try..."

Abuelita does have a special way of making me feel seen, but then again, Jordan does too. I look up from my hands and find the look in his youthful eyes revealing a soft kindness rather than a judgmental telling.

I focus on my breathing like Anne has taught me and dive in like I'm not going to suffer the consequences. "Do you ever feel like a big fucking failure?"

Jordan stares but doesn't answer, and it's making me feel silly for even asking. "Sorry, that was a stupid question," I say, rubbing my hand over my forehead and trying to pull back the words I've already let out.

He holds up his hand. "No, no, that's not it. It's just..." He drops his hand and lets out a slow breath. "Failure has always been a close friend of mine. Too close."

Jordan's admission has me considering that maybe I can share about my relapse. I know he'd been through the ringer with alcohol, but not to the extent that he saw himself as a failure. He seems like he has his shit together, unlike me.

"Doesn't it piss you off that God didn't step in and stop it all though? Anne said He knows about every failure, all of my suffering, and was there through it all. What the hell does that even mean?" I huff, resting my back on the chair and crossing my arms over my chest.

Jordan leans back in his chair too, blowing out air as he relaxes and thinks about my question. He lifts his arms up and over to cradle his head where his hairline and neck meet. I don't know why, but I'm so nervous to hear what he says next. "It means suffering happens. We all face it, but if anything, it teaches us that we can't deal with it alone."

I hug my arms tighter across my chest. Isn't that what I've been trying to do my whole life? Gritting my teeth and pushing through all the expected and unexpected life handed me.

I hear his words but fail to pull any comfort from them. I am still thoroughly confused by how God runs His whole operation.

"Remember when I told you a little about how Beau found me?" Jordan asks, dropping his arms and crossing them over his chest. I can't help but notice the shapes, colors, and lines forming pictures that tell a story written all over his arms. Each tattoo means something, I'm sure of it.

I knew Jordan was an alcoholic and that he was in jail, but the other details were a mystery to me. It isn't until now that I realize how much I want to hear it. "Not really, only that you met Beau when you were in jail and somehow that helped you."

His lips turn up into a small smile. "What Beau did was…" Jordan shakes his head. "He saved me. He legit saved my life. I had already tried to kill myself once because I thought I had failed one too many times and was going to try it again. It wasn't until Beau sat across from me and told me he wasn't going to leave that something in me believed him."

"Damn, sorry, that's…" I search my word bank while running a hand through my hair, and I can't seem to find any one that fits how shocking this is to hear about Jordan.

I look at him anew and notice how young his features look. The sandy blond hair on his head is full and thick while the sides are trimmed short; his eyes are a light, warm brown that soften all of his facial features. His beard is often trimmed short and edged perfectly, but today, I notice extra stubble that chases the long lines of his neck but nothing indicating a rough life.

What about your scars, Andrea?

I think of the physical scars I carry on my body. The tracks on my arms from the heroin needle jabbing into my flesh are the biggest reminders, but I have others too. Like the cigarette burns I have on my arms from myself and the back of my neck from Manuel. Or the two-inch cut on my forearm from a displeased customer. The physical evidence of a rough life marks me.

I have to look away from Jordan as he continues his story. It's almost as if those scars on my skin are glaringly obvious and I feel too raw and exposed.

"Both of my parents died at different points in my early childhood. My mother died shortly after giving birth to me and my father took his own life when I was only eight years old. We didn't live near any family at the time in rural Kentucky, so I was in a foster home until my Gram could be contacted. She took me in a few months later and raised me the best she could." He pauses for the space of a breath. "Losing your folks isn't easy at any age, I imagine, but as a young kid growing up, it destroyed me."

I listen with rapt attention even if I can't look directly at Jordan. I have a parent-size-hole in my own heart too, and he doesn't know how much his story is affecting me.

"My Grams was already in her early seventies when I went to live with her, and while she tried her best to raise me, the rage I had inside just came out sideways. I started drinking with some friends when I was sixteen and by the time I was seventeen, I had developed a habit that led me to robbing a rundown gas station and getting caught. I was tried as a juvenile and ended up doing a couple months of community service."

"What did your Gram say about all of this?" I have to ask even though I know what it feels like to live with the disappointment of others because of your failures—it sucks.

"She was pretty upset with me, but I think she also understood how much I was struggling. I did my service but it wasn't enough to get me to really change. When I was eighteen, I left a friend's party completely hammered and ended up getting in a car wreck." Jordan pauses his storytelling. One second strings to the next, and I wonder if he will continue. When he finally does, I feel every gritty confession.

"I was badly hurt and spent some time in the hospital, but what was worse was that I had hit another vehicle. It was a husband and wife." He pauses again. I hear the pain in his voice and I have to look at him. His mouth is in a tight line and he's shaking his head slowly, revealing the failure he had told me about earlier.

"I totaled their car and it almost cost them their lives. The wife... she... she became paralyzed from the waist down."

Shit. That is awful, I think to myself, but don't say anything out loud. What do you even say to something like that? Jordan has been looking at me this whole time, I've sensed it, but when he admits this final piece, his eyes close and he drops his chin towards his chest. I don't see regret in his downcast face when he looks up again, I see sorrow. Deep, deep sorrow.

"I felt horrible. Like the worst scum of the earth for ruining that woman's life. I was tried as an adult since I was eighteen, and I did some time in jail for it. While I was there and before I met Beau, I got news that my Grams passed away, and, well, I had no one left. I was overrun by depression and I wanted the harshest kind of punishment available—death. I started to believe that my life wasn't worth living. It wasn't until Beau showed up in my cell one day that I started realizing my life had some value." I can see all of his feelings written on his face: grief, remorse, failure, and... hope. The hope I see causes my breath to catch, it looks so natural on Jordan and now I don't want to look away.

"Beau was faithful to show up each week and was the kind of friend I needed," Jordan says with relief. I know how tenacious Beau can be when he has a mission in front of him. Hence, the car chase he took us on that could have taken all of our lives.

"After I got out of jail, Beau encouraged me to come to the Journey Center as a resident to have regular therapy and essentially rebuild my life from the ground up. I was still absent, wanting to get lost in the bottle and ignore it all." Jordan leans his arms forward on the table again, clearly remembering every piece to his own journey.

I want to reach for his hand, but I stop myself. Instead, I keep our conversation going, finding just how much I need his confession. "So what did you say when you realized God had always been there with you but never stepped in to help you out?" I know I must sound like a broken record at this point, but I can't get past it. I don't know why it bothers me so much but it does.

"I have had almost six years to process my life's decisions and my failures; they still wreck me. My pain hasn't gotten any smaller but God has just gotten a whole lot bigger. Forgiveness does that. Love can do that." His determination is revealed in the firm set of his jaw. It's painfully clear and also makes me feel like I can do really hard things, like facing the aftermath of my almost-relapse.

I've been fiddling with a curl of hair that is lazily hanging over my shoulder to give my hands something to do and my eyes something to look at when Jordan's face becomes too much. I'm more confused than ever and feel like I'll never make it out of my pit of failures.

"You seem so confident that God can forgive anyone." I look up at Jordan's earnest grin again, it's starting to make my heart expand inside of my chest. My eyes drop to my lap and my failures start talking again. "Some of us just aren't worth forgiving, I guess." I say barely above a whisper. I almost don't want him to hear me say this—it reveals too much—but of course he does.

"All of us need the reminder that we're worth forgiving; we are worthy of love. The people around us can teach this too."

I feel the swell of tears filling my eyes.

Worthy. Something I've never felt about myself. I'm too broken, too confused to waste forgiveness on.

"I failed... again. Last week. And I'll probably do it again," I say, trying to convince Jordan I'm a lost cause. "I can't promise it won't."

"It's a good thing that forgiveness isn't a one-time event. It isn't exclusive either," he says confidently, but with gentleness in his eyes. "The harder part can be forgiving yourself."

My stomach drops at the very thought of forgiving myself. I am my harshest critic, and if it were up to me, I would have considered myself a lost cause a long time ago.

For some reason *Abuelita,* Janet, Anne, Kit, and Jordan don't think the same thing though.

Jordan reaches across the table and touches my arm. The two-inch scar is just below his hand and the dichotomy couldn't be more apparent. His gentle hand against the marks from a beast. It soothes me in this moment and I don't want to be anywhere else.

"You're asking some really great questions," he says to comfort me. It's working this time.

I realize I haven't taken a full breath since the start of our conversation. I inhale deeply, craving air in my lungs, and then exhale, wishing my mind would slow down.

"Do you think you would want to come to church this Sunday? A community is a great place to ask these questions."

I pause to consider his invitation. "I don't know. Can I think about it and let you know?"

"For sure," Jordan says with a quick nod of his head.

"Thanks for talking to me about all of this. I can't say any of it feels any clearer but I avoided cleaning the women's bathroom for the last twenty minutes, so there's that."

Jordan's resonant laugh booms from his chest and catches me off guard. "There's that," he repeats with a grin.

We say our goodbyes, and I head off to clean the bathrooms, one of the chores I was responsible for getting done every day. I haven't been back to clean it since everything happened, when I was huddled in the corner, holding what I thought was my lifeline.

When I walk inside the stall today, I picture myself and what I might have looked like. Crouching to hide, knees pulled to my chest in shame, and tears staining my cheeks with the pain of my decision.

I'm sad for that girl. She did what she knew to feel better, to not feel alone, but that isn't me. At least, that isn't me now. Today, I have people behind me. The sinking feeling hasn't gone away, the need to appease my addiction is still there, but I have friends who aren't letting me go down without a fight.

CHAPTER 25
Goin' to Church

April 2012—Age 21

"Jeans will be fine," Kit tries to assure me.

We are almost late to the service because I can't decide on an outfit to wear. I convinced Kit to go with me. If I am going to be bombarded by a bunch of Bible-thumping know-it-alls, I want backup. There wasn't much convincing to be done though; it turns out Kit was just as curious as I was to see what this church thing was all about.

"Says the girl in a skirt." I eye her skeptically.

"What? I like to dress up."

"Naturally," I say, unamused but appreciating Kit's outfit all the same. My wardrobe had to take a hard left turn when I arrived at the Journey Center. The booty shorts, skin tight dress, and heels I arrived in weren't exactly practical anymore. I raided the onsite thrift store where every resident had access to choose a few pieces of clothing from regularly, and I found some items I liked.

It's a shot in the dark, but I finally decide the jeans and t-shirt I put on and took off multiple times in a fit of indecision will have to work for a morning church service. If we get kicked out for jeans, so be it.

Kit and I make our way to the church building located two miles away from the Journey Center and by the time we get there, I am thankful for the jeans that made the walk a little easier.

I'm staring up at the building they call a church and can't believe I'm doing this. I haven't been to church since I lived with Aunt Cindy the first time and I could only stomach going once. I felt different, and in a small crowd, that made me stand out. I'm worried this will be a similar experience.

I inhale sharply as we pass by the few people that linger outside and greet us with overly cheerful smiles. I exhale after crossing over the door frame and peer around at the unknown faces that are scattered around the room.

My senses are on overload as children rush around the room playing tag as their parents trail behind them trying to keep pace. The freshly brewed coffee in the front lobby area filters into this large auditorium with stadium-like seats and teases my sense of smell; the familiar scent of baked goods fills the spaces in between. I look to my left and there is a group of people spinning flags suspended on large poles practicing in the back corner, twisting about and highlighting the attractive colors as if preparing for a parade.

Flags? Why do they need flags in church? I think to myself.

The old and young are gathering and mingling in circles all around the open room, hugging one another with a cheerful gleam in their eyes all while balancing large books and cups of coffee. The large room centers around a stage with countless rows of seats linked together like arms interlocking at the elbow.

I turn to Kit who appears to be having the same sensory experience as I am. "Kit, um, where the hell do we go? I mean, shit, I probably shouldn't say hell out loud," I say nervously, lowering my voice considerably.

"Chill. I'm the only one that heard you," Kit says, looking around us briefly. "I think there are a few empty chairs in the back row over there." She points to a few seats on the other side of the sea of curious people. "Here, grab my hand so we don't get lost."

I look at our destination and pin my gaze there, searching for an anchor point in this storm of bodies and overbearing cheerfulness. We are stopped multiple times on our way to those seats by complete strangers who seem overjoyed to see us despite never having met before.

Do I know you? I can't help but question.

I'm not sure what to do with the noticeable attention. I'm a nobody to all of these people. I don't recognize a single human here and yet, I might as well be a family member.

I smooth a hand over my hair. "Uh, Kit. Did you know any of those people that just said 'hi' to us?"

"Not a soul," she mouthed before angling her smile my way.

I hear soft music playing in the background until a few people take to the stage and pick up different instruments that create a cohesive melody as each one joins in. The music continues to build, the lights dim, and words appear on the overhead screens that are bigger than one entire wall in our bunk-room. When the singers add their voices to the mix, I'm captivated by the push and pull of every sound.

I finally sit in my seat, ready for the show, when I notice everyone in the room stays standing. As the song picks up, so do the voices in the audience. I can't sit now, I'll be the only one. I stand back up, pretending like I was just bending to grab something. I tuck my curly hair behind my ear as the music gets louder, and I can feel the vibrations in my feet that trail all the way up my limbs. It's rhythmic and smooth while also loud and passionate. I like it and it makes me want to dance, but I don't know if that's allowed. It's not like I'm in *Abuelita*'s kitchen right now.

The flags begin to dance along with those holding them at the same time I see young children jumping and dancing in their seats and in the aisles. The beat picks up and the song soars to new heights. I realize then that I'm the only person *not* dancing. Eyes are closed, bodies are moving, and hands are grasping the air above them. I see the passion and witness the joy that this music brings to each and every person in the room, and what it brings to me too.

I look over to Kit who is studying the people too before meeting my eyes, disbelief and awe translates on her face and I know the feelings exactly. It's loud enough that the music would drown out any words I said, so I continue bouncing my eyes around the full auditorium, the sheer amount of movement has my gaze snapping from one side of the room to the other. I wasn't expecting this.

Off to the side of the stage sits a large, white canvas board with an even bigger drop cloth underneath it and multiple colors of paint are situated off to the side on a small table. The artist herself appears on the stage, picking up her round brush and sinking it deep into one of the colors before repeating the process as she mixes and twirls and mixes some more. She begins painting purposefully on the no longer white canvas before her.

Glad to see we aren't skipping arts and crafts today, I think, doing my best not to roll my eyes.

I shift my weight to my left foot and though my eyes are scanning the bodies on stage, I can't shake the feeling that I'm being watched. I casually do a one hundred and eighty degree spin each way until I lock eyes with an elderly woman a few seats down from me in the same row. I smile, hoping that will appease her, but it doesn't. She's still looking at me even though I've looked away and back again two more times. I decide to wave, which I immediately wish I could take back when she starts making apologies to the people in between us as she pushes in front of them towards me.

The old woman in the matching mint toned jogger suit whispers something to the woman who was sitting next to me and before I know it, the entire row is shifting down to accommodate my new neighbor.

When the woman looks up at me, I notice how much shorter she is now that we are right next to each other. Her hair is white and curly and I imagine this woman rolling her hair in curlers every single night since they are perfectly symmetrical.

"Um… hi," I venture to say over the music.

The woman's smile grows twice as big. "Hi, daughter," she replies, and I wonder if she has mistaken me for someone else, like her actual daughter.

I look towards the stage and back to the elderly woman. "Ma'am, are you looking for your daughter?"

She gives me a pinched expression. "What did you say?"

I try asking again, but it's clear she still can't hear me over the live band in the background so I lean closer to her ear. "Are you looking for your daughter?"

A confused look is painted on her face. "No," she replies.

"I just thought…" I stop not sure how to proceed. I consider just dropping it, but I feel bad if she is looking for her daughter and can't find her. "I just thought I heard you call me 'daughter,' but I'm not your daughter. Do you want me to help you find her?"

She waves her hand at me. "I did call you daughter and no, I've already found her," the old woman says, pointing at me.

I open my mouth to try and explain things further, but the beat of the song picks up and any hope I had of talking over the music is gone. I stand to my full height again, shaking my head side to side, trying to figure out where this piece of the puzzle goes.

When I turn my head back to the stage and notice the painting that has taken shape, curiosity and wonder are battling for the throne in my mind. I sense the emotion swelling and building inside of my chest like a fire with plenty of dry wood and oxygen to help it grow. I can't explain how or why, but the picture speaks to me. I see the anguish in the black and gray tones with a splash of red rage that makes me clench my fists beside me. The lines of blue remind me of tears and I can feel my eyes start to fill with them. The hope spelled out in yellow is what finally breaks me. It's what broke me almost a year ago too, but seeing it in paint makes me feel it in my soul. The painting doesn't take on an identifiable form, but the colors are enough to spur in me every emotion of the rainbow.

Keep it together, Andrea.

The tears are running down my face before I can call them back and try to gather some composure, which isn't there right now. The colors I see before me are a catalogue of my life. Every swipe of the brush adds more vibrancy to my past, present, and future. But I don't have a future. Right? I don't have hope. I have to get some air. I *need* to breathe. Suddenly, I'm sliding in front of people in our row to escape, unconcerned by my abrupt exit.

There's no time, Andrea.

You have to get out.

Run if you have to.

My pace quickens as I push through the double doors that will lead me to air. It's like all of the oxygen has been sucked out of the room and I am gasping; I'm inhaling and exhaling frantically, trying to get a deep breath. The fire that fanned into flame inside of me earlier has been extinguished, and in its wake, a chill that has me rubbing my arms despite the warm sunshine overhead.

Keep it together, Andrea.

I revert to my usual chiding but, this time, it doesn't work. I sit down on one of the steps outside and wait for the panic attack to let go of me.

A hand rests on my back; a movement that would normally cause me to jump in fear has me leaning in until I'm enveloped in someone's arms. There aren't any words that pass between us, but the hand that rubs my arm like it has been consoling me for years keeps me focused and grounded. My breathing slows and my emotions settle. I no longer feel the need to run, instead, all I want to do is stay right here in these arms.

When I finally look up and expect to see a stranger, all I see is a man who is anything but.

Jordan.

CHAPTER 26
Mija
April 2012—Age 21

I regrettably open my eyes the next morning, stretching my arms and legs and yawning wide as I push to sit up. My feet hit the floor and I prepare to stand when I receive a frantic command from my very concerned roommate that makes me startle.

"Don't move!"

My insides and outsides jump with adrenaline. "What's going on? Why can't I move?" My heart rate is now audible in our small room.

"Sorry, I didn't mean to freak you out. I just need to finish this. Can you just jump over them?" Kit asks, barely looking up from the sketchpad in her hands.

"You might as well have poured cold water on my head," I reply, peering down at the floor trying to understand what I need to "jump over." All I see are a couple pairs of shoes belonging to each of us and a few scattered clothes creating somewhat of a barrier between my feet and the floor.

"Can you just tell me what I'm supposed to be looking out for? I'm so confused and I really have to go to the bathroom," I say to Kit with a slight whine I am no longer trying to hide.

"The pants by your left foot. I am drawing them and don't want you to move them or else it will completely mess up my whole sketch."

Did she just say… pants?

My first thought is that Kit has to be joking. The pants had been dropped haphazardly near my bed even though they belonged to Kit. There doesn't appear to be anything special about this pair. If it wasn't for the focused look that her features reveal, I might have kicked them away from my side of the bed just to prove a point, but I resisted.

I watch as Kit looks from the pants in front of my bed then back at her work in progress.

"Okay… be back in a minute." I side-step the fragile pair of pants and shuffle towards the bathroom door in the hallway, just outside of our room. When I return, I catch a glimpse of Kit's drawing and the amount of detail and shading takes me completely by surprise.

"Kit! What the…? I had no idea you could draw like that? How did you learn how to do that and… when?" I'm so surprised by the details, I am positive my mouth is hanging open.

"Oh, yeah, I used to draw a ton but haven't done it in forever. It used to be the only way I could actually express everything that was going on around me. Since being here, I have started to dabble in it again."

If this was dabbling…

"When I saw that painter on stage at church yesterday, it just spoke to me. I *had* to draw. When I woke up early this morning, I couldn't exactly find anything that inspired me so I just started drawing what was in front of me. Hence, the pair of pants," she tells me, pointing to her muse with the point of her pencil.

"Oh my gosh. You are really, really good," I say to her. At Kit's reference to the painter at church, I remember the feelings it brought up for me. The hair on my arms rises to attention and I realize I've been fighting against these emotions, but I'm not winning.

"Thanks, I hope you don't mind if I keep those pants there for a little while. Now that I've started, I would really like to finish them."

If it was anyone else, I may not have caved, but this is Kit, my best friend. "Yeah, totally. I don't mind. I'll have to remember to move around them." At least they are Kit's pants and not mine.

I start dressing and preparing myself for the day ahead. Something that Anne and Janet encouraged was to have a solid daily routine. Between waking and falling into bed each night, my days are fully mapped out like a set course without many changes. I have never had this much routine in my life.

After I get ready, I go to the morning devotions with the entire program and when they finish, I come back to our room to do homework on my bed. Sure, there's a desk, but I prefer comfort while I read. At the end of every week, we have a check-in with our mentors and if we complete the required work, we can move on to the next phase of the program. I am on track to continue to the next lessons, and I feel accomplished when I look up at the clock and notice it's time to go to the kitchen to help *Abuelita*. I'm on lunch shift today. The crew I work with changes but the woman I'm really there to see doesn't.

I'm walking to the kitchen and feeling anxious to tell her about my weekend, namely the painting. I've been wanting to talk to her all morning. As I suspect, once I push through the swinging kitchen doors, *Abuelita* lifts her head from behind the stainless steel island where she has all of the meal ingredients for lunch that day and directs her beaming smile my way. A few of the other resident workers wave and continue their assigned jobs.

"*¡Hola, Mija!*" she exclaims. "Freddy, grab the celery from the refrigerator and start cutting, *por favor*, please," *Abuelita* orders, before turning back to me. "Andrea, *¿Cómo estás?* How are you?"

"I'm good," I say, pulling the apron over my head. "I got everything done that I needed to this morning, which feels good." I stall, wondering if I should even share about the painting that made me feel too many things.

Maybe I should just tell her later when there aren't so many people around, I start to reconsider.

"*¿Mija?* I can see you want to share something. *Dime.* Tell me."

I must have been doing a poor job at hiding my hesitation. I can't hide anything from her. She will have it out of me faster than I can think of an excuse.

"I had this weird experience yesterday that I haven't been able to shake," I start to tell her.

I sound crazy already.

"Well, I went to church yesterday and—"

Abuelita whips her head up from the work table where she is chopping vegetables and interrupts me before I can say the rest. "*¿Qué?* What? You went to church, *Mija?*" She sounds stunned at my news.

I was not expecting her reaction, but I continue anyway. "Yeah, I did. Jordan invited me." I don't tell her that he held me in his arms until my eyes ran dry. I'm still a little shocked I ended up there.

Abuelita's smile only seems to grow larger with every word I speak. I press on since I've already opened my big mouth. "Anyway, during the service, there was this painter on the stage. She painted a picture and I don't know why, but it made me feel a lot of things..." My words trail off and I'm unsure if I can explain the rest. As I try to retell what happened, I don't really understand it myself.

"What things, *Mija?*" *Abuelita* asks, seeking for the next layer of my heart.

I reach to grab a knife and cutting board so I can help cut more veggies for the soup we are making today while trying to conjure up some word that embodies how I felt.

I let out a breath and a word at the same time, "Hope."

Without further explanation, I reach for an onion and position it beneath the knife.

"Hope?" she questions.

I simply nod and slice into the white orb over and over again.

She thinks I'm crazy.

I shouldn't have said anything. I wish I could explain this better.

"*¡Dios mío!*" she says, her hand flying up to her chest.

"I know, I know; the painting thing sounds crazy, but —" I start to clarify, but *Abuelita* breaks in.

"Andrea, don't you see?" Her eyes are pleading. "You are starting to see you have a future. I knew there was a reason you were glowing today. *¡Lo sabía!* I knew it!" She's clapping her hands and drawing every eye in the kitchen to look in our direction.

"Shh, *Abuelita*! Everyone is looking over here. I already feel crazy telling you about this, okay?" A painting has never made me feel this way. I don't get how it could, but it has.

"I'm so excited, I can't help it! Do you know what this means, *Mija*?" *Abuelita* asks, both of her hands planted on the prep table between us. *Abuelita* Gloria is awestruck but, if I'm honest, I feel annoyed now. Hope never lasts long. It's here today, and likely gone tomorrow.

"*Mija*, it is like I have told you before. The noise of your past life is quieter; you are different now. You have hope for your life, for your future."

The knife I am using must not be sharp enough because tears are stinging my eyes as I continue to cut more uneven lines into the onion.

I set my knife down firmly. "I just don't get it, *Abuelita*. What's so great about it? Why does it make me feel like this? Like my heart is twice the size and I'm practically floating."

Abuelita doesn't take her eyes off of me and I feel her study me as I look down at my hack job. "Hope is *muy importante, Mija*, it is very important."

I wipe a few stray tears from my eyes with the edge of my apron. Does hope for someone like me exist?

Abuelita is moving around the kitchen island now like a woman on a mission. I turn to face her, leaning my hip on the counter for the support I need.

"*Mija*," she says again, but this time, she holds my face between her palms as she lifts my head to look into her eyes. "Do you know what hope means?"

My eyes are still swimming in tears as I look at her. *Abuelita* doesn't wait for me to come up with words that I don't have. "Hope means that this isn't where your story ends, *Mija*."

I've forgotten about the rest of the kitchen crew and instead cling to *Abuelita*'s words with everything I have.

"Your story is not over yet. You will make mistakes, but hope keeps us believing. It keeps us healing." *Abuelita* drops her hands from my face, but doesn't move away. "It's not our failures that define us, it's our hope."

I fight off the desire to drop my head and keep my eyes trained on hers, trying to soak up some of the strength she has. I've lived both sides of hope. The side that I wanted my story to end and apparently, the side where I don't. I'm still not sure if my failures make me a good candidate to believe in hope, but I'm starting to see glimpses of how *Abuelita* made it through losing her children. I'm starting to see how I can make it through losing mine.

"Have you ever seen hope in action, *Mija*?" *Abuelita* asks in a soothing voice.

Wendy's face comes to mind. She dealt with the worst of the worst and still found reasons to believe there was something to be recovered—like me. Maybe this is why I used up my one phone call to contact her when I got to the Journey Center almost a year ago.

I had been getting ready to start a full year program where I'd be going "dark" for a year and unable to contact anyone outside of the facility. I didn't want to call my Aunt Cindy, I had messed up her life enough, so I called Wendy. Her number was the only other one I had memorized. I can still remember the conversation vividly.

I picked up the phone and punched in the numbers that in perfect sequence would ring her cell phone, which she carried with her at all times. The phone rang three times before a voice on the other end answered.

"Hello?"

I paused. I could hang up now and she would never know.

I considered it, but I had already come this far.

Answer her.

"Hi, Wendy. It's me. Andrea."

"Andrea. Oh, Andrea. H-How are you?"

I knew I was surprising her. Hell, I surprised myself by following through with the call, but by sharing this news I wanted it to mark the moment; the moment where I move towards healing and kill off my demons.

"I'm good. I'm… really good, actually. I'm starting a program. And… I'm sober. I mean, it's been like two months, but still," I tell Wendy, though I'm not sure why.

"I am shocked, but in the best way. I am so proud of you. I can't even tell you how long I have been praying for a call just like this one," Wendy said.

"You have?" I asked. Wendy had always been in my corner, even when I didn't have one. She supported me through some of my toughest moments and I knew all of this because I lived it. At the same time, I still found it hard to believe that there were people who had my back.

"I have. You have been in my prayers since day one, Andrea, and you will be in them every single day you are in that program."

My eyes filled with tears. Damn. I swallowed hard. "I-I don't know what to say," I confessed. "Thanks," I finally said.

I shake my head, letting the memory of that call slip away. I look at my *Latina* grandmother again, and there is something there that tells me I can talk about Wendy.

I start slowly, cautiously. "I have given birth before. Twice. Well, thr— nevermind. The woman who helped me, she always had hope. It didn't matter that I had to call her because I was knocked up and needed help. It's like she saw a different woman than the one I saw."

"Ay, we could all use a friend who sees the best in us and not just the struggle."

"I don't know. At the time, I guess it just felt good knowing someone didn't think I was just some screw up," I admit. I'm not sure why I share this deeply personal part of myself that I had only shared in depth to Anne, in part to Kit, and not at all to myself. *Abuelita* seems to have this effect on me. My mouth speaks words that have been hidden inside for so long that they sound rusty and awkward, like shoes that are too big or too small and change how you walk.

"You have seen very difficult things in your life, *Mija*. It sounds like this woman came into your story when you needed her the most. Some might call her an angel. Others might call her a friend."

I inhale sharply as I reach behind me for the bread that will go with the soup. I need something to occupy my mind. Wendy's memory is causing my hands to shake, and I don't want to continue this conversation anymore. I'm unsteady as I try to digest *Abuelita's* words. The people I had in my life were usually after something from me; it was transactional. Wendy wasn't like that though. She was a lot less concerned by what she gained.

I put the bread back on the counter, not knowing what to do with it when a thought enters my mind. It pushes past the rest of my reflections and though it has never occurred to me before, now the question burns with a need to know inside of me. I have to know.

Why have I never asked?

"*Abuelita*, you have always called me *Mija*, since the first day I met you, but I never even asked you—what does that mean in English?"

"*Sí*, yes, I have always called you *Mija* because it always felt right," she confesses with a shrug of her shoulders.

"It means, my daughter."

CHAPTER 27
Building Bridges
April 2012—Age 21

I'm trying to focus on homework. It's critical that I stay on top of it so I can get my GED, but I can't get the conversation with *Abuelita* out of my head.

I was so caught off guard yesterday that my mouth dropped open and I wanted to bolt. "Wait, you've been calling me, *Mija*, for months now," I said in clear disbelief.

"Of course. Is there something wrong with that? Do you not like the name?" *Abuelita* replied with furrowed brows and concern lining her face.

"No, I don't mind the name," I told her before I knew how I felt about it. "That's not it. I-I just didn't know what it meant and now that I do, it just hits closer to home," I said on an exhale. She had been calling me *daughter* for almost an entire year and I had no clue. The old woman at church called me daughter too, and the uncanny coincidence is blowing my mind. I had always imagined what a real family would be like since mine always felt so far away.

Aunt Cindy was my family, I consider.

My one year blackout period is nearing its end, and I have been thinking about her more and more.

Will I call her?

Could I?

I don't have an answer for myself. I need more time to think about it. I shake my head at the same time I release the memory of my conversation with *Abuelita* yesterday. I have an hour before my appointment with Anne and with all of my chores finished I really need to finish this homework. I'm scribbling away while Kit sits across from me on her bed, flipping through a magazine.

"Did you ever want to leave? You know, in the beginning, when things were the hardest?" Kit asks, looking over her magazine.

"All the time," I say with a laugh. "I begged Janet to let me leave. I mean, my body was weaning from heroin, so my mind wasn't exactly in the right space," I explain to her. Those first few days at the Journey Center were pure hell.

Kit sets her magazine down. "I mean, after all of that. Did you ever want to leave after you detoxed and started counseling?" Kit's expression is serious, I can tell that much.

I sit up in my bed a little higher to give her my full attention and the question more thought. "There were times that things felt too hard; I mean, I almost relapsed, but I never wanted to leave more than I wanted to stay," I respond, wondering if that makes sense to me, let alone Kit. Even sitting on the bathroom floor with a heroin needle in my hand, I didn't want to get kicked out; I wanted to stay... I still do.

"I guess you have a point." Kit's face breaks into a smile.

I look at Kit and turn the question on her. "What about you... Did you ever want to leave?"

"Yeah, I did," she admits. "I wasn't even on drugs, but it's still hard to admit you need help, and that's exactly where I was at. Trapped with no way out and needing help," Kit says, looking beyond me and recalling her own memories.

"I think it's hard to admit anytime," I say to Kit, pushing aside my school book and sitting up further in bed. The word *help* wasn't even a part of my language dictionary before I walked through these doors.

There were plenty of times before the Journey Center when I lived on the streets that I thought about signing myself into rehab, but I never did because of how many failed attempts I had seen. Countless men and women walked into rehab one morning only to mosey on out within a week's time saying how it just wasn't the life for them. I thought that would be my story, too, and it almost was. The other side of a heroin needle does exist, but I'm still wondering how long I'll be on this side. Holding the heroin in my hand was a humbling reminder that my want for it is strong, but I'm in the process of getting stronger.

"I have to get ready to see Anne," I tell Kit when I move to stand, planting my feet on the floor in front of my bed when I remember.

The pants. Ugh, I almost stepped on *the* pants.

"Sorry, I know what you're thinking," Kit says with real remorse and a raised hand. "I promise I will finish up before the week is over," Kit tells me, doing her best to convince me of this.

I have to laugh a little at the ridiculous amount of concern that Kit, and now I, have for these pants. I'm not sure if they'll really be gone by the end of the week, but when I carefully step over them to get ready for my time with Anne, I consider gluing them to the floor. They've become something of a symbol for Kit, and I really don't want to forget about them, breaking their mold and Kit's heart while I'm at it.

I step into Anne's familiar office. The red, green, and gold jewel tone color scheme is so inviting, it makes me want to curl up on the couch and move in—I'm here often enough.

I'm telling Anne about my week so far, and I can't avoid telling her about last Sunday.

"So, I, uh, went to church last Sunday." I let the admission fall from my lips.

"Is that right? I didn't know you were planning on attending church. What did you think of your experience there?" Anne asks, genuinely curious.

Anne has been with me on this journey for a year, never pushing me past where I am willing to go, but giving me challenges that get me out of my shell that much more. She is looking at me now, waiting for me to share, and I don't know where I should start.

Should I tell her about the elderly woman?

Maybe I should just start with the painting?

Or I could scrap both of those ideas and ask why there were people waving giant flags. This one still has me scratching my head.

We talked for an hour, me telling and asking her so many things about my experience that I completely lost track of time. When I finally take a breath, Anne looks at me and then steers our conversation to action.

"I can see the change in the soft lines of your face today. I can see victory too and I want you to know how honored I feel to witness it," Anne tells me, raising a reverent hand to her chest.

I swallow, removing the lump that starts to form.

"I have another exercise for you," Anne offers slowly. "If you're feeling ready for another?"

How many tricks does Anne have up her sleeve exactly? I decide not to question the methods since my beating heart is living proof of their magic.

"Let's go for it. I'm ready," I say with an increased energy.

"Wonderful," Anne says with a smile. "I want us to start repairing some bridges."

"Alright…" I say slowly, waiting for the next assignment Anne wants to give.

She folds her hands and squints her eyes in question. "Who has been in your life whether in the distant or more recent past that you want to repair a bridge with?"

I could feel this coming. A name and face immediately pop into my mind and my stomach drops just as fast. "Aunt Cindy," I say almost as quickly.

I have turned my back on my aunt so many times. My hurt ran so deep that it pulled me further into myself and in turn, further away from her. I knew I needed to call, but it had been so long now without any words spoken between us.

Could I call her?
Did she want me to?

I look at my hands and then at Anne. *I can do this*, I try to tell myself, hoping I'm crazy enough to believe it. Or, at least crazy enough to follow through with it.

"I think that's a great choice. You've finished your first year of the program and you'll notice that second year students don't have the same restrictions on making calls or opening the door to family and friends again, if you want. You can decide how you would like to extend the invitation to repair this bridge. I would suggest a phone call but a letter will work too. Sometimes people will choose to write out their thoughts and then read them to their loved one over the phone or in person. It's completely up to you, but let's try to have movement on this before we meet again next week."

I nod my head, feeling unsure of how I'm going to do this again. I keep reminding myself that I've done this before and she had opened her arms last time, and the time before that.

I say goodbye to Anne and head back to my bunk room to sort out my thoughts. I'm walking back while sending up a silent prayer, or maybe it was more of a plea, that this will be the last time I have to build this bridge with my aunt.

I have a phone call to make.

• • •

I finally call a few days later when I find the courage. When I pick up the phone and punch in the numbers, I feel my stomach roll over on itself. I'm sitting in Janet's office while she works on some paperwork behind me. Her presence helps, but it doesn't make the sick feeling in my gut go away. I slowly push each button of her home phone number, delaying a second longer before I hit the last one.

Aunt Cindy has forgiven me before, but that doesn't mean she wants to make forgiving me a full-time job. I hit the last number and hold the receiver away from my face, trying to breathe through my nerves. A hand starts rubbing my shoulder, and I close my eyes. I can do this.

As much as my nerves tell me to hang up, it's this damn hope that puts the phone to my ear, listening to every ring until a voice echoes through the line.

"Hello?" the familiar tone speaks.

My eyes are still closed when my nerves morph into tears. I practiced every word I would say, but it's all gone; the words aren't there, only an abundance of tears.

Is it too late?

Will she forgive me?

"Andrea?" the voice says, and I nod my head like she can see me. A gasp escapes my mouth and I cover it with the back of my hand.

Aunt Cindy's voice softens when she says my name again, "Andrea."

My name has never sounded sweeter, and my heart immediately recognizes the solace her voice brings.

"How are you, sweetheart?" Aunt Cindy asks while I cry.

I choke on a sob, but the reassuring hand on my shoulder settles me and I find my voice. "Hi, Aunt Cindy. I-I'm good," I say in reply and really mean it this time. More tears baptize my face in a newness that I'm only now able to accept.

Forgiveness. Love. Joy. Reconciliation.

The call ends up being short because she is determined to come visit me at the Journey Center. "I need to see you, sweetie. I need to put my eyes on you and know that you are alive and whole. Where can I meet you? Can I come now?"

"Yeah, yeah," I reply, taking inventory of my Saturday schedule. "I'm free for dinner if you want to drive up?"

"I wouldn't miss it. I'll be there," Aunt Cindy says in a strong voice.

It takes her over an hour in traffic to get here, but based on her determination, she likely would have driven all night to get to me. I'm flooded with remorse when I see her tear-stained cheeks and red rimmed eyes. We hold one another in the lobby as our tear-filled hello is brimming with the promise of second chances. Or third… Maybe even fourth, at this point.

"I'm so sorry, Aunt Cindy." I need to get the words out before they consume me. "I-I made so many mistakes. I've given you so many reasons to turn away from me, but you haven't." I pull back to look at my aunt who has tears trailing down her face as well. She reaches up and brushes mine away with her thumbs and then holds my face in her hands.

"Oh, sweetheart. I forgive you. I want you to know, I will always be here for you. Your mistakes don't define you. You have too much good ahead of you," she says smiling at me before enveloping me in a tight hug. I don't want to leave this moment. My heart is so light, it might as well be floating above us like a balloon.

We are clinging to each other when I hear my stomach gurgle. Aunt Cindy laughs with me. "It sounds like it's time to eat," she proclaims.

I wipe under my eyes to remove any mascara that slipped down with my tears, and then I excitedly lead Aunt Cindy on a quick tour. I know I'm gushing about how great the Journey Center is, but I can't help it. This place has given me life and purpose. It gave me friends.

I finally lead us to the cafeteria where I know *Abuelita* has a meal waiting for us.

"¡*Hola, Mija,* this must be *tu tía,* your aunt!" *Abuelita* doesn't waste one step after exiting the kitchen and placing our plates on the table. She walks directly into the arms of my aunt, enthusiastically rubbing her back.

The warmth in my chest starts to grow, and I fear the smile on my face is permanently etched there. This is what an overwhelming sense of family feels like, I think. Family involves people that I never knew I had until now but, I have another realization, another feeling that I now have a name for—*love.*

I never believed I was capable of feeling love, or truly being loved. I've hidden behind a protective shield since I was little and realized that I never figured out how to put it down. The shield became like a second arm to me.

I have wondered how to convince myself it's safe to set it down and now I know how. It's love. It is love that is slowly disarming me, removing the shield and lessening the fear. I see love playing out before my very eyes as I listen to *Abuelita* and my aunt exchange kind words and heartfelt thanks.

Don't forget your babies. That was love.

Or when Wendy held you.

Aunt Cindy's acceptance. That was love, too.

Love has been here all along, I finally realize. It has followed me into every circumstance, acting as a light guiding me back to who I am. I guess if what Anne said was true, that God reaches out through the people around us, then love has a name.

"Andrea, *ven a sentarte a comer*," *Abuelita* says, "Come, sit down and eat! You both must be hungry."

I move towards these two women in my life who embody love. "Thank you," I say quietly, but loud enough for them both to hear. Gratitude is all I have, but somehow, I think it's enough. *Abuelita* surrounds me in a tight embrace, and Aunt Cindy squeezes my arm with a smile aimed right at me that makes her laugh lines show and her eyes crinkle.

This is my family.

Anne is right again; this bridge is worth rebuilding.

Love has a Name | Christina Hill

Part Three
The Redemption

CHAPTER 28
I Need You

April 2013—Age 22

"Andrea, are you almost ready to go, sweetie? We need to get going if we still plan to walk the two miles to get there," Aunt Cindy yells from the hallway.

"Yes, I'm just finishing up my hair now." I run the brush through my elbow length locks a few more strokes before deciding I'm ready.

"I wore my sneakers this time since I got blisters from walking in my flats last weekend," Aunt Cindy tells me from the hallway where she, undoubtedly, is checking her wrist watch.

"Alright, ready," I announce, walking out of my room and closing the door behind me.

"Where's Kit? I thought she was coming with us?" Aunt Cindy asks.

"She had to be at church early since she signed up to work in the kid's class this week. She will walk back with us though," I assure her.

Aunt Cindy turns her head to look at me. "Lunch, too?"

I know how important our Sunday afternoon lunch dates are to my Aunt Cindy. When Kit started joining us, she immediately became a part of our family, and my aunt has treated her this way ever since.

"Of course, she never misses it," I reply with a smile.

"Then let's get going. I need to walk off that caffeine I had with breakfast this morning. *Abuelita* certainly knows how to brew a strong cup of coffee!" Aunt Cindy says with a laugh. *Abuelita* did like to make strong coffee.

I fall into step with my aunt and we make our way down the stairs that lead us to the street.

I'm almost done with my second year of the program. Second year students still have weekly morning devotionals, studies, and jobs to do, but we have access to the world outside of the multi-block boundary lines that the Journey Center occupies. Some residents, like myself and Kit, choose to stay longer, if accepted, to continue working and saving up money. I have come a long way since stepping one high-heeled foot out of that mini-van and onto this campus, and I'm seriously ready for what is ahead for me here.

The sunshine is beating down on us already and it's only nine o'clock in the morning. My Aunt Cindy and I walk into church just before the music starts. We have our favorite seats already picked out because we sit in them every single week. The same elderly woman who called me her daughter has been as faithful as ever, greeting me with a knowing smile and a bounty of love in her arms. Turns out Gladys does have a biological daughter who lives in Washington State, and now she has an adopted daughter sitting next to her—me.

"Daughter, I am so glad you came back!" Gladys practically gushes as she approaches our row.

"Hi Gladys, it's good to see you too. You know I'm here every week, though," I say with a grin.

"Of course you are, dear! I am just glad you *keep* coming back," she tells me while leaning in and giving me an obvious wink.

"Me too, Gladys. Me too." I can't help but smile. Gladys sits beside us because our spot is actually hers. She invited me to sit next to her when I finally gained enough courage to walk back into this building. It would feel weird to sit anywhere else.

I lean in and give Gladys a quick hug before moving out of the way so Aunt Cindy can give her one as well. My aunt lives and works south of the city, but she is here every weekend without fail. I have drawn so much strength from her over the years, but our relationship has shifted. I'm not relying on her for survival anymore; I rely on her because we are family, more so than we ever have been.

When the service finishes, Aunt Cindy and I stand to leave, saying hello to our friends that we see often, but enjoy every encounter with like it had been weeks since the last. I hear my name being called from a distant corner and turn my head in time to see Jordan's hand waving at me above the mass of heads swarming the aisles as we attempt to exit.

"Andrea, hi! How's it going? It's good to see you," Jordan says, genuine joy spreading across his features at his greeting.

A smile spreads naturally across my lips. "I'm actually doing really well," I say, and I believe it. "How about you? It's really good to see you too. It's been like, what, six months since the last time we ate in the cafeteria together?" It's not like I've been counting or anything.

His warm, caramel colored eyes drink in the moment like my hazel ones must be doing. I can't look away, I've missed seeing him, but I fear that if I think about that, he'll disappear into thin air. I don't want that.

"Has it been that long? Dang. We'll have to fix that soon," Jordan says as his mouth tips into another smile.

"Someone else has missed you, too." I give him a knowing glare and then realize the mistake I made in admitting I had missed him. I clear my throat. "*Abuelita*, I mean, that's who I'm talking about."

His expression is amused. "*Abuelita* tells me all the time I need to come by the kitchen more often. I can't stand to disappoint her, but hopefully I won't have to anymore. I'm going to start helping out with the men's program before the year ends and another cohort starts up next year. They've been short a few leaders lately, and I've missed being around the campus."

My heart leaps, jumps, and skips at this news. It's like music to my ears knowing I will see him more often since the men's and women's programs have the same morning devotional time. Jordan has volunteered at the Journey Center since before I got here, but he had started spending more of his time and energy with the alcohol recovery group at the church after I finished my first year. He also holds down a paying job at the church too, so our cafeteria lunch dates have been nonexistent. I miss our deep conversations and the way *Abuelita* would tease him mercilessly.

He still has the short, dark beard that I remember too well and the killer smile that reveals two perfect dimples peeking out from behind his scruff. I remember now that his wicked smile is too good at melting hearts. I'm clearly not immune.

Before I can grasp at a coherent thought, Aunt Cindy touches my arm as she joins our party of two. I swallow hard and look away from Jordan's dimples that rendered me senseless there for a minute.

"Hi Jordan, it's wonderful to see you again!" Aunt Cindy greets him with a hug. "Tell me, how have you been? I haven't seen much of you."

Jordan has his hands shoved in his front pockets, his signature stance, and rocks back on his heels before answering. "Oh, you know, I've been around. I'm never far," he replies, looking over at me for some reason.

"You're always working on something, that's what makes me love you so much," Aunt Cindy says.

I want to blush at Aunt Cindy's forward comment.

"Ha! Thanks Aunt Cindy, I know I'll always have a cheerleader in you," Jordan says.

I haven't stopped smiling this entire time and now my cheeks are hurting. We continue talking until the swirl of people who were passing by us stops and the room is finally empty. We say our goodbyes and promise to catch up more soon. Aunt Cindy and I barely take a step before her head turns to look at me.

"My, my, if he hasn't gotten cuter!" she says, beaming. "And don't tell me you didn't notice," Aunt Cindy says, elbowing me in the side while she's at it.

"Aunt Cindy! I didn't think you would go for a younger man!" I say. My quick reply has her gasping and then laughing so hard that she grabs my arm and I have to hold her upright.

"Oh, honey, you know exactly what I mean." She raises her eyebrows and stares me down. "How old is Jordan anyway? Your age, I'm guessing."

"I think he's twenty-four," I say casually as not to encourage my aunt's antics.

"Huh, well, he had quite the smile when he saw you."

Did she notice that too?

"I'm sure he was just being friendly. He was a big part of my journey in getting to where I am today."

That has to be why his smile lit up the space around us, right?

"Honey, he looked as excited to see you as I am to see some lunch. Let's go eat!"

We can agree on most things nowadays... except where to go to lunch. I want Italian and Aunt Cindy wants Mexican food.

"Maybe Kit should decide again," I tell Aunt Cindy when we finally make it back to the Journey Center and sit in her car to wait for Kit.

"Where is Kit? I never saw her this morning and I thought she was going to meet us here, well, now," Aunt Cindy says, looking at her trusty watch.

"She'll be here soo—"

Before I can finish my sentence, Kit opens the rear car door and pops her head in first. "Were you looking for me?" Kit says with excitement.

"Perfect timing, we were just talking about where to eat today." Aunt Cindy turns her body to face Kit who is now settled into the backseat.

"Let me guess, I'm the tiebreaker again?" Kit says with an amused laugh.

"Surprise, I know how much you love the gig," I tell her.

"You know me so well," Kit replies before deciding on lunch for all of us. "Burgers, always. I mean, is there a better food group out there other than burgers?" Kit asks us both without really wanting an answer.

"Are you really saying that burgers are their own food group?" I ask with honest curiosity, turning my body around in the front passenger seat to look at her.

"Duh," Kit states.

"Burgers it is!" Aunt Cindy says while firing up her Mazda and pulling out of the parking lot to drive to our favorite burger spot a few miles away.

We pull into the parking lot and make our way inside where the server seats us at a table near the large garage door windows that are open and letting in a breeze that I'm sure has traveled all the way from the ocean. It's springtime now and the weather is warming up, making me want to spend as much time soaking it in as possible.

I look at Kit who isn't holding her menu because she has been here enough times to know what she likes. We all have been here enough times because, well, we can never decide on something different.

"Kit, how was the toddler class this morning?" I ask her, knowing exactly what it was like.

She gives a strained laugh. "I didn't know goldfish crackers could crumble that much. There was a layer of orange dust all over the room by the time we finished." Kit looks at us with a plain expression. "That's pretty much how it went."

I can't contain my laughter and almost spit out my water when Kit describes it. "Sounds about right," I reply, still trying not to choke.

"Even with all of the crumbs I find in my clothes afterwards, there is something about those kids that always keeps me coming back. They are adorable, and I—" Kit stops in the middle of her sentence and looks over at me.

I'm not expecting my face to reveal so much when talking about kids, but it does. That hole is taking the longest to heal.

Aunt Cindy looks over to me and notices my distress. "Oh, honey," she says before grabbing my hand that is resting on the table in front of me. Kit rubs my shoulder since she is sitting in the chair beside me and now my breathing is the least of my worries. A lump forms in my throat and I can't speak. I just shake my head back and forth, trying to remind my emotions that this is our lot in life. I chose adoption and it's hard. Like, really hard, even years later.

"I spoke to Wendy on the phone last week," my aunt begins to share. "She asked about you and gave me an update on the kids."

Two sentences is all it takes for my heart to plummet to the ground. I still don't know how to talk about my kids. They are both out there, somewhere, and I'm here, without them. It's a messy feeling that I haven't been able to sort into the right spot in my heart. Anne and I have had countless conversations about my birth children who are forging their own way in the world. My heart still clenches tightly whenever I think about them. The updates don't make it any harder than it already feels, and most times, it helps knowing they're doing well.

I've talked to Wendy a few times in the last year, getting news about the kids I placed into other homes. She keeps me in the loop even though I feel outside of it. I'm so proud of the little humans they are, but I never take any credit, because that's not how this story goes. I'm the one who muddled everything and that piece is the hardest to deal with. Both adoptions are open and their parents are willing to let me meet them, but I'm afraid of spoiling things further; tainting everything with my presence. What if I ruin their lives by not showing up and being a stable adult in their lives? I'm not sure that I trust myself yet to even try.

"An update... wh-what is it?" I ask, testing out my voice.

Aunt Cindy looks at Kit briefly who gives a few short nods. "Yes, of course. Everyone is doing great. Little Allison is six now. She is in kindergarten this year and loves every minute, especially art time."

I try to picture a dark-haired little girl with dark brown eyes (the only feature I can accurately recall from her biological father) in a painting smock, but still covered in paint from head to toe. I can imagine her painting with abandon like the girl had done on stage at church a year ago. I smile at the thought and and let my eyes fill with tears.

"Peter just turned two this month and is quite a handful, so I hear! He especially loves to climb and kick a soccer ball around whenever he gets the chance." Aunt Cindy says with a laugh.

I feel the familiar twinge of regret as Aunt Cindy speaks about Peter. I never held him like I did with Allison, and this fact hits funny every time his name comes up.

What would I say?

Would Allison hate me?

Would Peter let me hold him?

My aunt's voice brings me back to the conversation again. "Wendy told me that both Allison and Peter's families are getting together for Easter this year. She was wondering if you might be interested in joining too?"

I know this already since I talked to Wendy about it a few days ago, but I told her what I always tell her: I'm not ready. I want to be ready, but I can't pretend like these hesitations don't exist inside of me.

"I-I don't know, Aunt Cindy," I manage to say, and it's all I can do to keep the tears in my eyes.

"You don't have to make any decisions about it now. Just think about it. Pray about it. You know we are all here for you, darling," Aunt Cindy adds with a warm smile.

"Yeah, Andrea, you know we wouldn't let you do it alone," Kit chimes in.

I nod my head, not trusting my voice to carry the words that my heart is feeling right now. I've been afraid to build this bridge the most because it would lead directly to the past that I have been desperately trying to rebuild from. *Allison and Peter are just kids*, I remind myself. They are not the mistake; they are the gifts. The beauty that came from the ashes of my past mistakes.

Connor, too.

I can't think about the children that shared my body without thinking about Connor, the baby I named but never met. I hate that he isn't here even if I couldn't be in his life. Anne had been working with me recently specifically on inner healing after my miscarriage. She even organized a small funeral in remembrance of him where I had the opportunity to prepare and speak a few words. He isn't here on this Earth, but I remind myself where he is and that makes me smile, the first one since Kit told me about her time in kid's church today, which makes me start to laugh. The uncontrollable laughter starts spilling out of my body and before I can provide any explanation, I rock back and forth with deep belly laughs. All I see in my mind is Kit shaking crumbs out of her shirt.

"What's so funny?" Kit asks, and it only makes me laugh harder.

Pretty soon, we are all laughing. Aunt Cindy, Kit, and I are causing a scene with all of the giggles swirling around our table.

We finally stop when our waitress comes over to take our orders. When she leaves, Aunt Cindy looks at me again and says, "Oh! I keep forgetting to tell you. Patricia and I had lunch last week and she wanted me to extend a hello to you."

After reuniting with my aunt, my favorite nurse, whom I affectionately named Curls in the hospital so long ago, had become close friends with my aunt after I gave birth to Peter. When I first learned that her real name was Patricia, I told her of the nickname I had given her years earlier when we first met. She laughed until tears leaked from her eyes and told me I better not call her anything but Curls from now on. I happily agreed.

"Tell her I say hi. Maybe we can meet for dinner next Saturday?" I suggest.

"I will text her and see. She will be tickled that you asked," says my aunt with joy visible in her features.

We finish our lunch with less emotional outbursts of crying or laughter and make our way back to my aunt's car. I regain my spot in the front seat and stare out the side window, watching the cars move speedily down the street as my aunt pulls onto the road.

My kids are out there. They are living and breathing and enjoying life, and I want so badly to catch a glimpse of them. Scratch that. I don't want a glimpse, I want a full-blown, life-size, colorful picture of who they are and who they're becoming.

My arms ache to hold them, I realize, and I'm finally letting myself dwell on it. I look down at my empty arms and consider, for the first time since I said those painful goodbyes, that maybe this is the first step...

Realizing that I need them like they need me.

CHAPTER 29
That Smile

May 2013—Age 22

"Hey, Andrea!"

I turn around in line at the coffee shop to see Jordan right behind me. *Breathe,* I coach myself after seeing his heart-stopping smile light up the space around us.

"Hey, Jordan," I smile back and half-wonder if my smile causes his heart to skip too. "Coffee before devotionals is always a good idea," I say, pointing to the espresso machine behind me and knowing there could not be a truer statement.

One of the few activities that the men and women's groups do together is our morning devotionals. Since Jordan is helping with the men's group now, I see him every morning, and his presence is growing on me.

"Absolutely, fuel before any activity is a good idea," he adds and his smile doubles in size, which also doubles the palpitations happening inside my chest.

Ever since my Aunt Cindy mentioned Jordan's excitement at seeing me, I have been... distracted. I have seen and talked to Jordan plenty of times during the two years I've lived at the Journey Center, but something has shifted and I don't know how or why. I am more aware of our interactions together and it's a little unsettling.

"Can I buy your drink for you this morning?" he asks with a slight hesitation that I'm not used to hearing from Jordan.

I pause, wanting to know exactly why he is offering, but decide to blindly accept his offer. "Sure. I never turn down free coffee." *True.* If someone handed you a cup of coffee on the streets, even if they drank half of it, you take it. That could be your only meal for the day. "I'll get you one next time," I respond, wondering if I am assuming too much that there would be a next time.

"Deal," he says, moving next to me in line and extending his hand to shake on it.

I grab his hand, which dwarfs my own, and start pumping up and down as we look at one another, matching smiles on our faces. One of us needs to stop this handshake before it continues into tomorrow.

It's me who stops it, be it awkwardly, and I realize I'm not exactly sure how to be friends with a guy. Handshakes weren't the kind of thing I was used to doing with the opposite sex. My experience taught me that men only wanted one thing, and it wasn't a simple handshake.

I shake my head and remember who I'm talking to. This is *Jordan.* He smiles at me, and now he buys me coffee. I am repaving the roads in my brain to tell a different story: men aren't *all* after one thing.

"Graduation is just around the corner, you ready?" Jordan asks, stepping closer to me as he does.

"Yeah, I guess so," I explain with a touch of sadness in my words.

Jordan crosses his arms across his strong chest and leans closer to me. "I was sad when I thought of leaving here too... that's why I stayed," he tells me in a hushed tone.

I nod my head, but don't turn to look up at him. His sincerity is enough to make me want to cry, I can't imagine what the look on his face would do. "I'm thinking about staying too. I just don't know what I want to do yet."

He stands back to his full height. "I'm sure you'll think of a way to stay and if you don't, I bet Janet will."

We both laugh knowing just how much Janet loves her job, how much she loves me. It's not actually a job to her, it's a mission—a passion.

"Did you ever feel like... well, did you ever..." My voice trails off and I look away. There is something vulnerable in the words that want to escape from my mouth and I can't seem to let them out. I briefly look over at him, realizing I'm fumbling over words that he probably won't understand.

He looks down at me, patient and waiting. We are almost to the front of the line, but he isn't in a rush. So much so, that when the line starts moving, he doesn't move with it.

"Did you ever feel like you couldn't really help others when you felt so messed up yourself?" I ask in a moment of boldness.

Our reasons for being here are obvious. If anyone knows how shaky my road to recovery has been, it's Jordan, but if he knew my thoughts, he'd know how much help I still need. I've been sober for over a year, but that doesn't mean I don't think about getting high still.

Jordan looks at me with a soft expression. "Yeah, I did... I do," he simply states. "My first year was rough.

Detoxing takes a lot out of a person," he says, not even skipping a beat in the conversation. "And every day after."

I look down at my sneakers peeking out from under my jeans as I take the step forward that Jordan never took. He follows my lead.

"If we waited until we were perfect, we'd be waiting for the rest of our lives," he adds with a wink that I catch when I have a moment of weakness and look up at him. I think I might just melt.

I see a warmth in his features. He knew just as much as he saw. "Do you ever wonder what would happen if you didn't stay sober. You know, like a relapse," I ask and then immediately wish I hadn't. Maybe that is too personal, or at least too personal for coffee line conversation.

"Well, I have relapsed," he divulges as easily as if he's talking about the weather. "It was just before the end of my first year. I couldn't stop thinking about having a drink until it consumed me. I took a sip and couldn't stop. Beau found me passed out in my room and helped me get through it, but it almost seemed harder the second time. That's why I did another year of the program, because I didn't complete the first."

I know what it feels like to be consumed by a thought. It holds on until you do something about it. At first, I believed that meant I needed to appease the thought but now I know there's a difference between wanting and needing.

I nod and look up at Jordan. "Thanks for sharing. I guess I didn't realize it was that personal until it fell out of my mouth, sorry about that."

"Nah, I try to live with my story wide open," he says just before the barista calls us up to the counter to take our orders.

After ordering and picking up our drinks of choice—a latte for me and black drip coffee for him—we walk towards the small chapel on the sixth floor. As a converted hospital formerly run by nuns, the Journey Center made sure to restore the chapel to its full glory. I love how the place exhibits its rich history through ornate paintings on the walls and ceiling. The dark brown wooden pews appear uncomfortable to the eye, but hold you steady and expectant. The smell of time and history have become just as familiar to me.

As we walk towards the doors that will lead us inside the narrow space, I turn to look at Jordan just before he rests his lips cautiously on the edge of his hot cup and can't help noticing the strong line of his jaw. The facial hair covering it was intentionally edged to perfection, and I can't stop noticing. He is handsome, and I am very aware of it, something I have trained myself to become indifferent to.

It's like my senses are waking up, and Jordan is the first one my eyes have settled on, making my body openly respond to him.

"Here, let me get that," Jordan says, crowding my thoughts when his large frame reaches around me to grip the handle of the chapel door and open it wide for us to enter.

Both of his tree trunk arms are covered in colorful tattoos from wrist to bicep, and possibly further, but I'm not about to ask him to lift up his sleeves to show me. He knocks my resolve off kilter with a light brush to my shoulder before making contact with the handle, and a shiver climbs up my exposed arm at the contact.

My first coherent thought is that I *felt* it. My body has long since left the numb stage, but this is the first time I have felt the warmth of a man's skin and my body welcomes it. The second thought is that I haven't moved since Jordan touched me.

"Is everything okay?" Jordan asks, while holding the chapel door open and waiting for me to enter, respond or, really do anything.

I shake my head, telling myself I will work out all of these feelings later. "Yeah, it is. Thanks for opening the door for me," I say warmly, meaning every single word. My smile breaks the line of my mouth, revealing a big, toothy grin that makes my eyes squint and my cheeks rise to meet them. I walk past him, far enough away that our bodies won't touch, but close enough that I can smell the hints of his aftershave.

Pine. Orange. Vanilla.

I'm transported to the safety of my aunt and uncle's home; a candle burning in the living room, my aunt in the kitchen, my uncle reading the paper on the couch, and me curled up on the window seat. This is the place I felt the most safe, and here I am inhaling the scent on Jordan. It is bringing all kinds of comfort. Tears spring to my eyes at the memory, but I continue walking towards the seat I know Kit is saving for me.

My coffee tastes like pure heaven in every sip. I'm listening to the speaker but can't really hear anything or pay attention when I feel Jordan's gaze burning directly into the side of my face. My olive skin feels flush, and my hand rises to cool my cheek. I am instantly reminded of the warmth from Jordan's touch earlier that is now permanently burned into my skin like the tattoos on his arms. His lingering looks are, apparently, having a similar effect on me.

When was the last time that a guy made me blush?

This is the first time that I can remember having a difficult time focusing. Usually these times are filled with encouragement as I let the words of whoever speaks that morning wash over me and settle the turmoil in my mind and heart. This morning, it was Jordan's gaze that was doing all of the washing. I feel it in every glance. He might as well be holding me in his arms since he is filling my senses and causing my stomach to perform flips before landing a complicated dismount.

I take another sip from my empty coffee cup just to give me something to do. I'm also internally scolding myself to not look in Jordan's direction, which I'm failing epically at.

When the lesson is over, I stand up with my empty cup to recycle it and greet some of the other women who I have come to love dearly. I try to train my eyes on Kit and the other women we are talking to as I peer out the corner of my eye to see where Jordan is at.

My eyes wander to the opposite side of the room, where they remember seeing him, only to come up short. *He was just there,* I think. I do a quick scan of the room until they land on their intended target only to find Jordan's eyes waiting to lock with mine. He doesn't look away like he had been doing, so neither do I. We stand there for one too many heartbeats, his caramel eyes emitting an electrical current I feel all the way to my toes. I take a breath in, hoping my racing heart will settle down, but the intimacy of this moment is pinning me to the spot and making focusing on anything else difficult right now. I can't look away as my body temperature continues to rise. My hands are clammy and my mouth runs dry. All of this *feeling* happening without a single touch.

"Andrea?" I hear my name called but don't respond, assuming there must be another Andrea somewhere.

"Hellooo, Andrea?"

Kit. My head snaps back to her and now my neck hurts from the momentum of my quick movement. "Oh, sorry," I immediately say out loud, massaging my neck. "I think I... uh... I thought there was something..." My finger is pointing to something, though I'm not sure what, as my words come out jumbled. I try to gather my wits and remember what Kit and I had been talking about but I'm coming up blank.

Luckily, Kit only shakes her head and smirks at me before she starts talking to Dominique, leaving me to swallow hard and try to exit this chapel without looking in Jordan's direction again. I'm sure my emotions are written all over my face.

Things are clearly changing with Jordan, and I wonder if it's a change I am ready for.

CHAPTER 30
Worthy of Love
May 2013—Age 22

I wake up the next morning feeling tired but excited for the day ahead. It is the weekly adopt-a-block that the Journey Center organizes every Saturday and has become a staple in my calendar. We load up as much food as the vans can carry as well as clothing and fun activities for the kids we will meet. There are plenty of families who come to the Journey Center daily to receive these items but some of them don't have a car or money to hop on a bus and get here to receive a hot meal, pick through the donation bin, or the food pantry. This is why we decide to go to them, and it is equally as rewarding for all of us who serve. It has become the highlight of my week because of the consistent relationships we form in the neighborhoods we visit.

The morning sun is climbing higher in the sky as I walk towards the passenger van to prepare to leave. I am mere steps away when I see a familiar looking haircut on top of a pair of broad shoulders looking relaxed while talking to Janet.

I trade my slumped and tired shoulders for a straight back and bright eyes when I approach. My body has long since adjusted to sleeping at night, instead of working, but that doesn't mean I enjoy early mornings. I fluff my wavy hair to give it the appearance that I did more than just wake up and go, which is exactly what I did.

I approach the group, quickly running my hands down my hooded sweatshirt and hole-filled jeans to remove any wrinkles the floor may have given them. "Hi, everyone," I say, announcing my presence and trying my best not to reveal any pleasure in seeing Jordan here.

Friendly and familiar faces turn in the direction of my greeting and each of them lifts a hand or smiles in hello.

"Good morning, Andrea!" Janet says above the group. "I am just running through some of the jobs I have for people today. Jordan is jumping in late so we are moving a few things around." Janet nods toward Jordan who lifts one of his crossed arms to wave at me. I can feel my cheeks beginning to turn red and I give him what I hope is a casual smile. My heart is thumping loudly, but I'm far enough away, I hope he can't hear it.

"Oh, awesome," I say before clearing my throat to continue. "Janet, do you still have me serving with the kids?" I ask, hoping her changes won't affect me. Getting to work with the kids is my favorite part of these Saturday outings.

"Yes, I do, and I added Jordan to your group, too, since we can always use more hands with the kids. Their numbers seem to double every week we go since they tell their friends!" Janet says with a small laugh.

I smile in reply and move to get into the passenger van, but not before I see the smile lifting Jordan's cheeks.

"Here, let me," Jordan says, reaching out his hand to help me into the van.

I look down at his offer, remembrance of the time he helped me out of the van jumps to the front of my mind. Jordan must have sensed my pause because he took another step closer, but never dropped his hand.

When I reach out and our palms touch, I can't stop my hand from clenching his tightly; I'm clinging to Jordan in more ways than one, and it takes everything in me to get into the van and not dive into his arms.

I can feel Kit watching me with a curious look the entire time but she waits until we are seated to say anything. She bends her head close to mine. "Are you doing okay this morning?"

"Yeah, I'm fine," I say, clearing the memory from my heart and mind. "Did you know Jordan was going to be here today?" I whisper, not wanting to draw any attention to us in this confined space. "He has never come before."

"True, but now that he is a program director, I am sure he wants to get involved with the outreaches," Kit replies, like this should be an obvious enough reason.

"Oh. Right. That's a good point." My beating heart takes a quick dip at the realization that I am likely reading into things more than I should. Jordan is a leader and is likely just doing leader-ish things.

Our recent interactions have done something to me. Call it a short circuit in my brain or a full reprogramming happening in my body, but I am having a hard time seeing Jordan as just my friend. Something was happening, and I'm not sure if I should freak out or lean in to it.

When we finally arrive at this inner city neighborhood, miles from the Journey Center but still firmly within the city limits, I am reminded again why we come here week after week. These families have needs that need filling, and we have resources that need giving. We also have time and people to help, so we do. Every week. Rain or shine. Although, in California, it's mostly shine. It is pure delight to watch all of the kids and families rush towards the van in the expectation of our arrival each week.

Janet hops out of the front seat and swings the sliding van door open for all of us to exit. "Andrea, why don't you grab the water balloons we brought out of the trunk; it is shaping up to be a scorcher today and I think a little water fun would be perfect." Janet says before giving everyone else their marching orders too.

I walk to the trunk to find Jordan pulling out cases of food, water, and diapers that are sure to be gone in just a few hours. His large body takes up most of the space and most of the air around us. I pause at the edge of the open door and watch his intentional movements, captivating me until I see him notice my presence.

My attention snaps back. "Hey, Jordan. I just need to snag those water balloons right there," I say, hoping I don't sound too breathy.

"No problem, here you go," Jordan says just as I'm leaning in to grab the balloons. We are both unable to stop our forward momentum, and our bodies are now crossing paths in slow motion. My left shoulder bumps into his sturdy chest, and I almost lose my balance and topple forward when I feel two hands grip my waist. One hand is firmly planted on my stomach and the other is gripping my lower back doing the trick of keeping me upright. My body has forgotten all about the arm graze, and is fully invested in the here and now.

I know it's an accident. I should be embarrassed. Yet, all I can think about right now is how Jordan's hands feel holding me.

Well done, Andrea, I think, and I really mean it.

His hands are like a brand on my waist, and I am left feeling too aware while we both stand there, motionless. All of my senses are on high alert as every second our bodies touch sprouts more awareness. More desire. More wonder. We aren't moving and I don't know why since he has saved me from my fall and all is well now, or so I believe. I make the mistake of turning my face towards his to question why he is still holding me—why I am still enjoying it.

Our current position is close, so close, that when I turn my head our lips are only inches apart. I don't look away; I can't look away, and neither does Jordan. His eyes wander around my face before settling briefly on my lips. I *have* to turn away; I *need* to or else I am going to make an even bigger mistake. A mistake that doesn't have an undo button.

His heartbeat is fast beneath his chest. I know this because I am plastered against him with only his t-shirt and a few layers of skin between me and his heart.

He is looking into my eyes again and no coherent thoughts are passing through my mind. My head starts to lean in ever so slightly, so slow that I don't even register the movement until a voice startles both of us. "Everything okay back here?" Kit asks, saying each word just as slowly, or at least that's how I'm hearing it.

I jump out of Jordan's embrace like he is on fire and I am trying to save myself, which is exactly the case here. "Oh, yeah, fine. Totally fine," I reply to Kit, exchanging my uneven voice for an odd, high-pitched squeaky one.

"All good," Jordan simply states as he reaches for the balloons and hands them to me.

Oh, right. The balloons. That's what I was doing here, in Jordan's arms. "Thanks again!" I tell Jordan before escaping around the corner of the van to cover the red hue I know is stamped from my forehead to my neck.

I can't stop thinking about our collision for the rest of the afternoon. Especially when I started to lean in. How embarrassing. Did he lean too? I was too absorbed in my own bodily responses that I didn't notice his. I secretly watch him speaking to the families who came for food, I hear his laugh above the loud voices and music, and I watch him chase children with the full water balloons, bobbing and weaving like an expert.

Nothing has sparked between us before... why now? I ponder.

"Why, what?" Kit's voice makes me jump as she approaches from behind and comes to stand beside me where the sidewalk and grass meets, biting into a juicy, red apple. Did I just ask that question out loud?

"You have to stop scaring me like that!" I scold her while telling my adrenaline to chill. "Do you at least have one of those for me?" I ask, eyeing her delicious snack.

She holds up another apple, expecting my hunger before she even walked over here.

"Relax, it's only me. And don't think you can change the subject that easily, *amiga*. You said 'why now' under your breath as I walked up. What are you questioning?" Kit presses.

"I wish I knew," I reply, sinking my teeth into the apple, gathering a large, juicy bite in my mouth in case Kit pushes me further.

"It wouldn't have anything to do with that tatted man who had his hands on your waist earlier, would it? You know, the one who's had one eye on you too?" Kit says with a teasing smile.

"What?" My eyes flash to where I know Jordan is. I cross my arms and give her a sideways glance. "You saw all that? I don't even know what's going on but, apparently you do, so maybe you should tell me."

"Well, I am noticing you notice him and vice versa, so, spill it," Kit replies, taking another bite of her apple and training her eyes on me. "What's going on with you two?"

I exhale sharply. "Fine," I give in. "It's been two years since Jordan rescued us from the streets. I have never looked at him as anything more than a hero and a friend but something is… changing. I have seen him around a lot more and I don't know…" I can't admit what my heart feels. It's too vulnerable, and I don't know enough about what's happening yet to try and explain it. "I guess it's just because I am seeing him more now. That's probably it." I look down at my apple, like it holds the answer I'm seeking, thankful I have something else to look at now other than Jordan.

"It makes sense. You both shared an incredible experience together. And to be fair, you wouldn't have even been able to notice him before now. You know how Janet and the other directors are about relationships while in the program; it's discouraged," Kit reminds me.

She's right. When someone is enrolled in a program, regardless of how many years in they are, relationships are discouraged in order to focus on healing. "True. But don't you think I would have noticed how his light brown eyes sparkle when he smiles or the way his blond hair moves when he runs? Am I really even saying these things out loud right now?"

"Yes, you are," Kit giggles. "And that's okay! Andrea, you have been through so much in the last two years. Your ability of choosing the men in your life was pretty terrible," she adds with an expression full of disgust.

The faces of the men I had been with bursts before my eyes and immediately, I am all too aware of the woman I was. The woman who slept with men she knew and those she didn't to earn a buck. I'm not that woman now, but I can't remove the things I have done no matter how much I want to.

"I'm losing you. What did I say?" Kit breaks through my train of thought with a small nudge to my side, trying to pull me out of my head.

"Nothing. You're right. I don't really have the best track record with men," I admit.

Someone like Jordan won't be interested in someone like me.

I twirl the apple in my hand before taking another bite, tasting the sweet crisp flavor in my mouth before it slides down my throat. I sense the emotion climbing up as the apple goes down. I'm not sad that Jordan probably doesn't see me as anything more than a friend, and I'm not hurt by Kit's words, but it does force me to become too aware of the blemishes that will always be a part of my life, and I question what it means for my future.

I look over at Jordan again, his smile beaming brightly as he runs after a kid that just soaked the front of his shirt. My heart squeezes at the thought of how good he is. His heart, his mind, his soul, his actions. Everything adding up and pointing to the man my own soul is desiring.

In the course of my therapy, I have never considered the possibility of liking a man in a romantic way. I had been with plenty of men in my life, and I wanted nothing more than to push them all far away. Jordan is my exception.

"You're right, you didn't have the best track record," Kit confirms. "But that doesn't mean you can't start fresh going forward. You're a different woman now, Andrea, embrace her."

I don't reply, but I do watch as Jordan catches up with the kid who soaked him, tossing him in the air like he weighs nothing while the kid giggles and smiles the entire time. Jordan turns his head and sees me watching and lifts his arm to wave at me.

My heart is in trouble, but it doesn't keep me from waving back as it leaps ahead of my mind. I am stuck somewhere in the middle of knowing I am worthy of love and believing that it's true.

CHAPTER 31
Dance with Me

May 2013—Age 22

Abuelita has the music up loud when I walk into the kitchen that afternoon. She doesn't notice when I first come in because she is too busy bobbing her head and swaying her hips to Celia Cruz's song, *La Vida Es un Carnaval,* working up a sweat while stirring the spaghetti sauce. For every tear that I have cried on *Abuelita* Gloria's shoulder, there are twice as many smiles that this woman pulls out of me too, and it's happening again. A giant smile is painted on my face and all I can think is how good it feels.

She turns away from the stove and sees me, my hairnet and apron already on and ready for work, but that doesn't stop her.

"*Ven aquí, Mija*—come here, daughter! Dance with me!" *Abuelita* says loudly above the music, waving her hand to come closer to her. She is always drawing me in and encouraging me to let loose through dance.

"Let me just check the garlic bread first," I say, trying to evade her prodding.

"Freddy just checked it! Ay, it is time to move," she insists. I join her and we start slow with the basic salsa footwork so I can catch her rhythm. My feet don't always want to move this way and it has taken a lot of practice for me to master the basics, but I think I'm there.

"Rock forwards once. Backwards once. Reverse feet," *Abuelita* says out loud as my clunky footwork follows hers. I can't imagine high-top sneakers are the ideal shoe for this dance, but they're better than seven-inch heels.

I'm trying my best to keep up while *Abuelita* makes it look too easy by tasting the sauce, pulling out utensils, and directing people in their work all while keeping to the rhythm. I'm attempting to avoid the other cooks in the kitchen, but it's impossible at the rate *Abuelita* has my feet moving. I keep my eyes trained on the floor most of the time so I don't trip over our feet, or my flared jeans that skim the kitchen floor at my heels.

"I don't know how you cook a whole meal and find the energy to dance, *Abuelita*," I say with an out-of-breath laugh.

"This is how I stay young, *Mija*. Keep dancing and you will see." She is encouraging me forward with her hands and before I can argue, *Abuelita* is reaching for me again.

My feet are picking up speed as I try to keep up with her moves. She can still dance circles around me and does so often enough, but she's also the most patient teacher I can remember having. Her instructions are plain, but they are piled high with encouragement. *Abuelita* is fluid in her steps. The way she flicks her wrists and moves her hips while adding more spice and personality to every motion. It tells of the many years of kitchen dancing she has done.

"Salsa is all about feeling the music, Andrea. Do not focus too much on your feet or your body—they will catch up, I promise you. Feel the dance and your feet will follow," she coaches me. I listen even though my body still moves awkwardly. My mind follows the more intricate foot patterns she tries teaching me but the flow of my body is still trying to catch up.

My hips are a half-beat behind hers and it's starting to become obvious. "Is this right? I feel like my hips and feet are out of sync."

"Let the music draw you in. Don't overthink it." she tells me as if it's the easiest thing in the world. I let out another breath and try again. My toes are pointed, shoulders following in their direction, and my hips matching the beat of the song.

"There, that's it!" *Abuelita*'s smile shines clear in her expression. Her brows are lifted, eyes twinkling, mouth open and smiling, and cheeks puckered. If her facial expressions don't do the talking, her hands will. They are constantly bouncing up and down, in and out and all around her short frame.

We take another spin around the kitchen island, my basic steps nearly perfect and the sway of my hips causing me to take flight. I know what joy feels like: it's this, right here. I'm letting loose and it feels so freeing! *Abuelita* embodies joy like she's made of it, and in this moment, I am too.

I shimmy backwards to where the kitchen door and serving line meet before I bump into something hard but softer than the wall I assume I have run into.

Two hands have gripped the sides of my shoulders to steady my unbalanced body from collapsing altogether—again. I freeze, afraid to face the music behind me. Celia

Cruz is doing a fine job at singing but the anticipation between all of us rings louder. Much louder. My mind catches up to my body, which has been let loose (thanks to *Abuelita*) to feel the music, when I hear the voice just behind my head.

"Hey, Andrea, *Abuelita*."

Please tell me that walls can talk, I plead.

Abuelita's wide, brown eyes look directly at the hazel rings in mine. I stare back, unsure what to do next, but she doesn't seem to have that problem. I hear *Abuelita* burst into laughter, and I want to cover my face with my hands because I am mortified. *Oh no!* I whip around quickly, finding the rock solid structure I had just bumped into belonging to the smooth voice I have started secretly listening for. My eyes grow wide like a startled animal to find Jordan laughing along with *Abuelita*, his eyes glued to my reddening cheeks.

Heat. So much heat. In my face, my hands, my forehead. How long had he been watching me before I... before we...?

"Andrea has been working on her salsa. What do you think?" *Abuelita* asks Jordan and all I want to do is hide in the freezer.

My hands can't help but find the sides of my face to cool the sizzling temperature that has only gained momentum in the span of seconds.

"I can tell you have been teaching her everything you know," he says to *Abuelita* before looking back at me. "Great moves, Andrea." He slips his hands into the front pockets of his dark wash jeans; the t-shirt he wears works effortlessly to accentuate his upper arms.

I can't pull my eyes away until *Abuelita* clears her throat and my eyes find hers, my cheeks reddening even further.

"Of course, I taught her everything I know. Andrea is a great student!" *Abuelita* says with a flip of her short, salt and pepper colored hair that is covered by a hairnet, indicating her clear opinion on the matter.

"I heard the music from the hall and it brought me back to the good old times. I was planning to come ask for a dance before I bumped into your new partner," Jordan adds, nodding his head towards me. My hands have since left my face but they are a breath away from fighting another flare up.

"Ay, Jordan, you are always invited! You know you are my second favorite dance partner," *Abuelita* says while turning down the volume to her beloved Celia Cruz a few more notches. "Isaac, can you prep the salad, *por favor*," *Abuelita* asks, keeping the fluid motion of her kitchen operating smoothly at all times.

"Second, huh?" Jordan's eyes find mine again causing my breath to hitch as his smile lengthens across his handsome face revealing two dimples that make my breathing irregular.

I venture to use my vocal chords after his sudden use of that wickedly adorable smile. "Wait, you used to work in the kitchen?"

"I think most of us have at some point. I helped in the kitchen for a while, kind of like you, but I can see that I've been replaced." Jordan gives *Abuelita* a wink, and she starts fanning her face and giggling. I get it, he has this effect on most of us around here.

"I should let you gals get back to your dancing—" he clears his throat, "I mean, working." That smile is at it again, making my stomach do all sorts of fluttery things.

"Not so fast." *Abuelita* speaks up. My head turns in her direction wondering how else I can expect to be embarrassed today.

"My two favorite salsa partners must dance together now," she says pointing her finger between the two of us and waving for us to close the gap.

I pipe up first, wanting to give us both a way out of this, and fast. "Jordan is probably really busy and we have to finish up dinner prep in the next twenty minutes, *Abuelita*," I tell her, pointing at the clock on the wall like its the boss around here.

"I'm not busy," Jordan says without pause.

My mind can't pull up another excuse before the sound of a loud clap startles me. *Abuelita* is sealing the deal for me. My eyes snap to Jordan who shrugs and pulls his hands out of his pockets like he's going to hold mine.

I look back at *Abuelita* for help but she is positively enthusiastic about her idea. "Yes, this will be *fantástica*! Let me choose the song. We will finish dinner while you two dance."

I sheepishly look at Jordan, wondering if he is having second thoughts, but all I see is his tall frame walking towards me already and a distinct confidence in those light colored eyes of his.

He reaches out his hands towards me. "You ready?"

I stare at his outstretched arms. "Um, yeah, I guess so. I've never really danced with anyone else other than *Abuelita* before, I won't be very good." He needs to know what he is signing up for.

"That's okay, we'll figure it out together." Jordan looks down at his still open hands, waiting for me to grab them, but I'm frozen. My mind is racing, my body is still, and my heart is so loud, I can hear the beat in my ears.

Before I can come up with another short-lived excuse, *Rie y Llora*, starts playing through the speakers. "Freddy, turn up the volume!" *Abuelita* says, rolling her shoulders and waving at me to take Jordan's hand.

I put my hand in his, hesitantly, wondering if any sparks would shock me or not. His large hand is warm and inviting as his fingers close to envelope my hand in his. My hand might've been safe from sparks, but the jolt that occurs when his other hand rests on my waist is another thing entirely. Heat is coursing through my body at an alarming rate. It feels like the heat from his palm will burn a hand-shaped hole right through my apron *and* t-shirt.

We start off slowly so our feet can synchronize, just like I did with *Abuelita* minutes, hours, days ago? I can't tell because this afternoon has been going on forever already. I do know that I was far less nervous when I danced with her. The rhythm of the song picks up at the chorus, causing our movements to naturally speed up. Jordan doesn't skip a beat, and he's not even looking at his feet like I keep doing.

I look up for a brief moment, wondering what his secret is to such fluid movements, and his eyes never leave my face. He is so intent, I forget to breathe for a minute until I realize I need my breath if I'm going to pace myself through this dance. I can sense the timidity in my hips as we move; I know I'm holding back and I wonder if he can tell.

The few times I venture a look at him he's looking down at me, except for that one time I catch him winking at *Abuelita*, which of course sends her into a fit of laughter.

"Oy vey, Jordan, look at you go!" *Abuelita* encourages while simultaneously listing off instructions to the others.

My feet are moving quickly, trying to keep up with Jordan and the pace of the song. He is still gripping my hand when he spins me out, unexpectedly, but with a controlled ease and my hairnet almost goes flying off my head.

Wait, my hairnet?! That's right. I'm dressed for the kitchen, not dancing.

I'm stamped in embarrassment, but I don't have time to linger on this fact, however, before Jordan spins me back towards his body where I land with less grace and more thud, but it's hardly noticeable since his firm grip is holding me securely against him. I hold my breath, unable to release it in fear this moment will leave with it.

When I do speak, I hardly recognize my own voice. "Oh, sorry! That was a rough landing," I say through my labored breaths.

My gaze moves upward, the same mistake I made last time I was flat against his body, and I suddenly note just how close we both are. I am like a pancake on his chest, smashed so close our faces are only one movement apart.

I'm breathing harder now that my body is no longer in motion. I turn my head away quickly, avoiding the hooded look in his eyes that is surely a reflection of my own, but I can't find the strength to pull away completely. My body feels alive and not just because of the dance we just shared. Jordan's hand is sprawled across the middle of my back, holding me pressed closely to him. My chest is rising and falling, and I feel his heavy breaths moving the hair framing my face that have escaped from my hairnet.

My hand that was resting on his shoulder reaches up to push away the hair that has fallen into his face like it's been doing this forever. It's so natural. I am all too aware of the effect our close contact is having on me, but I can't stop my heart from taking charge. I had been transported out of the kitchen to a realm only Jordan and I existed in for a few blissful minutes, but the reality of many watchful eyes shakes me out of it. I pull my hand out of his and use my other to gently push off of his chest and out of the safety of his arms. My breathing is still heavy, likely even more so now that the thinking part of my brain is coming back to life.

I peer at *Abuelita*, conscious of the scene she has just witnessed, but all I see from her is an agreeable smile and with that she is moving around the kitchen to find Freddy or Isaac or really anyone.

I look back at Jordan who gives a small bow, never taking his eyes off of me. "Thank you for dancing with me, Andrea."

"Sure," is about all I can manage to get out through the breaths I'm working hard to take. I turn to the kitchen island to hold me upright.

"Thank you again *Abuelita*, I can always count on you," Jordan says, raising his voice so it carries across the kitchen to where *Abuelita* is telling Freddy something. I see a look pass between them and it makes me wonder.

No, no, Abuelita wouldn't plan something like this.

Wait, would she?

Would Jordan?

Jordan turns to leave and struts towards the door with more swagger than one man should be allowed to possess and starts to rock each foot backwards, then forwards in the recognizable salsa pattern. I try not to stare but his moves are perfect, and I admire how easily the rest of his body follows suit. He looks over his shoulder at me and winks as if I'm not already melting.

When Jordan's well-timed footwork sashays out the door, I turn my questioning eyes towards *Abuelita* without moving my body. She has a gleam in her eye as she matches my gaze and I feel transparent.

My mouth is open in surprise and I shake my head abruptly to break out of my trance. *"Abuelita,* is there something you want to tell me?" My breathing is still normalizing after our short dance, and I'm still holding onto the counter for physical and moral support.

"Sí, yes, he is a great dancer, you see!" she says motioning towards the doors that Jordan has just danced out of.

I lower my lids and study her intently, willing her to crack. "Hm. Is that all you want to tell me about that… dance?" I see the sparkle in her eyes before I watch the smile peel across her face.

"Ay, okay, you caught me," *Abuelita* replies, not the least bit concerned that I know. "I picked the song but it wasn't my idea."

"Wait… so… that… he…" I'm out of words just like I was out of breath. I want to point the finger at someone but I'm no longer upset about it.

"I am so glad you know each other. Jordan is a very good man, *Mija,"* *Abuelita* adds, like I'm not already failing to notice every time we are together and when we're not.

"Él es muy guapo también," *Abuelita* tells me with a wink and a giggle as she moves to the stove to stir the sauce and add another pinch of salt, Celia still serenading us in the background. I know more Spanish these days but *Abuelita's* words are too fast and I'm not able to follow her.

I tuck the stray hairs back into my hairnet as I look over at her, a teasing tone in my voice. "What are you saying now, *Abuelita?"*

"He is very handsome, no?" I had a feeling she read my face like a book after that dance. I thought I was the only one who felt the heat. I hoped I wasn't so readable, but the fluorescent kitchen lights must be telling a different story. I grab a few oven mitts to pull the garlic bread out of the oven to check that it is heated through and try to channel a relaxed version of myself.

"Yeah, sure. He's cute, I guess." *Very casual.*

Even though *Abuelita* is completely silent, I can feel the intensity of her smile behind me as I extract the tray from the steamy oven.

The conversation plays out in my head as we finish up dinner and begin serving it to the hungry residents and local community members. I put a slice of garlic bread in each of the to-go containers and try my best not to crack a smile as I recall Jordan's salsa moves when leaving the kitchen... or the feel of his hand on my back as it held me closer to his body... or the smile that was only for me.

Yeah, I remembered that too, and trying to pretend I didn't wasn't working.

CHAPTER 32
Thanks for Waiting
May 2013—Age 22

"Andrea, are you ready to leave? Did you want to go talk to someone first?"

I pull my attention back to Aunt Cindy, who is now standing patiently beside me and has been talking to me for who knows how long. I'm lost in thought and the memory of being in Jordan's arms while we danced in *Abuelita's* kitchen last week. I can't seem to shake it but, then again, I'm also not trying too hard. These thoughts run through my mind but never seem to tire, even with their constant replay.

I stand from my seat and follow her out of the row in the crowded church auditorium. "Yeah, sorry, we can leave," I tell her. My thoughts about Jordan are a muddled mess. I've never felt this way about a man, and here I am acting like the school girl I never was.

"Great, let's grab more coffee before we walk back for lunch. Oh! I also want to tell Gladys how good that book is that she let me borrow last week," Aunt Cindy replies.

"Sure thing. I could use another fill up too. Kit, are you joining us?" I turn back to look at her as she follows close behind.

"Absolutely," she says, gripping her sketchbook in her arms and hiking her side-bag further up her shoulder.

When we push through the front doors of the church several minutes later, we all welcome the fresh air. "I didn't think we were going to get out of there with all of those people swarming us like that!" Kit says with a laugh as the sunshine bears down and begins warming our chilled bodies thanks to the indoor air conditioning.

"I almost didn't! Gladys started chatting my ear off about her grandson," I tell them, rolling my eyes.

"She's just looking out for you," Aunt Cindy says with a small shake to my shoulder.

"You weren't much help when you asked about her nephew that she mentioned the week before," I tell her with zero surprise in my expression.

"What? I am an interested party just trying to help out my own niece!" Aunt Cindy counters back.

Kit laughs louder than our side conversation, and we both turn to look at her. "You know all of the old women at church are always playing matchmaker, Andrea. Gladys introduced me to one of the worship leaders a few weeks back and then just walked away. No 'goodbye' or 'see you later.' Nothing. She just dropped the mic, so to speak, and walked off."

"Only she can get away with something like that!" I respond through my own deep belly laughter.

Aunt Cindy and Kit lead the way on the narrow sidewalk back to the Journey Center. We haven't talked about where we will go to lunch, but I have a good guess where we'll end up.

We had only just started walking when I hear my name being called. I turn my head back to see Jordan's arm in the air waving me down. "Andrea, wait up!"

He really knows how to make a girl catch her breath while she's doing absolutely nothing, like standing. My heart jumps five feet in the air before I spin fully around towards Jordan and Beau as they make their way over to me. I take a look back towards the sidewalk, but Aunt Cindy and Kit haven't noticed that I've stopped.

"Hey, thanks for waiting. Do you mind if we walk with you?" Jordan asks. "I'm guessing we're all going to the same place."

"Oh, yeah, no problem." I wave them over to join me.

I'm giving myself a pep talk in my mind while quickly looking down at my outfit today, in gratitude that I'm not wearing my apron or hairnet. I have on a shortsleeved, coral colored blouse with a dark pair of skinny jeans and black flats.

Jordan, Beau, and I walk past the houses and businesses that are pressed into tight quarters and looking tighter every time a new building project starts. Beau talks about the foster care youth he is working with to support and educate them after they age out of the system, and it is fascinating to hear. It is so different from my own experiences. The Journey Center team really does have their hands in every aspect of community support networks; I can barely keep track of everything they help with.

Jordan and I listen attentively until Beau looks up to see the distance Kit and my Aunt Cindy have already traveled. "Hey, I'm going to go tell Kit something. I will catch up with you both in a bit," Beau says before running up ahead and leaving us behind.

I take a deep breath. Jordan and I are alone together but also completely surrounded by the activity of the busy street and active neighborhoods we pass through.

My feelings for him don't exactly make for good conversation, so I try another tactic to avoid the part of me that screams the loudest. "I imagine a lot of those foster kids who Beau is helping find jobs or education have crazy stories too. You were in foster care, right? What was it like?"

He clears his throat and tucks both of his hands into his back pockets. He looks completely at ease in my presence while I feel like there is a storm brewing inside of me.

"Most of my experiences were pretty tame. I had been in a couple of different families before being placed with my Grams. The last family that I lived with was my favorite, though."

"Oh yeah, why is that?" I ask, hoping more information about Jordan won't draw me in further.

"I was a preteen and in the most awkward phase of my life when I went to live with them. My voice was changing, my feet were too big for my body and I was hungry all the time," Jordan describes, his voice thick with memory and lined in laughter.

"You are just full of surprises today. I can't picture an awkward, pre-teen Jordan," I laugh, thinking about the young boy Jordan describes. It sounds nothing like him, but then again, we all go through an awkward phase.

He looks over at me and huffs out a laugh. "It's true, I promise. My shoes made me look like a clown walking around in them because they were so big," Jordan admits while shaking his head side to side.

"I'll have to take your word for it since I didn't know you back then," I tell him as my eyes lower to block the brightly lit sun. "Were there any other kids that you lived with?"

"Oh yeah. Five."

"Five other kids!" I say, more out of surprise rather than question.

"Yup. Two of the kids were adopted and three were biological. My foster parents didn't think they could have kids and were surprised with three."

"That would be a surprise—wow." I steal a look at Jordan who is starting to slow down. I peer in front of us to see why and notice the sidewalk is narrowing even more. I pick up the pace to walk in front of him and as I do, Jordan's hand finds my lower back, and he gently guides me forward.

My shirt is flowy and it tickles my skin beneath Jordan's lightly pressed hand on my body and it feels as if it is grazing my bare skin. It doesn't last long since only a few paces ahead the sidewalk begins to widen again and I already feel the loss of his hand. He drops it slowly but not without trailing his fingers across my back as he pulls away. I want to look at him to see if he notices my reaction and to see if I can notice his. I twist my head slowly to the side and see a relaxed expression that puts my own nerves at ease.

I exhale a breath and remind myself who I'm with. He makes my skin tingle and my pulse race, but I'm not afraid, and that feels like progress.

Jordan continues his story without a second thought to his effect on me. "There were a lot of kids in the house but I never felt like an added burden. I was a part of their family even if it was only for a few months. I actually kept contact with one of their sons, who is a year older than me."

"It sounds like that was a pretty special time for you. I mean, considering all of the other circumstances you were dealing with, it probably felt good to be in a stable family." I think about what stability has done for me, and I feel relieved. "My aunt is the only stable person I've ever had, and it has made the biggest difference in my life," I share, though I surprise myself by my willingness to do so. It is hard to think of Aunt Cindy's persistence to be in my life without tearing up. She has fought ruthless battles to see me as the woman I am today.

"I can see how much you mean to her and how much you love her too. Family is a beautiful thing," Jordan says in a tender voice.

"It is both a beautiful thing and a complete nightmare wrapped into one weird package," I add with a short laugh, bringing a lightness back to the conversation.

Jordan laughs at my description, and I love the hearty sound that it makes. It is doing nothing to slow my growing desire, but I choose to enjoy every minute of it regardless. His hands are back in his pockets again, and I see his tattoos moving beneath the flex and release of his arm.

"I didn't get it until I got to the Journey Center. Everything came alive through new friends, mentors, therapy, church. I saw what a family looked like," I explain, aware of how much this has changed me to find a group of people that surround me on all sides.

"I had a similar experience. Now the people here are my family," he confirms while nodding towards our final destination that I can now see in the distance.

We are walking through the parking lot when I see my Aunt Cindy standing outside the entrance, looking up at the sun with her eyes closed when we approach. "Oh, there you both are. I'm going to go grab my purse and I will meet you and Kit by my car. It's just over there," she says, pointing to her white Mazda nestled between the parking lot lines nearby.

"Sounds good," I say and watch Aunt Cindy walk towards the building I would call home for only a few more weeks.

Kit is still engaged in a conversation with Beau when I turn back to Jordan to offer a reluctant goodbye. "Well, it was great talking to you, Jordan. Thanks for walking with… us," *me*, I want to add.

I raise a hand to block the sun as I stare up at him and I see Jordan's intentions for a proper goodbye. He is facing me, extending his arms to either side of his body in a half circle: he is asking, inviting, waiting for me to stop him from hugging me. I don't. Quite the opposite, in fact. I open my arms and lean in.

His arms reach completely around my back and I turn my head to the side so I won't collide with him. My cheek is resting against his chest and I inhale deeply, smelling the familiarity on him once again and wishing the minutes that pass would somehow shift into hours.

I can feel my heartbeat in my ears as it drums loudly, or maybe that's his? The unique pattern of its beating matches my own. I entangle my arms around his waist and lay my palms flat against his back. Our bodies were in the shape of an "A," leaning on one another but maintaining some semblance of distance. Jordan, unsatisfied, tugs me closer to remove even more of that distance, and I feel the warmth of his body enveloping my senses. This place in his arms feels comfortable, and it feels safe. I'm not leaving.

My brain and body are both glitching from this close contact hug, and I can't make heads or tails of how I should act. I just *am*.

He speaks first because I can't based on how dry my mouth is.

"Thanks for waiting for me," he says, so quietly that I don't think the words are intended for me to hear, but I do. I'm not sure how to interpret their meaning. I assume he meant waiting on the sidewalk so he could walk back with me, but the way he says it has me considering other options too.

I close my eyes and let out a slow deep breath, wanting nothing more than to stay right here in this hug. I swallow so my mouth isn't so dry and I can find words to respond. "Sure, thanks for the conversation," I say quietly since my voice is muffled against his body that is surrounding all sides of me.

When our arms reluctantly release one another, I feel the remnants of his warm body on my suddenly bare arms and cheek. I'm aware of every inch of our distance. One of his hands trails down my arm and squeezes my hand before severing our contact altogether with the drop of his hand. The sun is shining high above us now, but a chill runs through me and makes me miss the embrace we just shared. He holds eye contact, speaking more through the expression in his eyes than he did with his words.

"Hey, Andrea, Aunt Cindy is waiting for us. You ready?" Kit calls out to me.

"Yeah, I, uh... coming!" I quickly reply, trying to recover from our hug. A hug! That's what is unraveling me: a simple hug.

I look at Jordan shyly, like we have just shared more in this parking lot. I'm no longer hungry for lunch. I only want to escape back into his arms to feel the safety and security I just found there. I reluctantly wave goodbye to

Jordan while turning to make my way towards Kit and the waiting vehicle.

I feel his eyes on me as I walk away, and now the sunshine feels unbearably hot.

CHAPTER 33

Graduation

June 2013—Age 22

"I'm so glad that's over," Kit says as we walk side-by-side back to the Journey Center. "I thought I would fall apart with nerves or fall off the stage altogether."

I laugh because I had the same fear, however irrational it was.

We had our graduation ceremony this afternoon at the church, and now we are officially done with the program. I honestly can't believe it. I'm so used to the work and my routines that I can't imagine them ending. In many ways, I don't want them to. They meant everything to me, and now that's all changing.

"Agreed. Walking on a stage with everyone watching was making me sweat bullets," I admit to Kit. "I'm just glad I didn't trip." There were so many eyes watching me, ones that knew me and plenty that didn't, and I was terrified I'd mess it all up. Now that it's over, I'm ready to celebrate.

"These gowns weren't really helping on that account," says Kit. "They're like wearing a sauna." She's holding up the black gown that is now draped across her arm.

Kit was offered a new gig in the foster youth program at the Journey Center. She has some unfinished business that she intends on making right as soon as she starts working. Kit grew up in foster care and so did her brother, who she hasn't been able to find any trace of for years.

There are so many feelings for both of us today. I'm nervous for the future since it will look different than my present, and change is still hard for me. Mostly, I'm excited for these possibilities. Janet asked me to work with her in the emergency women's shelter after graduation, and I realize there is really nothing else I want to do more than that. I want to be the face those women see when they don't think they can detox or walk away from the things that tried to swallow them whole. I want to tell them they can do hard things. I want to see the look on their faces when they do.

I look over at Kit, the woman I escaped with and the friend I have gained in the process. "Ugh, you're right, the gown was one step away from a garbage bag," I tell Kit. "But it was all worth it in the end." They are boxy and stifling, but still symbolize an accomplishment I never considered possible.

Kit leans closer to me and bumps my shoulder. "We made it through and now we get to eat! I'm starving. Did Janet say what we would be eating tonight?" Kit asks while adjusting her dress and running her hand through her long, dark brown hair.

"She didn't, but I know *Abuelita* was in charge of the menu so you know her famous tamales will be there," I tell Kit with a confident nod.

When we finally step foot onto the campus and approach the door to the cafeteria, the smell of meat encased in a corn husk hug consumes the air around us. *Tamales.*

"I guess that clears up any doubts about that matter," Kit laughs as my stomach growls in anticipation for the food just around the next bend in the hallway.

As we enter, I see all of the faces we have come to adore over the last two years smiling back at us. Joy-filled tears spring to my eyes, and I blink them away. I'm overwhelmed to see everyone in the same space, celebrating for reasons beyond graduating the program. We are survivors, and that is worth the whole of it.

Aunt Cindy spots me first and walks over with her arms already extended and inviting. "I am so proud of you, honey! You did it! You got your GED and you passed your program finals. I am just so thrilled for you!"

I see her pride, and I know my face is reflection of hers. Aunt Cindy reaches to pull me into a hug, and I cling to her tightly. I can physically feel the energy bouncing around the room as all of the happy graduates bask in the acceptance that none of us thought was attainable.

Abuelita isn't far behind my aunt when I see her waving her hand in front of her face to fend off the tears. It isn't working though, and the moment we embrace I can hear her tears echoing in my ear.

"*Mija*, you are so beautiful and you were beaming up on that stage!"

"Thank you *Abuelita*," I whisper for her ears only.

I move around the room slowly, congratulating friends, hugging the women I have watched detox from their drug of choice, and smiling at the family members who have been reunited with them. It's as much a day for our families as it is for us. It's the most beautiful mess of people I've ever seen.

Another light touch grazes my back. "Let's get some food, I bet you're hungry," Aunt Cindy says before patting the side of my shoulder and leading me to grab a plate and get in line. We fill our plates with all of the delicious food prepared by *Abuelita,* and the smell is enough to make me kiss her cheek as I pass through the line. My aunt leads us to one of the circular cafeteria tables and we join the swirl of stories from the last two years that are being shared.

I scoop some Spanish rice onto my fork and add to the conversation. "Remember the pants, Kit?" I say before taking a bite.

"Of course, that is still the best drawing I have done to date!" she replies proudly. I'm proud too, considering I never stepped on them.

I look around at the others sitting at our our table. "It really is. When Kit told me she was drawing a pair of pants, I didn't have very high expectations, but you have to see the drawing."

When my food is devoured and the conversation settles, I stand to track down the dessert that Kit says will blow my mind. I'm almost to the serving counter and ready to get a triple fudge brownie when a well-known shadow steps into my path. This time, I managed to stop before bumping into him.

"Hey, Andrea," I hear. "Congratulations!" Jordan says, giving my shoulder a light squeeze. He stands across from me, eyes sparkling and teeth gleaming.

His light touch makes me feel seen. "Oh, hey, thank you," I respond with a smile, feeling every ounce of his belief in me as the heat rises to my cheeks. I dip my head down, tucking a loose strand of hair behind my ear to hide the blush that is here to stay. I'm not a nervous person, but it seems whenever Jordan is around, I'm giddy, confused, nervous, happy—all of it.

Jordan's gaze lingers on my face. "You look really beautiful," he adds with a half-smile that causes my pulse to become visible through my skin.

Abuelita had noticed, and now so did Jordan but it sounds different coming from his lips than it did from hers. I feel every bit of what this word means today, body and soul.

I look up into his eyes with a smile, and I can feel my blush deepening. "Thank you. Everyone is dressed up on a special day like today," I say, grasping for neutral territory where the attention on me becomes the attention on we.

"Your dress really brings out the color of your eyes." Jordan's hand reaches to rub the back of his neck, adding to his boyish charm. I see such pure adoration in his eyes, and it feels weighty because it's directed at me.

I look down quickly, like my eyes are seeing more than they should, and shove my hands into the hidden side pockets of my dress. "I don't know, you should have seen the mannequin that was wearing it before me. She was the one who convinced me to buy it in the first place." Humor. Good. Neutral. Safe.

I lift my head and see his laugh building before I hear it. It starts as a painfully alluring smile and then his head tips back before a deep, rolling laughter sets in that I physically feel shake the ground beneath me. I join him and both of our smiles are wide.

"Okay, you win. That was a good one," Jordan says in between deep chuckles. He's shaking his head back and forth, and I can't help notice the color of one of his tattoos peeking up from the edge of his collared shirt. The warmth in my gut spreads when I see his smile and hear his next words. "I serve you with a compliment and you hit me with some humor. I like it."

The remnants of his laughter still lights up his face while he looks at me. I wish I could look down like I did before but his light-toned eyes are captivating, especially with admiration still shining in them.

"You're pretty special, Andrea," Jordan adds in a serious tone.

His desire and my scrutiny are at odds. "I'm not all that special," I say, scanning the other faces of the people in the room. My reply is painfully close to the truth. I've never been the girl to accept compliments with ease, but I'm finding that I want to learn how to accept Jordan's. I want to be the girl he says these things to, even if I don't know how to be her yet. If only this were another role I could learn, but it feels too vulnerable and important for just another act.

I glance down at my wedge heels, deep in my thoughts when I feel Jordan's finger grace the tender skin beneath my chin. He lifts my head so I can witness his insistent gaze but he doesn't drop his hand right away, and we are locked inside the intimacy of this moment for far too many unstable seconds.

Remembering where we are and who we're with, he drops his hand away slowly, but never his eyes. His gaze bores into every part of me, and I'm swimming in caramel and drowning in their power. Jordan tugs at the edge of his shirt collar but doesn't look away. I'm helpless to look anywhere else.

His low, steady voice speaks. "Do you remember what I told you the night we talked on Figueroa Street before you decided to come meet us?"

"I, uh, I... don't remember many of the details from that night. Just the highlights," I tell him because I can't think when he looks at me like that.

"I said you are worthy," his hand reaches for my hand. "Cherished," he adds, rubbing his thumb across my knuckles. "And far more precious than the rose I handed you, and I meant every word I told you that night..." His words drop off as my hand drops from his and I study his face for an indication of what he isn't saying. He opens his mouth only to close it again, and I see the turmoil he's wrestling with. I beg him with my eyes to continue, though I sense I may not be ready for it.

"I said those things before I knew you, really *knew* you, and now... I think they have only become more true. You are really special to me, Andrea."

My heart starts skipping to a new rhythm inside my chest and my lips separate at this admission. "What makes you say that now?" Fully aware that questions lead to answers, and they might be answers I'm not ready to hear. I tempt myself with knowing anyway.

Jordan starts to explain. "Because I——"

"Never mind, don't answer that." I cut in, backtracking when I realize what he might say. My mind and heart are at it again, fighting like young children over a toy neither of them can have. I can feel my heart racing faster and I sense the panic rising to the surface. What is happening to me? He is slowly upheaving another layer of my heart, and I'm not sure I'm ready. I let out a heavy sigh at the same time my mind is fighting to be in the driver's seat.

Jordan tries again. "I think when given a chance, roses are most stunning when they open up in full bloom," he pauses, and it takes everything in me to not look directly into his eyes. I'm looking over his shoulder, at his chin, his shoes, his hands moving rhythmically as he talks, but not his eyes. I won't look there because I know what I'll see. I know what I'll feel and it's too risky.

"You've opened up a lot in the last couple of years, and I guess what I'm trying to say is... I've noticed."

The words have been said. The words I've longed to hear but couldn't voice. I'm doubting my journey in this one reckoning moment and holding onto the last strings of my heart even if it kills me. "After roses bloom, they die," I say matter-of-factly.

Jordan exhales but continues despite my abrupt reply. "With care, the rose bush can survive through even the coldest of winters. The roses aren't dead, they're just sleeping," he counters.

"What about during the heat of summer?" My chin rises further in the air as if to prove him wrong.

"Still possible," he says confidently.

"What if I don't like roses?"

"Then we'll plant daisies, Andrea!" he says in a serious, slightly raised voice. I don't sense anger, only an undeniable earnestness.

My hands are balling into fists, trying to fight to protect my heart. "You sound so sure. What makes you think flowers are worth all of this trouble?"

"Only one of them is."

All of his chips are in at the same time I want to quit the game. I inhale sharply trying to manage the panic rising up in me. "I'm sorry, Jordan, I… I think I need to go right now."

I need fresh air before my knees fail me and I crumble to the floor. I brush past him hoping to find the air my lungs crave.

"Andrea, please… don't go. I'm sorry. I didn't mean to put you on the spot like that," he says to my back as I swim through the congregating people.

I'm frantic as I desperately try to push through the crowd, moving towards the open door that promises a full breath of air just beyond its frame. I burst into the night air, bending over and holding my throat with my hand, gasping and begging my body to keep it together, but it's not listening. I'm crumbling. My heart is too , and beating too fast.

I start walking through the full parking lot, forcing my body to move. What made me think I could play this game and not get hurt? Jordan drew attention to what had been pulsing between us, and in the light of his confidence, mine was shaken. He moved forward and I ran.

My breathing is still galloping at a frenzied pace when I reach the narrow sidewalk and see the long stretch of grass that lines it. I pull off the straps of my wedge heels and carelessly toss them at the base of a nearby tree. I rush to the grass and start running. I can't stop. My lungs are burning and my cheeks are wet, but I keep going. My mind and body are racing, but I feel invisible.

You aren't worthy of someone like Jordan.

You aren't worthy of anyone.

You're damaged, Alexandria!

The voice inside my head is screaming at me. When I can't take it another second, I stop abruptly and put one hand on my chest to feel it rise and fall with every breath I demand my body to breathe. I've run multiple blocks already, but it doesn't feel far enough. I want to outrun these emotions rising up in me. I wasn't ready for Jordan's confession, even if I knew it in my heart. I feel the weight of it now in the difficulty I have breathing. My thoughts keep saying I'm not ready and I'm not good enough. I don't trust myself enough to know if this is a lie or the brutal truth. Am I too far gone? Am I too unloveable? The panic is still coiled around my neck, tightening like a snake around its prey, and I need something to grab on to keep me in the present, to remind myself I'm not done fighting.

I sink down to my knees and grip handfuls of the soft grass in my palms. The blades are cold and stiff inside of my clenched fists. It's not enough. A surge of anger rises up through my core and out of my hands, and my fists start ripping up handfuls of grass one after the other. The only noise I hear are my pained grunts as I tear through the earth like the lies tear through my identity. My fingers ache with every dig I make into the gritty earth, but I don't care. I have to fight.

Nobody loved you.

Your own mother didn't love you!

Jordan can't love you.

"Stop! I don't believe you!" I scream at the voice in my head, desperate to be right.

You think these changes will last?

You're not worth the trouble.

My past is on full display in my head and I can't take it; it's too ugly for me to handle. "You're lying!" I groan, feeling the vibrations in my throat while raking the ground with my fingernails. The anger has been given full reign of my body, and I raise my hands high in the air and start beating the misplaced dirt with my fists. I'm fighting the voice in my head with everything I've got, but it doesn't seem like enough. I'm not enough.

"Where were *You* when I needed you? Where are *You*?" I point a condemning finger at the heavens above, and then back at myself. I feel sick with blame as I sit back on my heels, deflated by my rage and my lack. I want the lightning bolt to hit me; I need the earthquake to shake the ground I'm ripping up. I need something to confirm I'm more than who I was.

I want to feel something other than my shame.

It isn't Jordan's words that are undoing me, it's the lies that beat me up every chance they get. The lies that I created, believed, and adopted. I look down at my hands, my tears falling and mixing with the dark color of the dirt smeared there. They are throbbing from my digging, but the deep ache I have lived with all of my life is pounding in my chest to be let out. Could I let them? Could I surrender?

Jordan's words are causing me to face this girl, the one who has too much of a past to allow herself to be loved in the present.

"Why?" I choke out. "Why can't I forget?"

I want to let go of that girl, but she is just as much a part of me and there is no where I can run that would give me the distance I crave. She is me and I am her. I can't sit up any longer, and my body slumps further and further towards the unearthed dirt and grass until I am laying on my back staring up at the night sky. The sounds around me are all muted. I don't hear the cars in the distance, or any sign of life around me. My torment is too loud even though my body is no longer being ravaged by sobs or consumed by anger. I lay completely still as the tears slide out the corner of my eyes and trail down my temple, wetting the hair framing my face.

I'm here, Daughter. I've always been here.

Far beyond actual sound, I hear this voice reverberate off of the walls in my heart. It doesn't sound like thunder, hit me like lightning, or shake like an earthquake. This new voice in my head is so soft, whispering, but I hear it. It's the clearest voice I have ever heard. Where was the anger in this voice? The condemnation? The disappointment?

If love had a sound, it would be the familiarity of this voice calling me by name. The words comfort me, and it's like I can hear *Abuelita* call me *Mija*; Gladys mouth the name daughter; Aunt Cindy say I'm forgiven; Kit call me her friend; Jordan remind me I'm cherished. I feel warmth course through my body and a river of peace filtering into every fiber of my being as I lay there, stunned and motionless. All sense of time has vanished, like the lies I can't hear anymore. I try, but they aren't there.

This layer of my heart is peeling up at the corners. "You were always there, I just didn't know your name," I say into the darkness, but feel only in light of this reckoning. My tears start again as the lies fade into the background, and the truth of who I am finally surfaces.

I am loved, and I am worthy of love. A simple realization with a profound impact.

I wipe the tears from my cheeks with my dirt-stained hands then clutch them to my chest, focusing on my breathing like Anne has taught me. The suffering and pain have led me here; some decisions by choice and others by force, but there is no place I'd rather be than in this moment where I can feel myself covered in love and I actually believe it.

I close my eyes as I remember a song that was sung at church, the words materializing in my mind and on my lips as I whisper them into the silence around me.

Amazing grace, how sweet the sound
That saved a wretch like me
I once was lost, but now am found;
Was blind, but now I see.

The earth below holds me steady, and I open my eyes, seeing who I am with clarity for the first time in my life, scars and all.

Daughter, is who I am.

Loved, is what I feel.

Worthy, is what I'll always be.

CHAPTER 34
S.O.S.

June 2013—Age 22

Me: Can we meet today?
Anne: I have some time. Why don't you meet me at my office in 30 minutes. Sound good?
Me: I'll be there.

Thirty minutes later, on the dot, I stand outside of Anne's office pacing the narrow hallway, waiting for her to open the door and let me break down behind it.

After laying on the grass for God only knows how long on Saturday night, I finally made it back to my room long after the graduation party had ended. I felt tired and beat up, but lighter too. Waking up this morning, I can still feel some of that lightness, but with a heavy-handed dose of doubt. It's amazing to me how I felt so sure of what I heard only to question all of it again.

When the door finally swings open to reveal Anne's smiling face, I practically trip through her door with eager movements. The tears I have been holding spring to my eyes and pour down my tired face as I fall into my chair. I barely slept the night before after tossing, turning, wondering, and thinking of every failure I had ever had. The voice was back. I've been fighting with myself, but I don't know how to stop.

I avoided church yesterday knowing I would see Jordan there. Aunt Cindy was confused by all of my rash decisions from my hasty exit at the graduation party on Saturday night to canceling our weekly church and lunch date. She is worried. I am too, but I don't have words to explain why.

Anne moves closer, knowing her touch will be welcome, and starts rubbing my back. "Do you want to tell me what has happened to cause these tears?" she asks at the same time she sinks into the chair beside me.

"I wish I knew, Anne. I just feel so… so broken," I say through each gasp I take before the next rush of tears pours out of my eyes and down my distraught face.

Anne stays quiet and contemplative.

"Who has brought these feelings to the surface?" she asks, searching my face when I raise my eyes to her. I am safe here, in this room, and closed behind that heavy door.

"Jordan," I manage to whisper. "God… me, all of us, I guess."

Anne doesn't say anything to the explanation I give. Her silence encourages me to continue.

I wipe my eyes with the palms of my hands and allow the words to spill out of me. I can let this out just like I have done with everything else I've shared with Anne.

"It's not just what Jordan said but what he has made me feel. I don't know how to explain it all. I just feel really good when I'm around him until I remember how broken I really am. Then… then, it's like I can't stand myself." The truth sounds sensitive sitting between us. "I'm so broken," I whisper while looking down at my feet.

Anne's knees are nearly touching mine as she faces me with both her body and sincere attention. "Is there a reason why you're punishing yourself, Andrea?"

My head lifts slowly. "Punishing myself?" I ask her, but can't hide the surprise in my tone.

"It looks like you are still trying to punish the girl who was alone, hurting, and coping the only way she knew how to. You have forgiven her before. Empathized with her even, but you are back to holding the noose around your own neck, ready to pay the penance."

I wipe the tears from my cheeks, catching each new one that leisurely falls and feeling stunned by Anne's words.

"You are clinging to this brokenness like it defines you, like you have to wear this badge of shame for all you've been through. What would it look like to let it go?" she asks as I rub my hands slowly over my thighs, wondering what the hell this means.

"I-I don't know…" I reply, and I truly don't. Letting go of a past like mine is impossible. Now that a part of me can move on towards a future, I realize I haven't fully accepted my own forgiveness, and it's clear why. "I can't forget Anne. I can't forget the people who raped, abused, and used me. I can't forget the things I did to survive that torture. No matter how hard I've tried, those memories are seared into my mind," I admit, balling my hands into fists.

"Andrea, I'm not asking you to forget. God is not asking you to forget. That's not what forgiveness is about."

I try to let her words sink in, but they are only feeling skin-deep. She can see the doubt etched into my face as I stare at my fists while chewing on my lip.

Anne tries again. "Part of forgiveness involves purging every thought, feeling, and emotion that's been trapped inside. You have to let it out because otherwise the unforgiveness will find somewhere to go. It eats away at us until our bodies are suffering and our heart is behind bars," Anne says passionately while scrunching her eyebrows in concern. "Forgiveness isn't a one-time event. It happens every time we face a trigger, and each time, we need to give voice to those feelings that surface, but we also have a choice." Anne leans closer, as if that were possible and lowers her voice, "We can hang onto it, or we can release it."

Isn't that what I've been doing these past two years—learning how to release the pain so I can move forward? I've worked my tail off in therapy, thinking my layers had all been exposed, but I'm finding that there will forever be layers, and life is the journey of discovering new ones.

Anne hands me a tissue to wipe the tears that have fallen with my words. I can feel the redness rimming my eyes from their constant use, but I can also see how they are part of this release. My head turns to look at Anne when I feel her hand rub circles on my upper back, revealing her acceptance of me with a tender smile. I notice my body feels less rigid, and I'm setting down my shield, ready to stop fighting even if it's just with myself. I exhale a shaky breath as I lean into Anne.

She continues talking softly in my ear while I visualize my fists unclenching, my heart opening, and the forgiveness filling me like a cup being filled with water.

"I wish I could promise you that you'll never feel this way again, but I can't. Our stories don't define us, yet they are a part of us and because of that, each of us needs to learn how to accept and release," Anne explains, patting my knee and handing me another tissue. "Now, what you decide to do about Jordan is your choice. You can choose to walk forward and see what lays ahead, or you can walk away," Anne assures me.

I feel the peace of this moment washing over me as Anne affirms my say in the matter. I've lived so long as a slave that I forgot what it's like to live in freedom—to have a choice.

"Thank you, Anne. He is really good, you know."

"That he is, dear. That he is."

"Have you seen Jordan?" I ask as I walk up to the espresso stand.

"Hi to you, too," Kit says, pushing out a small laugh as she tamps down the coffee grounds to make someone's espresso. "No, I haven't seen him today, but why don't you check out the chapel?" she says, placing two shot glasses beneath the machine to wait for the pressed coffee to fill them.

I nod my head. "I'll start there. Thanks."

I'm determined to find Jordan before I lose my courage altogether. I've been thinking about what I'll say to him all night, and even though I'm no closer to knowing what will come out of my mouth, I'm ready. I think. No, I'm ready. I can do this.

I'm wearing my favorite light wash flared jeans with a teal colored t-shirt that brings out the blue hue in my hazel eyes and I feel like I could win the world in my simple outfit, or at least Jordan.

"You look gorgeous, girl." Kit winks. "Go get him," she encourages from behind the coffee bar.

I wave at her over my shoulder and walk towards the chapel to peer inside. It's completely empty so I search my mind for another place on campus I could look. He's usually at the Journey Center all day on Tuesdays, so where could he be?

I decide to check the lunch room; maybe *Abuelita* will know where he is. Heading down the few flights of stairs to the main entrance and into the cafeteria, I do a quick scan around the sparse tables with no luck. When I walk around the serving counter, which is completely empty of food, and push through the swinging doors, I half expect to see *Abuelita* and Jordan dancing. It's only in my imagination though, and I find *Abuelita* and her lunch crew wiping down the mess that always came with making a meal for hundreds of people.

"*Abuelita*, have you seen Jordan around?"

"*Sí*, yes, this morning he told me he works with the recovery group at the church all day. You'll find him there."

"*Gracias, Abuelita.*"

I turn to leave the way I came before I'm caught red-handed, or at least with lipstick on.

"Andrea?" *Abuelita* calls. My body slowly moves in a half circle to face *Abuelita*'s interest.

"I love Jordan. He is one of the best men I know," she tells me with love in her eyes. "But he would be a fool not to see how precious you are. You are a priceless gem, *Mija*. Don't ever forget."

"*Gracias, Abuelita. Tú es mi familia*—you are my family," I say proudly, finally able to share the Spanish I've been working on.

Her eyes grow moist with tears and both of her hands climb to clutch her heart. I blow her a kiss that she immediately pretends to catch in her hand, and I feel ready to continue my quest to find the man my heart has been seeking.

CHAPTER 35
Just Breathe
June 2013—Age 22

I spot him first, walking on the sidewalk coming towards me with a few other guys. I soak in the look of surprise and pleasure when he sees me. My stomach drops, and I'm completely caught off guard by how effortlessly handsome he looks today. I'm not looking at anyone else that surrounds him, only Jordan, because he's all I can see. As I get closer I notice his Adam's apple move up and down in his throat, highlighting the shadow of scruff lining part of his neck.

The heat of the afternoon has reached its peak, as have my nerves, and when I approach the group the conversation stops with my presence.

"Hi," I nod at the group of curious faces blocking the path. "Uh, Jordan, I was wondering if you had time for a quick walk?"

"Yeah, I have time," Jordan replies, looking at Beau, who I just noticed is there, too. I see Jordan high five a few of the guys or pat them on the shoulder to say bye, and I take the chance to finally start breathing again. Before I can blink, he's moving closer to me and pointing towards the sidewalk going the other direction.

I have a rough draft of what I want to say sketched out in my mind, but I haven't thought of where we could walk. He follows me until we round the next corner, walking side-by-side with unsaid words hanging between us when I notice we are heading in the direction of Echo Park. *Perfect.*

I inhale and exhale before letting the words in my heart take flight. "First, I want to apologize for walking out on you at the grad party the other night. I was really overwhelmed with everything and just needed some space to think and breathe."

"Of course, I'm really sorry that my words caught you off guard and made you leave your party early. I never wanted to hurt you," Jordan says with a soft tone that makes my shoulders relax.

"I know. You didn't hurt me, exactly, it was more like you highlighted some things that I was already struggling with. I had a chance to talk to Anne about everything, and I feel a whole lot better today than I did the other night."

He sighs, relief in his eyes. "I am so glad to hear that, Andrea. Truly."

Jordan swings his arms beside his body, accidentally brushing my arm in the casual movement. I close my eyes and gulp down my longing.

Breathe, Andrea. You can do this.

I talk with my hands in front of me while my legs quicken their steps. "I wasn't sure what to do with what you told me the other night. I got all tangled up in talking about flowers and then you said some things, but I wasn't sure if you actually meant them and... well..." My mouth is rambling just as fast as my feet are moving. Jordan is taller than me but even he is having to take greater strides than usual just to keep up.

"Woah, woah, woah. Hang on a minute." His hand reaches for my arm in one easy swoop and the touch shifts me out of my overtaxed mind.

I turn to face him, body, eyes, and soul. He's scanning my facial features, noticing every fear I've felt that is so plainly written there. I look away, trying to find the right words and coming up blank. "I–I…"

My head turns away and I see the park fountain in the distance, standing to attention at the center. The water pushes upward in a rush of activity and crashes down toward the pond only to do it all again. Its rhythmic motion helps center me. I try to gather my mashed up thoughts.

"What were you trying to say to me at the graduation party about… noticing me more?" The question slides off of my tongue without any reservations this time. I am ready for his answer. I want to hear what I ran from the other night.

"I got caught up in the metaphor, too," he says, rubbing the light stubble underneath his jaw. "I've been in knots these last few weeks trying to make sense of everything I feel."

"Me too," I admit on an exhale.

"I know what my heart feels but communicating it has been… hard." He is staring at the fountain now too, deep in concentration, almost tugging the same steady peace from the stream of water like I had done.

His words are like kindling for the fire he is about to start in my heart. "I really like you, Andrea. As in, I think about you as more than just a good friend and more than someone I helped get off of the streets. I have seen you blossom these past few months, no metaphor necessary, and I started noticing you and I wanted to know more… *want* to know more," he adds.

His words clothe me in the most gentle way. This man sees me. I'm not just a tool that serves a purpose, but a person to be treasured.

"I can't help but smile when your face lights up because I saw you when it didn't. The transformation you've gone through has made my head explode and my heart feels… settled when I'm with you. I didn't even know I was restless!" he says with a clipped laugh.

Fully loved while fully known.

My lips curve into a shaky smile at his comment and I feel the swell of emotion building.

"And another thing…" He's looking at me again, breaking through any of the barriers left that hide my heart from his.

"You are incredibly beautiful to the point that my eyes can't help but find you when I know you're there and even if I know you're not, I still look. I don't see a woman who's had a hard life; I see a woman walking in newfound freedom, and I couldn't miss this kind of beauty if I tried."

His confession is out and I don't feel the way I thought. I'm expecting the girl who freaked out at the grad party to show up, but she doesn't. Instead, I feel worthy and ready for this kind of affection, and it's revealed by the single tear that slips down my cheek.

"I don't even think you fully understand the effect you have on me," Jordan says, letting out a low, controlled breath as he takes a step toward me. The gap between us isn't any wider than a few inches, but it still feels too far. Jordan reaches for my hand and holds it delicately between his, moving his thumb steadily over my fingers in a repetitive circle like he did before.

The pace of my heart and the thrum of my pulse are working together in a fast motion. We study each other, the words Jordan just spoke echoing in the forefront of my mind. We have shared so much in the space of two years. No one else knew the struggles of losing a family and gaining one like Jordan did. He lived it and survived it, and now we are both thriving through it. We have each seen the dark side and chosen to walk in the light. Our stories intersect at a moment of clarity and healing that we are both leaning into.

My lips part and my mouth opens as if to say something, but I don't have words yet. It is all clicking in my head. All of it. The forgiveness, the wholehearted acceptance, and the love that runs through me like a current. It is different in some ways, but familiar enough to recognize too.

I squeeze Jordan's hand and take another step towards him until we are unnervingly close. My mind is filled with the memory of him handing me the rose when I was high and stuck in a tormented life without the possibility of love or hope. The possibility is now a breath away from me, staring at me like he did the first time we met and this time, I'm seeing it.

His eyes travel the journey around my face before returning home, seeking an answer with a quick look between my eyes and lips. I reach my other hand up in boldness to caress his cheek, and he leans into the feel of my skin touching his. Dropping my other hand, he instantly encloses his arms around my waist, settling on my back. The electricity between us is humming reliably while my hands slide up to the broadest part of his shoulders.

I hesitate, waiting for my body to freeze up the way it used to at a man's touch, but this isn't just any man. It's Jordan, and my body is responding to the close contact in a way I'm not familiar with, but I feel good about. I take a deep breath, waiting for my brain to catch up to my heart that is miles ahead.

"No man has ever seen those things in me," I say in a hushed tone, more for my acknowledgment than his. "I have never seen those things in me. I have never been here before. I don't know the rules here or the expectations. I'm afraid," I admit under the lightness of his affection.

He shakes his head. "It scares me too. More than you know. I haven't felt this way about anyone since I got sober, or even before that. But now that I have, I want to face those fears with you."

Tears prick the corners of my eyes as Jordan's hands move from my waist to cradle my face, ready to catch the tears that are falling. I grab his wrists for security and look up at him through my lashes, searching for assurance and seeing every bit of the love I feel chiseled into his features. We drink each other in, savoring the moment where two broken pieces just so happen to fit together and create something even more beautiful.

"Can I... maybe I could... kiss you?" Jordan asks hesitantly. His eyes are drifting from my eyes to my lips, waiting for my answer.

I still have a choice. I can pull back now to avoid the potential downfall in the future, or, I can lean into the possibilities. I can lean into hope, to love.

I nod my head, and Jordan dips his chin slowly, giving me every chance, every opportunity to change my mind but I don't want to. My hands steal around his waist as he gently tips my head up, which is still nestled between his strong hands, angling my face ever so gently until our lips meld together, softly at first and then sinking into the feeling we have both been curious about. I'm overwhelmed by the smell of Jordan's sweet pine, orange, and vanilla scent. I taste the salty tears that release from my eyes and bathe our connection in new beginnings. We move closer as if we are two magnets being pulled, cutting out any more distance that separates us. I sink into his embrace, clinging to the man who knows the pain of my past and accepts me still.

It is the joy of seeking and finally finding.

My body is alive in his arms, and I feel a rush of excitement at the possibilities we are exploring together. Our mouths are tightly connected, moving and angling when we briefly pull apart only to crash into the other once again. I have played the roles and done the acts, but there was never a heartbeat I cared for on the other end. Now there is, and it makes all the difference.

Our first kiss ends with a trail of second, third, and fourths until Jordan pulls his head away from mine with an audible groan. He rests his forehead on mine, "I wasn't expecting you."

I laugh at his reaction. "And you think I was expecting you? You haven't been my type for a long while, Jordan."

"Oh yeah, and what type is that?" he asks while circling his arms around my waist, settling another short kiss on my lips that I wish would last longer. He is staring down at my flushed face, waiting for my answer.

"You know, a knight in shining armor who will rescue me from the fiery dragon." My smile is teasing, but I hear every childhood desire I've had come to life.

"I think I fit the role perfectly, don't you?" he asks with a charming smirk. "At your service, my lady." Jordan releases me briefly to bend forward in an exaggerated bow.

I swat his shoulder in jest and pull up his large frame until he is flush with my body again.

"I didn't know your kind existed, Jordan. You are a gift, one I didn't know I was worthy enough for... but I'm learning how to see it that way. I really want to," I whisper.

"Alright, before you pierce my heart with any more of your compliments, let me be the true gentleman you believe me to be," he says, kissing my cheek and reaching for my hand.

The happiness I feel is painted all over my face. We start walking at a snail's pace towards the entrance of the park that will lead us back to the Journey Center.

"Would you let me take you on a date?"

"It depends..." I start, enjoying the question that is written on his face. "Will there be dancing?"

He answers my question with a question. "How did you know?"

CHAPTER 36
Roses are Red

June 2013—Age 22

I officially have nothing to wear.

I've been staring at my closet hoping an outfit will jump out and grab my attention, but nothing does. I'm brushing out the snarls from my wavy locks that are still drying from the shower and wondering if I should raid Kit's closet. My hair glows and bounces like it is ready for the night ahead; I just wish my clothing options felt the same way.

I've been waiting for this night to happen all week. Jordan is finally taking me out on our first date. I smile at the thought of seeing him soon. I don't know what his plans are, but I do know they will involve dancing, which is why *Abuelita* has been giving me crash course lessons all week in order to prepare. I'm coming ready this time with more fluid moves and no hairnet.

I abandon my closet to start applying my makeup. I prefer to keep it light and natural these days, opting for black mascara to fan out my lashes, a rose colored blush, and a delicate pink lipstick.

When I hear our bedroom door open, the one that we only have a week left to occupy before we move to our new house on campus, I see Kit traipse through it so I jump off of my bed to greet her.

"Kit! Where have you been? I've been pacing in front of my closet trying to find something to wear with zero help. It isn't going well, in case you were wondering." I'm not mad at her, but I am frazzled considering I need to meet Jordan in fifteen minutes.

"Geesh, sorry girl. I was gathering a gift for you from the guy waiting downstairs by the entrance," Kit says with a wink as she holds a slip of paper in front of her for me to grab. I can't help noticing the mixed bouquet of flowers in her other hand, my glare lessening by the second.

Kit sees my pause and waves the note in my face. "Don't just stare at it… here, open it!"

I take the slip of paper from Kit and unfold it, my fingers tingling in anticipation.

Pick your favorite flower and meet me in the lobby. -Love, Jordan

I look at the bouquet in Kit's hand that has a mix of colors, textures, greenery, and filler florals. However, on closer inspection, the bouquet looks… wild. No two flowers are the same. I recognize a few of them but the two that stand out make me laugh out loud—a red rose and a white, dainty daisy.

"So which flower are you going to choose? I know what you should wear tonight, too, by the way." Kit stretches her arm out and holds the bouquet for me to take as well.

I grab them carefully as I consider something. "Wait a minute. I didn't read the note out loud. How did you... did you already read it?" I lower my eyelids and glower at Kit.

"Well, I mean, it was a long walk up here with that note in my hands, screaming at me to take a peek the whole way, so..."

I give Kit a smirk and lower my nose to smell all of the different scents in the wild arrangement. "Okay, why don't you tell me what I should wear tonight then. I'm lost," I say.

"I'm not even sure why you have to ask. You know the one I'm going to choose, and you should absolutely wear it tonight." Kit's hands are on her hips now, trying to get me to telepathically read her mind.

She's my best friend, so, of course I can.

I walk to my closet and pull out the hanger that has what we both were thinking about draped on it, swirling about with every slight move of the hanger.

The dark green chiffon wrap dress is practically dancing already. I quickly put it on and admire its short, flute sleeves that drape around the curves of my shoulders and hangs just above my knees. Kit hands me a pair of nude strappy sandals with a slight heel that look elegant, but comfortable. I don't know why I didn't think of this option earlier; Kit is clearly right, it's perfect.

"That's the one!" Kit proclaims. "We're getting better at this," she says, pointing between my brain and hers.

The look on Jordan's face tells me everything I need to know.

"Wow. I, uh..." He's speechless, which is kind of the look I was going for. Jordan's eyes drink in the sight of me when I enter the lobby, roaming the length of my dress and leaving a wake of pleasure and delight. "So you do like roses best, huh?" he says with a more raspy voice.

The rose I plucked from the rest of the bouquet is held delicately in my left hand that hangs at my side. I draw my arm up with the rose and bring it closer to my nose so I can inhale it's pleasing scent.

"I guess I do."

"Why the rose?" he asks. A simple question with a hopeful answer.

"It seemed fitting considering it was the first flower you ever gave me." I had never received flowers from anyone before Jordan. The rose he gave me the first night we met was one that offered the promise of hope where it had all but died. Tonight, it represents the gift of love.

"I knew you were a rose kind of girl," Jordan says with a wink as he pulls me closer to him, brushing my loose, wavy hair away from my face.

"How could you tell?" I ask, so taken by the expression on his face that I'm surprised I have words to speak.

He gives me a knowing look. "If I recall, it has something to do with how strong they are," he says before kissing my forehead gently. "How delicate they look..." His lips sink into the smoothness of my cheek. "And how lovely they smell," Jordan finishes, nuzzling his nose into the tender area of my neck. He kisses it softly as my heart rate picks up speed beneath my skin.

He pulls back to his full height without kissing my lips, and I'm disappointed so I reach my hand up behind his neck and draw him closer until our lips press together. It isn't a lingering kiss, like the others we've shared, but it seals the excitement we both have in this moment.

"You look really great tonight, too," I tell him when I pull away. He's wearing a white button-down shirt with the sleeves rolled up just above his forearms, dark jeans, and a pair of soft brown ankle boots. I can't pull my eyes away from him, and I'm so glad I don't have to.

Jordan reaches for my hand with a thankful smile and we walk outside into the warm summer night towards his car. He opens the passenger door for me, and I can't tell if I want to smile or cry at the memory I have. I look up at Jordan with love in my eyes.

"What is it?" he says with a worried inflection to his voice.

"Just something my Uncle Roger used to say." I climb into the seat and adjust my dress as I watch Jordan walk around and climb into the driver's seat.

Jordan starts to buckle his seatbelt. "Did you want to share?"

I start to speak through my smile. "He would ask me if the boys I was interested in would open doors or carry my books." I release a small laugh. "He would have liked you."

"I'm sorry I never got to meet him. It sounds like he was looking for a knight in shining armor for you as well," Jordan says with a wide grin as he puts the key in the ignition and backs the car up.

"Yeah, you could say that. It took me a while to find one, but I'd say it was worth the wait." The dam has broken, and I have enough feelings to fill a lake. No, an ocean.

"Are you going to tell me where we're going?" I ask.

"Do you want to know or would you prefer to be surprised?"

"I want to know," I reply. "Surprises aren't my thing."

"That's fair. Have you ever been to Santa Monica?"

"No, I haven't. Isn't that on the water?" I say, my face scrunching as I try to recall.

"Yeah, it's a cool beach town that has a pier full of rides and carnival games. I thought we could grab some dinner and then…" He drums his hands on the steering wheel to build the suspense of what's to come. "Salsa dancing at the 3rd Street Promenade. We can check it out, maybe jump in for a few songs…"

I've been waiting for this all week, hence the extra hours spent with *Abuelita*, but that doesn't mean I'm not nervous. Jordan was really good at dancing when we were in the kitchen and I'm still worried I may not be up to snuff.

"Does that sound fun?" he asks, sensing my pause.

"Yeah, yeah, that all sounds great. I'm just… nervous, I guess."

"What are you nervous about?"

"For one thing, you are a really good dancer. What if I step on your toes or make you fall?" I ask with a slight laugh, realizing how silly this all sounds when I speak it out loud.

"I don't know if you've noticed, but I'm kind of a tank," Jordan says, waving his hand in front of his body to indicate as much, bouncing his eyes between me and the freeway.

"Good point. Okay, I probably won't make you fall, but what if I fall?"

"I won't let you fall, I promise."

"And what about your toes? You don't care enough about them? I could break one with this heel you know," I tell him jokingly.

"I care about my toes, but I care about you more."

The smile spreads across my face as smoothly as butter on toast. "Alright, Mr. Suave. Hopefully you feel the same way when your feet are black and purple tomorrow," I tease him.

"Oh, I will." His quick look at me warms me all the way through. "Maybe I should be the one worried about your mad dancing skills. I know all about your private lessons last week."

"What! *Abuelita...* I should have made her swear not to tell you."

"You know she can't resist my charm," Jordan says with a full grin. He's right. *Abuelita* loves Jordan like a son.

I decide to take a different approach here. "You're right, maybe you should be worried about keeping up with *me*," I say with a confidence I don't actually possess.

"True, I guess you'll have to teach me a few of the moves I may have forgotten since the last time we danced together," he says, still smiling as he looks over at me. That smile is out to get me tonight. I feel the tension between us rising, and all I want to do is to be in Jordan's arms, dancing or not.

I peer out the window, trying to settle my racing pulse. "I will," is all I can say through my anticipation.

The remaining twenty minute drive passes in easy conversation, belly laughs, stolen looks, and an eagerness for the night ahead. When we arrive, the town is busy and finding parking proves almost as difficult as it would in downtown L.A., but Jordan eventually swings into a spot, and we make our way towards the restaurant, hand in hand, only letting go when Jordan hopped out of the car to open my door again.

We walk a short distance to a restaurant called 45 Santa Monica, and we are seated on the private upper balcony that looks down at the restaurant's bustling activity and mingling conversations below.

"This is officially the nicest restaurant I have ever been to before," I whisper to Jordan as the server leaves to fetch some water. I feel a sudden weight of my missing etiquette in this environment as I stare at the place settings on the table.

What should I do with all of these plates?

The table settings look equal parts complicated and pristine. An anxious cloud settles over me as I look to Jordan and back down at the silverware.

Jordan, sensing my rising panic, leans towards me in his chair and rests his hand on my arm. "What do you think we should do about all of this extra silverware?"

A laugh bubbles from behind my lips at his apparent lack of silverware knowledge too and the panic all but disappears with his honesty.

"Remind me to punch Beau for giving me this recommendation," Jordan says, lifting his menu to review it.

"Noted," I say with a nod. "But let's wait and see if the food is any good at least," I add with amusement lingering in my expression.

We both ordered the steak, which tastes like heaven in every bite, and I know every other steak will pale in comparison from now on.

"Remind me to hug Beau for telling me about this place." Jordan says, licking the remaining flavor from his lips.

"We both will!" I reply, my stomach feeling satisfied by my choice.

Even with silverware occupying our hands and a table between us, the line of connection holds strong. A touch on my arm, a nudge to my knee, or a thumb running the length of my jaw don't leave me guessing how Jordan is feeling. Our gazes are never far from one another. The woman I see in the reflection of his eyes is who I long to be. It's who I am.

Our conversation is easy, and I want to soak in every second listening to his voice and hearing the passions of his heart.

Jordan reaches for my hand resting on the table when our food is devoured. "You told me once that you had a couple of children..." Jordan starts, broaching the topic carefully.

"Sort of," I begin, wondering if I can finish without feeling every crack in my heart.

"You don't have to share if you're not ready." He squeezes my hand, resting his cheek on his other hand that is propped up on the table by his elbow.

"I want to." It's true this time. I've had more and more conversations about my kids lately. I can't get through the day without thinking of them, and they are just as much an extension of me even though we aren't together. "I've had two children," I pause, dissecting the look on his face to see if I can find any emotion that ignites my shame. I don't, so I press on. "Both are with adoptive families, and..." my voice lowers when I think of Connor. "I had another baby that didn't make it. I miscarried."

"Oh, Andrea...I'm so sorry," Jordan says, empathy filling every word.

I shake my head slowly in remembrance of all that I've lost, but all that I still want to gain. "None of it has been easy."

"Have you been able to see them?"

I look up at Jordan. His question is legit, but it still stings. "I haven't. You remember Wendy?" He nods so I continue. "She hosted a call with me and each of the adoptive families before graduation. We've talked about getting together when I'm ready. I'm just hoping one morning I'll wake up and be ready, but that hasn't exactly happened yet," I explain, reaching to take a sip of my water.

"Do you think this is something you'll ever be *ready* for?"

I don't hear a challenging tone from him, only a desire to understand.

"Probably not. It doesn't stop me from wishing though. I know Kit, Aunt Cindy, and Wendy would be there to support me. I know I'd need it."

"Add me to that list," Jordan says with such confidence that I want to cry right here in the middle of this crowded restaurant. My eyes start glistening with tears, so I drop them and stare down at my empty plate.

"I think that's really amazing that you chose the path of adoption. That's very brave of you." Jordan's hand rubs the length of my upper arm rhythmically, giving me the strength I need to continue sharing.

"I think I'm starting to see the beauty in it," I reply, letting my emotion settle.

I reach my hand towards Jordan's cheek, my palm spanning the length of it as my eyes thank him for accepting me. All of me. The pieces that I thought would be my undoing were feeling the tender caress of healing. His eyes reflect love, safety, respect, kindness, and admiration.

"Check please!" Jordan raises the other hand he has been leaning on, and I see something flash across his face that I once knew only as lust, but on Jordan's face it reads as devotion. I'm creating new memories in place of the ones that ripped me apart.

After paying for the meal, Jordan leads me out of the restaurant and onto the busy sidewalk with his hand resting on my lower back and purposefully guiding me towards the promenade. The sounds of trumpets, congas, and maracas fill the night sky the closer we get to the open outdoor space that is filled with dancing bodies.

Trees with hanging lights line the expansive street that only appears smaller because of the crush of people twirling and rotating at both fast and slow speeds. I look on and notice a varied group of expert and amateur couples gyrating to the upbeat tones that ring in my ears and beat in my chest thanks to the live band. We look at this activity with awestruck amazement, watching all of the movements competing for the attention of our eyes.

"My toes are ready to get bruised," Jordan declares with his other hand extended towards me in an invitation to join the mass of dancing bodies.

I suck in a breath.

"Don't worry, Andrea. I got you." He reaches for my other hand when I don't place it in his. "You've had all the extra practice with *Abuelita*, so, let's see your moves," Jordan says casually, setting my nerves on edge while simultaneously making my knees tremble with his smile that I can't look away from.

"Your smile is going to be the death of me." My comment slips out before I can think better of it. I bite down on my lower lip.

Jordan pulls me closer to his body, placing one hand on my waist and cradling the other in his large grip. "Not before the look in your eyes kills me first," he whispers into my ear, sending a pulse of awareness through my entire body.

I don't have time to think before he's spinning me out, drawing me near, and dipping me backwards expertly. My back is straight as I hover above the ground; the only thing keeping me from plummeting to the ground is Jordan who has me cradled in his arms.

Here goes nothing.

You are confident. You are brave. You are worthy.

The song, *La Negra Tiene Tumbao*, starts playing, surrounding the night sky above us and reverberating off my limbs. It spurs on the pace of my feet and Jordan, never skipping a beat, twirls me around so my back is facing him. I dip under his arms from left to right before he spins me back to face him, flush against his chest and breathing heavy after only the first few moves.

His right hand finds the curve of my waist following the back and forth motion of my hips. "Remember, I've got you," he tells me. His face is so close to mine, the heady feel of being in his arms renders me silent. All I can do is nod.

Jordan spins me away from him, my wavy hair flying loose and free to trail down my back only to curl around my neck when he draws me back. He trades one of my hands for the other and repeats this again. The nerves are falling off with every rotation and quick foot pattern as I try to remember all that *Abuelita* has taught me.

Let the music draw you in.

Your feet will catch up with your body.

I focus on the beat, letting my hips move rhythmically side to side while my feet glide forward and back. I feel the energy of the song filter through my body, filling every part of me with a carefree sensation. I don't hold back like I did before when we danced in the kitchen. Instead, I ride the wave that the music creates—the one Jordan is riding too.

I feel the warmth of his hand at my waist again and the other one that cradles my own, sensing the energy there. His gaze is boring into me, watching every motion with an intense desire that I feel all the way down to my bare toes.

When he spins me again, my flowy dress tangles around my legs and my back connects to his chest. I feel his breath tickle my ear as he leans closer. "You are captivating."

I lean my head back so I can see his face, our lips only a brush away when I push off of him and start dancing again, challenging him to follow me when I look into his eyes and raise one of my eyebrows. My right hand is still in Jordan's while my left rises to play with the dark tendrils of hair tumbling down my back and around my shoulders. The music has drawn me in. We are a vision, he and I, the only ones dancing in a sea of people.

This is freedom. Every movement I make, the chains of my shame, unworthiness, and anxiety are loosening as my body leans into the expression of this moment with Jordan. My hips sway as I dance around him, my hand drawing a full circle around his midsection as I go.

The fluidity of his movements become more recognizable to me with every song that blares through the streets of this city near the ocean. My hair tickles our bare arms and my shoulders shimmy effortlessly to the beat. There is no routine. No second guessing. Just movement. I have shed every bit of timidity and I am fully immersed.

When another song ends and the world around us slows to a stop, Jordan doesn't release my hands but gathers me closer to him. Nestled into his powerful form, a flood of joy courses through me. I smile up at him, feeling the heat glistening on my forehead and the lightness in my spirit elevating.

Jordan bends his chin closer to my face, chasing the curve of my lips with his own. I can no longer deny him after the cat and mouse game we've been playing. My heart rate doesn't slow when I am encircled in his arms, and it's as if my body is still dancing. He kisses me like it is the first time; the newness of our budding relationship is still fresh to my taste buds. The crowded streets fade away, and all that stands is the love that courses freely between us.

I am completely sober but intoxicated by this feeling. He deepens our kiss and my whole body responds. My knees soften, yet, they still manage to keep me standing, and my arms grip the back of Jordan's neck, tracing his hairline and relishing in the feel of us together. This is a piece of my redemption.

Full. Sweet. Complete.

I hesitantly break our kiss and rest my forehead on Jordan's chest. The hands that just a moment ago held my face and willingly tangled in my hair now cross around my lower back, holding me with such admiration.

"Remind me to thank *Abuelita*," he finally says, breathless.

My head tilts back. The beaming smile that lights between us like firecrackers holds all of the satisfaction my soul could have hoped for, all of the victory that I didn't believe existed, and all of the love that my heart is capable of.

"We both will," I tell him before closing the small gap between our lips.

EPILOGUE
To You From Me

Four-months-later
September 2013—Age 23

I walk around the house anxious, wringing my hands and fluffing pillows. I'm looking to water plants we don't have. Anything to distract myself while I wait.

Today is the day. After months of gaining courage, attending multiple therapy sessions, and buckets full of encouragement, I am finally ready. Or, as ready as I'll ever be.

I'm meeting Allison and Peter, my birth children, for the first time today.

So many people I love are here in this small house with me—Jordan, Aunt Cindy, Kit, Wendy. We moved into our new home located just a stone's throw away from the main Journey Center campus a few months ago. The commute is great, considering I can wake up fifteen minutes before work starts and be back home and in my sweatpants even sooner.

I've been working in the women's emergency shelter alongside Janet for the last few months and though it has been a rewarding experience, working on this floor has also challenged me too. I am speaking to younger versions of myself who are just coming off of drugs and seeking a life that is completely *other.* I am watching the bravery of these women, and I'm left astonished by every victory they choose, however small, because the path is never easy. It's anything but linear.

My journey has had its own plot twists along the way, but eventually, it deposited me here, living with my best friend and a couple of new ones, cherished by a man I wasn't expecting, doing work that gives my soul purpose, and awaiting my first meetup with two, small humans I gave life to. The very same kids that have always reserved a piece of my heart, if not the entirety of it.

I spoke to Wendy on the phone last night and she gave me the pep talk I needed to be prepared for their visit. "Little Allison is seven years old now and her parents, Sarah and Anders, are just the sweetest. They have been talking to Allison about you since she was born, and she is beyond thrilled to be meeting you," said Wendy with a kind assurance.

It means the world to me knowing that I wasn't as much of a stranger to Allison as I had thought. Sarah and Anders had been talking about me to her this whole time. Even while I was living in the dark without a hope in sight, they were praying for me and believing for more. I had always had people cheering me on, I just didn't know it then… but I do now.

Wendy continued. "Peter is two and a half years old, and you will adore his chubby little cheeks and big hugs!"

I listened to Wendy share more about Peter's parents, Todd and Angie, and I settled deeper into my new bed, letting the stories of the lives I had missed fill the crevices of my soul. As Wendy likes to say, I was now *clothed and in my right mind*, which means it's time to meet my kids. That day is here, and it is equal parts exciting and terrifying.

Wendy arrives early and watches me flutter from one room to the other. "You're making me dizzy, Andrea! Here, come sit down, they will be here soon," Wendy states as she pats the couch cushion beside her. Jordan is setting up a few snacks in the kitchen before popping back into the living room upon hearing Wendy's command.

He smiles at me when I finally sit and then he moves around the couch to rub my tense shoulders. "You can do this. We are all here with you," Jordan confirms quietly enough for only me to hear, but we both know that wouldn't be possible in a room with these ladies. They are each watching me intently, gauging my responses and silently praying for the nerves that are floating around my body like they are actually visible to the naked eye.

"I know how difficult these first meetings can feel, but I want you to know that you are courageous, Andrea. You have seen the darkness in a lot of people, but now, it's time to see the light in these children," Wendy says while grabbing hold of my sweaty palm.

"We are all here with you, sweetheart," Aunt Cindy adds from across the coffee table.

I take a breath, willing the fast pace of my heart to calm.

You can do this.

You have waited so long for this.

It is the only thing I ever really wanted after I started on this healing journey—to meet my children face-to-face. Now, it's time.

Before I can fret any longer, there is a knock at the door.

"I'll get it," Kit states as she stands up from the living room chair and makes her way to the door. I stand on shaky legs and take a deep, calming breath, choosing to siphon the strength from the others here in the room who are now standing around me.

My eyelids close as I focus on calming my rapid breaths. I hear the voices first and my ears try to sort out the tones and inflections to the individuals they belong to.

"Hi, come on in!" I hear Kit greet everyone.

"Thank you, we are so happy to be here!"

"We appreciate you inviting us."

I hear the shuffle of shoes being removed and purses being hung before bodies filter into the living room. I open my eyes and let my irises settle on the people filling my vision. It doesn't take long before I spot *her*. The girl I had kissed goodbye in a sterile hospital room so many years before.

Allison.

I can't help notice her dark curly hair that matches my own. I'm no longer in the living room of our new home, I'm in a hospital bed holding a small baby girl for the very first time. I'm kissing the top of her head and sighing in relief. I'm wishing I had never been in the position of birthing a child and knowing I couldn't imagine my story without her. When I look at Allison now, I see that baby girl that was brought into this world in turmoil, but has always held a peace I didn't quite understand. I felt it then and I feel it now.

Love. Wholeness. Redemption.

I know I'm staring without blinking, but I can't look away from her achingly familiar features. She is every bit of the little girl I first laid eyes on when I was fifteen. Her soft, rounded cheeks I ran my finger over when she was a baby are now slender, revealing the seven years that have passed.

I want to reach out to her. I lift my hand only to let it drop again knowing I haven't earned that place, but I want to.

"Hi, Allison," I say just above a whisper.

"Hi," she responds in an equally small voice.

I can see her studying me. Maybe she sees my remorse or senses the nerves creeping up. My eyes start to fill with tears and I don't hold them back. I welcome them like the companions they've become on this journey—my journey. Joy and sadness are co-mingling when I feel a smile lift the corners of my mouth. No more words pass between Allison and I, but I hope my presence tells her I want to rewrite the end of our story. Together.

When Sarah drops her husband's hand and walks towards me, encircling me in a hug that comforts the fifteen-year-old girl that had to make the toughest decision, I choke on my sobs. I'm gasping into her shoulder and clinging to her so tightly that I have to remind myself to ease up.

"I have wanted to do this since we first held Allison as a baby. We never had the chance to meet you then, but this is what I would have done," Sarah says softly, filling the stillness of the room with her melodic confession. I can hear the sniffles and quiet cries as the years of an awaited reunion are finally realized.

"You chose to give us a gift, Andrea, and for that I can never find enough words to say *thank you*. You will always be a part of our family." Sarah's words are soothing the doubts

I have carried every single year since that first goodbye. I never realized how much I needed her arms around me. She's holding me together in this moment, and we both feel it.

My head pulls up from Sarah's shoulder and Wendy has a box of tissues at the ready. I grab one trying to appear less shaken by such an uncommon experience of hugging my daughter's adoptive mom. My hands are shaking as I attempt to dry my eyes.

Allison's adoptive father, Anders, smiles, and I notice the gleam of moisture on his face, too. My emotion is thick in my throat when seeing this. I wish I had words to express myself, but all I have are tears saved through time and unlocked with the key of forgiveness. I feel it so strongly. These families don't see me as the girl who messed up, they've only seen the woman redeemed by grace and baked in hope.

A small body emerges from the group gathered in the living room, having his fill of the quiet ambiance, he gives a hearty screech as he toddles towards me. We all let out a relieved laugh that cuts through the intensity of this moment. His arms are flailing as I bend down to greet the young boy I have never met before.

Peter.

His deep brown eyes lock with mine for a brief second, and I watch the wheels of his mind moving as he explores the space around us. He is curious and attentive as my own eyes memorize every detail of the sweet face I have only ever seen in pictures. I see every bit of wonder in him. He is a miracle; a child born into addiction and saved by God's healing touch. I know it's true, because this miracle is trying to climb onto the coffee table and grab the books spread out on top of it.

I carry my regrets for never having seen or held Peter after he was born. I'll never forget what could have been. I didn't want any of my shame to rub off on him. Forgiveness of self is just as important as forgiveness of others, and I am fumbling my way through it.

Angie walks closer to us, scooping up Peter in her arms to avoid a fall and extending her other to embrace me. I step closer, holding them both with a reverence I have for the strength they possess. I feel the clutch of a hand on my shoulder and when I lift my head and try to see through blurry eyes, I notice Todd's equally tear-filled ones staring back at me, clear and genuine. I look over at Aunt Cindy who moves a hand to her heart, overcome by the depth of this reunion.

Everyone in the room is speaking the language of tears.

My heart is soaring when I speak next. "Th-Thank you all… for coming today," I manage to choke out. "I-I never thought this would happen, to be meeting all of you. I just didn't believe it would happen, but you did… I can see that now. Thanks for never losing hope in m-me." My voice is unsteady as the emotions in the room are too dense to wade through. Jordan's strong frame stands just behind me now and as he curls his arm around my shoulders, I lean in, my eyes absorbing my family that has tripled in size.

"We love you, Andrea. We've loved you since the first moment we found out about you and every day since," Todd tells me. The room echoes in similar agreements, and I'm confident in the love that is dousing me from head to toe. It's full and complete, causing my heart to burst.

Allison moves from her mother's side and steps in front of me in the ever-decreasing space around us. I am gazing straight into a younger version of myself when I look at Allison; it makes me inhale sharply to catch my breath. I can't believe she is here. My knees bend and connect with the hardwood floors, staring up at this precious face and taking in the years I have missed. I memorize the green of her eyes and the rosy hue to her skin.

I have missed her so much.

She's here now, and so am I.

In this moment, I offer to Allison what I always wanted as a seven-year-old girl. I extend my arms in a welcoming embrace, half expecting her to turn away from me, but she doesn't.

She slowly walks into my arms, closing the gap and the years that have separated us. I hold her in a hug, remembering how many moments I had wished for exactly this as a young child and receiving everything but. I feel my heart being knit together with Allison's, now and forever. I couldn't forget this if I tried. I'm not sure how much time has passed since I welcomed her near, but it will never feel like enough.

A gentle greeting bounces off the walls of the front entryway and it brings a severe comfort with it. "*¡Hola! ¿Cómo están?*" *Abuelita* emerges through the door holding two giant bags in each hand.

I unfold out of my daughter's arms, extending a hand towards Allison, which she grabs without reservation. *Abuelita* looks around at all of us, seeing the well of tears we can't seem to fill. "Oy, am I too early? I thought everyone could use some food but I will come back!"

"No, no, *Abuelita*! You are right on time," I say in a voice filled with fresh emotion while inhaling the familiar scent of corn and a mix of ethnic spices.

"Did you hear my stomach growling all the way from the cafeteria, *Abuelita*?" Jordan asks while moving to envelope our dear grandmother in a hug.

"You know I cannot stop feeding all of you!" *Abuelita* says as she sets the bags down on the coffee table and turns in circles taking in the faces around her.

"I am so happy to meet you all! I have heard so much about you," *Abuelita* says before turning towards Allison who is still gripping my hand. "Especially you, *Mija*."

Abuelita smiles at Allison and then winks at me. She knows what it has taken to get here, and I love that *Abuelita* loves me all the same. Peter, who has been exploring the confines of our small house for the last few minutes, emerges from the kitchen, his mother Angie on his heels as he makes a beeline for the food.

"Ay, Peter is hungry!" *Abuelita* exclaims and bends down to tousle his hair but not before whispering to him. "I bet you like dancing too, *Mijo*, I can tell these things!" We all laugh as Peter attempts to peel open the bags and *Abuelita* is trying to distract him with dancing.

The conversation flows around the living room and eventually carries out into the yard where we thoroughly enjoy the food *Abuelita* has made for us. Allison and Peter explore as I listen to story after story of the memories that have been piled up for such a time as this. Home videos, pictures, and descriptions bring the past into full focus. I thought I would be reminded of every moment I've missed, and I am, but I'm also reminded of the beautiful life my kids have experienced because of my choice. I feel as if I have cried more tears of delight today than I ever have before.

They are safe. They are happy. They are loved.

I absorb everything, drinking deeply from every look, every touch, and every conversation. *What once was lost, has now been found.* It's taken years of pain, addiction, and discovery to get here and the suffering has only made my love grow stronger.

Eventually, everyone starts to trickle out and make their way home as the sun goes down, but not before making plans for the next time we will see each other, a visit I am already looking forward to.

Kit claims exhaustion and goes to bed early after crushing me with one more big hug. "I'm so proud of you, friend. You did the impossible."

"Thanks for sticking with me through everything. I am glad you got to share today with me," I tell her.

Kit squeezes my hand and waves goodbye to Jordan.

I walk him to the door and we're standing under the light of the moon when he turns to face me, tangling his hands in my hair and tipping my face to look up at him. My arms encircle his waist and for the span of a few heartbeats, we stare at one another; full thoughts passing between our eyes.

"I love you so much, Andrea," Jordan says faintly.

"I know you do," I smile teasingly.

"Oh, you do, eh?" he says tickling my side and causing me to squirm.

"Hey, no fair," I pout, but not for long. "I love you too, Jordan. So. Much."

He lowers his mouth to match mine, kissing me gently before deepening the kiss and sealing the fullness of the day's events in one, swift action. When we break for air, Jordan opens his eyes to search mine. He knows my insecurities, the hardships, and the struggles I've faced. He also knows the victories, the freedom, and the love I have discovered.

"Hang on a minute. I'll be right back," Jordan says before jumping off the porch and running to the side of the house.

"Wh-what?" I stand there, stunned and cold from the loss of his arms around me. Jordan disappears around the corner of the house and I'm left wondering what in the world he is up to. I didn't think he had left anything behind; he would have walked through the house if he had forgotten anything.

It doesn't take long until I see Jordan walking towards me, arms hiding something behind his back. My expression is equal parts question and thrill at what I might find there. He has that boyish grin on his face and his hair is all messed up from his quick sprint.

He's standing in front of me again, pulling one of his arms free from behind his back. There's a beautiful rose standing to attention in his fist.

"What in the world, Jordan? Do you just carry roses around with you now?" *Impossible man.*

"If they weren't so sharp, I might consider it, especially when you smile like *that*," he admits with a wink that he knows makes my heart beat faster. "You actually have a rose bush on the side of the house. I saw it a while ago and I've been waiting."

"Waiting for what?" I take the rose from him.

"For it to bloom, of course."

"And, was it worth the wait?" I ask him, touching the soft silk of the petals.

"Always," he says, shaking his head once and training his eyes solely on mine.

I want to cry again, as if I haven't just spent the entire day weeping.

In a hushed voice, Jordan washes me with the promise he made when I first met him, but adds to the promise that has since changed my life—our lives.

"You are worthy, cherished, and far more precious than this rose, Andrea. I want to remind you of this every single day because no words have ever been more true. I want to spend every moment staring at you, pouring my love on you, and soaking up how alive I feel when I'm with you." He pauses, stepping closer and securing his hands on my lower back, tracing invisible circles with his thumbs. When he leans closer and lowers his voice, I soften at his question turned statement. "Marry me."

My heart drinks up his words as they fall from his mouth and I feel the full weight of Jordan's promise, his petition, all in this single rose. I look up at him with the full adoration of my love. I'm not surprised. I am only overjoyed that these words have finally been spoken and there is only one answer that I can give.

"Yes," I say without hesitation.

Shortly after Jordan leaves, I fill a cup of water from the kitchen and position it sacredly next to my bed with the rose leaning inside of it against the rim. I pull out my worn journal and my favorite pen from the corner desk and curl up on my new bed ready to write out the words that want to pour out of me. I don't want to forget anything that's happened today. It was all too good. I need something to mark this moment and nothing feels more right than writing it out. I write with a consistent stream of tears marching down my cheeks as the words fill the lines of the pages.

Love has a Name | Christina Hill

Future Andrea,

You have grown a lot these last two and a half years. You have done things that you didn't think were possible to do, like making peace with your past, forgiving yourself, accepting others' forgiveness, and reaching out to build relationships with your kids. That's right, the children that were there at your lowest points are seeing you at your highest. What a gift that is! Don't ever forget that. Keep building that bridge because those kids are worth it. They are loved by so many people, you included, and will teach you more about love than you could ever hope to know. Let them.

You are no longer defined by your addiction. Victory is yours. Walk forward as the evidence of healing. You experienced nothing short of a miracle when you ditched your needle for freedom. The struggle will be there, because the addiction was real, but you are an overcomer. Your heart is lighter and your countenance brighter because of it. You are no longer bound by chains but you have been freed! Hang onto this freedom.

I hope you always live in the fullness that God designed for you. You know what this feels like now. Lean in. You are worthy just as you are, just as He said you were. When you were broken, distrusting, and burdened, you were always worthy, but now you can see it. Lead out of this place where you know your identity. If you can do this, you'll be just fine. Better than fine, actually.

Lastly, love as if your life depends on it—because it does. Love is what saved you. Love pulled you out of the pit of despair and placed you on solid ground. Love created a family. Love gave you the gift to see, hear, touch, and experience. Find love and you'll find God. After all, Love has a name.

With love always,
Andrea, Mija, Friend, Sister, Beloved

Author Notes
(Contains Spoilers)

In 2020, our family welcomed our fourth child, the first by way of adoption. Every adoption has a story to tell and while our family grew by one more beautiful baby, it was not lost on us that another family had one less child in their arms. I am forever grateful to our son's birth mom for the choice she made to place her child in the waiting arms of our family.

During the adoption process, we heard countless stories of women's journeys to and through adoption from our advocate/facilitator—let's call her Judy. It was Judy who shared story after story of birth mothers that she had worked with and the heartbreaking realities of their situations. The birth mothers and fathers she has helped are innumerable, but she remembers every name, every child, every adoptive family, and everyone involved. She has bore witness to some excruciating backstories and heart wrenching births, but her mission is simple: Love the *one*.

She has helped so many *ones* in her years of doing this hard work, but you just can't even fathom the lives that have been changed because she loves with everything she has. Our family is one story among the thousands.

Judy mainly facilitates adoptions, joining children with their forever families, but her heart beats for the birth mothers. She pursues them relentlessly, like Wendy did with Andrea, and she stays in their corner years after they choose to adopt their child, rooting them on, and loving them no matter where they are in their story. My prayer is that every birth mom would have a Judy in their lives.

The Journey Center is also a real place, but I have changed the name. There are so many programs doing fantastic work to see that women are supported and cared for on their way towards healing. The rose ministry that was highlighted in chapter nineteen is also real. A team of people will often accompany a former prostitute to the streets to build relationships and help provide for any needs they have. When a woman chooses to leave the streets, it's no small thing. The car chase scene that Andrea and Kit experienced was based on a true story. The rescuers in real life did, indeed, call ahead for backup and tons of ex-cons, former drug dealers, rough-looking men that were in the program lined the streets to scare off the pimps and, it worked.

The wild stories and seemingly impossible situations are endless, but so is the redemption. Let us be the advocates for the women and men who are stripped of their choice, and empower them with the ability to choose freedom. The need is great and the impact lasts for a lifetime.

If I could leave you with one encouragement, it would be this. Find the *one* that you can love relentlessly. The homeless person on the street, the neighbor, the stranger at the grocery store, the prostitute, the foster kids. There are so many people hurting and most are but a stone's throw away from us. Find this person and love them like your life depends on it, because their life just might.

Please note I have adapted every story for the privacy of the individuals involved. My main character, Andrea, reflects a compilation of stories and is not tied to one individual person. Every story is unique, including Andrea's.

If you are interested in seeing my inspiration for some of the characters, scenes, outfits, etc. discussed in this book, you can find me on Pinterest @authorchristinahill.

I also love connecting with readers on Instagram and TikTok: @authorchristinahill. If you loved the book, please consider writing a review on Amazon and GoodReads. This is such a tangible way to help indie authors and for the message of this book to reach more beating hearts.

With all of my love,
Christina

Acknowledgments

Writing a book takes more than a village, I'll tell you that much! I had so many people willing to help light the way. I could fill a book with all of the names. The indie author community is so strong and welcoming and I could not have figured this out without any of them. Thank you to every author that answered my messages and offered all of your wisdom and insight. Special thanks to Caitlin, Marie, Lindsey, Tracey, Janessa, and Peyton. I was able to do this because you paved the way and were willing to share, teach, and help. You're all phenomenal.

My husband, Samuel—Your role in this book has been the greatest and most influential to me. You were there when the idea was a spark and you are here now with the final product. You were the first to read the entirety of the book prior to anyone else and when it was at its most raw stage. Thank you for providing your ideas, perspective, encouragement, and tears to make this story come to life. Thank you for also caring for our home and family when I needed those extra evening and weekend hours to write and edit. We did this, babe. You and me.

Thank you for also being willing to cringe your way through the lovey dovey parts, even though they aren't your favorite.

Mom and Dad—You have encouraged me with every crazy idea I have ever had! Each and every one of them have been so different but you were also just as supportive in each endeavor. Writing this book has been no different! You have cheered me on every step of the way before even knowing what I had written. Thank you for your endless belief in me.

Jimmy—My brother, your nursing knowledge has been so helpful in making this story believable and real. Thank you for talking shop about the different drugs and how they affect a person's body. Your stories are unfathomable but have been immensely educational. Thank you for teaching me and responding to my random texts about drug symptoms. I love you even more for it!

Erica—You are the best sister-in-law a girl could ask for! You agreed to read through and edit my book while teaching, being a mom, and pregnant. I can't tell you how much this has meant to me to have your detailed eye look through everything. You're amazing.

My kids, the Fab Four—You kids have been there for every big and small celebration for this book. Thank you for screaming and providing endless amounts of high-fives when I shared each milestone. Your unending support is what dreams are made of, and is exactly what I needed to see this thing through. I love you all so much. I know you are watching me and because of that, I hope you know you can do the crazy hard things!

My friend, Brenda—Thank you so much for being a well of information as I peppered you with thousands of questions about L.A., homelessness, addiction, and double checking my Spanish. You played tour guide when I came to L.A. and I value every hour, minute, and second you spent helping me with this book. Also, your photography skills are insane! You captured every piece of what I wanted for this book cover. THANK YOU!

Beta readers—Thank you to each and every one of you who put eyes on this book at one point or another! Janessa, Marie, Tracey, Caitlin, Erica, Katie, Janell, and Peyton. You gave it the punch it needed to become what it is today. The time you took to make it happen, means the world to me.

Special shout out to my 7th grade English teacher, Janell, for also being willing to read and edit this book in its infancy. Did you think the girl always getting caught making out with her boyfriend in the hallway would be sending you her book? Teachers are the best. Thank you!!

My editor, Annie—Your unmatched skill and know-how has been invaluable to this process. When I say I could not have done this without you, I mean every word. You absorbed every panic-edit I had like the champion you are. I appreciate you and your hard work so much!

To everyone at the "Journey Center" who was willing to answer my questions, share their stories, and give feedback on this book. Diane, Lissett, and everyone else who shared your personal stories. The magic of this place has only increased in your eyes over the years and that speaks to the greater mission you are a part of. I hope the whole world gets a glimpse into the things God is doing in and through your organization!

Our Birth Mom—This book is dedicated to women who have been in the position of choosing adoption but you were my first introduction to the magnitude of this choice. You have taught me so much through your decision to place your son in our arms. I promise to always tell him about you and how freaking brave you are! You made an impossible decision for his sake and that speaks volumes. You are our family by choice and we will forever be tied together by the love of this little boy. Thank you for your gift. I love you with my whole heart.

Our Son—You are the reason this book even exists. Your name means *Breakthrough* and for good reason! We all came together in unity over your life, cheering you on and pouring out our love. Your story has pierced my heart since the moment we found out you would be ours. I am inspired daily by your little life because you are a living and breathing miracle. I have watched you overcome and seen you thrive beyond understanding. I love you, sweet boy. To the end of my days, and beyond, I love you.

About the Author

Christina is a lover of love who has been writing stories in her head since middle school. She also holds the titles of 'mom' and 'babe' and lives on an island in the Pacific Northwest with her four children, husband, and cat.

When Christina isn't reading or writing, she is wrangling her kiddos, homeschooling, taking baths, baking, or watching **PBS**.

For more information, visit www.authorchristinahill.com.

To Love Again
Coming September 2022

Kit Lopez is finally healing and stable after being rescued from the streets of L.A. where she made a living as a prostitute. When her identity of caring for her family shattered, she was left to pick up the pieces, and needed a job to support herself. That job nearly broke her—body, mind, soul—and now Kit wonders if she can still fix everything, and find the one person her heart beats for—her younger brother, Jacob.

Her current job in the Foster Care Youth Program at the Journey Center is what's keeping her going, and believing the impossible for her little brother that she let slip through her fingers when they both went into the foster system. Kit's time to find him is running out since Jacob is about to turn eighteen and will age out of the system. She realizes more than anything, she needs help. The one thing Kit hates asking for and had promised herself to never need.

When longtime friend and rescuer, Beau Colson, extends support and more, Kit realizes quickly she is at risk of losing her heart. In order to move forward, she'll need to face the demons of her past, the love being offered in her present, and grapple with a future that may not include her brother. Kit just hopes that love is big enough to conquer her fears.

PROLOGUE

Goodbye

June 16, 2011—Age 20

The cold night air wafted in through the open van door causing a shiver to chase the length of my spine, and the hair on my arms stood on end. I looked down at my shaking hands and wondered for the hundredth time what the hell I was thinking.

I started rubbing my hands methodically up and down my arms to keep them from revealing my fear. My arms were covered by my favorite jean jacket that was supposed to shield me from the cool air that touched the rest of my bare skin, but I couldn't fend off the iciness that seemed to penetrate beneath. I was already here, sitting like a wounded animal hiding from her predator, hoping this sanctuary wouldn't be discovered. How I managed the courage to make it this far was beyond me. Maybe it was the look in Janet's eyes as she held my hand, or maybe it was the rose that the man with the warm brown skin and kind eyes handed me. Either way, it sparked something in me that I couldn't deny; like paddles connecting to my chest and jolting me out of my state of oblivion. I was *alive* after believing I was the walking dead.

Gloria a Dios.

The familiar phrase leapt from the recesses of my mind as though Janet had said it aloud from her spot in the backseat. I angled my head in her direction slowly just in case she had said something, but Janet was looking down at her watch, seemingly unaware of the shock that coursed through me at those words. It couldn't have been Janet who said it. That tone could only belong to one person: my mother. It had been years, but I would know the inflection of her voice anywhere. She always used to use that phrase —Glory to God. It had become her life motto the moment my Spanish-speaking father taught her how to say it. My mother was white, religious, and an addict. All reasons that my father should have run far away, but instead, he only ran closer.

Why was I thinking about her now?

I shoved the familiar phrase and the unwarranted memories out of my mind just as another woman was walking towards the waiting van. She climbed in hesitantly, checking the backseat to be sure there weren't unwanted visitors joining us. A classic move when you are accustomed to always watching your back on the streets. Things happen. Unplanned events that leave you exposed or scarred, usually both. I looked on as the blond guy, who introduced himself as Jordan, handed her a water bottle and blanket. He had offered me the same, but I didn't need those. I needed a gun, or a knife at least, knowing what we were about to do and the dangers we now faced.

I tucked a piece of my long, straight, dark hair behind my ear while the girl and I studied each other, silently agreeing to an alliance should this deal go sideways as they do sometimes. Street life in L.A. was anything but predictable, and I had learned to roll with the punches— literal and figurative.

"I'm…" she paused. "Andrea," I heard her say, barely above a whisper.

"Mercedes," I said with little feeling. "Actually, no, it's Kit." I hated my street name. I carried it around like a weight around my neck, paying penance for my choices. It disgusted me. I would rather be Kit though, even if I didn't like her either.

I looked forward when I heard the two men climb into the driver and passenger seats in front of us, watching as they prepared this vehicle for takeoff. My head turned to peer out the window once more, expecting dark, shadowy figures to appear outside of the car, acting with swift movements to pull me from this seat and whisk me off to sudden death.

Death. That's exactly the kind of punishment I would be facing for being in this van.

I couldn't die. Not yet. I hadn't found Jacob yet, and I wasn't about to leave this world without finding out the real story of what happened after we entered foster care. I was doing this for him, I told myself as I yanked my eyes away from the windows and forced myself to take a deep breath. Everything I did was for him. Whether it was working different blades to earn money and potential pieces of information that would lead me back to my brother or getting in a van with strangers that promised to help me, I did it. I would do it.

The car started moving just as fast as my lips were silently moving. I was sending up the prayers I had heard my mother pray time and time again. I didn't know what value they had. The prayers didn't work for her, but maybe they would for me. My eyes stayed closed as we traveled down the L.A. city streets until my fear forced them open to scan our surroundings. It wasn't until the words I dreaded most were spoken that the panic began to overtake any semblance of calm I tried to embody.

"Andrea, Kit—get down on the floor and don't sit up or look out the window, we're being tailed and I don't want anyone seeing you two," said Jordan with a serious but calm demeanor. "Janet, you too," he added.

Before I could second guess my next move, I dropped to the floor of the van faster than I had fled to the van earlier that night. "Oh shit! I knew I shouldn't have come! They always find you. No matter what, they track you down," I declared out loud to the earlier version of myself who had made the decision to follow these strangers to a supposed freedom. The man driving wrenched the steering wheel, and the car careened around another bend in the road. The gas pedal had to be nearly to the floor if I had to guess, but I couldn't open my eyes. I wouldn't.

I had been fully catapulted into the darkest corners of my fear and dreaded every moment of what my brain told me would happen next. The terror was evident in my screams, and I channeled every bit of my sanity into the promised protection of my mother's prayers.

Save me! Someone. Anyone. Dios Mio.

My adrenaline was at its peak now, with every screech of tires on the pavement, and I no longer had a grasp on reality. The words that I thought were in my head were escaping out of my mouth in quick succession. The van took another turn and my body pressed into the side of the bucket seat, the speed of the vehicle itself threatening to kill me.

I heard Janet's attempt to comfort me, but it did little to assure me. "We won't let them get you, Kit. Your pimp and his men will realize this soon enough."

She may have been a former prostitute on these streets, but did she know the kinds of pimps that were out there these days? They controlled everything on Figueroa Street, where the 110 and 10 freeways meet, and fear and survival mingled.

I'm going to die. I'm going to die. Oh God, I don't want to die! Help. Please!

My pleas grew stronger, filling the small space of the van with the unhindered rush of frenzied emotion. My heart was thumping wildly inside of my chest, sweat gathered on my brow, and an instinctual will to survive had me clenching my fists tightly and pounding the floor of the van, ready to fight whatever threat came. I had turned from a wounded animal awaiting a predator to an enraged beast, ready to fight to the death if it came to that, and I was certain it would.

Fear lived beneath the surface of every encounter I had on the streets. Some prostitutes were on drugs, which was easy to see by the glazed look in their eyes, but not me. I wanted a clear head and a sharp sense of my surroundings at all times. I had seen enough shit out there to know I needed my sanity in order to survive. Andrea had that glazed look in her wide, terror-filled eyes. Maybe this is why she was quiet now, laying on the floor of the van without so much as a squeak. My senses were sharp, but that didn't mean I was too terrified to face the demons that plagued me. The demon that stole my money, forced himself on me, and then sold me like a common box of crackers at the grocery store. I was nothing to my pimp. I lived every day of my life afraid of what he could do to me. Today topped all of those days combined.

You are nothing.

I own you, bitch.

You don't think I could kill you?

Threats. They were only threats, weren't they? At this moment, I believed the threats of my pimp were about to be proven true. The tears streamed down my face and the thick layer of black mascara that I had coated my lashes with before work was burning my eyes and mocking me. The voices around me were muffled. I couldn't tell who was speaking or what was happening. All I knew was the piercing screech of my terror materializing in front of me, and the strongest will to live I have ever experienced.

You have to survive.

You can't let him down, again.

Don't you dare give up!

The dichotomy of words being spoken in my mind were warring for rulership over my decisions. I didn't know which to believe, but time was not on my side. Before I could decipher anything further through the mess of tears, the recognizable sound of battle had just crushed the side of the van that I was crouching by. Bullets. One... two... three bullets rang out, deafening the voices around me and causing our driver to punch the gas pedal further to the floor. I gripped the seat in front of my head and shrieked louder at the impending reality: our lives were a breath away from death. Time became nonexistent. My memorized prayers were silenced. The voices in my head came to a screeching halt just as the battered metal box on wheels hit a bump and immediately stopped.

Death had found me.

Fear had devoured me.

It would all be over soon, I hoped.

My body shook uncontrollably, and my hands that gripped the seat in front of me to keep from rolling around the vehicle moved to cover my face waiting with expectation at my fate. Heavy breathing from five utterly exhausted bodies filled the silence that my whimpers hadn't stolen already, and I waited. And waited.

Nothing.

No, no. That's not right.

Where are the other bullets?

Where are the hands that controlled me?

It felt like an eternity waiting to meet my Maker, and solidify the misery I felt in the depths of my soul.

Goodbye. I'm so sorry, I failed you.

I will miss you so much, Jacob.

I love you.

My final words were sealed upon my heart and spoken out loud between the cracks in my speech and the restlessness of my body. My world became small in those final moments, and I realized how little my life really was. A wisp. A flash. I didn't want this world, not if I couldn't have my brother Jacob in it. My eyes clenched tightly and my whole world went dark.

Love has a Name | Christina Hill

Made in USA - Kendallville, IN
81529_9798985719901
05.10.2022 1520